Christmas at the Beach Hut

Christmas at the Beach Hut

Veronica Henry

ORION

First published in Great Britain in 2018 by Orion Books,
an imprint of The Orion Publishing Group Ltd
Carmelite House, 50 Victoria Embankment,
London EC4Y 0DZ

An Hachette UK company

3 5 7 9 10 8 6 4

A CIP catalogue record for this book is
available from the British Library.

ISBN 978 1 4091 6665 8

Typeset at The Spartan Press Ltd,
Lymington, Hants

Printed and bound in Great Britain by Clays Ltd,
Elcograf S.p.A.

MIX
Paper from
responsible sources
FSC® C104740

www.orionbooks.co.uk

For Claire McLeish, who always makes sure my
stocking is full – Merry Christmas, my friend!

Dear Everyone,

I do hope you aren't one of those people who hates Round
Robins. As someone who gets excited about Christmas
almost as soon as the clocks go back, I love hearing what
other people are up to, but if you don't then please feel free
to bung the Kingham family update in the bin! No boasting,
I promise. We haven't been to the Caribbean or bought a
second home in Cornwall or a mid-life crisis E-Type Jag...

Simon is busier than ever and spends a lot of time
in London as that's where most of his building projects
are – luckily the high-speed train from Birmingham
means he doesn't have to stay over too often. Becoming a
partner at the beginning of the year has meant a lot more
responsibility for him, as the MD, Colin, is taking a bit of a
back seat but he's enjoying the challenge.

The twins are studying hard for their mock A levels – or
so they assure me! There is no more thankless task than
persuading teenagers to revise. Hattie was Snow White in
the skating club's Christmas production and Luke's finger-
boarding Instagram account has more than 20k followers.
No, I don't understand it either but at least it's safer than
actual skateboarding!! Photos below! I can't bear to think
of the two of them heading off to uni next September. So
please come and stay in our empty nest come autumn. Our
little bit of Warwickshire has lots of gastropubs so we can
offer you bracing walks and Sunday lunch by a roaring log
fire. Bookings open!

I've just taken voluntary redundancy from Craven Court
after nearly twenty-five years of organising events and

weddings for them. The hotel has been bought out by a big group run by a dynamic young team who all look as if they are still at school! They are making lots of changes so it seemed the perfect time for me to have a change too. I finish work three days before Christmas – it will be a whirl getting everything ready but I can't wait to have a proper break for the first time in years and make this our best Christmas ever at Pepperpot Cottage!

With love for a Merry Christmas and a wonderful New Year,

Lizzy, Simon, Hattie and Luke xxxxx

THREE DAYS BEFORE CHRISTMAS

I

'What are you doing?'

Harley stood on the landing, fists clenched. He could see the man looking around his room, like a landlord eager to spot something wrong so he could hold on to the deposit. He was checking out the vintage album posters, the acoustic guitar leaned against the wall, his *Star Wars* advent calendar, hung up by the bed.

The man turned and smiled, teeth white in his tanned face, the collar of his stonewashed rugby shirt turned up, his hair playboy-long: a Peter Pan look that didn't fool Harley.

'Just checking everything's in order.'

Harley could see that the top drawer was open on his chest of drawers, and his Christmas cards had been knocked over.

'You've been moving my stuff.'

Tony gave a little shrug. 'I'm just making sure...'

'Making sure what?'

'I don't want any funny business.' He gave a little nod, as if reassuring himself that this invasion of Harley's privacy was totally reasonable.

Harley felt a rush of heat inside him; a surge of adrenaline that had nowhere to go.

His room was on the top floor of the house, what would have been the maid's room when this was the holiday villa for a wealthy Victorian merchant. The landing was filled with light from a big round window that looked down to the harbour. He'd loved that view when they'd first moved here; loved watching the boats come in and the fishermen land their catch.

He knew what Tony meant by funny business. Drugs. It was the kind of assumption people like Tony made about people like Harley. Just because his dad was black. And in prison.

'Leave my things alone.'

Tony walked out of the room and stood in front of him. Harley was conscious that the man was a few inches taller and a good deal broader and heavier – twelve stone to Harley's ten. But Harley was fighting fit – he trained at the boxing club every day, and ran four times a week rain or shine.

Tony's eyes were wintry – as cold as the icy sea outside. 'This is my house,' he said, his voice dripping with menace. 'If you don't like it, you can go and live with your dad.' Then his face broke into a smirk. 'Oh, wait . . . You can't, can you? Not where he is.'

He started to chuckle.

Harley stepped forward. 'Say that again.'

Tony's eyes slid sideways as if he was looking for back-up. He realised that the staircase was right behind him. Suddenly he didn't seem so confident.

'I'm just having a laugh,' he said. 'Can't you take a joke?'

He was nervous. Harley could tell that by his body language. He was so close he could smell his breath.

Chocolate. He'd been eating chocolate.

'Have you been eating my advent calendar?'

Tony blinked. 'Only today. Number twenty-two.'

'I hadn't opened it yet!'

Tony gave a shrug. 'You'll have to wait for tomorrow.'

'My dad sent me that.' Harley stared at him levelly, daring him to say something.

He could see Tony rooting about for a suitable riposte, trying on a few for size, then rejecting them. He wasn't as brave as he made out. In the end, he gave a weak smile and a jerk of his head. 'Out the way, there's a good lad.'

Harley didn't move. 'Don't go in my room again.'

For a moment, there was silence. Harley could hear a thrumming in his ears as his heart whooshed blood around his body. The pressure was so intense he felt sure he might explode.

Then Tony lifted a hand and prodded Harley in the chest with his forefinger. 'It's not *your* room,' he said, accentuating each word with a tap. 'You keep forgetting that bit. This is *my* house. If I want to kick you out, I will.'

With each tap Harley felt the pressure rise even more. He had always heard about red mist. And he was surprised, when it came down, that it wasn't a jolly Christmassy red, but a deep, dark, dangerous red the colour of blood.

He put his hands up and grabbed Tony's shirt, giving him a sharp shake, like a dog with a rat.

'Easy, boy.' Tony stepped back until he was right on the top stair.

It would only take one push. No one knew Harley was at home, so they wouldn't suspect him. It would look like an accident. Poor old Tony Brice, falling down his own stairs. And just before Christmas too.

2

Mick the Post strode down the high street, pulling his trolley behind him, dressed in shorts and a fleece because he always wore shorts, whatever the weather. *'Oooh, you make me feel cold just looking at you...'* people would say, but he hated being trussed up. He liked the zingy feel of the air on his skin. And it wasn't even that chilly. Just... nicely crisp. It had to get well into the minuses before he put proper trousers on.

He felt much more purpose at this time of year. Nowadays, most people's post was whittled down to speeding fines and parking tickets and unsolicited bumph. Their faces didn't light up when they saw the postman coming any more. But Christmas was different. And his trolley was bulging, because this little town was full of the kind of people who still sent Christmas cards.

Astley-in-Arden was far enough out of Birmingham to have its own identity: small enough for you to feel a part of it, yet big enough to have a selection of shops and restaurants that meant you didn't have to go too far afield if you didn't want to. There was a wide high street lined with a mix of mellow red-brick Georgian townhouses and black-and-white timber cottages. Nestled amongst the history were all the conveniences of modern life:

dry-cleaners and wine shops and a decent Indian take-away. Astley-in-Arden was as perfect as you could get.

It did Christmas well, too. The oak trees that lined the pavements had strings of lights woven into their bare branches: tiny pinpricks of silver that lit up the streets. The shops went all out to look festive, their windows hung with tinsel and baubles. There was a towering Christmas tree in the marketplace and pupils from the local school sang carols there on Saturday afternoons to raise money for charity, their golden voices soaring skywards.

All Astley needed, thought Mick, was a sprinkling of snow to make it the perfect Christmas-card scene. He looked up into the sky with an experienced eye, but there was no sign of snowfall, just a few gentle clouds meandering about with no sense of the urgency everyone else seemed to have. Everyone had gone up a gear today. With only three days left before everything shut down for the silly season, time was running out.

Mick lowered his pace as the shopfronts dwindled and the houses began, his deliveries slowed up by greetings and thanks from homeowners rushing to the door to see what he had brought, wondering if the presents they had ordered online would arrive in time. If not, there would have to be a last-minute mercy dash into the larger town of Leadenbury, nearby, or Birmingham itself. He could sense their panic. Every year, people left things to the last minute. They would never change.

Eventually he drew to a halt outside Pepperpot Cottage. At the far end of the high street, heading out on the road to Stratford-on-Avon, it was one room wide and three storeys high with a pointy thatched roof, giving it the appearance of a Georgian silver pepperpot that must have been the inspiration for its name.

He was burrowing about in his trolley for the sheaf of cards addressed to the Kinghams when the front door popped open and there stood Lizzy Kingham, in fleecy pyjamas covered in reindeer, a pair of flashing antlers perched in her curls along with a dollop of cake mix and a dusting of flour.

The front door opened straight into the living room, and behind her a staircase led upstairs. Mick glimpsed wonky walls and sloping floors and inglenook fireplaces: he had never been inside Pepperpot Cottage but he longed to, for it was the kind of house that enticed you in, always full of laughter and music and cooking smells and a warm glow. Right now, the scent of spicy chocolate and the ubiquitous sound of Slade on the radio drifted out of the kitchen.

'Mick!' Lizzy said. 'I've caught you at last. I've usually gone before you get here. But today is my first day of freedom. I finished work last night. Hurrah!' She brandished a bottle of red wine with a gold ribbon wrapped round it. 'This is for you. Simon says it's a good one.'

'You didn't need to worry,' said Mick, but he took it gratefully. The days of tipping postmen had long gone, but a few of his regulars gave him thoughtful gifts and he preferred them to hard cash. 'Oooh – Châteauneuf-du-Pape. I shall enjoy that. Thank you.'

'Well, a very merry Christmas to you,' said Lizzy, and took the cards from him. She began leafing through, stopping at one with a little frown, then she looked up, realising she was being rude.

'Something smells good,' offered Mick.

'Mincemeat brownies. You're ten minutes too early.' Lizzy made a face. 'I've got three days to get everything sorted. I'm never going to do it.'

'You will,' said Mick. 'Everyone makes far too much fuss.'

'But I want it to be perfect.' Lizzy looked anxious. 'I haven't even got my tree up yet. Can you imagine?'

Mick chuckled. 'The sky won't fall in because your tree's not up.'

She stared at him in mock indignation. 'It's not Christmas till the tree's up!'

'It'll be all right,' said Mick. 'Everything will happen in good time.'

Lizzy nodded. 'Let's hope so.'

She smiled and her blue eyes twinkled at him, but Mick thought she looked tired – and something in that sheaf of letters was bothering her. He could tell because she kept glancing down.

'Good luck with it all, then,' he said, grabbing the trolley handle.

'Thanks, Mick,' she said, raising a hand, then she disappeared back inside Pepperpot Cottage, shutting out the mouth-watering smells and a rousing chorus of Merry Christmas Everybody.

3

Lizzy scurried back into the kitchen and sat down at the table. She was surrounded by all the detritus of baking – empty mixing bowls and wooden spoons – and there was flour everywhere. She ignored the mess as she sifted through the cards until she found the slim white envelope with the crest she had spotted earlier: Missingham Manor Hotel. Her heart was thumping as she opened it. Surely it was good news? They wouldn't waste a stamp otherwise, would they? Most prospective employers just sent an email, if that – more often than not you were left dangling, working out for yourself that if you hadn't heard after two weeks, you weren't wanted.

She pulled out the letter and unfolded it.

She knew immediately, because there were just two lines. *We thank you... unfortunately... details on file...* She swallowed down her disappointment. She would have been perfect for the job. She ticked all of the boxes.

When she'd taken voluntary redundancy, she had told herself she wouldn't start job-hunting until after the New Year. After all, she'd never had a career break – only six months after the twins were born, which was hardly respite. And Simon had told her not to worry about getting a new job straight away. But she couldn't resist applying when she saw them come up, and this would have been her dream. Missingham Manor was a fairy-tale hotel in the Cotswolds – yes, it would mean a longer journey to work but once the twins were at uni come September she wouldn't be needed around the house so much. At all, in fact.

Anyway, it didn't matter how far away it was because she didn't even have an interview. She gave herself all the usual platitudes – *they probably promoted someone internally; don't take it personally* – then crumpled up the letter and shoved it in the bin. She turned to the other Christmas cards instead, trying to smile at the greetings and messages, but she could feel herself blinking back tears.

She looked up as a smell of burning curled across the kitchen. She leapt to her feet and opened the oven door: two baking trays of mincemeat brownies, ruined. She pulled them out of the oven and put them on the side, staring at them in dismay. She'd got up early to get ahead with the Christmas baking. She was going to have to start all over again.

The doorbell rang, making her jump. She switched off the oven and ran to answer the door. On the doorstep was Hattie's new best friend, Kiki, who had recently arrived at the twins' school mid-A levels. Lizzy could see why Hattie was drawn to her, with her shaggy russet bob and her fedora hat and her purple suede coat with the fringing. Next to her was another girl in black leather leggings, an outsize mohair jumper and a heavy mane of glossy red hair. At the kerb was a shiny white SUV with blacked-out windows.

'Hi, Mrs Kingham,' said Kiki, fixing Lizzy with her

slightly mad eyes; turquoise with pinprick pupils. Lizzy hoped they were like that naturally – she wasn't sure about Kiki yet. 'Is Hattie ready?'

'Oh shit,' said Lizzy, remembering Hattie was going into Birmingham shopping. 'I was supposed to wake her up. I'm so sorry. Come in, come in. Hattie!' She called up the stairs, then peered outside at the parked car. 'Is your mum waiting? Get her to come in too.'

'I'm Kiki's mum,' smiled the girl with the leather leggings, holding out her hand. 'I'm Meg.'

Lizzy stared at her for a second, then took her hand. 'Oh God, sorry. You look so . . .'

How could she be Kiki's mother? She looked the same age as the girls. Though on much closer inspection, maybe she was older than she appeared. Just a very few wrinkles at the corner of her eyes; pale skin with a dusting of freckles; very Julianne Moore.

Meg laughed. 'I've always looked the same age. It'll all go horribly wrong one day. I know it will.'

'Shall I go up and get Hattie?' asked Kiki, who'd obviously heard this conversation a million times.

'Sure,' said Lizzy, and Kiki legged it up the stairs. 'Come through to the kitchen,' she said to Meg. 'Would you like a coffee while she gets ready? I'm so sorry. I was supposed to get her up at half eight but I completely forgot.'

'Hey, it's not your responsibility,' said Meg. 'She has an alarm on her phone, right?'

'I suppose so,' said Lizzy. Meg had a point, but Lizzy always felt as if everything was her responsibility; her fault. 'Thanks for taking them into Birmingham. I haven't got the time. I've got so much to do still. I only finished work last night and I'm so behind...'

She led Meg through the living room, keenly aware that it was in a mess, that the decorations weren't up, that the cards weren't on display, then through into the kitchen.

'It's no problem. I need to go in. I have a load of stuff still to get. It's never-ending, isn't it?' Meg looked around the kitchen and its chaos approvingly. 'What an adorable kitchen.'

The kitchen wasn't big, but it was cosy, with its quarry tiled floor, a fireplace lined with shelves and a huge picture window that looked out over the walled garden. The Kinghams ate in here too, at an old pine table with mismatched chairs. There were years and years of clutter jostling for space on the shelves and the walls. It needed a major de-clutter and a deep clean, thought Lizzy – now she was jobless there would be time...

'Thanks,' she said, discreetly putting her hand up to remove her antlers and depositing them on the kitchen table, conscious she was still in her pyjamas. 'I have been up for ages, by the way.' She pointed at the smouldering ruins on the side. 'The Great British Burn Off...'

Meg wandered over to inspect them. 'Oh, they look fine. Just a little bit singed. Stick a load of icing sugar on them. No one will notice.' She broke off a corner. 'Yum.'

'Coffee?' said Lizzy, and Meg nodded.

'I just want to say,' she said, sliding into one of the chairs, 'I'm so grateful to Hattie for making friends with Kiki. It's been tough for her, moving school in the middle of her A levels, but she had a bit of trouble at St

Margaret's. It's so lovely that they're friends. Hattie's a good influence.'

Lizzy glowed with pride. There was nothing nicer than praise for your children.

'The two of them get on well. She loves coming over to you.'

Hattie was slightly in thrall to Kiki, whose father made pop videos and a *lot* of money.

Meg smiled. 'I'm taking a back seat in the business while she finishes. My husband's away more than ever so I think it's important for me to be around.' She blinked and for a moment there were tears in her eyes. 'I worry that I wasn't there enough when she was younger and it made her go off the rails a bit. I think she's back on track now. She seems to be working hard.' She sighed. 'When does the worry stop?'

'Hey,' said Lizzy, putting a cup of coffee in front of her and sitting down at the table opposite. 'We all do the best we can. We can't hold ourselves responsible for everything.' She patted Meg's hand. 'Isn't that what you just said to me?'

Meg gazed at her. Lizzy wondered what issues she was mulling over in her mind; what her fears and worries were. She recognised the combination of panic and anxiety in Meg's face, for she felt it herself, constantly. The fears for your children only grew bigger as they did, as they became people in their own right and started making decisions for themselves. Not always good ones.

'You're right,' said Meg. 'We're too hard on ourselves. But it's tough. I might only look thirty, but I feel a hundred and eight.' She laughed and lifted her coffee cup. 'Anyway, cheers. Here's to burnt brownies. Who cares?'

I do, thought Lizzy. She'd wanted two trays of perfection, and to be standing in front of this stunning woman looking like a respectable human being, in a house that didn't look as if someone had dropped a bomb.

'Mum!' Hattie burst into the kitchen, Kiki in her wake. 'You were supposed to get me up!'

She looked different lately, thought Lizzy, the glamorous influence of Kiki and Meg apparent in her newly bleached hair sporting a streak of kingfisher blue, her skater's figure perfect for the tight military blazer and minuscule velvet skirt she was wearing. She looked fantastic.

Lizzy felt a pang, recognising that any influence she had over her daughter's sartorial style had finally evaporated. For a moment, she remembered a smocked gingham dress and a pair of red sandals with little brown feet buckled inside.

'Come on, Mum,' said Kiki to Meg, who was finishing her coffee.

Hattie and Kiki were as agitated and keen to go as young racehorses.

Lizzy beckoned Hattie over, rummaging in her handbag, and gave her twenty quid.

'Here's some money for lunch,' she said, sotto voce.

'I'm not sure that will be enough,' Hattie whispered back. Lizzy raised an eyebrow.

'Well, it's all I've got,' she said, fixing her daughter with a meaningful glare.

Hattie hesitated, and Lizzy could see her processing a choice of possible replies. Then she smiled and leaned in to give her mother a kiss. 'Thanks, Mum.'

'Make sure you're back by sixish,' said Lizzy. 'We're doing the tree tonight, remember? As long as it arrives...'

They always decorated the tree together, as a family, but they'd left it very late this year – not for want of Lizzy trying. She'd been badgering Simon for days to get the tree delivered. He had a contact who could get them cheap, but this year's tree still hadn't materialised. Simon had promised it would arrive today. In the meantime, he wouldn't let Lizzy get one from somewhere else.

'He's only charging thirty quid for a six-footer, straight to the door,' he'd told her before he left for work this morning. 'That'll cost you seventy anywhere else.'

'Yes, but it's no use if it doesn't turn up.'

'It will. Today. I absolutely promise.'

'You said that yesterday. And the day before.'

'He's given me his word. It'll be here by lunchtime.'

'Great. We can decorate it tonight. I'll do the usual.'

They always had lasagne, and Lizzy always played the soundtrack from *The Snowman* while they were doing it. For the last few years she'd had to fight for it, as the twins wanted their own music thumping away in the background, but she always won. It was her tradition and she knew they secretly loved it; they teased her when she cried when 'Walking in the Air' came on, because it was so heart-soaringly joyous. The decorating of the tree was Christmas to her, when they all came together and made the house ready.

Lizzy walked Hattie, Kiki and Meg out to the front door and waved them goodbye. As they climbed into the SUV, a flat-bed truck with a huge Christmas tree on the back careered to a halt behind it.

Lizzy gave a wide grin and pointed madly at the van so Hattie could see it, giving her a double thumbs-up. Hattie gave her a discreet thumbs-up back then turned away. To be fair, no one wanted their pyjama-clad mother waving at them from the doorstep.

'All right, love? Where'd you want it?' grinned the Christmas-tree man, clambering out of his cab. 'I've got a peach for you here, the pick of the bunch. Nothing but the best, your husband told me.'

Lizzy clapped her hands in delight. Simon hadn't let her down.

Christmas was going to be perfect.

4

Back in the kitchen, she did all the washing-up, cut the brownies into tiny little squares, throwing away the burnt edges, and dusted them with icing sugar as Meg had suggested. She'd make some chocolate fridge cake later, with cranberries and pistachios – she couldn't burn those, but her inner Nigella would be satisfied.

Then she called up her Christmas spreadsheet on her iPad: an alarming plethora of presents still to be bought and wrapped, food to be prepared, chores to be time-tabled, tasks to be delegated . . . There was still so much to be done. She felt a little bubble of panic but then told herself it was fine: she'd left work, she had nothing to do but concentrate on Christmas.

As events manager at Craven Court Hotel, she had always been run off her feet during the festive season, firstly with the office parties they held every night in the run-up – three-course dinner, half a bottle of fizz and a DJ for £24.95 a head meant they were always full to bursting – then getting the hotel ready for the guests who had booked their Indulgent Christmas package: three nights including a present from Santa (cashmere gloves for the ladies; leather wallets for the men).

So Christmas had always been a mad scramble.

Snatched lunch-hour shopping trips. Favours called in to sneak the afternoon off for carol concerts and nativity plays. Broken resolutions to make everything from scratch which inevitably ended in buying luxury mince pies and sausage rolls and Christmas cake from Marks & Spencer, paying extra to make up for her culinary neglect. One year she'd actually had to pinch a box of crackers from the hotel as she'd forgotten to buy any. And she always had to go in on Christmas Day just to check everything was running smoothly: that Santa hadn't turned up drunk, they hadn't run out of pigs-in-blankets and the fairy lights on the box bushes outside hadn't fused. Everything had to be perfect.

This year, it was time for everything at Pepperpot Cottage to be perfect. There had to be an upside to voluntary redundancy.

To be fair, her 'voluntary' redundancy hadn't been all that voluntary. But Lizzy could read between the lines. The new regime wanted to get rid of the dead wood. They didn't want a middle-aged events manager. They wanted someone young and vibrant who had their finger on the pulse of social media and the latest cocktail craze. Lizzy had seen, in the brochures for the other hotels in the group, the skin-tight cheongsam dresses the staff were expected to wear and had thought *Oh dear*.

'Take the money and run,' said Simon cheerfully. 'And if you don't want to get another job straight away, you don't have to. I'm earning enough these days. Take some time out.'

Lizzy looked at him, puzzled. It would never have occurred to her not to work. She wasn't a lady who lunched.

Or a gym bunny. She'd always been a working mum. Not being one wasn't an option.

It was funny, though. Back at the end of the summer, when she'd 'volunteered' and they'd said thank you and told her when her last day would be – 21 December – she hadn't batted an eyelid. She had felt confident that she would be able to find another job. But now, confident was the last thing she was feeling. Especially after the rejection from Missingham Manor. It was the fourth *thanks but no thanks* she'd received.

She took in a deep breath and told herself to forget about applying for jobs for now. She could have the rest of December off, as a reward for all those Christmases she had worked round the clock and run herself almost ragged, juggling everything and smiling constantly. This year she was going to really enjoy every moment, soak up every detail – and hopefully get a rest into the bargain. It was a terrible time of year to look for work anyway, so she would hit the ground running in the new year, refreshed and filled with resolution.

She looked up at the clock. It was nearly half ten and she still wasn't dressed and she had a doctor's appointment at quarter past eleven – one of the many things she was shoe-horning into this three-day window.

She ran up two flights of stairs to the twins' rooms at the top, and knocked on Luke's door. There was no reply so she went in tentatively. He was still fast asleep, the curtains drawn.

'Luke!' She tapped his shoulder and he stirred, rolling onto his back with a groan.

'Hey, Mum,' he mumbled.

'Listen, I've got to go out. Will you do me a favour?'

'Yeah, yeah. Course.' He looked up at her with bleary eyes.

'Can you get the decorations down from the attic for me? Put them by the tree in the living room? They're just by the water tank – three boxes full. You can't miss them. They've got Xmas Dex written all over them.' Lizzy knew, when explaining to men where to find something, you couldn't be too precise.

'OK.'

Lizzy looked around the gloom of the bedroom. She could see plates and mugs and clothes strewn everywhere.

'And can you have a bit of a tidy?'

She hated nagging. It had been a long, hard term for both of them with their mocks looming after Christmas. But there was no need for squalor. They could indulge in that as much as they liked once they were students.

'Yeah. Sorry, Mum. I know. It's disgusting. I'm a slob.' Luke gave her an endearing grin. 'But it's my job.'

'I'd be very worried if it was tidy in here. Anyway, I'll be back later this afternoon but if you could sort your bedroom and get the decorations down you'll get a gold star from me. We're doing the tree tonight – it's just arrived, thank God.'

Luke nodded. 'Cool.' He reached for his phone and started scrolling through his apps. She'd lost him, thought Lizzy. He'd be counting his Instagram likes – there was little point in any further communication. She bent down and ruffled his hair fondly. He batted her hand away with a smile, not taking his eyes away from his screen.

'Attic. Decorations. Don't forget.'

'Love you, Mumma,' he sang. It was the twins' mantra

– their way of telling her she didn't need to go on a minute longer; they'd received the message and understood.

He didn't look up as she left the room.

Lizzy ran down to her bedroom, jumped into the shower then pulled on a pair of jeans and her Christmas jumper. It had a pudding on the front with a sprig of holly. Usually the jumper put a smile on her face and put her in the spirit, but when she looked in the mirror an image of Meg, with her slender legs and that mane of hair that was artfully tousled to look not-done, flashed into her head. She tried to tug the bottom of the jumper over her bum to get the same outsize effect that Meg had sported, but either it had shrunk or she had got bigger because it only just reached past her waistband.

Looking in the mirror also reminded her she had been meaning to put an application of Frosted Chocolate Brown through her hair for weeks, but hadn't had time. And it was such a messy business and got all over the bathroom and the towels. Anyway, flashes of grey were fashionable right now, weren't they? Wasn't getting older all about embracing your imperfections these days? Flaunting the flabby bits? Celebrating the silver?

It didn't matter, she told herself. She was going to the doctor, not a fashion show. But she felt a sense of gloom creep over her. That insidious mix of uncertainty and panic which had become all too familiar of late, and which she couldn't control. She would be bobbing along quite happily and it would sneak up on her. She had, initially, blamed the redundancy, but it wasn't just the redundancy that was making her feel like this. There was something else, something she didn't like to think about:

the fact that, come next September, there would only be two of them in these four walls. Every time she thought about it, she felt that cold iron fist around her heart, that needling in her stomach and a terrifying sense of dread that had, eventually, sent her to her GP a month ago.

'I feel as if I'm going mad.'

The GP had looked at her, raising her eyebrows to indicate she needed more information.

'Everything seems pointless. Especially me. And I can't sleep. I wake up at two and lie there for about three hours worrying. Then I fall back to sleep and can hardly drag myself out of bed come morning. I've got no energy. I've put on about a stone. And I feel...' Lizzy grasped about for the best word. 'Full of dread. But I've got nothing to worry about. Well, no more than most people...' She gave a helpless smile. 'Though my twins are going off to uni next September, so there's that.' She took in a deep breath. 'Sometimes I just want to crawl out of my skin and run away.' She finished with a sigh, and to her horror felt her eyes fill with tears. 'Oh God.' She put her fingers up to her face and wiped them away. 'Sorry.'

'I think,' said the doctor, 'that what you are feeling is quite normal, given your age.'

Lizzy nodded.

'Well, yes. But I didn't expect to feel so overwhelmingly awful.'

'If things don't get better, we can look at prescribing something. Antidepressants. Or HRT. But they don't work for everyone and I think it might be better in the first instance to see if you can plough through.' She wrote a list. 'Cut back on caffeine and alcohol and spicy foods.

Get plenty of exercise and fresh air. Take up something that will help you relax. Yoga or pilates.'

She'd handed Lizzy the piece of paper. Lizzy looked down at it doubtfully. It didn't fill her with confidence.

This morning, she was going back to see the GP again. She'd had a month to put the doctor's suggestions into practice, but if anything she felt worse, as if she wasn't in control of anything. As if life was dictating terms to her, rather than the other way round. She'd always been so positive and upbeat, but now it all felt like wading through treacle. Small things became big obstacles. She'd tried to hide it from everyone – Simon was under enough pressure without worrying about a hormonal wife – but she felt she needed someone to tell her it was OK to feel like this and that it was normal and that it would get better. That she would feel like herself again.

She gave herself a thumbs-up in the mirror, telling herself that asking for help didn't make her a failure, then spent fifteen minutes looking for her car keys. Which turned out to be in the car.

This happened *all the time*. Further evidence she was going completely barmy.

She arrived at the surgery with two minutes to spare. She walked up the steps, trying to count how many times she had been inside this building. Until she'd become pregnant with the twins, she had barely darkened the surgery doors. Thereafter it had felt as if she was there every week for one thing or another for her or for them. Blood tests and check-ups and jabs. Mastitis. Colic. Chicken pox. Ear infections. Eczema patches. Smear tests. The appointments had tailed off for the twins when they reached their teens and became more robust and she herself hadn't been in for anything until the appointment a few weeks ago.

'So there's been no improvement?'

Lizzy sat in the plastic bucket chair opposite Dr Redmond, fiddling with the end of her scarf, wondering if she was wasting the doctor's time. She'd made the appointment last week when she'd found herself in tears in the loo at work over something trivial. Now she felt a bit of a fraud.

'I'm so up and down. Sometimes I can cope no problem, then something happens and I fall apart. It's so silly...' She gulped. 'And sometimes... sometimes I feel as if it wouldn't matter if I wasn't here.'

Dr Redmond, about half her age, slender in black trousers and a navy cardigan, her dark bob smooth and sleek, looked at her with her head tilted to one side, as if seeing her for the first time. 'Have you had suicidal thoughts?'

Lizzy had to consider her reply. 'No. But sometimes I think I'd like to go to sleep in a warm, fuzzy place where I can just curl up. And not wake up.'

This time the doctor looked concerned. The last time she was here Lizzy had thought she looked rather bored; as if she had wanted something juicier to diagnose. Now, though, she sprang into action.

'I think perhaps we should try some antidepressants. Just to get your head over the parapet and help you feel less... overwhelmed?'

She began typing into her computer. Lizzy's heart started to beat a little faster. When on earth had she become the sort of person who needed antidepressants? She was one of life's sunbeams. Nothing got her down.

But she realised, as the prescription edged its way out of the printer, that she felt a little green shoot of hope in her heart. She reached out for the slip, hoping this really would be the answer and she might start to feel like herself again, instead of a grey shadow. She half listened while the doctor gave her instructions about how to take them, warning her they wouldn't work straight away, advising her to avoid alcohol, then stood up, murmuring her thanks.

She walked out of the consulting room and back through reception, wondering how many people knew what she was holding in her hand. None, of course. They would have no idea and probably cared even less.

As she stepped outside the prescription fluttered in the breeze and for a moment she was tempted to let it go and watch it fly across the car park. After all, were the tablets really going to make any difference to how she felt? It scared her to think that was what she needed to navigate life.

She stuffed the prescription into her bag and wrapped her coat round her, determined to pull herself together. Apart from being made redundant and facing an empty nest, she had nothing serious to worry about. And she *must* make the most of the good things. It was Christmas time. She was looking forward to tonight, to decorating the tree and sitting round the table with a big lasagne and a couple of glasses of wine and laughing with Simon and Hattie and Luke.

She got in her car and sat there for a moment. For the past few months she had felt like the proverbial swan, gliding down the river with her feet desperately paddling away underneath the surface where no one could see. Now she had asked for help. She had done the right thing, she told herself. She felt better already.

She decided she was going to ignore the annoying to-do/shopping list that was weighing her down – the fresh flowers that needed buying, the dry-cleaning that needed picking up, the extra few stocking fillers she had to buy – and head straight for Leadenbury. Her farewell present from Craven Court had been an extremely generous voucher for Inglewood's department store.

She was going to spoil herself with something new and luxurious to wear on Christmas Day. She imagined something casually glamorous, with a pair of black suede ankle boots (high, but not fall-off-and-break-your-ankle-after-one-glass high). Perhaps she'd even get a makeover at one of the cosmetics counters; contour her face with some of that shimmering highlighter that gave you cheekbones.

Her spirits lifted. Tablets shmablets – all she needed was some retail therapy.

5

Inglewood's was a family-run department store in Leadenbury, the little market town five miles from Astley-in-Arden. Lizzy preferred shopping in Leadenbury to braving Birmingham, which won hands down in terms of choice but was rather an ordeal and made her feel anxious. She couldn't cope with the city traffic or the parking or the crowds these days, and she was grateful to Meg for running the gauntlet with the girls.

Leadenbury was a tad old-fashioned but Lizzy had her secret parking spot and her favourite coffee shop. And Inglewood's had had a revamp recently – once it had been a bit mumsy and frumpy, full of lambswool jumpers and calf-length skirts, but one of the younger members of the Inglewood family had given it an injection of life. It might not be Selfridges but it was a lot less intimidating.

Inside, the shop felt very jolly. As part of their new image they had made a big effort with their decorations and it shone and sparkled, with merry Christmas tunes being played at just the right volume and the air filled with the scent of cinnamon and cloves.

As she rode the escalator up to the second floor, Lizzy felt calmer; a cheering sense of anticipation washed over her. It was important to reward yourself, she thought.

She might still have a list of things to do as long as her arm, but it was important to put herself first for once. Self-care, that was what it was called these days – she'd read about it in a magazine and thought the expression sounded slightly dubious, but she was all for it.

As she plunged herself into the clothes section, she gave herself permission to get exactly what she wanted. Age was just a number, as was your dress size. She might be a bit tubbier round the middle than she had been, but she still had a great cleavage and great ankles.

It was a real luxury, having the time to look through all the Christmas outfits: emerald green satin, silver sequins, black feathers and white cashmere. She was spoilt for choice, but finally settled on a cranberry red velvet dress with flattering drapery and batwing sleeves. She found her size and took the dress towards the changing room.

As soon as she walked in, she stopped in her tracks.

In the middle of the floor was a woman, hands on hips, looking at herself in the mirror with adoration. Lizzy couldn't ever imagine doing that. She had taken to avoiding any glimpse of her reflection if she could help it of late.

This woman, however, clearly loved what she saw. She was Amazonian, her hair a striking white blonde crop which showed off her cheekbones. She wasn't beautiful, but she carried herself with such confidence it made you think she was. She was trying on a white crêpe sleeveless jumpsuit, the sort of outfit that would fill any normal woman with dread.

Amanda. Simon's ex-wife and the mother of his two children, Lexi and Mo.

The last person Lizzy wanted to bump into in a communal changing room.

The last person Lizzy wanted to bump into – ever.

Next to Amanda was a pile of clothes that had already been tried on, rejected and thrown on the floor. Lizzy knew full well she wouldn't waste any time putting them back on the hangers. She'd leave that to the assistant, the one who was standing next to her nodding in admiration.

'We do have a range of hold-you-in underwear,' the assistant was saying. 'If you feel the need.'

Amanda flashed her a glance. 'I don't think so. There's only a slight bump where you can see my Caesarean scar.' She patted her non-existent stomach.

Lizzy clapped her hand over her mouth, trying not to laugh. How could she actually say that?

'Silver heels, I think,' said Amanda. 'And silver nails.'

'Oooh, yes,' said the assistant with relish, then caught sight of Lizzy standing in the doorway. 'Did you want to try that on?'

'No, I'm fine,' Lizzy squeaked, backing out of the changing room before Amanda spotted her. She couldn't bear the humiliation of trying on her outfit next to her. Amanda looked like the Snow Queen in the white jumpsuit; Lizzy would look like the Snowman.

Amanda dragged herself away from her reflection and gave a cry of recognition.

'Lizzy!'

Lizzy shut her eyes. She could just run; fling the dress at the assistant and bolt for the exit. But that would be weird, and she didn't want any instances of erratic behaviour getting back to Simon's mother. She was already paranoid about the two of them talking about her behind her back.

Instead, she smoothed her hair down and lifted the corners of her mouth into as big a smile as she could manage.

'Hi, Amanda,' she managed.

'Come in! No modesty here. All girls together.'

'Actually, no. I've changed my mind. I thought I wanted something new but I don't at all—'

'Come on. Spoil yourself. It's Christmas! Time for us women to put ourselves first for once.'

Lizzy raised an eyebrow. Amanda always put herself first. She always had. It was a skill Lizzy secretly admired. She had tried to analyse how she did it: basically by not giving a monkey's about anything or anyone else, ever. Annoyingly, it didn't seem to have done Amanda any harm. No one liked her any less, and she always got what she wanted.

Amanda was looking at the dress over Lizzy's arm.

'Oh, that dress is gorgeous. It would look amazing on you. It wouldn't suit me at all. You've got boobs whereas I haven't. Try it. Go on.'

Lizzy hesitated. Was Amanda being genuine or was she luring Lizzy into a trap so she could humiliate her? She wasn't going to risk it.

'No. I've got nowhere to wear it, even if I did buy it,' Lizzy managed lamely.

'Don't be silly,' said Amanda. 'You don't need a special occasion. It's Christmas!'

'It would suit your colouring,' said the assistant. 'And it's very forgiving. There's a lot of stretch in it.'

33

'We all need a bit of stretch at this time of year.'
Amanda patted her non-existent stomach again.

Amanda never ate anything. In the twenty years she
had known her, Lizzy had never seen a cake or a biscuit
or a crisp pass her lips. She looked at her watch.

'I haven't really got time now . . .'

Amanda motioned for the assistant to unzip her, then
let the jumpsuit fall to the ground and stepped out of it,
standing in front of Lizzy in just her lacy high-cut pants
and a push-up bra.

'By the way, thank you so much for stepping in and
having Cynthia.' Amanda reached out and started putting
her clothes back on.

'What?' Lizzy was startled.

'It's not every day you get offered a half-price chalet in
Val-d'Isère. I couldn't possibly have turned it down. Perks
of the job.' She shimmied into a pair of skinny jeans and
zipped them up without even having to breathe in.

'Sorry,' said Lizzy. 'I think I'm missing something.'

'Mo and Lexi are so excited about coming, but there
wasn't room for Cynthia.' Amanda disappeared for a
moment into a black polo-neck jumper, then her head
popped out. 'It's only a two-bed chalet.' She ruffled up
her hair till every strand was back in place.

Lizzy took a deep breath, trying to make sense of what
Amanda was saying.

'You're going skiing for Christmas?' She tried to keep
her voice level. 'But it's your year.'

Lizzy and Simon took Christmas in turns with Amanda
to have his children and his mum. Lizzy had been glad
it wasn't their turn this Christmas: it was always quite
cramped in Pepperpot Cottage and there was twice as

much washing-up and noise with the extra guests. She loved Lexi and Mo and the twins got on well with their half-siblings. Now they were all older the age gap had closed, and even though Mo and Lexi were in their early twenties they loved to revert back to being teenagers – there was always music and board games and raucous laughter.

But Cynthia was another story.

'I spoke to Simon. He said no problem. Surely he told you?' Amanda's smile edged a little wider, sensing a spanner in the works – though being Amanda she would just swan off to the Alps regardless.

Lizzy shook her head. 'He hasn't said anything.'

'Oh dear. Well, I know how busy he is these days. He must have forgotten. She won't be any bother for you. She's no trouble, is she?'

Lizzy blinked. Not trouble, exactly. But she didn't want Cynthia at Pepperpot for Christmas.

She'd always had a slightly uneasy relationship with her mother-in-law. Cynthia thought the world of her son's first wife and had been gutted when Simon and Amanda split. Lizzy had always felt a pretty poor replacement. Cynthia had never said that she was a disappointment, not in so many words, but Lizzy was aware how successful Cynthia thought Amanda was, with her luxury travel agency, Sand and Snow.

And she was conscious of all the things Amanda did for Cynthia: the lavish bouquets of flowers on her birthday, the tickets for her to go and see Michael Bublé and Alfie Bose, the holidays. Amanda had once told Lizzy that Cynthia thought of her as 'the daughter she never had'.

Lizzy couldn't begin to compete with Amanda's showy generosity, and felt overshadowed by her.

And then, four years ago, not long after Simon's father, Neville, had died, Cynthia had done something awful. Something awful that only Lizzy knew. Distraught, Cynthia had sworn Lizzy to secrecy. Lizzy had kept her side of the bargain, but as a result, the less she saw of Cynthia the better. Lizzy didn't want to sit through Christmas hiding the truth from Simon and the children yet again. She found it exhausting, pretending to make Cynthia welcome when in reality she couldn't ever forgive her for what she had done. It was sheer luck that it hadn't ended in tragedy.

Tempting though it was, she couldn't say any of this to Amanda. She wondered what Amanda would say if she knew the truth about her ex-mother-in-law? Loyal Lizzy had kept her mouth shut for four years, because she wasn't a troublemaker, and she didn't want Simon to be worried about his mother.

She knew she was going to lie down and roll over, because she couldn't betray Cynthia. If she protested, there would be an outcry and she would have to tell the truth. So she would keep quiet. Amanda would waft off to Val-d'Isère and Cynthia would come to Pepperpot.

Everyone would get the Christmas they wanted, except Lizzy. How was that fair?

Amanda was nodding at the assistant to take the jumpsuit to the till for her, picking up her bag. Lizzy knew she couldn't carry on this conversation. She would probably end up bursting into tears and making a fool of herself. She knew from experience she would end up looking like the unreasonable one. The unstable one. It happened every time.

So she turned quietly and walked out of the changing room.

6

As Lizzy wove her way back through the dresses that had only a minute ago been so tempting and enticing, her mind raced. She was burning with the injustice.

Why should she put up with it? They *couldn't* spring Cynthia on her, three days before Christmas. She felt angry, because she knew they all thought, 'Oh, Lizzy won't mind.' That she would selflessly set another place at the table and organise everything.

Well, maybe this time she wouldn't. No one had had either the nerve or the courtesy to let her know the change of plan, and this year was *her* Christmas. The one she wanted. She wasn't going to be manipulated. She was going to behave like Amanda and put herself first.

She pulled her phone out of her bag and called Simon. She was, for Lizzy, extremely cross. She didn't even say hello when he answered, just snapped at him.

'When were you going to tell me about your mother?'

'What?'

'I've just bumped into Amanda in Inglewood's and she says your mother's coming to us for Christmas.'

'Oh shit.' The expletive was heavy with the dread realisation of a man who knows he's messed up.

'So you knew?'

'Amanda said they might be going skiing and she'd get back to me. But I didn't hear any more so I thought it was off.'

'Well, as far as Amanda's concerned she's hitting Val-d'Isère tomorrow and it's a done deal.'

'She was supposed to confirm it.' Simon sounded defensive.

'You should have warned me it might happen.'

'I didn't want to stress you.'

'Well, I'm bloody stressed now.' Lizzy could hear her voice rise.

'Lizzy, it's fine. I'll sort everything that needs sorting. Not that we need to sort much. It's only one extra person...'

'It's Cynthia. That is not *only* one extra person. That's a military campaign.'

'Rubbish. It's one more chair and a few more spuds.'

Lizzy shut her eyes and stepped onto the escalator.

'I'll have to get her stuff for a stocking. She can't just sit there empty-handed while we open ours. I'll have to get extra food, and a Christmas pudding without cherries in, because she doesn't like cherries, and we'll have to rearrange everything in the kitchen to fit an extra place, and our morning will be interrupted because *you* will have to drive over and get her... And I'll have to make sure everything is perfect in the spare room and put the best linen on the bed—'

She paused for breath.

'I'll make it up to you,' said Simon.

Lizzy felt limp with frustration.

'I wanted it to be just us. The last Christmas before the twins leave home.'

'They're not leaving home. They'll be back next year.'

'You don't understand.'

'I can't tell her not to come.'

'No. Tell *Amanda* to tell her not to come. Tell Amanda we have other plans and it's up to her to sort it. She's the one who didn't confirm.'

'I can't do that, Lizzy.' There was panic in Simon's voice.

'Why not? It's exactly how it would work if it was the other way round.'

'But it's not. And she's my mother, not Amanda's. She only goes to Amanda because of Lexi and Mo. She's *my* responsibility.'

'So my Christmas gets ruined because of what everyone else wants?'

She could hear her voice go up an octave and several decibels. The people in front of her were turning round to look at her. She was surprised, though, by the sympathetic smiles she was getting.

'Do you know what would be nice?' Lizzy lowered her voice, but it was a bit wobbly. She was *not* going to cry. 'If you stuck up for me for once.'

Simon didn't reply for a moment. She heard him sigh. 'Did the tree arrive?'

Lizzy didn't answer straight away.

'Yes,' she said eventually, cross that now she was supposed to sound grateful even though she'd wanted the tree at least a week ago. 'Thank you,' she said through gritted teeth. 'I'll see you later.'

She hung up and put her phone back in her bag. A woman nudged her.

'I feel your pain. Christmas is a nightmare. I wish it

could be cancelled. Get yourself a bottle of Baileys and it will all be all right.'

Lizzy smiled as she reached the bottom of the escalator. She held her head high as she walked out through the cosmetics hall, breathing in the mingled scents. She pushed at the double doors and headed out into the street where the icy air hit her. She took in a big gulp of it and told herself she wasn't alone. There were women everywhere trying to keep a smile on their faces in pursuit of the perfect Christmas. She mustn't take it personally.

Across the street there was a market stall selling hot chocolate and doughnuts. Vanilla-scented steam floated along on the notes from the Salvation Army band, reminding Lizzy she had had no lunch. Her mouth watered: sugar was just what she needed. She was about to set off across the street when she felt a hand on her shoulder and turned, half expecting a word of reassurance from another sympathetic shopper.

'Excuse me, madam.'

There was a black-clad security guard standing in front of her. He had INGLEWOOD'S written on his left breast. She smiled.

'Yes?'

He nodded towards her handbag. 'Have you paid for this item?'

She looked down to see the velvet dress still slung over her arm, hooked behind her bag.

'Oh my God!' She looked back up at him in horror. 'I didn't realise. Honestly. I was going to try it on in the dressing room and then I bumped into my husband's ex and I just forgot I had it.'

The guard looked at her, stony-faced. He had a toad-like expression and bags under his eyes.

She thrust the dress towards him with a smile.

'Here. Sorry. I was going to hang it back up. I hate people who don't hang things back up after they've tried them on.'

He held out his arm.

'Perhaps you'd like to come with me so we can discuss it in private?'

'What?'

'I need you to come with me.'

He was firm and formal and the meaning was very clear. He was trying to usher her back to the shop.

Lizzy felt her cheeks flush scarlet. Her heart was pounding. People were looking at her as they walked past, disgust and accusation on their faces.

'Just take it back,' she said. 'Please. Honestly. I would have turned round as soon as I realised. I don't even want it. I don't even know if it fits!'

He took the dress, shaking it out on its hanger for all to see, and nodded towards the shop entrance.

'This way, please.'

She looked around in disbelief. She supposed she could do a runner, but what if a member of the public bundled her to the ground like a common criminal? She had no option but to do as he asked.

'It's a misunderstanding. But if you insist.'

It didn't really get more mortifying than being marched through a shop with a security guard. Lizzy tried to put a smile on her face that signified her innocence and his lack of judgement.

The guard led her to a small office in the bowels of

the building. Inside, a woman of about her own age was waiting. Her name badge indicated she was Shirley Booth, assistant manager.

'Mrs...?'

'Kingham,' said Lizzy. 'There seems to have been a bit of a mistake.'

Shirley nodded, expressionless. 'Let's deal with the formalities first.'

The next few minutes passed in a blur as Lizzy was seated and filled out a form, giving her name and address. She found herself going along with it, too shaken to protest, with no idea of her rights or what she was supposed to do.

'We need to take your photograph,' said the guard, holding up a camera.

'What? Why?' Lizzy put her hands to her hair. Ludicrously. This wasn't a fashion shoot. It was a mugshot.

'To put on our database. In case we have to ban you.'

'Ban me?' The prospect was both ridiculous and horrifying. She sat up straight. 'I've been shopping here for longer than I can remember. I spend a fortune. I bought a new hoover in here last week!'

She said it as if hoovering and shoplifting were mutually exclusive.

The security guard didn't crack. 'We take shoplifting very seriously. And we circulate photographs to the other shops in Leadenbury. With the police cut-backs us shopkeepers have to look out for each other.'

They were going to take her photograph and notify every shop in town that she was a shoplifter? Lizzy felt sick. She turned to Shirley. Surely a woman would understand?

'I wasn't shoplifting. It was an honest mistake. I don't even want the wretched dress. I was going to put it back. I didn't even try it on!'

'You came out of the changing room with it over your arm and went straight down the escalator,' said the guard.

'I was on the phone to my husband. His ex-wife had just told me we've got his mother for Christmas.'

'Classic diversion tactic. Everyone tries that.'

'You are joking. Please tell me this is a joke.'

Shirley sighed and pressed a remote control. 'I'm afraid we've got you on CCTV.'

Suddenly there Lizzy was on the television screen, gliding down the escalator talking into her phone, the dress over her arm.

Lizzy sat back in her chair, bewildered. 'I don't know what to do. I wasn't stealing it. Am I supposed to call my lawyer?'

'We should be calling the police. This is a serious offence.'

Lizzy suddenly grabbed her handbag and rummaged about in it, producing the vouchers.

'Hang on a minute. I came in here to spend these. Why would I steal a dress when I've got the means to pay for it? It doesn't make sense and you know it doesn't.' She thrust the vouchers across the desk.

'Sometimes it's the richest people that nick stuff.' The guard remained unmoved.

Lizzy hated him, with his mean mouth and the way he talked through his nose.

'I suppose you've got a quota? A target number of people you've got to catch to keep your job?'

He raised an eyebrow. 'You walked out of the shop with a dress over your arm. I didn't exactly frame you.'

She turned to Shirley, who was frowning at the frozen image on the screen. Lizzy's face was a rictus of fury and despair as she spoke into her phone.

Lizzy tried appealing to her better nature.

'You must know what it's like. Trying to keep everyone happy at Christmas. I took my eye off the ball for one second and made a mistake. Where's your sisterly solidarity? We're all in this together. We're supposed to support each other, not stitch each other up.'

Shirley and the guard exchanged glances. The guard rolled his eyes as if to say *we've got a right one here*.

Lizzy sat back and crossed her arms. 'Fine. You can do what you like. Arrest me if you want. At least I wouldn't have to face the mother-in-law-from-hell in prison.'

There was silence for a moment. Then Shirley seemed to make a decision.

'Right,' she said. 'You're free to go.'

'What?' said the guard. 'You can't do that. It's not our policy.'

'It was obviously a case of seasonal stress.'

'You haven't fallen for that old chestnut? You're going soft.'

'I know what it's like,' said Shirley. 'Everyone moving the goalposts, expecting the earth, making their little demands without giving a toss how it might affect your plans, not thinking for a moment that you might like to put your feet up for five minutes or stop having to make lists ... And in the meantime you have to do everything, even buy and wrap your own bloody presents because everyone else has better things to do ...'

45

She trailed off, suddenly looking embarrassed at her diatribe.

'Well, quite,' said Lizzy. 'You've hit the nail on the head.'

'I don't know what you're on about,' said the guard.

'Exactly!' chorused the two women.

As Lizzy picked up her bag and made to leave, the manager gave her a complicit grin.

'Have a merry Christmas,' she said with a wink.

'Thank you,' said Lizzy. 'I'm going to make sure I do.'

7

Lizzy drove home feeling stunned. Had that really happened? She replayed it in her head, every excruciating moment. She didn't know whether to laugh or cry.

All she'd wanted was a Christmas dress. Instead she'd been humiliated. First by Amanda, looking like a goddess and pulling rank. Then by being arrested in full view of everyone in front of Inglewood's. Anyone could have seen her. *Amanda* could have seen her, being frog-marched through the shop. There was every chance she had. Lizzy cringed at the thought.

It doesn't matter, she told herself. You're doing the tree tonight. It will all look lovely, and you'll have your family, and they will love you and keep you safe and make you laugh.

She might even tell them what had happened that afternoon. Maybe after a glass of wine she would be able to see the funny side. She was so sensitive at the moment she never knew how she was going to feel about anything.

She told herself to forget about Amanda. And she would just have to be gracious and welcome Cynthia. She couldn't ban her mother-in-law from the house without betraying her confidence. It was their secret. Lizzy had made a promise, perhaps against her better judgement, but mostly to protect the husband she loved. It was ironic that she was being punished for that loyalty, but she wasn't going to let the cat out of the bag.

It was hard work being a good person sometimes.

Back at home, the house was quiet. She walked through the living room and saw with a flicker of irritation that the boxes hadn't been brought down from the attic yet. Surely Luke wasn't *still* in bed? She didn't mind a reasonable lie-in, but she had a rule that everyone should be up by lunch. She trotted to the top of the house, tapped on his bedroom door and opened it.

His bed was empty. The curtains were still shut, and the plates and cups she'd asked him to move were still there. She swallowed down her disappointment. His clothes weren't on the floor any more, though. He'd obviously gone out in a rush, not bothering to do any of the things she'd asked. She sighed.

She loved her children, but they could be spectacularly selfish. She knew that wasn't unique to them, not by any means, but it was very wearing. Yet again she was backed into a corner and given a choice she didn't want to make: get cross and be a nag, or do what she'd asked to be done herself.

She chose the latter. She didn't want to spoil tonight by phoning Luke and moaning. No doubt by not chastising him she wasn't teaching him a lesson, but she didn't have the heart for another confrontation today. Instead she pulled a chair out of his room and put it on the landing, pushing at the hatch to get into the attic. She hated the loft ladder with a vengeance. Pulling it down until the bolt snapped into place made her jump every time: she was terrified of getting her fingers caught.

She finally got all the boxes of decorations down, puffing and sweaty from the exertion of scurrying up and down a ladder she still didn't trust, then carried them down to the living room.

Every year she pulled everything off the tree in a desperate panic, because she would always forget it was Twelfth Night and was terrified it would bring bad luck even though she wasn't really superstitious. So now here she was, faced with a tangle of tinsel and glitter and shards of shiny broken glass. Her heart sank at the sight: it was going to take ages to sort through it all and put it into order. She just wasn't the sort of person who wound the fairy lights neatly around empty Pringles tubes – although she would be this year. This year she was going to be on it.

The tree was standing proudly in a red pot in the corner next to the fireplace. Six feet high, plump and triangular, with evenly spaced branches – Simon had done her proud, she had to admit, and it had been worth waiting for. It was so perfect it almost looked fake, but the scent of fresh pine filling the room proved it wasn't. Though you could probably get fake trees that smelled these days, thought Lizzy. You could get fake anything. Fake reindeer, fake polar bears, fake snow . . .

She'd looked up a Winter Wonderland 'Treetorial' Workshop on the internet. This year she was determined to take things up a level and throw herself into a Nigella/Kirstie world of magical indulgence. Without, of course, sacrificing any family traditions, as that would be far too traumatic – not least for Lizzy. She knew there would be an outcry if she threw any of their old decorations away and she wasn't that much of a control freak.

Besides, the workshop had taught her how to revamp

her tree decor by 'gonging up': giving your old decorations a new lease of life by stringing them up with sumptuous bows. She'd splurged out on several spools of burnt orange velvet ribbon that made her mouth water.

But first she had to go through the boxes and throw away anything broken, then sort everything into size order. Apparently, you put your big balls in the middle of the tree, for depth, and the smaller ones on the outside.

How had she survived Christmas until now, without professional tree-decorating tips?

Painstakingly, she began to go through the boxes – nearly twenty years of accumulated Christmas bling. Every single bauble brought a memory with it, from the half a dozen wooden elves she had bought for their first Christmas at Pepperpot Cottage – they'd had the tiniest tree imaginable – to the feathery flamingos she'd bought the year before. Then there were the glue-encrusted offerings made by Hattie and Luke at nursery. She found two little clay plaques with their handprints, painted gold, and felt the prickle of tears. Their lives were in that box of decorations, marking the years.

Most poignant of all was the battered satin angel with the white feather halo she had bought for the twins' first Christmas. As soon as they were big enough they took turns to put it on top of the tree when they'd all finished decorating. Whose turn was it this year? She couldn't remember, but she would find out later. The twins would know. The poor old angel was battered and grubby and had seen better days, but she was irreplaceable. Anything else on top of their tree was unthinkable. Lizzy gave her a scrub with a damp dishcloth and fluffed up the feathers and put her to one side, ready for the finale.

She felt quite drained when she'd finished, but eventually she had everything laid out in order. Planning and preparation were her new watch words. Farewell to chance and chaos, she thought.

She decided she would give 'gonging up' a trial run. She cut off a length of velvet ribbon and threaded it through the metal hook on a particularly lurid Santa caked in neon glitter. Try as she might, she couldn't get the ribbon to do what she wanted. She was aiming for a big fat bow with a nice plump knot in the middle, so she could then cut a v into the ends of the ribbon to give it a florist's flourish. But her bow just looked limp and creased and mean. There was nothing sumptuous about it.

Frustrated, she flung the decoration back into the box. She was useless. Utterly useless. She wasn't Kirstie bloody Allsop. She was ham-fisted, unimaginative Lizzy who couldn't create magazine perfection to save her life.

She told herself to calm down. Decorating the tree was supposed to be fun. It wasn't a competitive sport. It wasn't something to be judged on. It was their lovely Christmas tradition. Surely the tree was supposed to be a reflection of how your family had evolved, not a benchmark of good taste?

She sighed. It was just that she had wanted it to be different this year. She'd wanted to spend time making everything look – well, not perfect, but stylish and interesting enough for people to take note and remark.

She'd pictured the tree as six foot of luxe sophistication at first glance, but on closer inspection the delighted guest would spot the kitsch and retro baubles of yesteryear, the home-made offerings lugged home by the toddler twins, and exclaim at Lizzy's genius, her artistic eye, her cleverness in mixing the nostalgic with the 'now'.

'Oh, you are clever! I wish I had your knack,' she imagined someone like Meg saying.

She looked at the bare branches doubtfully then decided to give it one last try. She cut a fresh piece of ribbon and threaded it through the loop, then twisted it into a bow – and suddenly there it was, absolutely perfect. She stood back and stared at it in delight, pleased she hadn't given in. She held it up to the tree, admiring the effect, feeling a ripple of satisfaction at her achievement. Maybe she needed to do more of this kind of thing? The feeling of achievement was lovely...

She remembered the prescription in her handbag. She went into the kitchen and took it out and looked at it. Would taking them be an admission of failure? A realisation that she couldn't cope with the ordinary, the day to day, the mundane? There was nothing to justify taking them. No bereavement or divorce or trauma. Did she really need antidepressants? Or should she, as they say, just 'get a life'? Do more of the little things that until now she hadn't had time for? Like tying velvet bows?

Of course she didn't need antidepressants. She was just a middle-aged woman facing up to some changes in her life, she thought. She tucked the prescription behind the Indian takeaway menu on the noticeboard and carried on tying bows until she had got it down to a fine art.

8

The sun was leaching from a pale wintry sky faster than Harley could walk. He'd just managed to catch the last bus, and it dropped him on the esplanade with a wheezy hiss of its brakes and a puff of diesel. He was the only person to get off: a massive contrast from the summer months, when the driver could end up waiting more than ten minutes for the streams to disembark. Summer in Everdene was a short, sharp spike bringing much-needed visitors and money. Winter was long, dark and filled with weather: storms and freezing fog and terrifying waves that showed no mercy.

As he jumped onto the pavement he eyed the beach in front of him. Today the sea was quiet and calm; the tide was edging its way in nonchalantly across the pale-pink sand that would soon turn to grey. The fading light bounced off the bay: a rich deep turquoise that would soon turn to navy.

Hardly any of the shops along the front were open. Everdene was too far off the beaten track to be a lure for tourists at this time of year. The Spar shop had a few straggly trees in nets propped up outside. The Ship Aground served mulled wine and played seasonal anthems on a loop. The locals would all be heading home from whatever job kept them sustained, if they were lucky enough to have one. They might venture out later, for a drink, but for now the little seaside town was settling down for the evening as the lights went on and plumes of smoke began to curl from the chimneys.

Harley shifted his rucksack onto his shoulder and strode towards the beach. He wanted to get to the hut before dusk, because the darkness here was as dark as night ever got, and the light from the few street lamps didn't reach far. The sky overhead would be as flat and black as an iPhone screen. If there was no cloud the stars would be little pin pricks of hope, like fairy lights strung across the horizon.

He was still wound up from this morning's confrontation. He could still see the hostility in his adversary's eyes; smell the sourness of his distaste and feel the man's fingertips on his chest. He knew what Tony wanted. For him to lose his temper. So he could make Harley look like the bad guy. For months and months he'd been chipping away at him. Little jibes. Verbal jabs. Loaded remarks that no one but Harley would understand. Tony was everything that Harley hated: racist, sexist, narrow-minded, controlling... He had a small-town mentality that, combined with being a big fish in a small pond, made him think he could behave how he liked and treat people how he wanted. Of course, what most people saw was the smiling, successful charmer: Tony rarely let his mask slip. He had to Harley, though. Harley could see right through his performance.

And Harley couldn't put up with it any more. He had to get out before he lost control. Luckily, boxing had taught him when not to fight back. His coach had drilled into him how to keep his temper. Nevertheless, he had a limit, and he could sense that his limit was approaching. He was afraid of his own anger.

The cortisol was still pumping through him, making his blood fizz as he headed towards the slipway that led down onto the beach. The air cooled him a little, wrapping itself round him, damp with sea spray. Gradually he was able to breathe again, and he filled his lungs with ozone, letting the fury dissolve. He tried to visualise it leaving him, drifting off along the beach in rivulets.

That man was not worth his anger.

But he still felt a knot inside him. A tangle of helplessness and fear. Was he a coward, to leave the two people he loved most in the world with the person he hated the most? Harley didn't want to spoil Christmas for Leanne and River. His mum and his little brother were more important than he was. Tony viewed Harley as a threat, that much was clear, and maybe without him in the house things would be easier.

He could feel the cold of the sand through the soles of his trainers. As he reached the end of the slipway and turned left, the wind jumped out at him, gleeful with spite, and he blinked, pulling his padded jacket tighter. Head down, he walked parallel to the shore. To his left, the row of beach huts began, protected from above by the dunes.

He knew each and every one. When they were first built, back in the sixties, they were simple wooden structures, with very basic sanitation. Only a few originals survived. Over the past decade, a slew of wealthy middle-class families had swooped in, putting in every mod con until Everdene looked like Nantucket, all white and blue and grey weatherboards. Some were the last word in luxury: state-of-the-art fridges with ice-makers and fancy cookers with pizza ovens and charcoal grills lurked behind the shabby chic frontages. Some were holiday lets, changing inhabitants every week; some were lived in all summer by families who decamped from their city homes. Some were only opened occasionally.

It was one of these Harley was heading to now. A shrewd businessman had bought the Lobster Pot in the late seventies for his wife and children to escape to while he worked. It was still in the same family. His daughter now lived in Dubai: Caroline Openshaw descended about three times a year, leaving it empty the rest of the time. Her family usually came over for Christmas and Harley had got everything ready for them, but he'd had a message earlier that week to say they wouldn't be coming. At the time, he had thought nothing of it, but now, after his altercation with Tony, it was serendipity.

'Feel free to use the hut if you want,' Caroline had said in her email. 'No point in it sitting there empty!'

She was one of the more generous owners. Harley had a summer job as a caretaker for several of the beach huts. He did running repairs, took deliveries, filled the fridges with groceries and wine, liaised with cleaners and babysitters and taxi drivers to make sure the summer crowd didn't have to lift a finger. Once there had just been his boss, Roy, tending to their needs. Roy had been there when the huts were first built. Now, he supervised a team of six, most of them local college kids. As jobs in the area went, it was a good one: it meant Harley could leave the house and hang out on the beach at Everdene nearly every day in the holidays. And there were always pretty girls to chat to.

They loved Harley, with his cinnamon skin and light-green eyes. There was no one else like him round here. He was exotic and glamorous: a hint of rum and reggae. Even though his dad came from Handsworth, not Trenchtown, he was more authentic than some of the surfing guys that tried to emulate his look. He didn't show off about being the real deal, but he knew the girls could tell. And with his skinny jeans rolled up and his faded T-shirts and his intricate tattoos, he had a rock 'n' roll glamour that was irresistible.

Of course, just like Tony, people made assumptions, thought he peddled dope for the holidaymakers, but that was for idiots. On the contrary, Harley was squeaky clean; he had the occasional beer when the sun went down, but for the most part he lived for his fitness and his art. He had done several murals for cafés and restaurants in the area, all with a sea theme. People couldn't get enough of mermaids and pirates, it seemed. His dream was to go to art college. It was a fantasy at the moment, though. He couldn't afford it, and he didn't want to leave his mum. Not yet.

He'd had to step away for the time being, though. He didn't know if it was because of Christmas, but the atmosphere seemed to be getting worse. And Harley knew his presence antagonised Tony. That he only had to breathe to wind the man up. So maybe if he made himself scarce, tensions would ease.

Though part of him didn't want them to, because he wanted his mum to see the truth. Why couldn't Leanne see what Tony was really like? Was she really taken in, just because he was captain of the yacht club and was on the local council? Was she really impressed by all of that? Maybe she was, because Tony was such a contrast to Harley's dad . . . Maybe she'd been drawn to Tony's respectability?

His pretend respectability. Sticking on a blazer for a council meeting didn't make you a good person. It made Harley even more uncomfortable, the fact he was supposed to have respect for Tony's status. Yes, Tony could make things happen in Tawcombe – licences and planning permission – but he usually only made them happen if he could benefit in some way. He always had an ulterior motive.

Harley's biggest fear was that Tony and Leanne would get married. She and his dad had never got round to it, and Harley could sense that Leanne wanted a ring on her finger for security. For River. Even though River wasn't Tony's. If that happened it would be even more difficult to make her see the light.

'He's a good man,' Leanne would tell Harley, over and over. She was still pathetically grateful to Tony for the roof over their heads. She couldn't see that the price was her freedom.

Harley saw things she didn't. Harley heard things she didn't. He didn't want to crush his mother's dream, but it was getting harder and harder for him not to say what he thought about the unnecessary rules and expectations Tony forced them to live under. It had all been very chilled out and relaxed that first summer. Barbecues and boat trips. Once they'd moved in, though, Tony had begun to change. Tidiness and quietness were enforced. The house didn't feel like a home. No shoes allowed inside, no loud music, nothing out of place...

Leanne didn't seem to notice what was happening, like a lobster put into cold water and gradually heated up. Harley had, though, because he didn't have the disadvantage of thinking himself in love.

'It's his house,' Leanne would protest, if Harley complained. 'We have to respect that. We're very lucky.'

It was an impossible situation. He couldn't stoke things up and bring them to a head just to prove he was right, because that would be dangerous. But if he didn't, the situation could go on for ever. It was unbearable. For Harley, at least. Leanne seemed to be able to put up with it. But she'd always been able to put up with a lot. It was both a strength and a weakness.

Was it irony, how opposite Tony was to his own father, who had lived in a whirl of chaos and impulsivity? The volume had been turned up to ten whenever Richie was around: the sparky kid from Handsworth who'd made it to grammar school, against the odds, and done well for himself, becoming a financial advisor – until it all went wrong and he was done for fraud... Then there had been raised eyebrows and mutterings. People loved to judge.

Richie had protested his innocence and insisted that he had been conned by his partner, Aubrey Fennel, but Richie's signature was all over the paperwork. The paper trail led right back to him: the bulk of their clients' money had been plunged into a high-risk investment scheme which relied on the stock-market falling. And it hadn't.

Just because Aubrey had managed to abscond with the remaining funds, didn't mean that Richie wasn't responsible for what had happened to his clients' money. The police made an example of him. Financial advisors were supposed to be trustworthy. He had given the profession a bad name. He had to be suitably punished. Four years in gaol, and his assets were used to repay the victims.

Harley remembered how one day they'd had everything; the next, nothing, for with Richie's prison sentence went his business, and therefore their house. And Leanne couldn't bear the shame, for some of Richie's clients had been their own friends.

So she had fled Birmingham with Harley and River, fled the gossip and the speculation. Which was how they'd ended up down here, in what Leanne had hoped would be paradise, and a fresh start for her and the two boys.

Harley trudged on, passing the hut where two girls from London had had a big party last summer, after their GCSEs. It had all got out of control, with dozens of their mates getting far too drunk, and one of them had nearly drowned. Harley had helped the two girls clear up the next day – the hut had been trashed, and they were hysterical. They were idiots. Rich idiots. The girls had been super grateful to him.

The light was nearly gone. The sea was pewter-black now and the temperature had dropped. He quickened his pace. He knew this stretch of beach better than anyone, he knew every single hut, every knot of wood. You could have dropped him here blindfolded and he would have been able to tell where he was by the smell: the clean gusts of air, sharp with salt and the faintest trace of seaweed, like opening an oyster.

At last, here it was. Wide and sprawling, with a balcony at the front and wooden steps, it glowed white as whalebone in the semi-darkness. He went round the back of the hut and dug in the sand until he found the little tin where the spare key was kept. Time and again he'd suggested a new lock on the door, with a code for security, but for all their money and international jet-set lifestyle, Caroline seemed to want to keep the traditions of the hut, out of sentimentality perhaps, and having an old key in a rusty tin was part of that.

He slid the key into the lock and pushed the door open. Caroline might want to keep the key in a rusty old tin, but the inside of the hut had been renovated with no expense spared. Harley flicked the light switch and a warm glow filled the room.

The walls were wooden, washed in pale cream paint. There was a mezzanine with a double bed in the roof and two sets of bunk beds at the back behind thick linen curtains. The living area was open plan with a small kitchen hand-built from driftwood, and two low-slung couches flanked a wood-burning stove, a pile of fresh logs stacked neatly either side. The floorboards were covered in sheepskin rugs that felt like walking on clouds.

Harley felt the stress in his body ebb away. He breathed in, relishing the calm, the silence, the lack of tension. The hut seemed to pull him in and give him the hug he needed. He could almost hear it whispering that every-thing would be all right. He flumped down into one of the couches, cocooned in its velvety softness.

He shut his eyes. He had feared that he might not be able to shut them without seeing Tony's face in front of him. Or hear his taunting barbs: the ones designed to make Harley lose his rag and make the first move. It had taken all his strength not to react. He was never, ever going to give Tony the pleasure of making him lose his temper.

He had to retreat, to work out his next move. He'd read the *Art of War*. This was a tactical withdrawal. He could let Tony think he had won, for the time being at any rate. Though he had no idea what to do next. After all, he was only a boy, with no money, no power, no influence. Still, he felt sure something would present itself.

He will win who knows when to fight and when not to fight.

There was something else he had to think about, too, but he didn't have room in his head for it right now. He put his hand in his pocket to feel the card inside. He'd taken it off his chest of drawers as he left the house. He felt a pang of sadness for a moment as he imagined his dad writing it. Did they have a shop in the prison? How did he get the advent calendar? For a moment, he had a flashback to the two of them queuing for *Revenge of the Sith* – Harley had only been about five, but his dad had brought him up on *Star Wars* DVDs and he had been sick with the excitement of it all, holding his dad's hand and jumping up and down.

He didn't want to think about his dad yet. It was added pressure and the situation was already complicated. He could think about him once he'd figured out what to do about Tony and his mum. He'd better text her and tell her he was staying out – he quite often did so it wouldn't ring any alarm bells yet. He could have a proper conversation with her tomorrow, and tell her the truth. That he wasn't coming back. That he wouldn't be there for Christmas.

He fired off a text then picked up a fleecy blanket that was folded on the arm of the couch and wrapped it round himself. He longed to sleep, but he didn't quite feel comfortable using one of the beds, even though Caroline had told him he could use the hut. He still felt awkward about taking her up on her offer. He knew if he told her his situation, she would probably tell him to stay there as long as he liked. But he didn't want to tell anyone what was going on, because that made it real.

He had nowhere else to go, though. You couldn't crash at any of your mates' over Christmas – it was family time. He would hide here for the time being. No one would see him or know he was there. Just while he gathered his strength, sorted his head out and worked out what to do.

In less than a minute he was fast asleep.

9

At five o'clock, Lizzy made herself a cup of tea and ate two luxury mince pies, peeling off the lids and loading it up with squirty cream underneath. She was the only person in the house who liked them, but they tasted of Christmas – buttery and spicy and sugary – and she relished every crumb.

Then she set about assembling the lasagne. She wasn't the greatest cook in the world, but she could rustle up stodge. It was one of the things Simon had appreciated when they first got together, the fact she actually ate. He had groaned in ecstasy the first time she'd made him spag bol – not a gourmet recipe, just mince and Dolmio with handfuls of grated Cheddar flung on top – but to him it was manna.

'You have no idea,' he said, shovelling it in with abandon. 'You have *no* idea. Amanda only ate Cup a Soup and slices of lean chicken breast and grapefruit.'

Lizzy had extended her repertoire and improved her methods and ingredients over the years, though it was still bog-standard family grub. Lasagne was their family favourite: now she made it with proper sauce, not out of a jar, and she made her own cheese sauce stringy with mozzarella. The horrors of the afternoon faded even further as she chopped and grated and stirred and sang along to *Now That's What I Call Christmas.*

By six o'clock the lasagne was ready to go into the oven. Lizzy had made two long loaves of garlic bread as well, laden with butter and fresh parsley. She wrapped them in foil ready to pop in at the last minute.

She was just congratulating herself once again when her phone rang. It was Hattie.

'Mum! Kiki says we can go back to hers – they're going carol singing in their lane. Meg says she'll drop me back after. But there's going to be loads of really cool people there. Do you mind?'

'Oh,' said Lizzy. She knew what that meant. Kiki lived in a ritzy neighbourhood alongside a handful of minor pop stars and local footballers. Hattie was obviously hoping to hang out with the great and the glamorous. She couldn't, just couldn't, tell her to come home. She didn't want to stand in the way of her daughter's fun.

'No problem,' she said, trying to keep the disappointment out of her voice. 'The others will be back in a bit.'

'Love you, Mumma. I'll text if I see someone cool.' Hattie rang off. Lizzy could picture her face, alive with the excitement and anticipation of hobnobbing with the stars. The teenage equivalent of a toddler's excitement at their stocking. It made her feel unspeakably sad.

Never mind, she thought. She'd do the tree with Simon and Luke, and maybe Hattie would be back in time to put the angel on the top – Lizzy was pretty sure Luke had done it last year.

By seven, neither Luke nor Simon had come home. Lizzy frowned and picked up her phone. She'd been so busy singing and dancing around the kitchen to George Michael, she'd missed a text from Simon.

Been dragged out for a drink by the girls in the office. Would be bad form to refuse. I'll escape as soon as I can. X

She knew, if she phoned him, that he would come straight away. But who wanted to beg? She certainly didn't. She wanted him to be here because he wanted to be, because it mattered. Because he'd remembered. But he didn't seem able to remember anything important. Or maybe he was afraid to come home and face the music? She didn't think so. She wasn't a scary wife. Or a scary mum.

Though she was starting to feel like one. She could feel resentment beginning to build up. She wasn't scary, but she wasn't demanding either, so she thought the least they could do was respect the one evening she'd asked of them.

She was not going to cry. She swallowed down a lump, then dialled Luke.

'Hey, Ma.' She could hear pounding bass, but that didn't help her narrow down where he was.

'Just wondered what time you were coming home?' She did her best to keep even a hint of accusation out of her voice. She wasn't going to mention him forgetting to bring down the boxes.

'Oh shit. Um . . .' She could picture Luke's panic, visualise him scratching his head under his beanie, looking round at his mates. 'What time do you want me? I'm at Hal's. We're doing all our Insta stuff so we can load it up over Christmas.'

She fought down the urge to scream at him that he should be at home. That he'd promised, only that morning. That he was rude and inconsiderate, and how could a stupid Instagram account featuring stupid baby skateboards be more important than his own family, his own mother?

But she didn't. Of course she didn't.

'Don't worry,' she said. 'The others aren't back. Sort your Instagram out.'

'You sure?' He had that uncertain tone that teenage boys used when they weren't entirely sure if their mums were being sarcastic. Because deep down they still cared for and were still scared of their mums, but it didn't mean they wouldn't push it to get what they wanted. 'You're really sure?'

He wanted her blessing. She sighed.

'Totally sure.'

'Love you, Mumma.' There it was again: the twins' stock phrase usually warmed her heart, but now it set her teeth on edge.

She knew he'd forget her as soon as he hung up. Knew his attention would be diverted by whatever he was doing with his mates. Knew that he hadn't given doing the Christmas tree a second's thought. A wave of desolation hit her.

Desperation at the doctor's. Humiliation in the changing room. Degradation in the street. And now desertion. And no one to listen. No one to pour her a glass of wine or give her a hug or tell her she was important.

She looked inside the oven at the lasagne. It was perfectly golden, and around the edges she could see the sauce bubbling up. It needed eating now, this minute. If she turned the oven off and left it, it would deflate, the cheese would turn from gold to brown and the lasagne sheets would be leathery. She turned the knob anyway, then pulled the dish out and slammed it on the kitchen table.

She felt anger bubble up inside her, as molten as the melted cheese. How could they all do this? They knew how much this meant to her. Didn't they? Maybe she hadn't voiced it loudly enough. How much she loved welcoming Christmas into the house, with the people she loved best, watching the branches of the tree turn from bare to laden, the tinsel and the baubles catching the light. The scent of apple logs crackling in the grate, mingling with eucalyptus, cloves and cinnamon.

What was she supposed to do? Issue a written invitation?

Bugger them. Bugger them all. If they didn't need her or care about her, then she didn't need or care about them.

She had done her very best to behave well, to swallow her disappointment, to bend to Amanda's last-minute changes, to welcome her mother-in-law despite her misgivings.

Bloody Amanda. How on earth did she still have such control over their marriage? Amanda and Simon had divorced over twenty years ago, yet somehow she managed to have an influence on what went on in their daily lives. Simon *still* seemed to dance to her tune and not Lizzy's.

Thank goodness the children were older now. When they had all been smaller, it had been a constant battle. Amanda would change the arrangements to suit herself. She would expect Simon to drop everything in order to have Mo and Lexi when something came up she wanted to do. Yet she would also cancel their weekends with him at the last minute or be difficult about timings, so Simon and Lizzy could never plan anything. Lizzy tried to be patient, because the important thing was for Mo and Lexi to feel secure and loved and wanted, but when Hattie and Luke came along it made it very difficult to be as flexible and relaxed about arrangements. Yet somehow Amanda always managed to make Lizzy feel as if *she* was the unreasonable one, the demanding one. It simply wasn't worth putting up a fight, so she always capitulated.

And it was still happening, even now! Everyone was supposed to change their Christmas plans to suit Amanda, who would be swanning off to Val-d'Isère with her outsize Chanel sunglasses and nary a thought for anyone else. Well, Lizzy wasn't cooperating any more.

She remembered her adolescent fury at some imagined slight when she was thirteen. Preparing to run away, thinking how sorry they would all be. This was a similar feeling: the same indignation and self-pity. But underlying it was a desperate suspicion that she didn't matter. That if she ran away, no one *would* care. That they might, in fact, heave a sigh of relief.

They'd manage without her. They could carry on their social lives, not have to worry about her timetable, sort out their own food as and when they wanted it. They might miss her for a nanosecond, the first time they ran out of loo roll or if she wasn't in to sign for their packages or if they wanted a lift somewhere, but they'd soon find a way to get round it.

She paced round the kitchen, nibbling her thumbnail. Every time she looked at the lasagne, she grew more indignant. Every time she thought about Cynthia sweeping in through the front door, she shuddered. Every time she recalled how Simon had rolled over and given in to Amanda, she ground her teeth with rage.

She grabbed her copy of *Delia Smith's Christmas* off the bookshelf, leafed through it until she found the Christmas Day cooking schedule, then laid it on the kitchen table, marking it with a folded copy of the Ocado order due to arrive the next day.

She tore a piece of paper out of a notebook. It was hard not to write something self-pitying and passive aggressive, so she went for matter-of-fact.

Hi everyone. I've decided to go away for a few day and have some me-time. Everything you need for the perfect Christmas is right here. Delia is foolproof so just follow the instructions. All the presents are in my wardrobe and will need wrapping – Sellotape and scissors in kitchen drawer. Check the fairy lights before you put them on the tree.

Love mum (Lizzy) xxxxxx

Then she went upstairs and started to pack.

Half an hour later, stepping out into the cold air, she still couldn't believe what she was doing as she trundled her suitcase to the car. She opened the boot and flung it in, stuffing a tote bag full of books in next to it.

No one had called her to see if she was all right or tell her they were on their way home. They didn't have a conscience. They didn't bloody *care*. But they'd expect everything to be just as it always was: just as it had been for the past eighteen years, from the satsuma in the toe of their stocking to the tipsy trifle she made on Boxing Day. Well, it was all there ready to be sorted if they wanted it. Ocado was bringing the satsumas and the sherry and the trifle sponges. All that would be missing was Lizzy.

She started the engine, checking the petrol gauge. Three-quarters of a tank was plenty.

Lizzy's car ate up the miles as she hit the motorway a quarter of an hour later. There was something reassuring about the journey. She had done it so many times in the past, although not for a long time – Simon liked the sun, so they always headed to the airport on holiday – but there was a rhythm to it she hadn't forgotten. Even now, as she joined the M5 and saw the sign for the South West, she felt the same flutter of anticipation she had felt at sixteen. Then it had meant summer and sunshine and the promise of freedom. Madonna and Hawaiian Tropic and bottles of Bud. White denim cut-off shorts with cowboy boots. Her and Caroline in the back of Caroline's mum's Volvo, both trying to be cool, but also trying to be convincingly well-behaved and responsible and adult so she might leave them at the beach hut unchaperoned for a few days...

Now it meant... what? She wasn't sure. Nevertheless, the butterflies were there. She realised she hadn't felt them for years. Having butterflies was one of those things you grew out of without noticing: that fizzy warmth in your tummy you got the night before something exciting that stopped you from eating. She had missed the feeling. Anticipation was a big part of any adventure.

And that's what this was. Her adventure. Her chance to

change things. It was the first time she had felt anything positive for a while: the butterflies had shoved aside the sense of unease she'd had for the past few weeks. She felt defiant and elated and turned up the radio.

Chris Rea was singing 'Driving Home for Christmas' and she thought: ha! 'Running Away from Christmas' more like. She hummed along with her new lyrics, keeping her eye on the speedometer, responsible even in her solo *Thelma and Louise* moment. Her Honda didn't care for going much over seventy anyway, but she didn't want a speeding ticket.

Running away wasn't going to change who wielded the power in the long run. That was always going to be the person who had no conscience and no consideration for anyone else. But at least for the next few days, Christmas was going to be on her terms. She was going to please herself and no one else, from the minute she woke up. She would eat what she wanted when she wanted, read what she wanted, watch what she wanted, sleep when she wanted... And maybe the penny would drop with everyone else that *she was an actual person*.

She knew where she was going. Everything she needed would be there. She could see Caroline's scrawl in her Christmas card: *Poor Richard has done his knee in so no coming home for us this year. We were hoping he might recover but he can't face the flight. So it will be 30 degrees and a poolside lunch for us. I know that sounds luxury but what I wouldn't give for a snowflake and a roaring log fire... Anyway, feel free to use the hut any time you like. I'd rather somebody got the use of it.*

It would be there, the key. She could feel it now, heavy and cold. The lock would be a little stiff. That was the salt. But the door would open eventually, though it might take a little push of encouragement. She hadn't been there for a very long time. She hadn't needed to. But she did now.

IO

Just before midnight, Lizzy sang along to Jona Lewie as her car snaked down the steep hill towards Everdene.

'*Ba da ba da bam bam, ba da ba da bam...*' That was it. She was going to have 'Stop the Cavalry' on the brain for the rest of the night now. She could never get rid of it once she'd heard it. Did she wish she was at home for Christmas?

No, she thought, remembering standing by the bare tree like a spare part, waiting for someone to turn up. Waiting for one single member of her family – she didn't mind which – to acknowledge her existence.

Everything was shrouded in darkness. Even the street lights had gone off as she drove down the esplanade. Most of the lights in the houses had gone out too. She shivered slightly: she had the heater on, but she could feel the wind buffet the side of the car as it hit her from across the water she knew was there but couldn't see. All there was in front of her was an expanse of sky and sea, too dark to see the join.

She swallowed. She realised she had never been to Everdene in winter. She had always known it shrouded in the soft blanket of a pale-grey summer night, not this hard blackness.

She pulled into the car park next to the beach. She turned off the engine and felt a frisson of fear. In her haste she had completely forgotten to bring a torch. What an idiot. Maybe she should sleep in the car and wait until morning? No, she would freeze. It wasn't that far; she knew where she was going. In ten minutes' time she could be in the warm.

She had no alternative now, she realised. There wouldn't be anywhere else to stay in Everdene. No cosy little seaside hotel she could stroll into — they were all shut for the winter.

She tugged her car keys out of the ignition, picked up her handbag and rummaged about in it for her phone, remembering it had a torch — not a very powerful one, but it might help a little. As she burrowed about amongst the pens and combs and packets of Polos, she couldn't put her hand on it. Then she realised she must have left it plugged in on the side in the kitchen. She hadn't put it in her bag before she left.

She was in the middle of nowhere, in the pitch dark, without a phone, and no one knew where she was.

Suddenly her impulsiveness felt like foolishness. The adventure had lost its allure. Panic wriggled inside her. What wouldn't she give to be snuggled up at home in her own bed?

Come on, she told herself. Don't bottle it now. You're not afraid of the dark.

She slid out of the car. The wind sliced through her, taking her breath away, as she ran round to the boot and took her case out. Maybe she should just take out her night things? It would be difficult to lug her case across the sand. She opened it swiftly and groped about for her sponge bag and her pyjamas, stuffing them into her handbag. The wind was whipping at her hair and she pulled the hood of her jacket up, threw the suitcase back in and slammed the boot shut.

She set off across the car park. She could hear the waves pounding the beach, determined and repetitive, like a school bully punching a hapless new boy. She felt very small and very alone. This was foolhardy. The beach huts loomed before her, shadowy and silent and unhelpful. There were more of them than she remembered, and she feared she wouldn't be able to find her way. She trudged on, head down, as the wind whistled between them. Twelve, thirteen . . . she would know it as soon as she saw it. Only a few more moments and she'd be able to slip inside and get warm.

At last! She saw the familiar balustrade that marked the edge of the veranda. Straight away she was taken back: two teenage girls sitting in their bikinis and cowboy hats, sipping lukewarm bottles of Budweiser in the early evening sunshine, scanning the beach for talent.

She ran round the back of the hut to the corner where she knew the key was buried. Her fingers burrowed in the cold, damp sand until she found the tin. She pulled it open with freezing fingers.

Empty.

She hadn't for a moment thought it wouldn't be there. It was always there. It had been for decades. She stood for a moment, staring down at the empty tin. How could she have been so stupid?

She went back round to the front of the hut, up the steps, and tried the door, just in case. Of course, it was locked. She leaned her head against it and groaned. She remembered with a sick lurch that she had run the petrol tank to nearly empty. The indicator had shown she had thirty miles left when she'd turned off the main road. At the time she had thought it was plenty to get where she wanted to go: she could fill up the next day. Right now, there wouldn't be a petrol station open for miles. Fifty, probably.

She swallowed down a sob. She'd be found frozen to death the next morning, being pecked by seagulls. Yet again she thought of her bed, the lovely cosy million-tog duvet she'd bought when they did the makeover last summer. Why on earth had she stormed out? Amanda was the drama queen, not calm, placid Lizzy.

Suddenly she found herself bathed in a pool of light from the beach hut window. Lizzy gave a little scream and stepped back, her heart pounding, as the door swung open.

Standing there was the most beautiful boy she had ever seen, his skin like burnished gold in the lamplight, his hair a tangled halo of dreadlocks, his eyes light green and startled.

'Are you all right?' he asked, his voice husky and gentle.

'Sorry. You made me jump,' said Lizzy, her hand on her pounding heart. 'I wasn't expecting anyone to be here.'

He must be about Luke's age, she thought. She was racking her brain as to who he could be – a friend or relative of Caroline's? Or maybe Caroline had rented out the hut without telling Lizzy – because why would she tell her? Her invitation to use the hut was longstanding. Lizzy had never taken her up on it until now, but perhaps she should have double-checked.

'Mrs Openshaw didn't say there were guests arriving,' the boy said, looking wary.

'I haven't booked it. Not officially,' said Lizzy. 'Caroline said if I wanted to use it over Christmas, I could.'

The boy gave a wide smile. 'She said the same to me.'

'That's Caroline,' said Lizzy. 'Generous to a fault.'

The boy nodded his head towards the inside.

'You better come in. Quick. It's freezing.'

Lizzy hesitated. 'I've got nowhere else to go,' she admitted. 'And I've got no petrol. I'm Lizzy, by the way. I was at school with Caroline.'

'I'm Harley,' said Harley. 'I'm the caretaker. I look after quite a few of the huts.'

'We used to come here every summer. I haven't been here for...' She tried to work it out. 'More than twenty years.' She laughed. 'I go and stay with her in Dubai instead. Much warmer.'

She walked in past him, and he shut the door behind her.

'Oh my goodness,' said Lizzy.

Lizzy looked around the hut. She hardly recognised it. When they were kids, it had been like a glorified shed, with camp beds and a primus stove, an ancient sink and an even more ancient loo. Now it looked like an Instagrammer's dream, a cosy refuge done out in cream and dusty grey-blue.

'Caroline told me she'd done it up, but this is like something out of a magazine.' She must have spent more on this hut than Lizzy and Simon had ever spent on Pepperpot Cottage. 'It used to be really scruffy. There was a big old smelly sofa and a rickety table and nothing worked. This is amazing.'

'This is my favourite hut,' said Harley. 'Some of them are even more done up. This one still feels homely.'

Lizzy took in the fluffy cushions and the thick rugs and the blue-and-white-striped linen blinds where once there had been hideous orange and yellow flowery curtains. She saw there was a cable-knit blanket stretched over the sofa: Harley must have been curled up underneath it when she disturbed him.

'Are you staying here tonight, then?'

'I was going to. I had a bit of a falling-out at home.'

'You and me both,' laughed Lizzy. 'Though, actually, I left before the falling-out.'

Her face fell slightly, as if she was remembering why she was here.

'Same.'

They looked at each other for a moment, both feeling awkward about the situation.

Harley cleared his throat. 'I was hoping Mrs Openshaw wouldn't mind. I knew they weren't coming for Christmas and I just thought...' He looked incredibly nervous. 'I didn't have anywhere else to go.'

'It's OK,' said Lizzy. 'I don't think Caroline would mind one bit.'

'The beds are all made up. I got everything ready for them when I thought they were still coming. There's the double bed up on the platform or the bunks.' He indicated the sofa. 'I thought it was a bit cheeky to use a bed so I was just going to crash on the settee.' He moved towards the kitchen. 'I hadn't got as far as getting the fresh supplies in. There's no milk, I'm afraid. But I think there's beer in the fridge? Leftover from last time they were here?'

He looked at her, anxious to make her feel welcome.

'I'm fine. I stopped on the motorway for a coffee.' Suddenly Lizzy longed to lie down and close her eyes. 'To be honest, I just want to go to sleep.'

'If you don't want me here, I can go.'

Lizzy looked at the boy, nervous energy and anxiety rolling off him. Yet underlying that was a peace and a calm. He moved with a grace most young men of his age didn't have: she thought for a moment of Luke's lanky frame, all elbows and knees.

'But you don't have anywhere *to* go.'

'No. But you've got more right to be here than I have.'

'Not really. And it's far too late for either of us to find somewhere else.' She smiled at him. 'It's quite funny, really. I think Caroline would be tickled pink, the two of us ending up here. Waifs and strays in her beach hut.'

Harley still looked doubtful. He obviously felt as if he had been caught doing something he shouldn't, yet Lizzy trusted him and believed his story.

'Look,' she said. 'Let's both crash here for tonight and take a view in the morning.'

Harley nodded. 'I'll put some more logs in the wood-burner. I didn't want to use up too many just for me, but you need to warm up.' He walked across the room and pulled open the glass door of the sleek wood-burning stove tucked away in the corner. A gorgeous scent of woodsmoke filled the hut as Harley tugged a couple of logs from the neat stack at its side and lobbed them in. 'It should heat up pretty quickly.'

Lizzy felt a wave of tiredness. The long drive and the cold were catching up with her, as well as the emotion of doing something so out of character. It made her uncertain, for a moment – she felt a little tug of home-sickness, a momentary longing for Simon.

She buried it.

'I think I will go to bed, if you don't mind.'

Harley pointed at the mezzanine. That hadn't been there in her day – Caroline must have got a clever carpenter to put in a platform with a little ladder.

'That's the biggest bed – it's comfier than it looks up there. And you can pull the curtain across.'

'If you're sure?'

She got changed in the bathroom and did her teeth. Once there had been a grotty old loo and sink and a rather makeshift shower behind a plastic curtain – you had to be careful not to let the water leak everywhere and there was always a lot of mopping up to do afterwards. Not that there was any incentive to stay in there long as the water was always lukewarm. Now, the walls and floor were covered in glittering silver and grey mosaic tiles, and the rain-forest shower was behind a thick glass screen. It was still snug in there, but now it was slick and luxurious and everything worked.

She paused at the bottom of the ladder up to the mezzanine, feeling a bit self-conscious in her pyjamas.

'I've locked the door,' said Harley. 'Not that there's anyone around at the moment.'

She smiled. 'Night,' she said, and tried not to laugh at the absurdity of the situation. She could sense he was a good kid. You could always tell a lot by the way a child looked at you, and Harley had met her eye not with a brazen confidence but a quiet honesty.

She crawled into the bed and pulled the duvet over her. The sheets were stone-washed linen, the pillows ridiculously soft. Everything smelled of lavender. She was in a cocoon and nothing would induce her to leave it. Tomorrow she could wake up and think about what she'd run away from, and what she was going to do. But for now, all she wanted to do was sleep.

II

Simon flung himself into the back of the taxi with a slight sigh of relief.

He loved going out in Birmingham. The city had a sophistication to it now that it had never had when he was young. His boss, Colin, had asked him at the last minute to take the younger ones out for a drink as it was their last day in the office.

'I'd have done it once,' he said, 'but they wouldn't want me along any more.' He'd given Simon a handful of twenties and a pat on the back. Simon understood his role. It was more important than ever to keep staff morale high, as poaching of anyone remotely competent was rife, so Simon knew he couldn't really say no. He was representing Colin and he would earn brownie points both from his boss and his underlings.

He'd swept them all off in an excited gaggle to a cocktail lounge in Edgbaston with glitzy decor and exotic drinks: the atmosphere had been hedonistic and indulgently festive. By eleven o'clock everyone was starting to unravel and Simon wanted to escape before anything went too horribly wrong. No one was snogging anyone they shouldn't yet, and no one was crying, but inhibition was definitely heading out of the window.

Not that he was responsible for anyone's behaviour out of the office, but as second-in-command he couldn't just ignore it when people stepped out of line right in front of him, so it was better to remove himself from the equation. Out of sight was out of mind. What goes on at Christmas, etc.

It took him a while to say his goodbyes – the girls were getting particularly amorous and playful and he had to disengage himself from their embraces. Then he put the rest of the money Colin had given him behind the bar for them to carry on drinking and called an Uber, which took ages to arrive. This was probably the busiest night of the year, as pretty much everyone had knocked off work and was in the mood to celebrate.

He slumped back in his seat, trying to block the odious waft from the scented pine tree dangling from the rearview mirror. Did cab drivers put them there on purpose to torture their inebriated passengers? Surely they didn't want them to throw up?

A cab ride all the way home was a luxury but he'd missed the last train, and he was pretty sure Lizzy wouldn't mind driving him in to pick up his car the next morning. He'd stopped after three cocktails because he couldn't hack it these days and he would still feel rough tomorrow. He was a bit cross with himself: he shouldn't be kicking off the holiday with a hangover, but at least he'd sent his staff off feeling loved and looked after.

The city was looking its best at gone midnight, the night sky bright and star-studded, as if reflecting the lights that were strung along the streets and inside the windows of the shops and restaurants. He felt a sudden fondness for the city that had given him so much opportunity. He stretched out his legs with a sigh of satisfaction at the thought of nearly two weeks off. He loved his work but he never really switched off. You had to be ahead of everyone else all the time. There was only so much business and you had to fight for your slice of the pie.

He shut his eyes as the cab sped through the outskirts of the city and eventually into leafy Warwickshire, passing through several small villages before they reached Astley-in-Arden. He loved the little town where they lived. And he loved Pepperpot Cottage, even though it was far too small for them, really.

Lizzy and Simon had realised when the twins were about six that it simply wasn't big enough for a family of four. Yes, there were enough bedrooms – four, albeit snug – but only one bathroom, and no dining room, only a living room and just enough room in the kitchen for a table that could seat four comfortably, six less comfortably and eight if four people had a table leg between their own legs. They decided it was time to sell and move somewhere with more space and a larger garden.

Pepperpot Cottage was snapped up for a good price. But although they scoured the area, increasing their radius in direct proportion to their rising panic, Lizzy and Simon could find nowhere that felt like home. In the end, they had gone for a very swanky new-build five-bed near Stratford with all the mod cons and three bathrooms. 'Architect-designed', boasted the particulars, but as Simon pointed out, who else would it have been designed by? A dentist? A lollipop lady?

The day they were due to exchange, Lizzy had woken up sobbing.

'I can't do it,' she wailed. 'We mustn't leave Pepperpot. It's our home.'

'But we're exchanging today! Completing in two weeks.'

Tears streaming down her face, she grabbed him by the hand and pulled him out of bed, leading him downstairs to the kitchen, opening the top half of the stable door that led into the garden. Sunlight streamed in, together with the scent of honeysuckle.

'It's beautiful, our garden,' she said. 'That new garden? It's sterile. There's nothing in it. A larchlap fence and a lawn.'

'We can soon make it something.'

'But not that. It will never be that.' She grabbed his hand again and led him into the living room, pointing to the worn oriental rug in front of the inglenook fireplace. 'Look. That's where we made them. Hattie and Luke. How can we leave?'

'We can take the Magic Rug of Conception with us,' joked Simon.

Lizzy shook her head. 'I'm not leaving.'

He stared at her, starting to realise she was serious.

'You're mad. Everyone will be furious.'

'I don't care,' said Lizzy, crossing her arms. 'This is my house. My children's house. It's where they belong. I'm not moving.'

Simon groaned. 'What's it going to be like? When they're teenagers? When they have their giant gangly friends back? When we're all trying to get into the bath-room at the same time?'

'People live in much smaller houses than this.'

'But... the double garage? The integral dishwasher – you clapped when you saw that. The *dining* room.' Simon looked shell-shocked. He had totally got his head around the move; he was looking forward to a house which didn't need constant maintenance, where the wind didn't whistle through the windows and the lights didn't trip every five minutes.

'I'm not signing,' said Lizzy. 'You need my signature and I'm not signing.'

'You've already signed everything. The paperwork's at the solicitor, ready to go.'

'I'll phone and stop them. We haven't exchanged. It's not too late.'

'You've got last-minute nerves, that's all. It's a big change.'

Lizzy shook her head. 'You'll have to drag me out of here kicking and screaming. I'm not going.' She sat down on the sofa firmly, as if she was about to be forcibly evicted. Simon scratched his head. He knew Lizzy well enough to know she wasn't joking.

He sighed.

'I'll call the solicitor, then.'

Here they still were, over ten years later. And no one cared that there was only one bathroom because they'd sorted out a kind of rota and they'd all learned to be as quick as they could. The house was just off the high street, so it was the place everyone hung out in, coming for drinks before going out for dinner, and back for coffee afterwards. And the kids hung out there too, because it was easy to go back there at lunchtime from school. Simon and Lizzy had an easy-going open-house policy and the best-stuffed freezer in Warwickshire. At any time of the day or night you might find someone pulling a pizza out of the oven or smothering a tray of chips in mozzarella or scooping out balls of ice cream.

It was a family house, battered and worn around the edges. Anyone buying it would replace the scruffy old pine kitchen and rip out the bathroom with its leaky shower and temperamental toilet. Every now and then Lizzy would get a kitchen brochure and fantasise, but she would push it to one side and say, 'The thing is, I'm quite happy really. It's comfortable, and that's all that matters.'

Other men were envious of Simon and his undemanding wife. They all seemed to be under pressure with constant plans for refits and renovations and extensions and life-changing new equipment.

'How can anyone spend two thousand pounds on a fridge-freezer?' one of his friends asked in despair, and Simon couldn't answer him. He was grateful, though, for Lizzy's contentment. Not because he would have begrudged them spending the money, not at all, but it must be hard to live with dissatisfaction. Lizzy didn't *want* things, generally, and if she did, she got them herself without trying to manipulate him or play some sort of guilt card.

That was why he loved her so much. Because she only put her foot down about things that were really important to her. Which was why her objection to Cynthia coming for Christmas had unsettled him earlier. It wasn't like Lizzy to be so vociferous. But she had probably been a bit stressed, and she never liked it when Amanda pulled rank – that was probably what was behind it. She'd have calmed down by now, he was sure.

Simon sneaked up the front path, opened the front door, slipped off his shoes and crept up the stairs. He wasn't going to wake Lizzy. Neither of the kids were still up either – there were no lights on or music. He looked at his watch and realised it was nearly one. Shit – time must have flown. He'd fully intended to be home by midnight.

He slipped into the spare room to save Lizzy the horror of his inevitable snoring. It was standard for him and his mates these days to be banished: he was one of the lucky ones who hadn't been permanently booted out of the marital bed. But he didn't want to inflict the noise on Lizzy, who rarely complained. Some wives, he knew, were much less forgiving. Two of his friends were forced to wear unsightly anti-snoring contraptions before they were allowed under the duvet. Lucky for him his snoring only reached antisocial levels when he'd had a few. Like tonight.

He dropped his clothes to the floor, went and had a wee and brushed his teeth as quietly as he could, then clambered into bed.

TWO DAYS BEFORE CHRISTMAS

12

'Road trip!!!!' sang out Jack, closing the boot of the Saab as carefully as he could. They were only going away for five days, but it was packed tight with everything they needed, and everything they didn't need as well.

There was certainly enough food to feed an army. The details had said there was a convenience shop in the village and a supermarket about eight miles away. Jack was not leaving anything to chance. His idea of hell was fishing around in a dilapidated shop freezer for oven chips. So all the food they needed for the next few days was carefully packed up in cool boxes and insulated bags.

There wasn't a single sprout or mince pie; not a chipolata or a chestnut. In fact, nothing reminiscent of a traditional Christmas whatsoever. Christmas lunch was going to be a lamb shoulder, cooked long and slow in coffee and treacle and star anise and fennel seeds that would melt down into syrupy spiciness, the tender slices served on a pillow of buttery polenta.

Yep, maybe he was obsessed with food. Maybe it was all he thought about, but it stopped him going crazy and thinking about the things that caused him pain. Planning food, sourcing food, cooking it, eating it, sharing it gave him purpose and momentum and comfort. Nothing much else did.

Except Nat. Of course Nat. His buddy, his partner in crime, his raison d'être. He looked in the rear-view mirror to check up on him and smiled. Nat was holding up his *Sesame Street* book, looking at it as intently as if he was reading *War and Peace*, a little furrow between his straight brows, even though at only just three he couldn't possibly read yet. He was a good traveller. Music and plenty of pit stops and bags of cubed cheese and date and apple would keep him going.

Jack's heart gave a little jump of pride and love. He hoped he was doing the right thing; that Nat wouldn't be scarred for life because he was turning his back on Christmas.

It had been easy to fob everyone off. He told friends he was going to family, and family he was going to friends, and they all believed him because they respected his wishes and his privacy and didn't want to push him into anything because they knew this was a difficult one...

Would it ever not be a difficult one?

He couldn't face any of it. The sounds. The smells. The taste. The rituals. The decorations. The music. The television programmes. It actually made him feel ill. He could feel the panic rise. The scent of cloves made him gag. The sound of jingle bells made his chest tighten.

The beach hut had seemed like a stroke of genius. He didn't want to go to a hotel – no escape from Christmas there. A cottage would be dull and middle-aged. He was an anxious flyer so abroad wasn't an option. (Was he becoming too anxious about life? He should watch that.)

A beach hut would be a boys' adventure. It would be

way too cold for swimming but they could explore the coast path and poke about in rock pools and maybe get the kite up. The hut they were borrowing had a well-equipped kitchen, and he'd downloaded a bunch of films onto his laptop.

And they had Clouseau with them. He was tucked up in his basket in the boot, snuffling away. Clouseau wasn't particularly outward bound but he might like the beach.

If anybody had told him that a fugly little French bulldog would go some way towards filling the hole in his heart, he would never have believed them. He had got the puppy for Nat, because someone had told him it was important for a small boy to have a confidante, and he didn't want their relationship to be intense and pressurised. A dog would spread the emotional load, he thought, and he was right.

But it was Jack who scooped up the velvety grey bundle and held it close in his darkest moments. It was Jack who whispered in Clouseau's ridiculous ten-denier ears. Who took comfort in the wisdom in his kindly brown eyes. Clouseau was silent and wise and flatulent and better than any therapist.

In fact, since Clouseau Jack had been doing so much better. He'd moved on from the anger phase.

'Stop being so bitter,' his sister, Clemmie, had pleaded with him at the beginning of the summer. 'It's not good for you. It's not good for Nat.'

'I'm never angry with Nat.'

'No, but he deserves a happy dad.'

Jack had looked at her, incredulous. 'How can I ever be happy again?'

'You will be,' said Clemmie. 'You will be, I promise. Not the same kind of happy. A different sort of happy.'

Jack shook his head. 'You've got no idea...'

'Don't forget she was my friend too.' Clemmie was starting to get cross. 'You don't get to hog all the grief.'

Jack stared at her. 'Did you really just say that?'

'Yes. And here's another thing. Maybe it's easier to be angry? Maybe that's the coward's way?'

Jack didn't know what to say. 'How can I help what I'm feeling? It's just there, inside me.'

'I don't know. But I know this isn't what Fran would want for you.'

'So what am I supposed to do? Go out dancing? Get on Tinder? Apart from anything, I've got Nat to look after, remember?'

'I know it's difficult. And of course you've got a right to be sad. But I hate seeing you like this.'

'Like what?' Jack raised his eyebrows. 'Fat? Go on. Say it.'

He'd always been a big lad. Tall and broad, well over six foot. Which was OK when he was young and still played rugby. But now, with the metabolism of a thirty-six-year-old, it wasn't so easy keeping lean, and he'd stopped going to the gym once Fran had got really poorly.

Clemmie sighed.

'You're not fat, Jack. But you will be if you're not careful.'

'So I take comfort from food. It's better than drinking myself into oblivion, isn't it?'

'Of course it is.' Clemmie knew she had to choose her words carefully. 'I just don't want you to self-sabotage, that's all.'

'Did Mum and Dad get you to tell me I'm a porker?' Jack knew he was being unfair, and unkind. Clemmie was staunch and brave and nothing but supportive. But he felt defensive. He knew as well as she did that he had put on nearly two stone in the past two years. He was tall enough to carry it off, so far. But if he carried on . . .

Clemmie pointed at Jack. 'You know what Fran would say.'

'Yep.' He nodded. Fran would tell him to stop wallowing. 'I do know what Fran would say, because I hear her voice in my head every minute of the day. And you're right. She'd call me a fat bastard.'

Clemmie winced. Her face softened. 'No, she wouldn't, Jack. Don't do that negative self-talk.'

'Don't do that therapist-speak,' he shot back. He was going to cry. Dammit. 'Can we change the subject?' His voice was tight with tears. 'I've had enough of tough love. You don't have to tell me any of it. I *know*.'

He'd listened to Clemmie, despite his protestations, because he'd always heeded his sister's advice. He'd started walking when he got Clouseau, cut down his carbs, dropped a stone in three months, and somehow his anger had melted away with the fat. By autumn, he had even gone on a couple of dates – Clemmie had babysat for him, and had reassured him before he left the house, because he was surprised at how nervous he had been. In the end, they were pleasant enough girls, but they weren't as interesting or fun or infuriating as Fran. Not even close. He had been polite enough to text each one afterwards, too, and tell her something kind so she wouldn't feel rejected when he didn't ask her out again, but neither had replied. They must have sensed that his heart wasn't in it.

As autumn faded and December approached, he'd begun to dread Christmas. It was too much. Both because of the good memories and the bad ones. So he decided to take Christmas out of the equation. It was much easier that way for everyone. No one had to worry about the elephant in the room.

As he negotiated their way through Ealing and out towards the M4, it was still dark, the street lights still on, only one or two corner shops showing signs of life. Nat had woken at six as he did every morning, and Jack had figured they might as well get on the road as quickly as possible. They could be at the seaside just after lunch.

'OK, buddy?' He looked again in the mirror and Nat stuck his little pink thumb up.

Next year, he thought, he would do the whole family Christmas thing, because he would be stronger. And of course he'd packed Nat's stocking and presents, and some silly crackers. He couldn't ignore Christmas completely, but doing it somewhere else away from everyone and all the traditions, would make it just about bearable. He hoped he wasn't being selfish. Nat was young enough not to have any preconceptions. Besides – the seaside? It would be brilliant.

He turned up the Hot 8 Brass Band. You couldn't not smile when you played the Hot 8 Brass Band. Nat was bellowing along tunelessly from the back seat.

I love you, man, thought Jack, putting his foot down. The sooner they got to Everdene, the better.

13

Lizzy woke and stared in puzzlement for a moment at the white tongue-and-groove ceiling above her. Where on earth was she? She pushed aside the remaining fragments of sleep, trying to get her bearings. She could see a porthole, with a patch of pearly grey through the glass. She peered round and saw she was on a high platform, cocooned in baby-blue linen—

The beach hut. She remembered now. Her crazy moonlight flit. Her arrival in the pitch dark. And . . .

She peered over the edge of the mezzanine to the room below. Harley was still fast asleep on the sofa, curled up under the blanket, dead to the world as only teenagers can be. She felt a rush of maternal fondness, even though he wasn't hers. It was such a tricky age, that cusp of boy to man, that complex navigation of adolescent angst and trying on a bigger pair of shoulders. She wondered about his home life and what had caused him to run away. She hoped that sleep was helping him sort things out. Your subconscious could unravel your problems while you slept, she found.

Although she wasn't sure hers had unravelled. She didn't want to think about them yet.

She pulled her clothes towards her and put them on,

then clambered out of bed and over to the ladder that led up to her eyrie, scrambling down it with as much elegance as she could muster. She plopped onto the floor and padded over the floorboards to open the door.

There, in front of her, was the reason she had run here. It was the crispest and brightest of winter days: the kind that made everything pin sharp in the silver sun. The sand gleamed pale pink and glittery, and beyond it the sea shone like Bristol glass, only an occasional frothy white meringue of a wave breaking the surface. The sea air slid into her lungs, so sweet and fresh she had to gulp it in. A breeze wrapped itself round her, sensuous and seductive, greeting her like a lover. *What took you so long?* it seemed to ask.

Then the cold suddenly hit her. She grabbed her coat from the hook just inside the door and pulled it on, then stepped out onto the veranda, putting the door on the latch and closing it to so the freezing draught didn't wake Harley.

Now it was daylight she could see the row of beach huts, and for a moment she gasped. They were all so different now. And there were so many more of them. A lot of them were bigger, too, with elaborate additions: decking and pizza ovens and outside showers. A far cry from the slightly ramshackle huts they'd once been, though Lizzy thought she preferred them scruffy and a bit rough round the edges. There was an air of competition that hadn't been there when they were young: beach huts were a status symbol now.

She walked down onto the sand. It was eerily quiet, except for a few keening seagulls and the distant murmur of the waves – the tide was a long way out, and she seemed to be the only person on the beach. Judging by the car park last night, there weren't many people down here. Everdene was remote and the weather here could be harsh, so it probably wasn't a popular destination for Christmas. Lizzy was grateful. The fewer people she came into contact with, the more quickly she could clear her head. And there was something very liberating about being the only person on the mass of sand, the sea in front of her the only thing between her and the coast of Wales. She stretched out her arms and looked up at the sky, a swirl of grey cloud like a pale blanket above her.

This was what she was craving. Peace and solitude and time to think.

She wanted to whoop with excitement at the exhilaration and do a little dance, but she didn't quite dare. If Harley happened to see her, he might think she was bonkers. She looked at her watch instead. Pound to a penny no one at Pepperpot would be up yet, though she did wonder what Simon had thought when he'd come home to an empty bed. If he'd even noticed. He'd have been the worse for wear so would probably have gone into the spare room. Hattie and Luke certainly wouldn't have noticed her absence.

She still felt defiant about running away. Not only was it a statement, it was a chance for her to get some distance. If she was at home, she would already be up making lists, trying to get ahead with the baking, doing last-minute dashes to the shops, finding the time to wrap all the presents (even though she no longer had to hide from small prying eyes to preserve the legend of Father Christmas, she liked to keep everything secret). She could feel the tension inside her already just at the thought

– that desperate feeling of running round in circles while everyone else did exactly as they pleased.

And all of this was before taking the root of her anxiety into consideration. Amanda and Cynthia. Cynthia was the tangible problem, but it was Amanda underlying it, as ever. She had always been a source of tension in their marriage. How could she still have such an influence on their lives?

Lizzy thrust her hands deep into her pockets and began to walk down to the sea's edge. It was a long way out. She might actually get some exercise while she was down here – something she hadn't done for herself for ages. She quickened her pace and felt her mood lift immediately. She lifted her face to the breeze and breathed in salty gusts of airborne sea.

Bloody Amanda, she thought. But then, if it wasn't for Amanda, she would never have met Simon in the first place. She remembered it as if it was yesterday, although it was twenty years since Amanda had come to see her to book her wedding. Her *second* wedding, which Lizzy remembered thinking was a little unfair because she hadn't even had one yet . . .

'The thing is, we're going to bring you loads of great publicity. Our wedding photos are going to be in all the local papers and magazines. So I think you should give us a good discount.'

Amanda once-Kingham and about-to-become-Fantini had sat back in her chair and smiled at Lizzy.

Even at ten o'clock in the morning after a workout in the gym she was immaculate, her hair glossy and shining. She wore a leather miniskirt, a black polo-neck jumper and sky-high court shoes. She crossed her legs, wrapped in high-shine tights, and tapped her pen on her notepad expectantly.

'I'm afraid it doesn't quite work like that.' Amanda might think Lizzy was a pushover, but Lizzy knew all the tricks and more.

Amanda's smile widened but her eyes narrowed. 'There are plenty of other places we could go who'd be thrilled with the exposure. Craven Court is our first choice, but...'

Lizzy stifled a sigh. It never ceased to amaze her how wily brides-to-be could be. There was little romance in the planning of a wedding these days. They were hustlers, out for what they could get. If ever she had to deal with a man, it was much more straightforward. They made their choices and asked her to send them the bill.

'Amanda – at the end of the day your wedding venue is your decision. All I can do is tell you what we can do, and for how much, and assure you of my closest attention from start to finish.' She held up brochures for the three packages they offered. 'I imagine you will want the platinum package. It is the most expensive but you get what you pay for: the ballroom, *vintage* champagne, a five-course dinner, a live band as well as a DJ...'

Amanda looked down sulkily at the brochures. 'Of *course* platinum.'

Lizzy cleared her throat and spoke in a confidential tone. 'If you can't afford it, then I promise you the gold package is equally wonderful. And you wouldn't have to pimp your wedding photos.'

Lizzy knew the barb would hit Amanda where it hurt. She would never usually intimate to a client that they couldn't afford what they wanted, but there was no point in being subtle. She could see straight through the sickly syrup Amanda ladled on. It wasn't charm, that wide smile that went nowhere near her eyes, that little-girl voice with the breathy laugh, the way she touched you on the arm repeatedly when she spoke to you, trying to reel you in and make out you had some sort of special relationship.

She knew her, by sight and reputation, because Amanda used the gym and spa attached to Craven Court and came in several times a week to use it.

'She's in the middle of a messy divorce,' Kim the gym receptionist had confided in Lizzy a year or so ago. 'Her kids are sweet. It's such a shame. She brings them in sometimes at the weekends. She leaves them in the crèche for hours.'

Kim's disapproval was implicit. Lizzy could see Amanda made the most of her time in the gym. She was toned and tanned and groomed and plucked – all the things Lizzy wasn't. She had free gym membership as a perk of the job but never seemed to find the time to get in there. Anyway, at the end of the day she wanted to go home to the little house she'd just bought and carry on with the decorating: she was determined to do it all herself. Painting the spare bedroom was far more satisfying than sweating on the cross trainer, and decorating burned calories because she'd read it in a magazine: 326 calories an hour *and* you had something to show for it.

No sooner was the ink dry on Amanda's decree absolute than more gossip ricocheted round the hotel faster than a ball round a squash court. She was having a fling with Fabio Fantini, the Italian footballer who played for a local team and who came to Craven Court to use the gym and have massages.

'She didn't waste any time,' Kim told Lizzy. 'There's a rumour they've been having sex in the sauna.' She wrinkled her nose in distaste.

Lizzy didn't want to think about it. And she would have done anything to get out of helping plan Amanda's subsequent wedding, but unfortunately she didn't have a choice. She also knew that she had to make the day as perfect as she could, because Amanda was the sort of person who could make life very difficult if she didn't get what she wanted.

She was not going to give her a discount though.

'Oh dear,' said Amanda. 'I thought you'd understand. The thing is, there is going to be a lot of press attention so we might as well both benefit.'

Lizzy sighed. Amanda wasn't going to give up. 'We have our own publicity strategy. It doesn't involve exploiting our guests. Our focus is the wedding, and making sure the bride and groom have the most memorable day they can. That is our reward. We don't want the day compromised.'

Amanda looked away. Lizzy could almost see her brain ticking over, looking for a new angle.

When she looked back, there were tears swimming in her eyes.

'This is my chance to get it right,' she said. 'I thought marriage was for ever when I married first time around. It turned out that my husband had other ideas...'

'Oh,' said Lizzy, not entirely convinced by Amanda's performance.

'It's pretty awful,' said Amanda, 'when you find out the father of your two children has been cheating on you.'

'I'm sure,' murmured Lizzy, even though she couldn't

help feeling Amanda was laying it on a bit thick to get what she wanted.

'Luckily Fabio is very strong. Very moral.'

Very rich, thought Lizzy, who had seen his penis extension of a car.

'That's why I want everything to be perfect,' Amanda reiterated.

'I understand,' said Lizzy. 'Everything *will* be perfect. I'll make sure of that. But the price is the price.'

Two days later the manager of Craven Court called Lizzy into his office.

'Amanda Kingham says she offered you her wedding photographs and you turned them down?'

'I didn't think it was appropriate.'

'Of course it's appropriate. The two of them met here. We'll get great coverage. Give her fifty per cent off whatever she wants. We can't let this opportunity slip through our fingers.'

Lizzy didn't think she had ever been so angry. She felt manipulated and outmanoeuvred and humiliated. Amanda had gone over her head and the manager had pulled rank.

'No problem,' she said, her fingers tightening round her pen. Was a Bic ballpoint an offensive weapon?

Why everybody was in thrall to Amanda and Fabio she couldn't fathom. They were hardly Posh and Becks. Lizzy demurred graciously and resolved to make the wedding as fabulous as she possibly could. She knew Amanda would be poised ready to catch her out and pull her up on anything that wasn't exactly to her liking. So she went above and beyond the call of duty, sourcing the most dew-drenched and lusciously scented flowers, ordering the most spectacular cake (three foot of hand-carved chocolate), devising an unforgettable menu with the chef and quite literally rolling out the red carpet for the happy pair to walk down on their arrival from the registry office.

If Amanda wanted to be splashed all over the local papers, Lizzy was going to make sure Craven Court was the star.

Everything was set fair on Amanda's wedding day. It was April at her most inviting; soft and gently warm. Lizzy stood in the centre of the marquee that the hotel put up for larger weddings and drank it all in. Everything was a symphony of cream and deep red, the colour of Fabio's team. There were scarlet satin bows on the backs of the gold chairs, crimson roses wrapped in ivy trailing over the tables and an arch of red balloons in the shape of a heart for them to walk through on arrival. None of it was to Lizzy's taste but she had to admit it looked pretty stunning. Amanda would be delighted.

She frowned as she tweaked the snow-white linen table-cloth on the top table. Why was it that she wanted to please Amanda when she couldn't bear her? Was it fear or was it to prove a point? It really was most extraordinary, how she got everyone to do her bidding. Even her ex-husband was coming to the wedding. Lizzy was baffled by this until she realised he was going to be unpaid childcare.

'Simon's going to look after the children,' Amanda told her. 'It's very important for me that Mo and Lexi are there, and for Fabio of course. As of today he'll be their father too. But obviously I can't look after them.' She flashed a smile and Lizzy saw that her teeth were several shades whiter than they had been at their last meeting. 'And Simon and I are totally amicable for the children's sake, so it seemed to make sense. I didn't want to have to leave them with a nanny on such an emotional day.'

Or pay for one, thought Lizzy shrewdly.

Lizzy was expecting Amanda's first husband to be a smooth operator, a little bit flashy. She certainly wasn't expecting to like him. But she warmed to him at first sight when he turned up at the reception in a very well-cut grey suit, a child in each hand. He wasn't classically handsome, but had dark brown hair swept back from his forehead, kind brown eyes and a smile that would make you drop what you were doing to help him. She wouldn't have put him and Amanda together at all: he was far too charming and polite, and Lizzy had expected someone brash. No doubt he'd had something that Amanda wanted at the time. Stability, perhaps?

Today, he wore a slightly exhausted, put-upon expression that he tried to disguise. He was clearly finding the wedding torture: having to explain his presence to surprised mutual friends and be introduced to Amanda's new social circle while keeping the two little ones under control. Mo and Lexi were the only children invited, two-year-old Mo dressed up in a little suit and four-year-old Lexi in a white lace dress that was a copy of her mother's. Everyone ooh-ed and aah-ed over them, and Amanda posed for endless photos before shooing them back to Simon.

Lizzy made a point of making sure he was all right.

'Just order anything you want from the bar for them. And if it gets too noisy there's the hotel lounge – there's a big television and lots of board games in the cupboard.'

Simon gave a wintry smile of thanks.

'They should be fine. They're good kids. I've only got

to stay here until eight.' He rolled his eyes. 'At least, those are my instructions.'

Lizzy put a hand on his shoulder. 'It must be hard for you.'

Simon didn't answer for a moment. 'As long as she's happy,' he said. 'When Amanda's happy, everyone's happy.'

And it seemed as if Amanda was happy. She posed in front of the balloon arch with Fabio and all his teammates while the photographer popped his bulbs in a frenzy of excitement. Dinner was seamless, the bride and groom cut the cake and then joined each other on the dance floor for the first dance, 'How Deep is your Love?'

How deep are your pockets, more like, thought Lizzy, and felt a momentary twinge of sympathy for Fabio, who was gazing into his bride's eyes, totally under her spell.

'I'm off now,' said the photographer. 'I've got the money shots. I'm going to get back to the darkroom and get them to the papers as quickly as I can.'

'Thank you,' said Lizzy.

Later, she watched Simon on the dance floor, carrying Mo and holding Lexi's hand while they jiggled along to 'Dancing Queen'. Amanda was on the other side of the dance floor, arms high, slinking and shimmying with her bridesmaid cohorts while Fabio stood on the sidelines nursing a glass of champagne and eyeing his new wife with Italianate jealousy.

Lizzy thought how brave Simon was, and how wonderful of him to have the grace to put his children first when he could so easily have refused to play ball. He was being so gallant looking after them both. Little Mo had obviously had enough, his head drooping onto Simon's shoulder. What a lovely father he was—

Suddenly Mo's head snapped up. He arched his back, opened his mouth and vomited out a stream of purple liquid all over Simon's shirt and jacket. Simon froze in horror, clasping Mo as tightly to him as he could to avoid the sick getting everywhere.

Lizzy ran straight over. She could see, out of the corner of her eye, someone pointing out the drama to Amanda, who shrugged and melted away from the dance floor before anyone got any bright ideas about including her in a rescue mission.

'Oh my goodness, you poor thing,' Lizzy said to Simon. 'And poor Mo. Poor little boy.'

Mo, by now, was crying. Simon looked utterly shell-shocked.

'I'm so sorry. It's so hot in here – he gulped down one of those drinks a bit too quickly. I hope it's not all over the floor ...'

'Only a tiny bit. Don't worry about the floor. We can get that cleaned up.' Lizzy signalled over to the bar staff to come and deal with it. 'Come with me,' she said to Simon, holding out her hand to Lexi, who was staring up at everyone with wide eyes. 'Come on, Lexi. Let's go and see if we can find a room, eh?'

'I'm so sorry,' said Simon again, mortified.

'Don't be silly,' said Lizzy.

She led him to a spare bedroom she had put aside for any guests who decided they might like to stay over at the last minute. Simon strode beside her along the softly carpeted corridor.

'I can't thank you enough. This is a complete nightmare. Luckily I brought some spare clothes for the kids ...'

Simon managed an anguished smile over the top of

Mo's head as she put her pass key into the lock and opened the door to let them inside. It was a small double bedroom with an en suite, all done out in the hotel's signature chintz, with lots of frills and flounces and cushions. Lexi bounced onto the bed with glee.

'Lexi – don't jump. This isn't our room,' her father told her, looking panic-stricken.

'Oh, don't worry,' said Lizzy. 'She probably needs to let off some steam. They've both been so good.'

'Apart from the projectile vomiting.'

'It wasn't his fault, poor lamb.' Lizzy smiled at Mo, who was snuggled into Simon's shoulder, looking at her out of the corner of his eye. He had his father's long eyelashes, noted Lizzy. 'Come into the bathroom. If you strip Mo off and give him a quick blast in the shower then you can get cleaned up while I look after him and Lexi.'

'You're an angel.'

'It has been said.' Lizzy grinned.

'I've got clean clothes for the kids in this bag.' Simon indicated a holdall he was carrying on his other arm. 'But I'm not sure what I'm going to wear. I think my trousers have escaped but no way can I put my shirt or jacket back on.' He looked down at his stained clothes and made a face.

'I'll go and look in lost property for you. We get lots of things left behind. If you don't mind wearing a stranger's shirt?'

'It's better than a shirt drenched in Fruit Shoot vomit.'

They both laughed.

'We send the clothes to the laundry so they'll be clean.'

'You're an absolute star.'

He looked at her with gratitude in his eyes, but also

something else Lizzy couldn't identify. Whatever it was, it made her blush. She grabbed the remote control from the bedside table.

'Come on, Lexi,' she said, feeling a bit flustered. 'Let's see if we can find the children's channel.'

She turned the television on and started to flip through the stations. Simon headed for the bathroom. He shut the door behind him and Lizzy gulped.

Oh God, she thought. He's absolutely bloody lovely.

For a moment she wished she wasn't looking so buttoned up in her dull hotel uniform, with its flared navy knee-length skirt and boxy jacket that managed to disguise any hint of femininity. But then she reminded herself he wouldn't be interested in her. He'd been married to Amanda – he obviously went for high maintenance and glamour. Lizzy's curly hair was tied back in a scrunchie and the make-up she had put on first thing this morning had long worn off. She was too busy keeping the wedding guests happy to touch up her lip gloss.

Five minutes later Simon posted a pink and clean Mo out of the bathroom door wrapped in a white towel. Lizzy scooped him up and plonked him on the bed next to Lexi, then rummaged in the bag Simon had left on the floor for clean clothes.

'Right, you two. Shall I get you some food?'

'Chipth,' said Mo.

'Pizza,' said Lexi.

'I think we could get a pizza and chips here pretty quickly.' Lizzy picked up the phone and called room service. *Scooby Doo* was blaring out but she could still hear the shower in the bathroom. She made herself go a bit pink thinking about Simon standing in it.

Ten minutes later he came out, dressed in one of the white towelling dressing gowns the hotel supplied. It was a little small for him, stretching over his broad shoulders and only just done up.

'I've ordered pizza,' squeaked Lizzy, noticing his shapely calves. 'If you hang on here I'll go and see what clothes I can lay my hands on for you.'

When she came back he was lying on the bed in between Lexi and Mo, watching *Scooby Doo*. She arrived at the same time as the food.

She handed him a pair of jeans, a checked shirt and a sweater.

'Oh,' he said. 'Thank you so, so much.'

He really was pathetically grateful, as if he was unused to people being kind or helpful.

She laughed.

'It's not a problem at all. Nip into the bathroom and get dressed and I'll look after these two.'

As the bathroom door closed, she sat down in between Mo and Lexi.

'It must be nearly your bedtime,' she said to Lexi.

Lexi shook her head. 'We're staying till the end.'

'I don't think so, surely? It'll be midnight before it ends.'

Lexi considered this.

'What does midnight look like?'

Lizzy thought about it. 'Well, it can be very dark. But it's quite special. You know the story of Cinderella? When the clock struck midnight, she had to leave the ball?'

Lexi nodded. 'She lost her shoe.'

'She did. But she found her shoe eventually. And her prince.'

Shoes and princes, thought Lizzy. That pretty much summed up her job. People finding the man or woman of their dreams. Then spending as much money as they could in one day to celebrate the fact. It was ironic that she spent her life making people's dreams come true, yet she had no prince of her own. She was too busy. Too... unsure of what she wanted. And if she was honest, still not over Tom—

The bathroom door opened. Simon stood in the doorway, looking even more attractive now he was in casual clothes.

'I'm not sure about the blue...' He grinned, holding his arms out for inspection as if he had just come out of a changing room.

'I think it suits you.' Lizzy genuinely did.

'Listen, I better get these two home. It's way past their bedtime. I should have taken them at six but Amanda wanted them to stay for the cake and the first dance.'

'Do you need a cab?'

'No – I'm fine to drive. I made a decision not to drink today. Self-preservation.' He made a face. 'Drink always makes you feel vulnerable, don't you think?'

Lizzy wasn't really a big drinker. She started talking nonsense after one glass then fell asleep after two. But she knew she was unusual. 'It must have been a strain for you.'

He shrugged. 'Yeah, well. It was my own fault.'

Lizzy frowned. 'Was it?'

Simon's eyes flickered over to the children, who were paying him no attention whatsoever, mesmerised by *Scooby Doo*.

'I... um... got a bit distracted by someone else when

I was married to Amanda. There wasn't anything really going on but...' He shrugged. 'Amanda didn't take very kindly to me taking another woman out for dinner. She found the receipt. It's the most expensive pizza I've ever eaten.'

'Oh.' Lizzy was surprised by his confession. Amanda had been telling the truth after all. Although she had implied more than just a pizza had been shared.

There was a bit of an awkward pause. For a moment Simon looked as if he wished he hadn't said anything. He pulled the sleeves of his jumper down nervously, then looked at her.

'I wanted you to know that,' said Simon. 'In case you thought I was some sort of saint.'

Lizzy privately thought that anyone who could put up with Amanda for any length of time was definitely a saint, but it wasn't her place to comment when Amanda was paying the bill.

'Nobody's a saint, are they?' she managed finally. 'We all make mistakes.'

Simon nodded. 'Mine cost me my marriage. And I can't forgive myself, because of the children. I broke up the family.'

He looked desolate.

'She could have forgiven you. Taking someone out for a pizza doesn't sound like such a huge crime.'

Simon's eyebrows shot up. 'Amanda – forgive?' He laughed a hollow laugh. 'Now that is an interesting concept. Let's not talk about it any more. It depresses me.'

Was he still in love with Amanda, Lizzy wondered? Was that the root of his regret?

He held out his hand for her to shake. 'Listen – I owe you big time. Thank you. I'll get the clothes back to you.'

Lizzy took his hand. It was warm and dry and her hand felt just right in his clasp. 'Don't worry about the clothes – they've been in lost property for weeks.'

'You've been really kind.'

He still didn't let go of her. They looked at each other. Lizzy gulped. What she was feeling was not very professional. By the look on Simon's face, he was feeling something too. But she needed to get back to the wedding party. She'd been away long enough. It would be just her luck for something to have gone wrong and for Amanda to be on the warpath.

She drew her hand out of his. If they held on to each other any longer it would be odd.

'It's all part of the service,' she managed with a shaky laugh. 'I better go.' She ruffled Mo and Lexi's hair. 'You be good for your daddy, you two.'

They could barely tear their eyes from the telly. Simon laughed. 'Don't take it personally. *Scooby Doo* always wins.'

'I'll try not to,' said Lizzy. She slipped out of the room and closed the door gently, then leaned against the wall in the corridor outside. Get a grip, Lizzy, she told herself. Simon was the sort of man who made every woman feel like the centre of the universe when his attention was on them, be they waitress or paramour. He had natural charm and warmth: she mustn't mistake it for anything meaningful.

She put her hands to her mouth and breathed in and out. Her heart was tripping over itself. What was the matter with her? She'd never felt like this before . . .

Now, standing on the beach at the water's edge, Lizzy relived the feeling. There were turning points in your life when something shifted, when you just knew something was going to happen, and that moment in the hotel corridor had been one of them. She looked down at the sea, the waves teasing her by coming up as close to her as they dared then trickling back where they had come from. She stepped backwards – she only had her Skecher trainers with her and she didn't want to get them wet.

She'd better go to the car and get her stuff then nip to the shop for some supplies. She was longing for a cup of tea. She turned, facing the wind full on, feeling it whip her hair into an even wilder mass of curls and sting her face. She wondered if this day was going to be a turning point too, if it was going to help her become the woman she wanted to be instead of the woman that suited everybody else.

14

Simon woke valiantly at half past seven. He cocked his ear for the sound of Lizzy up and about – the kids definitely wouldn't be up yet – but the house was still quiet. Lizzy must be having a lie-in, though she didn't care for lying in bed much. Not that she was some paragon of virtue; she simply preferred being up and doing nothing, pottering about in her dressing gown and slippers, drinking tea, listening to Chris Evans on the radio, wandering about in the garden if it was nice. But perhaps today she'd decided on a snooze. He'd nip down and make her a cup of tea. She didn't need to give him a lift to the office; the Christmas traffic would be mad. He'd get the train.

He crept down the stairs which led straight down into the living room, ducking his head under the black beam on the way down. He flicked the lights on as he reached the bottom. In the alcove by the fireplace was a splendid Christmas tree in an earthenware pot. Next to it were several boxes and bags full of decorations.

For all its jolly roundness, the tree seemed a bit resentful at having to stand naked in the corner of the room. Simon frowned. A memory snaked its way back to him: Lizzy had mentioned them decorating the tree with the kids last night. Somewhere amidst the chaos of yesterday it had slipped his mind. She hadn't mentioned it when they'd spoken.

No, he thought. She definitely hadn't. She'd mentioned his mother, though. Last night's cocktails curdled in his stomach as he recalled the Cynthia Conundrum. There was absolutely nothing he could do about it. He couldn't tell Amanda she couldn't go skiing. He couldn't tell his mother she couldn't come for Christmas.

Lizzy would understand. He knew she would. She would have calmed down by now and resigned herself to it. He was cross with himself for not following up with Amanda, but he wasn't surprised she'd just gone ahead and done what she wanted without getting back to him. Why did you always forget people's shortcomings? Some kind of misguided optimism, perhaps.

Feeling the unsettled self-loathing of the slightly hungover, he walked into the kitchen. Tea and toast was what he needed.

As he turned on the light, he frowned. The table was laid and in the middle of it was a dish of lasagne. Was this some sort of trendy Christmas innovation he didn't know about? Lasagne for breakfast? Something Jamie or Nigella insisted was the new culinary must-eat?

He went to touch it. It was stone cold.

At Lizzy's place was an open copy of Delia Smith's *Christmas*, much loved and covered in gravy stains. There was a piece of paper on it with her familiar scrawl. At first Simon thought it must be a list, but on closer inspection he realised it was a letter. He picked it up.

It was addressed to him and Hattie and Luke.

Hi everyone. I've decided to go away for a few days and get some me-time. Everything you need for the perfect Christmas is right here. Delia is foolproof so just follow the instructions. All the presents are in my wardrobe and will need wrapping – Sellotape and scissors in kitchen drawer. Check the fairy lights before you put them on the tree.

Love mum (Lizzy) xxxxx

He read it, disquiet growing inside him, his hand shaking slightly. He stood for a moment, read the note again and looked around the kitchen, almost expecting Lizzy to be standing there with a grin on her face.

But she wasn't.

He charged up the stairs with the note in his hand, ducking again to avoid the low beam, and bowled into their bedroom.

The room was painted very pale blue, with a feature wall covered in bird cages and parakeets – Lizzy had agonised for ages over wallpaper samples when they'd redecorated last summer.

'I want it to be like a boutique hotel,' she'd said.

Simon wasn't sure what that meant, but it turned out to mean floor-length curtains, lots of very annoying cushions and a flat-screen telly. But he did his best to fulfil his wife's dream with his DIY, knowing full well that their clutter would never allow them the 'boutique hotel' illusion for very long. Lizzy had loved the makeover, and had made a valiant effort to keep things tidy.

Now, the room was resoundingly, balefully silent. The curtains were wide open, letting in the first of the slurry-grey light, and the bed was made. He pulled back the duvet and put his hand on the sheet underneath to see if there was any residual warmth. There wasn't.

His heart began to beat a little faster, uncertainty and panic pooling in his stomach. He went back out onto the landing and shouted up the stairs.

'Hattie! Luke!'

Of course there was no reply. He ran up to the third floor and poked his head into Luke's room but there was no one there, which wasn't unusual. Luke often stayed over at one or another of his mates. He rapped on his daughter's door, then opened it with caution.

'Hat – have you seen your mum?'

The room smelled sweet, a mix of a hundred different scents: sugary perfume and fabric conditioner and incense sticks and hairspray. Hattie was fast asleep. He could just make her out in the semi-darkness, the only glimmer a string of fairy lights across the top of her headboard. She was curled up on one side, her hair spilling across her pillow. She changed the colour of it as often as she changed her clothes these days. Right now it was peroxide white with several glossy blue streaks. He didn't like to think of the chemicals that had gone into producing the effect. He'd said nothing. With teenagers, you picked your battles.

'Hat! You need to wake up.' He walked towards the bed, avoiding the clothes and shoes scattered across the floor.

Hattie stirred with a groan. 'What is it?'

'When did you last see Mum?'

She stretched out her arms and lay thinking for a moment. Simon felt a tug of impatience.

'Hat?'

'I dunno.' Hattie scrunched her face up in thought. 'Yesterday morning? I went into Birmingham to do some shopping. I called her about... five? I told her I was going carol singing with Kiki.'

'What did she sound like?'

'She sounded... OK. I guess. I don't know. I was in Selfridges. It was really noisy.' Hattie sat up and reached out for her phone. 'Why?'

Simon handed her the note.

'I can't see. Can you open the curtains?'

Simon flicked back the red gingham and looked out of the window at the empty drive.

'Shit.'

Lizzy's car had gone.

He hadn't noticed last night. He wouldn't have noticed much last night, to be fair.

Hattie looked up, frowning. 'What does this mean?'

Simon spread out his hands. 'I don't know. She's not here. There's just a cold lasagne on the kitchen table and that note.'

Hattie looked baffled. 'Well, didn't you see her last night?'

'I stayed out as well. I had a work thing I couldn't get out of. Then I slept in the spare room.'

They looked at each other.

'She wanted to decorate the tree,' said Hattie slowly. 'She told me she was going to do it with you two.'

'Me and Luke?'

'Yes. I wouldn't have gone if she'd said she minded. Or if I knew you weren't coming back.'

'I don't think Luke came back either.'

Simon could see her processing the information. He longed for her to come up with an explanation for Lizzy's disappearance he hadn't thought of. A sudden memory. He felt like a small child waiting for reassurance from a parent. But if anything Hattie looked more worried than he did. Which was worrying in itself, because Hattie never usually worried about anything but herself. In the most feckless and charming teenage girl way.

'Me-time,' he said. 'How can she want me-time at Christmas? Christmas is about family.'

'Yes. But we weren't here. Were we?'

'Is she punishing us?'

Hattie shrugged. 'I don't know. She has been a bit funny lately, though. Don't you think? Not quite herself.'

Simon nodded. 'Since the thing at work.'

'I thought she didn't mind? She told me she didn't mind.'

Simon sighed. 'I think perhaps she did mind. You know how good your mum is at putting on a brave face.'

This was the whole problem. Everyone assumed Lizzy didn't mind about things because she was brilliant at looking on the bright side. 'Never mind, no one's dead,' was her favourite saying when something bad happened. She was always there to catch everyone when things went wrong. But maybe there had been no one to catch her. Maybe the redundancy had hit her harder than she let on.

Hattie picked up her phone. 'I'm calling Luke. I think he was at Hal's last night. I saw some of their videos on Instagram.'

Simon rolled his eyes. Luke and his mates spent hours doing videos of miniature skateboards they rode with their fingers. They built ramps and mini skate parks for them. They had quite a following, and several sponsors, and a lot of prestige from their peers. It was a cult that was baffling to most people, as all good cults should be. Luke would have been up all night, no doubt, garnering Instagram likes.

'He won't be fit to communicate yet.'

Hattie dialled anyway.

'Poor Mum. I feel awful. Where do you think she's gone?'

'Let's not panic yet. Maybe she's left the note to make a point and she's just gone to Waitrose.'

Even as he spoke the words, Simon wasn't convinced. The house felt different. There was no energy in it. No Radio 2 in the kitchen, no Lizzy singing along, no rich aroma of freshly roasted coffee curling its way up the stairs. No coconutty steam coming from the shower.

'Luke!' said Hattie as her brother answered. 'We've got a crisis. Mum's done a runner.'

'We don't know that yet!' Simon hated hearing Hattie vocalise it.

Hattie covered her mouthpiece. 'I have to tell him that or he'll just go back to sleep.' She took her hand away. 'Get home as quickly as you can.' She looked up at Simon. 'He wants to know if you can give him a lift?'

'My car's still at work.' Simon looked at his watch. He should be on his way in by now if he wanted to get it back – he was pretty sure the car park would be locked over Christmas.

'No,' said Hattie to Luke. 'You'll have to walk. Hurry up.'

She hung up, then looked up at her dad.

'Have you tried calling her?'

'I didn't think of that.' Why hadn't he thought of that? Panic, he supposed.

Hattie pressed her mum's number and waited a few moments.

'It's gone straight to voicemail,' she whispered.

'Leave a message,' Simon whispered back.

'Mum? It's Hattie. We found your note. What's going on? We're worried about you. Are you having a meltdown? We're a bunch of selfish pigs and we don't deserve you. Come baaaaaaack!'

She hung up.

'I need coffee,' said Simon.

Hattie scrambled out of bed. 'She won't have gone far,' she said. 'Mum's not a drama queen. Not like Amanda.'

'Yes, OK,' said Simon hastily, not wanting to be reminded of his ex-wife's shortcomings. Hattie and Luke were very wary of Amanda: slightly in awe but also slightly disapproving.

'Is that why you married Mum?' Hattie asked. 'A bit of stability after all the histrionics?'

Simon heaved a sigh. There were a million reasons he'd married Lizzy.

'I married her because she was kind. And she made me laugh.'

Hattie nodded. 'Yeah. Mum's pretty funny.'

'She's not a practical joker, though.' Simon frowned. 'Which is why I'm worried. We need to find her.'

Ten minutes later, Luke came bursting into the kitchen. It never ceased to amaze Simon how his son had gone from a small boy with short red sticky-up hair to a six-foot warrior with dark auburn curls, inevitably spilling out from under a trapper hat or a beanie or a baseball cap. He wore a rotation of long-sleeved T-shirts with a plaid shirt tied round his waist: a look that gave Simon a twinge of nostalgia for the early nineties. But if ever the kids played Nirvana and he was tempted to sing along, one look from either of them soon stopped him. He needn't think he still had teen spirit – he was way too old.

'Mum didn't say she minded,' Luke said, panic spread across his freckled face. 'If she'd said it was a problem, I'd have come back. She said the lasagne would keep and we could do the tree today.'

'Is it a Thing, though, decorating the tree?' asked Simon, slightly mystified. 'I had no idea it was a Thing.'

'We always do it together,' pointed out Hattie.

'Yes, but not in a big deal kind of a way. We just all muck in as and when. Don't we?' Simon was desperate for reassurance, trying to justify why he had been remiss.

'It must have meant more to her than we realised?'said Hattie.

'She can't have just run away,' said Luke. 'Where would she go?'

'Let's phone her again.' Simon picked up his phone and dialled Lizzy's number.

Lizzy had given her smart phone back to the hotel when she'd left, and just had Luke's very old Nokia, which she claimed to love. 'I don't have to worry about losing it or smashing it,' she would say.

They all jumped as it rang, plugged in to its charger by the kettle. They looked at each other.

'She hasn't taken her phone with her,' said Hattie helpfully.

'No shit, Sherlock.' Luke rolled his eyes.

'Well, she can't have gone far. No one goes far without their phone.'

'Unless they don't want to be contacted. Anyway, you know Mum hates mobile phones. She's always forgetting it or losing it.'

Simon picked up the phone and scrolled through it, in case there were any clues.

'Her last call was to you, Luke.'

Luke looked a bit baffled. 'Why didn't she say she minded?' he asked. 'If she'd said, I'd have come home.'

'Because that's not what Mum's like,' said Simon, furious with himself. 'Let's go through everything. See if we can find out where she's gone.'

'What time did she leave?' asked Hattie. 'Was she in bed when you got back last night?'

There was a pause.

'I don't know. I slept in the spare room, remember. The snoring thing . . .' Simon looked abashed.

Luke gave a snort. 'You're such a warthog.'

'Didn't you go in and say good night?' demanded Hattie.

Simon looked at his daughter. 'Did you?'

Hattie bit her thumbnail. 'I didn't want to wake her up.'

'Well, nor did I.'

Luke looked between the two of them. 'You mean Mum wasn't even here and neither of you noticed?'

'At least we came home!' Hattie hit back.

'We don't know she wasn't here.'

Simon looked around the kitchen, feeling slightly stunned. He looked at the table, imagining Lizzy laying it – she'd put out Christmas napkins with Rudolph on, and proper wine glasses. She'd obviously been looking forward to them all eating together. He felt sick with guilt.

With Lizzy gone, the house lacked energy and purpose. Not that she was driven or bossy or organising, but she had a spirit. Even now they were all slightly at a loss, the air slack with indecision. He needed to rehydrate and get some food inside him before he could function. He knew himself well enough to recognise that. He picked up the kettle and took it over to the sink, wincing at the roar of the water as it gushed in.

'Can I have a bit of lasagne?' asked Luke. 'I didn't get any dinner.'

'No,' said Simon, whisking it away and putting it in the fridge. As soon as they found Lizzy, they could all sit down and have it together. 'Make some toast.'

He pulled a loaf of bread out of the bread bin by its bag and slung it next to the toaster. He was being short because he was angry, with himself mostly, but also the kids, for being selfish. It wasn't just him who'd let her down. They all had.

'So what are we going to do?' Hattie was scraping at the nail varnish on her thumbnail, leaving specks of green glitter on the tablecloth. She always did this when she was nervous.

'I'll check her emails. And her Facebook.' Luke pulled out the kitchen table drawer and felt for Lizzy's iPad with its flowery cover.

Since they'd got her the iPad for her birthday four years ago, they were used to her having it on her lap while they were all watching telly, choosing plants for the garden or ordering books or looking at photos on Instagram. She had endless crushes on outdoorsy or creative types, preferably both – Monty Don, Kevin McCloud, Rick Stein. She stalked them religiously on the internet, liking their posts and buying their books and attempting to recreate their worlds in her own haphazard, Lizzy-ish way: bouillabaisse and raised beds full of herbs. Nothing ever worked out quite right but she was very cheerful about it and would then move on to the next object of her affection.

Luke typed in her password. They all knew her password. Lizzy wasn't the type to have secrets on her iPad. He started scrolling through her apps and messages.

Simon suddenly felt nervous. What if there was something awful on there?

'I don't know about this,' he said. In his mind, he suddenly conjured up a sturdy, kindly, weather-beaten gardening type who she had met – where? Stranger things had happened. Lizzy wasn't classically beautiful but there was no doubt men were drawn to her: her warmth, her kindness, her laugh, her twinkly eyes...

And had he been paying her as much attention as he should? Had he been as reassuring about her redundancy as he could have been? Or had he just left her to flounder? She'd been a bit subdued and anxious, although he had told her not to worry about getting a job straight away. He was doing better than ever at work; his bonuses were rolling in. He hadn't said they wouldn't miss her salary, because he didn't want to belittle her contribution, but he didn't want her to feel pressurised either. He wanted her to do whatever made her happy.

Guilt and gin collided in his stomach and started to climb his gullet. He pushed it down with an ill-disguised belch that he managed to turn into a cough. Images of Porn Star Martinis floated past him, washed down with chasers of gut-stripping cheap champagne. He reminded himself it had been his duty to stand in for Colin, to shepherd the younger ones, put money behind the bar, keep morale up.

He looked at the note again. It must be a joke. She really must have got up early and gone off to beat the crowds somewhere, leaving this to shake them up a bit.

Only Lizzy was never sarcastic. It wasn't her style. He felt sweaty with panic: too much drinking always made him anxious, even without a reason to be so. He tried to collate his thoughts. Car. He needed to get the car. They couldn't do anything without that.

'There's nothing weird in her emails,' said Luke. 'Only orders for Christmas stuff.'

'Don't look,' said Hattie. 'You don't want to know what you're getting. Let me see.'

She tried to take the iPad off Luke, but he snatched it back off her.

'Oi!' said Hattie, tetchy with the stress of it all.

'There's nothing there,' said Luke firmly, and shut the iPad back in the drawer.

'Guys, I need to get the train into Birmingham and fetch the car. Why don't you hold the fort here? Maybe do a bit of tidying up? I bet Mum will be back by lunch.'

Even as he said it, he didn't believe himself. The note was so unlike her, it unsettled him. But he had to put on a brave face for Hattie and Luke, who were both looking uncharacteristically distressed. It was a funny age, this – teenagers could be so insouciant, yet it didn't take much to rattle them: a change in routine or an unexpected event.

And Lizzy's bombshell was *totally* out of the blue.

What the hell were they going to do if she really had run away?

15

The walk from the sea's edge to the car park took longer than Lizzy expected. The wind was against her and walking on damp sand was strenuous. She'd be as fit as a flea if she did this every day, she thought. And a windswept walk on the beach was much more pleasurable than jumping on a treadmill or joining an aerobics class.

And you could think, out here in the fresh air without the demands of everyday life interfering. She wanted to figure out who she really was and what she wanted. It wasn't that she was unhappy with Simon but that she felt she was losing control of her life. That everything familiar was slipping away from her and that she was being eternally compromised by all the baggage of marriage. Of course you had to compromise, but she felt as if she was the only one doing it. Which wasn't really compromise, was it?

She supposed what she wanted was everyone to recognise that, without her having to tell them. Running away was her way of shocking them into thinking about her. Was that dishonest? Or was it passive aggressive – which seemed to be the greatest crime you could commit these days? *Something* had to change, even though her marriage was fundamentally sound. She and Simon were made for each other. It was other people who got in the way.

She smiled as she thought back again to what they now referred to as Operation Fruit Shoot. It had been two o'clock before she had got home the night of Amanda's wedding – an occupational hazard. It had been no wonder she was still single because she always seemed to end up working on a Saturday night, and was home so late that Sunday was often a write-off.

It had been quite a struggle to get rid of all Amanda's wedding guests, who wanted to linger on and drink the bar dry. Then she had supervised her team of cleaners to sweep through the marquee and make it immaculate. She never left the mess for the next morning. She gathered up the lost property – two pairs of very expensive high heels, a pair of glittery earrings and someone's car keys. Presumably they'd got a taxi home and would realise the next morning their keys were missing.

She opened her front door, kicked off her shoes and headed for the kitchen to make a cup of tea, wondering if Simon had got home safely with the little ones. She remembered the touch of his hand and the look in his eye. As she trickled the last of the milk into her cup of tea, reminding herself that she needed to do a supermarket trip the next day come hell or high water, she realised that tonight was the first time for a long time she had felt drawn to someone.

She took her tea up to her bedroom and crawled under the duvet. Tomorrow she would finish painting the spare room and start putting it back together. Nesting always made her safe. It was satisfying, building a home, even if it was just for one. She'd go to the antiques market tomorrow and see if there was something she could pick up to renovate: an old chest of drawers or a little bedside table. Projects like that absorbed her and made her feel uplifted, even if she wasn't very good at it; it was sort of mindless and constructive at the same time.

On Monday morning a huge bouquet of lilies arrived at Craven Court reception. Lizzy walked past them – flowers often arrived for guests, so it was nothing out of the ordinary. But the receptionist called to her.

'Lizzy! These are for you. At least, I think they are.'

'They can't be.' Lizzy walked over to have a look. Her heart was lolloping like a baby rabbit across a lawn.

On the envelope was written: *To the Wedding Organiser with the curly hair and the forget-me-not eyes.*

'Forget-me-not eyes,' breathed the receptionist.

Lizzy looked at the words, turning them over and over to see who else they could possibly mean. She was arguably the wedding organiser, and she had curly hair – she put up her hand to feel whether this was still the case, and yes, her head was covered in a mass of ringlets – and her eyes were certainly blue, though she would need to check her *Observer Book of Wild Flowers* to ascertain if they were the exact hue of a forget-me-not.

'Open it!' Kim urged.

She pulled up the flap of the little envelope that came with the flowers.

Thank you so much for rescuing me on Saturday. Would you have dinner with me so I can thank you properly?
Simon

Underneath was written his phone number.

'Oh my goodness,' said Lizzy, thinking that this was probably the best and most exciting moment of her life so far.

'Ring him. Ring him now!'

'I can't.'

'You can! He's just sent you a huge bunch of flowers and asked you out for dinner.'

Lizzy buried her nose in the lilies while she thought. They had a heavy sweetness that was intoxicating and she felt a little removed from reality. Did he really want to take her out for dinner? Or was he just being polite? She turned the little card over in her fingers, reading the number. She couldn't imagine having the nerve to dial it. What on earth would she say to him when he answered?

'Right,' said Kim, swiping the card off her and picking up the reception phone. 'If you won't do it, I will.'

She started pressing the buttons.

'No!' squeaked Lizzy.

'Hello, Mr Kingham? I have Lizzy Matthews on the line for you?' Kim held out the phone.

Lizzy shut her eyes in agony. She reached out one hand and Kim pressed the phone into it. She put it to her ear.

'Hello?' she managed.

'Aah,' said Simon. His voice was warm and amused, and achingly familiar. 'So your name's Lizzy.'

'Yes. Thank you for the absolutely beautiful flowers. You shouldn't have.'

'I know. I should have brought them in myself. And asked you out to dinner face to face. But I was too nervous.'

'Nervous? Of me?'

'Not of you. Of what you might say. So would you? Have dinner with me?'

Lizzy swallowed. 'Well, yes. I'd love to.'

By now she had opened her eyes and could see Kim clapping silently.

'Tonight?'

My goodness, he was really keen. 'Tomorrow,' said Lizzy firmly, thinking of all the restoration work that needed doing.

'I'll book a table at Pinocchio's,' said Simon. 'For eight o'clock?'

'Perfect,' said Lizzy. She loved Pinocchio's, the buzzy little Italian restaurant in Leadenbury. 'I'll see you there.'

She handed the phone back to Kim, who bounced up and down in her chair with delight.

'I've got a date,' Lizzy said in disbelief. 'You don't think it's a joke? Or a trick?'

'For God's sake,' said Kim. 'No, I don't. This bouquet has been sent by a man who is seriously smitten.'

'Smitten,' said Lizzy, not feeling at all like the sort of person anyone would be smitten with.

Kim picked up the phone.

'Right, I'm booking you in for an MOT in the spa. Eyebrows, facial, bikini—'

'I don't need my bikini doing,' protested Lizzy. 'That's going a bit fast.'

'It's psychological,' said Kim. 'If you're all trim and tidy down there, it gives you confidence. Trust me.'

Lizzy wrinkled her nose. Trim and tidy? Never mind her bikini line, what was she going to wear?

Six months later, Lizzy and Simon were arranging their

own wedding. They were sitting in her kitchen, writing out a guest list over a bottle of Australian Shiraz.

She loved the way he fitted into her house. It had felt as if he belonged there the moment he'd walked in, whether he was sprawled on her sofa watching telly or curled up under her duvet. She still couldn't believe it when she opened her eyes and saw his dark hair on her pillow.

'We want Mo and Lexi there, don't we?' asked Lizzy. 'I hate those po-faced weddings where they don't invite children.'

'Of course. I expect my mum will look after them,' said Simon, filling in the names on the diagram of the top table Lizzy had drawn.

Lizzy frowned. 'But surely your mum will want to enjoy herself?'

'I suppose so...'

'Won't Amanda look after them for you? After all, you looked after them at her wedding.'

Simon looked at her and sighed. 'I'm not even going to ask.'

'It can't hurt to ask.'

'Honestly, Lizzy. It's just not worth it.'

'Is she really that selfish?'

He sighed and topped up her wine, pushing it over to her. 'Can we not talk about Amanda? This is about us. As far as I'm concerned, from now on, Amanda isn't part of my life any more.'

At the time, he had seemed so definite. She'd had no reason to disbelieve him. But as Lizzy reached the beachside car park, she reflected on the irony of those words. Twenty years on and Amanda was still pulling the strings. Lizzy didn't know why she couldn't take control of the situation. Was she that feeble and ineffectual? Or maybe Amanda was more important than she was?

Maybe by running away she was enabling *everyone* to have the Christmas they really wanted, relieving them all of duty and tradition and obligation. Maybe she was doing them all a favour.

She opened the boot and pulled out her case and the tote bag of books she'd hastily packed. She decided she would spend the afternoon curled up by the wood-burner with her slipper socks and a hot chocolate and read, without interruption. Her Christmas, her way, safe in the knowledge everyone else was doing just as they liked too. It would be absolute bliss.

16

Simon stood on the station platform, anxiously looking down the line, his eyes flicking up to the departure board. He wanted to get in and out of Birmingham as quickly as possible. He'd considered a taxi but the train would, on balance, be quicker because the traffic would be terrible. But not if the train was delayed... He shivered in the cold air, then felt a surge of relief as the nose of the train appeared round the corner and headed determinedly for the station.

Moments later he was squashed up amongst the panic-shoppers heading into town for their last-minute present buying, sporting a mélange of fake fur, reindeer antlers and flashing earrings. He managed to slink into a window seat. He felt queasy, and he wasn't sure what was causing it: his over-indulgence, his fear for Lizzy or the smell in the carriage, a mixture of a hundred noxious perfumes, the alcohol-infused sweat from last night's hangovers (including his own) and stale cigarette smoke.

He sat hunched up in his seat, arms crossed, head down, urging the train to go faster. In the absence of company or a newspaper, he had no choice but to use the journey to think things over, and it made him uncomfortable.

He cursed himself yet again for going out the night before. Why hadn't he remembered Lizzy mentioning the tree? Why hadn't he left after one drink? He could easily have done that. Why hadn't he left at a reasonable time, instead of stumbling in after midnight no good for anything?

Because he'd wanted to feel young? Because he'd wanted to go out with a bunch of young people and drink and laugh with them? Because he was vain and selfish and shallow and insensitive? Thoughtless at best. Self-indulgent at worst. What kind of a man did that? One who was afraid of getting old. One who didn't deserve the love of a woman like Lizzy.

Simon knew he didn't look his age yet, because he dressed well and appropriately, and he went running three times a week to keep any paunch at bay. But there was no denying his hair was getting thinner, his widow's peak more pronounced, and he had to keep it much shorter because there was nothing more tragic than a middle-aged man with thinning long hair. And there were a few streaks of silver in it. Yes, it was quite distinguished – or was that just what you told yourself, or other people told you, to soften the blow of the ageing process?

He'd had the urge to let that thinning, silvering hair down a bit. There was nothing more sinister to it. He certainly wasn't going to chat up any of the girls in the office. Yes, there'd be a bit of banter, but the thought of anything more intimate made Simon shiver. He lived in horror of being thought predatory.

He'd seen it often enough. Men his age, dressed up in too-tight skinny jeans and fitted jackets and *Peaky Blinders* haircuts, homing in on glamorous thirty-somethings, thinking that their wealth and their sophistication and charm made them contenders. He'd seen the young women catching each other's eyes and smirking. He would never, ever put himself in that situation. He wasn't that kind of a man.

Though he had been once, he reminded himself.

He was sweating now; the train carriage was overheated. Every now and then a cluster of twenty-somethings started a rousing chorus of 'Rocking Around the Christmas Tree' and tried to get everyone to join in. Simon just couldn't find it in him.

'Cheer up, mate, it might never happen,' said one of them to him.

He sighed, pushing back his hair and wiping his forehead with the back of his hand. Another ten minutes and they'd be in Birmingham.

Nina.

Nina had been his downfall. Or had she just been the catalyst? They hadn't had an affair. He could put his hand on his heart and say that. Although what constituted an affair? Did having feelings for someone other than your wife signify infidelity? An emotional betrayal?

Nina had run the photocopy shop two doors down from his office, where Simon often went to have brochures and leaflets printed out. They would get into conversation while he waited and their friendship had blossomed from there. Nina was kind and reassuring and gave him support at a time when he was floundering helplessly, trying to keep his high-pressure job going with two small children and a wife who made constant demands. After having Mo and Lexi eighteen months apart, Amanda seemed to want her life to stay the same: late nights out and lie-ins. Simon had been quite happy to drop down a gear and enjoy his family; Amanda seemed to have no notion of family or the fact that marriage was a compromise.

Amanda had been impossible. When he described it to her, Nina had been appalled by Amanda's expectations and lack of consideration. Gradually, she had given him the courage to start standing up for himself.

'You're being pussy-whipped,' Nina used to tell him, because she was straight talking and, although she was five years younger than him, very perceptive.

Amanda didn't like the new assertive Simon. She liked things her way. Her eyes narrowed every time he put his foot down. When he told her they were a team, and not in competition with each other, she had been mystified. Amanda didn't really do teamwork.

'What's got into you?' she demanded, when he refused to look after Lexi and Mo one Saturday while she went to the gym. He suggested they should all get in the car and go for a walk in the nearby forest instead.

'I'll take you for tea afterwards,' he promised, and she looked at him as if he was mad.

'Tea?' she said, as if he'd suggested eating their own arms.

The thing was, Amanda didn't do simple pleasures. She only did expensive, self-indulgent ones, and he should have realised the implications of that before he married her.

He'd asked Nina out for a drink one night when she'd stayed late to print some urgent mailshots for him. A casual invitation; not a date, but a thank you. They'd gone up the road to a new gastropub and a drink had turned into Nina saying she was hungry and Simon suggesting pizza as he was too. Four Seasons, she had ordered. He could still remember how it was exactly divided into four: ham, olives, mushrooms and artichokes.

'I don't want to go home,' Simon said to Nina when he asked for the bill.

She looked at him, unable to deny the easy, relaxed atmosphere between them that begged to be taken further.

'Don't even go there,' she said, looking upset as she pulled her jacket off the back of her chair.

'Shit, I didn't mean to offend you—'

'You haven't. Not at all.' She locked her eyes on his, and he saw something in them: confusion and fear and sorrow. But also a warning. 'It's just... wrong.'

Simon pushed the receipt into his jacket pocket as he led her to the door and they said goodbye. Nina walked off very quickly, not looking back, and he wondered what she really thought – if she'd been tempted, if she wished, like him, they'd met under different circumstances. Regret followed him home, taunting him. For a moment he had dreamed of something better, something equal. A kinder, gentler relationship would make him a better husband and father, he was sure of it.

Amanda had found the dinner receipt. When Simon had started standing up for himself, Amanda had become suspicious. She was on high alert. It was only two pizzas and a bottle of Chianti from the pub down the road from the office, but it was all the evidence she needed.

Now, Simon wondered if he had wanted Amanda to find the receipt all along. He felt bad for Nina, who was horrified to have triggered the end of his marriage, even if it was making him unhappy. By then, she was seeing someone else, a trainee lawyer who made her eyes sparkl

Simon knew Nina would never have wanted a relationship with him; that she would always have felt tainted by his broken marriage.

But then, a miracle had happened. He had met the person who he was meant to be with. His darling Lizzy: comfy, funny, kind – from the moment she'd rescued him at Amanda's wedding, had dealt with the fountain of vomit without turning a hair, he had known she was the one.

He sat back in his seat and closed his eyes for a moment. They felt gritty from lack of proper sleep. He drifted off slightly and the clamour in the carriage faded into the background. If he could wish for anything, it would be that Lizzy would be at home when he got back, making sausage rolls ready for when they got back from the crib service in Astley on Christmas Eve. It was one of their traditions, even though they weren't religious. It was always a social event and they often asked people back for drinks afterwards.

He sighed and looked at his phone. His heart leapt when he saw a text, but he realised it was from Lexi, on her way to the airport. He pressed call.

'Hey, dad!' said his eldest daughter. 'We're just about to go through departures.'

'I just wanted to say have a good trip. Everything ok?'

'It's all cool. Mo went out with work last night so he's hanging, but that's his problem.'

Simon chuckled. 'Him and me both. He can sleep on the plane. Is your mum ok?'

It was funny. He still worried about whether Amanda was happy, even though he was no longer responsible for her. And even though she was partly responsible for Lizzy's disappearance because of her selfishness.

'Oh, you know Mum. She'll be as happy as a clam once she's in duty free.'

Amanda would be hoovering up as much merchandise as she could carry.

Simon wondered whether to mention Lizzy going AWOL, but decided there was no point in drawing his older children into the drama. Not yet. He didn't want Amanda knowing, speculating, gloating...

He sighed. Maybe he shouldn't vilify his ex-wife at every opportunity. It was toxic.

'Have a good time. I'll call you on Christmas Day.'

'Merry Christmas, Dad. Got to run.' Lexi gave a squeaky kissing noise and hung up.

For a moment, he wondered what life would have been like if he and Amanda had stayed together. Would they all be making their way to the departure gate together? It didn't bear thinking about. No Lizzy. No Hattie and Luke.

Where *was* she? Me time. Had she gone to some spa? Had she got on a plane to go somewhere?

'The next stop is Birmingham Snow Hill,' intoned the passenger announcement and suddenly everyone jumped to their feet and started gathering together their belongings. Simon felt rooted to his seat. Now they were here, he longed to stay on the train and let it take him where it would. Except he knew the final destination was Stourbridge, and that wouldn't help anybody. So he got up and manoeuvred his way to the exit, ready to bolt up the platform.

'All right, mate. Let the dog see the rabbit.' Someone

elbowed him out of the way. He didn't care if he was being pushy. Time was of the essence.

It took him ten minutes at a fast pace to get to the Georgian building that housed his office. He clicked the fob on his key ring that let him through the security gate, hoping to get away without being seen. There shouldn't be anyone here today – the office had officially closed for Christmas the day before.

'You look rough.' Colin came bowling out of the back entrance, beaming, in his usual uniform of black polo shirt, tweed jacket and baggy chinos. Of course he was here. He would probably be here tomorrow as well, right up to the wire. He came into the office six days a week, but that's why the company did as well as it did. He paid well and was generous about time off, because although he himself had a shocking work–life balance he knew you got the best out of people if they could see there was a point to it all. He might live for his work, but that didn't mean everyone else had to.

Simon was fairly sure Colin was grooming him to take over when he retired.

'Someone had to look after the troops,' he responded cheerily.

'Well, much better you do it than me.' Colin might be a multimillionaire, but he was down to earth. No swanky cocktails for him. 'I'd have taken them all down the Bricklayers' Arms for a pint and a pickled egg.' He chortled, and Simon couldn't help smiling despite his hangover and his worry. He admired Colin. Colin could spot the cracks in a building and the dodgy fine print in a contract from fifty paces. And he had nerves of steel.

He could play the long game. Simon admired him for it and wished it came as easily to him.

'Well, have a good one, mate,' Colin said, patting Simon on the back.

'I hope so . . .' Simon paused for a moment. He would trust Colin with his life. Should he confide in him? 'Only I've got a bit of a problem at home.'

Colin raised his thick, unmanaged eyebrows. Once dark and his best feature, they were running wild now they were turning white. 'One of the kids?'

Simon sighed. 'No. Lizzy.'

'Is she unwell?'

'No. It's a bit more complicated than that. She's . . . gone missing.'

Colin did a double-take.

'What?'

'None of us have seen her since yesterday.'

'Bloody hell.' Colin sounded shocked. 'Lizzy? But she's . . . sound as a pound, Lizzy.'

Once or twice a year Colin took Lizzy and Simon out for a slap-up dinner with his wife. He believed firmly in family. And he and Lizzy had always got on famously.

'I know. Which is why it's so worrying. I came down this morning and there was a note. Basically saying *sort yourselves out, I'm off.*'

Colin turned the information over in his mind. He was a thoughtful man; instinctive but never impulsive. 'It could be her age.'

Simon frowned.

'Kid gloves, Simon. You have to treat her with kid gloves. As if she's a piece of precious china. And generally speaking my advice to you is keep your mouth shut. You can't ever say the right thing.'

'Tell me about it.'

'Be on your guard,' Colin warned him. 'Even the most mild-mannered and sweet-natured woman can turn into a monster at this time of life.'

Simon looked at him warily. He knew Colin wasn't a 'new man'. That he would probably still refer to 'the wrong time of the month', which Simon knew you just couldn't do these days. But he understood life and how it worked. This was, Simon knew, the voice of experience.

'We were supposed to help her decorate the tree last night,' he admitted. 'We forgot. All three of us.'

Colin winced. 'Oof. Well, in that case you're best off going and buying her something to make up for it. Something she's got her heart set on.'

'Lizzy's not like that.' Amanda had been. An offence like that would have needed a whopping great present.

'A holiday,' said Colin. 'Book her a holiday. Venice or Santorini would be my advice.'

'There's no point in booking anything until we find her,' pointed out Simon.

Colin nodded. 'Sit tight. She'll be back. It's ruddy Christmas, isn't it? Too much pressure. That's why I take my lot to the Lygon Arms in Broadway for lunch and let someone else have the stress.'

Simon could imagine Colin, cheery and red-faced at the head of the table, with his various offspring and their children ranged down each side, while waiters rushed around pouring vintage wine that Colin wouldn't want to drink (he'd have a pint of bitter) but would happily foot the bill for.

He opened his car door and slid into the driver's seat as Colin patted his roof in farewell. His hands were shaking as he put them on the steering wheel.

Oh Lizzy, he thought. You silly sausage. Where on earth are you? We *need* you.

17

Harley pulled back the curtains to let in the morning light. It slid past him, tentative and pale, pushing aside the shadows. He touched the end of his nose: it was icy cold. The air inside the hut had a brisk edge to it, so he loaded up the wood-burner again.

He was surprised not to have woken earlier – the seagulls usually provided him with an alarm call so he was used to getting up early. He'd seen that last night's unexpected visitor had gone. She wasn't on the mezzanine and her coat had vanished, though she had left her tooth-brush in the bathroom so perhaps she'd gone for milk.

He reached out for his jacket, slung over the arm of the sofa, and pulled the crumpled card from his pocket. It was cheap and flimsy and most of the glitter had already fallen off, which made him feel a bit sad. He supposed there wasn't much choice in prison. He tried to picture his dad writing it. Had he been in his cell, chewing on the end of a splintered biro? Or siting at a table with a load of other prisoners, choosing his words while everyone bantered around him? He had no idea what life was like for his father, he realised.

He read the card for the hundredth time since it had arrived with the advent calendar. Luckily he had found the parcel before his mum. She wouldn't have taken it off him but it would have upset her. Any reminder of Richie always did.

Dear H,

This is a really silly present and I know you are way too old, but the truth is you are never too old for Star Wars. Anyway, I hope you have a great Christmas. I think about you and River all the time. And there's something else I want to say. Now you're eighteen, you can come and see me whenever you like. The thing is, H, I totally understand why your mum doesn't want anything to do with me. I let her down. I let you all down. But I would really value the chance to explain everything to you. How easy it is to make the wrong choices for what you think are the right reasons. I'm your dad, so it's up to me to teach you what's right and wrong. And I know I did wrong. I'm enclosing my prisoner number and the number you need to call to arrange a visit. It would mean the world to me. You and River are the things I am proudest of in the world and I don't want to lose you. But there's no pressure. It has to be your decision. Anyway, have a great Christmas and hug your brother from me.

I love you, H.
Dad xxxxx

Harley let out a heavy sigh. Every time he read the card he got more confused. He'd hoped that by leaving the house things would be clearer in his mind. He put the card back down on the thick glass of the coffee table then fell back onto the cushions of the sofa with a groan.

Never mind worrying about his dad. He needed to talk to his mum first, about what he had done, before he made any decisions about visiting prison. He picked up his phone, his thumbs hovering over the keys, not sure how to articulate how he was feeling.

The door opened and he saw Lizzy, red-faced and struggling with a variety of bags and a small suitcase.

'Hi!' she said. 'You were fast asleep when I left.'

He jumped up. 'You should have woken me. I'd have helped.'

He took the case from her and carried it in. She followed, breathing hard.

'I've got provisions,' she said. 'Tea and coffee and milk, and bacon and eggs. Do you fancy a cooked breakfast? It's all I can think about. I'm ravenous.'

'Sounds awesome,' said Harley, smiling at this micro-whirlwind of a woman, and surprised to find how pleased he was she hadn't disappeared. 'Shall I put the kettle on?'

'Definitely!' Lizzy humped two bulging carriers onto the kitchen work surface. She started unpacking the food she had bought and set to making breakfast.

She was impressed with the new kitchen. She could remember her and Caroline struggling to cook with a two-ring gas burner and a very small microwave: endless baked beans and spaghetti hoops; hard-boiled eggs and bags of ready-salted crisps. And sausage sandwiches with rivers of tomato sauce. They hadn't worried about carbs in those days.

Now there was a sleek induction hob and a shiny four-slice toaster in gleaming copper that matched the kettle.

It was all pretty impressive, but Lizzy thought that she preferred the old hut, with its flaws and foibles. They'd used enamel plates and plastic beakers and mismatched glasses that Caroline's mum had brought down; things that would ordinarily have been thrown out but had a second lease of life.

'This is better than my kitchen at home,' she told Harley, cracking a brace of eggs into the frying pan next to the bacon. 'Can you make some toast?'

This hut might be luxurious and slick, but it didn't have as much character. Not that she was complaining – beggars, she thought, can't be choosers. She admired the chunky hand-thrown mugs and the matching crockery in pale turquoise, and the different-sized glasses depending on what wine you were drinking.

The two of them sat at the table in companionable silence to eat their breakfast, the sun outside growing more confident as it shone in through the window, like a new arrival at a party, who's had a glass of wine.

'The thing with here,' said Harley eventually, 'is you can forget all your worries. It feels as if nothing bad could ever happen.'

'I know,' said Lizzy. 'I haven't been here for years, but that's how I always used to feel when I came here with Caroline.' She looked sideways at him, thoughtfully. 'Do you want to talk about it?'

He wiped a crumb from the side of his mouth. 'I can't go back home for Christmas. Well, I can't call it home. It's not home. It's my mum's boyfriend's house.'

'Oh dear.'

'I want it to be like when we first moved down here.

153

Just me and Mum and River, my little brother. We only had a small flat but it felt like ours.'

He swirled the last of his tea around and looked down into it as if there might be a solution there.

'The trouble is,' said Lizzy, 'things don't stay the same. Ever.'

Harley looked up. 'I know. But I hate him. Mum's . . . boyfriend. Whatever you want to call him. Tony.' He spoke the name with distaste. 'I've tried really hard to see his good side. And figure out what Mum sees in him. But . . .'

He slumped, defeated, unable to find the words.

Lizzy put her hand on his arm. 'It is difficult, you know. Being a step-parent. I've done it. My husband has two children from his first marriage and I found it really hard. I still do. The family stuff.'

Harley looked at her. His eyes were rock-pool green, glassy with trouble. 'He scares me.'

He said it so matter-of-factly it made Lizzy's tummy turn over.

'Do you mean he's violent?'

Harley considered his words carefully.

'Not exactly . . .'

'But?'

'Yesterday, I felt as if he . . .' Harley struggled to articulate what he was feeling. 'It's as if he's goading me. As if he wants *me* to have a go at *him*. He was taunting me. He was looking in my room. Making sure I hadn't got a big stash of weed in there or something. Like, just because my dad's black I must be a drug dealer. And he knows it winds me up.'

'It sounds like his problem, not yours.'

'I can't stay in the same house as him.' Harley looked defiant, his eyes flashing with the injustice of it all. He looked as if he might be on the verge of tears. 'I nearly lost it with him. He was right in my face, giving it . . .' He did a yapping motion with his hand. 'He wanted me to touch him. I know he did.' He put his head in his hands, then looked up. 'Then he could prove to Mum I'm a waste of space, like my dad.' He gave a half-smile. 'It's all a bit of a mess, really.'

Lizzy looked out over the sea, thinking carefully. It was a tricky situation and she didn't want to advise him badly.

'Maybe a little bit of time out *is* what you need,' she said. 'It's just a shame it's happened at Christmas.'

'Mum will be gutted. She desperately wants everyone to get on and for us to be like a family. And it's not me. It really isn't. She doesn't see what he's like.'

'Have they been together long?'

'Two years now. And he was great to start with. We thought everything was going to be OK again. We'd had a bit of a tough time. My dad got sent to prison. Everyone always assumes drugs. But it was fraud. Dad was smart. He was a financial advisor. But not smart enough. He lost all our money.'

'That's awful,' said Lizzy.

'I know. He and his partner invested it in something high risk they shouldn't have touched.'

'Ouch.'

'He lost our friends' money too. That's what Mum couldn't forgive. And she hated all the gossip. The way everyone dropped her when they found out. So we moved down here. She used to come here on holiday as a kid. She thought it would be nice for River to grow up by the sea. And she thought I'd be better going to college here than in the city. I think she thought I might go off the rails without a father figure.'

'You don't seem like an off-the-rails type.'

Harley grinned at her. 'Of course I'm not. I'm an angel.'

'So what are you going to do? You ought to tell your mum where you are. She'll be worried.'

Harley looked down at his phone. 'I told her I was at a mate's last night. So she won't be worried yet. Maybe I'll just text her. Tell her I'm not coming back.'

His face crumpled with the stress of it. Lizzy put a hand on his arm. 'It's always better to do these things face to face, you know. Trust me, as a mum, that's what I'd want. A chance to talk it over.'

She felt anguish for Harley's mother and what she'd been through. And the agony of being torn between two people you loved who didn't see eye to eye.

'She's out all day. She's selling stuff at the Candlelight Market in Micklestone. She makes wreaths.'

'Wreaths?' Lizzy looked alarmed.

He laughed. 'Christmas wreaths. Not funeral ones.'

'Oh, I see. Well, why don't we go? I could drive you. A Candlelight Market sounds just the thing.'

'Does it?' Harley didn't look convinced.

'Yes. I haven't had a chance to do anything like that yet this Christmas. Wandering around buying stuff you don't need and eating things you shouldn't.' Lizzy's eyes were shining. 'Micklestone's not far, is it?'

'It's about eight miles. And that would be amazing,' he said. 'Because I can't go back to the house. I just can't.'

Lizzy jumped up. 'Well, come on then. I like a plan. Let's get our skates on.'

Harley couldn't help but feel heartened. There was something comforting about Lizzy. She didn't judge, and she had insight. He opened his mouth to ask what had happened to her, why on earth *she* was here, but she was already clearing the plates and taking them over to the sink. She was slightly hyper, slightly overexcited, as if she was covering something up, and there was something about her body language that told him not to ask. Not just yet.

18

Cynthia struggled awake from a not-very-interesting dream – even her dreams were dull these days – to see her mobile inching its way across her bedside table as if it was determined to throw itself off the edge. It always did that when she put it on silent/vibrate and it still unnerved her. She reached for it listlessly and tried to focus on the name that was flashing up. Without her glasses on she made an educated guess that it was Amanda.

'Hello?' She could never leave a phone unanswered, even if it was someone she didn't much want to talk to. Cynthia wriggled her way up until she was leaning against her mink-grey velvet padded headboard. How many sleeping tablets had she taken last night? If it was two, that would explain why she couldn't gather her thoughts. It was a naughty habit, but the oblivion was so tempting.

'Cynth! We're in the departure lounge. Drinking Buck's Fizz.'

Amanda sounded jubilant. She must be phoning her from the airport. Cynthia felt a pang. 'Lovely.'

'Listen. I thought I ought to phone you. I wanted to give you the heads-up.'

'On what?'

'I don't think Simon has told Lizzy you're coming to them for Christmas.'

'Oh.' She tried to remember the arrangements that had been made. Oh yes. Amanda had promised she'd square Cynthia having Christmas with Simon, thanks to her last-minute skiing plans. That had only been a few days ago. Cynthia hadn't spoken to Simon about it yet – she knew this time of year was hectic for him at work. She was going to give him a ring tonight, to see what time he was coming to pick her up, and what she could bring.

'I bumped into Lizzy yesterday and she had no idea you were coming, so I think he's forgotten to tell her. And to be honest, she was a bit . . . funny about it.'

'Funny?' Cynthia felt her chest tighten.

Amanda sighed. 'I don't want to tell Simon off for not telling her because then he'll get cross with me. But she didn't sound very happy.'

'Oh.' No, thought Cynthia. She wouldn't be.

'You know how organised she is and she'd probably planned everything down to the last potato. Lizzy's never been very spontaneous or flexible. Everything is always such an ordeal for her.'

Cynthia frowned. That was patently untrue. Lizzy was very capable and easy-going, totally unlike Amanda who had very specific priorities and was very controlling. The two women couldn't be less alike.

'Well, the last thing I want to do is upset Lizzy,' said Cynthia, wishing the conversation would go away. That she hadn't answered the phone.

'Talk to Simon. He'll smooth things over. He probably just forgot to mention it. You know what he's like when he's under pressure.'

Amanda spoke as if Simon's preoccupation with work was still a daily irritant to her. Cynthia felt nettled. Her son was a grafter like his father had been and there was nothing wrong with that. She was very proud of him. She was about to say something when Amanda cut her off.

'Oh, our flight's being called. Got to run. Merry Christmas, Cynth. I'll bring you back some duty-free.'

She rang off.

Cynthia sighed. She dropped the phone back onto her bedside table and tried to assess the level of fug she was feeling this morning. She welcomed fug; clarity was alarming as it brought everything into sharp focus. She liked her edges fuzzy, which was why she went to bed as late as possible then took sleeping tablets. Heaven forbid she should wake up bright-eyed and bushy-tailed.

But the truth had cut through the fug. Of course Lizzy was disgruntled that she was coming. Cynthia had known she would be. She'd hoped they could get through it by pretending, like they usually did. But Amanda had hit her Achilles heel, making her acutely aware of the rift between her and her second daughter-in-law.

The one she infinitely preferred, though she could never admit it to anyone.

She swung her legs out of bed. The champagne carpet was luxuriously soft under her feet and she wriggled her toes for a moment before fishing about for her slippers. She walked over to the window and pulled back the curtain. The day was throwing a grudging light over the six dormer bungalows that sat in a circle in Copperfield Close, as if there were people elsewhere who deserved the light more.

Cynthia had never much cared for the word 'gated'.

She had a horrible feeling that the gates were to keep the residents in, rather than intruders out. Copperfield Close felt like a very expensive prison, but as Simon had pointed out when she moved from their rambling family home after Neville died, the move was as much about the future as it was about now. Which basically meant it would still suit her when she started to lose her marbles or went off her legs.

She could never argue that the bungalow wasn't impressively appointed. Every comfort had been considered, every eventuality. Everything was controlled at the touch of a button. Even the curtains could be closed when she was away from home via her phone. Every cupboard was soft-close; appliances could be turned on and off with the flick of a finger. She didn't even have to fill a kettle – boiling water came out of a special tap. The carpets were deep and soft; the curtains long and thick; the lighting was dimmable.

Cynthia never had to think about anything. Every bill was paid by direct debit, her readings sent by remote control. She could sit on her sofa all day and not move and her life would still go on. The fridge would be stocked, the interest on her investments would be put into her current account, the laundry and dry-cleaning would be collected and redelivered in cellophane and put back in its place. There was a regular delivery service of groceries, prescriptions, whatever you needed. In Cynthia's case, boxes of wine arrived and were placed in her temperature-controlled wine fridge by a faceless helper. There was a team of them, in pale green tabards.

And if she wanted to go anywhere, she pressed a button on her phone and a driver in a white Mercedes would glide to her front door. She had told Simon that she didn't want to keep a car any longer, that it was more economical to rely on taxis and buses than keep Neville's Jaguar on the road. She'd told him a friend from the golf club had bought it. The lie was effortless for why would he not believe her?

It all made her feel as if she might as well not be here. Yes, she was ladies' captain at the golf club, but there were plenty of people waiting to jump into her size fives. Yes, she was on several charity committees. Yes, she played bridge. Yes, she indulged her passion for musical theatre on a regular basis. She was busy, busy, busy yet she felt empty inside. Without Neville, it all felt pointless.

Christmas made it infinitely worse. Neville had always been such a jolly Christmassy sort. He embraced it fully, and he had lots of traditions that began in early December, making it a month of both celebration and generosity.

The first weekend in December they would go into Birmingham to do the Christmas shopping. Neville made a list of gifts for his staff, and the two of them would work their way through Rackham's from the top floor, analysing what was on offer, comparing possibilities, debating colours, until every member of staff was catered for. Then they would go and choose that year's wrapping paper and ribbon.

Afterwards they would go for tea at Druckers, the Viennese patisserie. This was Cynthia's favourite day of the year, sitting surrounded by their carrier bags with a beautifully set table between them and a plate of cream-filled pastries and cakes to devour. In those days you weren't made to feel guilty about cream and sugar and carbohydrates. A little of what you fancied did you good

– or even a lot, from time to time. They would always leave saying they didn't need anything else to eat that day.

In the evening, they would wrap the presents together. They laid everything out on the dining table. Neville would carefully measure and cut the right shape and size of paper, Cynthia would wrap, and they would share a bottle of champagne while they labelled everything up, writing something thoughtful to each recipient. Cynthia would pop two jacket potatoes in the oven, because she knew that by eight o'clock they would feel hungry again despite their earlier indulgence, and when they finished wrapping she would serve the jacket spuds filled with butter and grated Cheddar with a dollop of coleslaw on the side.

Now, it was a different picture. Neville was gone, his engineering business had long been sold and there were no staff members to thank this Christmas for their loyal service, even though she was still living off the fruits of their labour. Thanks to Neville's business skills and risk-taking and careful financial planning he'd made a big profit from the sale. Because he was jolly and ruddy-faced and full of jokes people thought him a bit of a buffoon but he was far from foolish. He had left her a wealthy woman.

She couldn't bear thinking about it, the hole he had left when he died. Being his right-hand woman had been her raison d'être. He had never made her feel like just a housewife. Or a trophy wife – even though that's what everyone had thought she was, for she had been so glamorous, with her tiny waist and her dancer's legs and her halo of white-gold hair, petite next to Neville's bear-like bulk.

Cynthia had never had a shred of personal ambition – two years at ballet school had been enough; she might have had the legs but simply didn't have the guts or the backbone – but she was ferociously ambitious for her husband and his business. She was that woman in the quote: 'Behind every successful man . . .' And she bloody well worked hard for it, from the moment she brought him his poached egg in the morning to turning on the electric blanket at night.

He had never belittled or demeaned her or made her feel like the little woman. He worshipped her. He valued her opinion. Every night they talked things over. He made decisions based on her suggestions. She knew every member of his staff and had views on how they should be handled. They had been a team, and now she was alone she felt rudderless. He'd been gone nearly five years and still she had found nothing to fill the emptiness she felt inside.

There was only one thing that had made it less painful. She thought she had the perfect formula. She measured it out carefully, so people didn't talk and she didn't make a fool of herself. She had a list of rules. Never before midday. Never more than three glasses an hour. And never more than one bottle a day.

Of course, sometimes she broke her own rules, but that was the nature of the beast: it made you forget your principles. It mostly happened when she was with people. She needed her crutch even more when she was in public, for she didn't know who to be, how to be. And of course, other people urged you on, filled up your glass, and she found it hard to say no.

The next day she would resolve not to overindulge

again. A little was enough to numb the pain, after all. A lot just added to her anxiety the next day. Why could she never learn that? Surely she had learnt her lesson, after what had happened?

Cynthia leaned her forehead on the glass of the window, limp with despair. Why had Amanda done it? Why did she have to swan off and leave Cynthia feeling even more unloved and unwanted than usual?

It's not Amanda's fault, you fool. It's your own.

Even now, the memory made her shudder. Her cardinal sin. The shame. The realisation that Lizzy would never trust her again because of what she had done. The awful deal they had struck...

It was no wonder Lizzy didn't want Cynthia coming to them on Christmas Day. Oh God, how humiliating. There was no way she was going to go to Pepperpot Cottage now, even though she had bought everyone's presents with enormous care. Of course she wanted to see Hattie and Luke, but she didn't think they'd be bothered. Seventeen-year-olds didn't care about that kind of thing.

Not like when they'd been small. They had loved coming to see their grandparents, running up the gravel path outside the house and fighting as to who would get to ring the doorbell. There was a train set for Luke and a doll's house for Hattie – the same ones that Mo and Lexi had enjoyed. She had loved their chubby little arms round her neck and the way they wriggled when they sat on her knee and she tried to read to them.

She turned away from the window. She wasn't going to think about it. She wasn't going to live in the past. Instead she picked up her phone. Her hands were shaking as she found Lizzy's number. She cleared her throat so her voice wouldn't waver, threw back her shoulders as if she was about to go on stage with the Royal Ballet and breathed in to give herself courage as the answerphone clicked in.

'Lizzy? It's Cynthia. I think there might have been a bit of a mix-up. Amanda seems to think I'm coming to you for Christmas Day. But as soon as Amanda told me she was off skiing I made other arrangements. I do hope that hasn't inconvenienced you. Let's make plans to swap presents after Christmas.' She paused for a moment, not quite sure how to ring off. 'Happy Christmas,' she added quietly.

She hung up quickly. She could already imagine Lizzy's eyes rolling as she listened to the message, but also her relief. Cynthia imagined her knife and fork being whisked away with a flourish.

Outside, she saw the fairy lights spring to life on the two conifers that flanked the entrance to Copperfield Close. The automatic timer had snapped on, reminding everyone that this was the season to be jolly. Cynthia shut her eyes. One tiny risk. One stupid decision and she'd messed up everything. She had lost any hope of being welcome at Pepperpot Cottage ever again.

19

Simon's heart sank as he drove back onto the drive at the side of Pepperpot Cottage and saw Lizzy's car was still not there. He had secretly been hoping that she would have turned up while he was gone. But no. The drive was defiantly empty.

'Hey,' said Mick the Post, striding up with his trolley behind him. 'Not so many today. Thanks for the wine, by the way.'

'No worries,' said Simon, but he didn't want to engage in Yuletide pleasantries. He took the proffered mail and hurried inside, to find Hattie and Luke still in the kitchen.

'Should we open this, do you think?' he asked.

Along with two Christmas cards was an official-looking envelope with Lizzy's name typed on the front.

'It might be a clue,' said Hattie.

'That's what I thought,' said Simon, and started to lift the flap without thinking too much about what would be inside. Some hideous diagnosis of a terminal disease or a massive debt or a letter demanding damages? A ransom note?

He pulled out the letter.

'It's from Inglewood's.'

'There's a voucher.' Beady-eyed Hattie spotted it in the envelope and pulled it out. 'Fifty quid! Bloody hell!'

Simon read out the letter.

Dear Mrs Kingham,
    Please accept our full apologies for the misunderstanding in our store today. Be assured that we will not be taking the matter any further. We wish you season's greetings, and as a token of our goodwill we enclose a voucher for you to spend at your leisure.
        With my very best wishes for a peaceful Christmas,
        Shirley Booth
            Assistant Store Manager

'Misunderstanding?' said Simon. 'What do you think happened?'

'Maybe Mum got stuck in the lift and wigged out?' suggested Luke. 'You know she hates lifts.'

'She never goes in the lift at Inglewood's,' said Hattie. 'She always uses the escalator.'

Simon sighed. 'We better go and find out. I need to get her a present anyway.'

'Haven't you got her a present yet?' Hattie looked at him accusingly.

'Yes. But I think I need to get her something better.'

Instinct told him that the slow cooker he'd got her from Argos wasn't going to do the job. To be fair, she had asked for it. But it showed little imagination and less generosity. He hadn't even had to leave his desk. He'd ordered it online and had it delivered to the office. It was in the car boot, waiting for him to wrap it in some leftover paper that he would pinch from her.

He felt ashamed. Lizzy was brilliant at presents. They were always thoughtful and funny and personal and often had a theme, even if it was just a colour scheme. One year she had got them presents that began with their initials – he'd had socks, slippers, swimming goggles, a sweater, a bottle of Shiraz and a Stereophonics CD. None of the gifts were highly original on their own but by linking them she had made them special, somehow.

'Get dressed,' he told the twins. 'See you outside in ten.'

He hoped that this wasn't too little too late, and prayed that on Christmas Day she would be sitting in the living room ripping the paper off a huge pile of presents with her usual smile. That she would absolutely realise how much he bloody loved her. How much they *all* loved her.

20

Cynthia had forced herself to get up and get dressed. She had a long shower, then put on a pair of cream slacks and a gold jumper in honour of the time of year, blow-dried her hair and put on a full face of make-up. Appearance was everything.

She sat at the table for two in her kitchen. There was a glass of ruby red breakfast juice in front of her and a plate with two slices of granary toast. She could never face food until about eleven. Her appetite had vanished after Neville died, and she hated eating on her own. She nibbled one of the triangles, but it felt like dust in her mouth.

The space opposite her felt more glaringly empty than ever. Neville should be there, sipping his tomato juice, waiting for his poached egg to reach peak firmness – he liked them hard, not runny, so he could cut them into four and spread their pale yellowness onto his English muffin.

Oh, how she missed looking after someone. It was an overwhelming need that wouldn't ever be fulfilled now. No one needed her. They had their own lives, their own support systems. She felt superfluous. Surplus to requirements.

The days stretched out in front of her. Christmas Eve tomorrow, then Christmas Day looming, black and empty. What was she to do? Where should she go? Everyone else on the close would be trotting off to friends and relatives. She'd seen a couple of them head off earlier today, laden with luggage and presents.

Were there friends she could go to? She could make up some excuse as to why she wasn't with her own family. A bout of illness? But you had to know someone very well indeed to gatecrash their Christmas Day, and she didn't feel confident enough to call anyone, for fear of hesitation or a false 'Of course you must come to us' accompanied by out-of-sight grimacing and eye-rolling.

As a widow, she felt a nuisance. Easy to overlook. She could just stay in bed for Christmas, she thought. Make her way through the side of smoked salmon and the couple of bottles of champagne and the box of white chocolate truffles that were sitting in the fridge. She'd had them delivered, originally to take to Amanda's. She never turned up empty-handed.

She spooned some more marmalade onto her toast to make it less dry.

Buck up, Cynth, she told herself. She was not going to let the chain of events crush her. There must be something she could do; some constructive way she could spend the day. It was probably too late to book a hotel somewhere or fly to warmer climes. She chewed her toast, turning over the possibilities.

She remembered an article she'd seen recently about people helping out the homeless on Christmas Day, serving them dinner, entertaining them, bringing them into the warm to make them feel included at a time of year when one could feel very alone.

She felt a surge of enthusiasm for her idea. This was the way forward. In fact, she would do this every year, so she wouldn't ever need to feel unwanted again. And Neville would have approved as well. He'd done so much for charity. Quietly. He wasn't one of those men who wanted to be pictured in the local paper handing over money. He was discreet. And he'd believed that charity begins at home. She remembered him dressing up as Santa at work: all the factory workers would bring their children in on the last Saturday before Christmas and he would give every one of them a present. He might have made a lot of money but he gave away more than people realised.

She looked up homeless charities in Birmingham on her iPad. She was shocked by what she read: how many homeless there were, their stories, their bleak futures. She was cheered by the possibility of offering them warmth and company, even if it was only for one day.

There was one charity in particular that caught her eye – not the biggest, but it seemed to have great success in turning round the people it helped. There were lots of stories of people who had lost everything, including their self-respect, but had found their way again, picking themselves up and going on to lead happy lives. She wanted to be part of that. How wonderful, to give someone hope.

She remembered a film she'd watched recently. Diane Keaton falling in love with a man who lived wild in the woods near her Hampstead house. Maybe that could happen to her. She'd strike up a relationship with an entrepreneur who'd fallen on hard times. She'd give him something to live for, give him a reason to get himself back on his feet. They'd fall in love, travel the world . . .

She couldn't help laughing at herself. She was getting carried away. She might not fall in love – how could she, when she still loved Neville? – but she could make a difference.

Galvanised, she picked up her phone.

'My Christmas plans have fallen through unexpectedly,' she told the person who answered. 'I want to offer myself to help out at the refuge over Christmas. I don't mind what I do – peeling spuds, washing-up. I don't mind getting my hands dirty.'

She was somewhat surprised to hear a sigh.

'I'm sorry, love,' was the reply. 'We've got all the help we need. We're never short of offers at Christmas. It's very popular, helping out on Christmas Day. It's the rest of the year we have a problem with.'

There was an implied criticism in her tone.

'Oh,' said Cynthia. 'Are you sure there's nothing I can do?'

She was fazed by the response. Somehow she'd imagined a cry of joy, profuse thanks and being welcomed with open arms. Not that she was in it for the glory.

'What about a donation? Money is what we need. You can set up a direct debit via our website.'

'I see.' Cynthia could tell by the weariness in the girl's tone that she was not the only person to have had the same bright idea. 'Well, of course. I'll do that straight away.'

'Thank you and merry Christmas,' the girl replied, her reply automatic and far from heartfelt.

Cynthia put the phone down. She felt somewhat crestfallen.

By the time she had phoned a third charity, and got pretty much the same response, she felt utterly despondent. She couldn't even give herself away on Christmas Day. Everywhere she turned, a door was shut in her face. She felt even worse than she had after she'd finished her conversation with Amanda. She hadn't thought that was possible.

She walked over to the fridge and pulled out one of the bottles of white wine resting in the bottle rack. She didn't even look at her watch. She knew it wasn't midday yet.

She didn't give a figgy pudding what the time was.

21

'Mrs Kingham accidentally left the store with one of our dresses yesterday. Our security guard apprehended her outside the shop. She still had it over her arm.'

Shirley Booth, the assistant store manager, was looking at Simon with a mixture of pity and curiosity. He felt as if he was an object of interest; as if she had heard something about him and wanted to see it for herself. He wasn't sure he cared for her scrutiny, especially as she had initially refused to give him any details about yesterday's incident, until he had explained that Lizzy had gone missing.

He and Hattie and Luke were standing in Shirley's office. He'd shown her the letter.

'You mean you arrested her?' he asked.

'We took her into the office for questioning. I could see it was a mistake after just a few minutes. I'm highly trained. I can spot a liar at fifty paces. I could see Mrs Kingham had made a genuine mistake.'

'Mum would never, ever nick anything,' said Luke. 'She's just not that sort of person.'

Shirley smiled at him.

'You'd be surprised. We have the most respectable people in here stealing things. And we have to take it seriously. We have zero tolerance on shoplifting. Times are hard and people don't see it as stealing.'

'Don't they?' said Hattie.

Shirley shook her head sadly.

'The amount of times people tell us that the prices we charge cover our losses. As if that makes it OK.' She nodded over to a TV screen in the corner. 'We've got hours of CCTV – sometimes we scroll through it just for fun, to see the people we've missed. It's better than telly.'

She chuckled at the thought.

Simon sighed. 'How did she seem to you?' he asked. 'When she was in here?'

Shirley put her head to one side, as if considering how truthful to be.

'Like all of us. Stressed out by Christmas. She said she didn't care if she ended up in prison because at least she'd get some respite.'

'Did she really say that?' Simon was shocked.

'I can tell you, I'd be right there with her. Christmas is a special sort of hell.'

'Hell?' Simon looked baffled. 'I thought it was supposed to be fun.'

Shirley Booth gave a hollow laugh.

'Spoken like a true man.'

Simon shot her a glance. He didn't like her tone.

'Thank you for the voucher,' he said. 'Or were you worried she might sue?'

Shirley looked at him. When she spoke, her tone was soft.

'I just thought she needed spoiling,' she said. 'If the manager found out, I'd probably get the sack.'

Her words hung in the air, the criticism not just implied, but blatant.

Simon tried not to flinch. He felt a ripple of anger at this woman for judging them. Yes, they had been thoughtless, but no more than that.

'Thank you for your time,' he said stiffly. 'Come on, you two. Let's go.'

The three of them went back out to the front of the store and stood at the bottom of the escalator, slightly shell-shocked.

'She was a bit harsh,' said Hattie. 'Christmas is fun. And Mum loves it.'

'She does do everything, though,' said Luke. 'To be fair.'

'Because she wants to,' said Simon. 'Trust me. I spend a lot of time asking what I can do to help. And she always says she's got it under control.'

'It's because she doesn't like asking or admitting she needs help,' said Hattie. 'We should just have done things, without being asked.'

'Or remember the things she *did* ask,' said Luke gloomily.

Simon looked at his watch. It was heading for lunch and he had run out of ideas about what to do next. He hoped beyond hope that by the time they got back Lizzy would be home, laughing at herself.

'Right,' he said. 'We need to get her a present. Hattie, what do you think Mum would like? More than anything?'

'What's the budget?'

'There is no limit,' said Simon. 'Your mum is priceless. Doesn't she need a new handbag? The strap on hers keeps snapping.' Simon was proud of himself for coming up with such a practical suggestion.

'She's always going on about those coffee machines,' added Luke. 'When she comes to pick me up from Hal's. They've got one and she always raves about it.'

'Good idea.'

'And I think you should choose her some perfume,' added Hattie. 'I'm pretty sure she ran out.'

'OK,' said Simon, mentally adding up the tally so far, though he didn't care what it came to. He'd mortgage the house up to the hilt to get her back and make her happy. 'Let's get started. Hat, you choose the bag because I haven't a clue. Luke, go and check out the coffee machines. I'll do perfume.'

He looked at Hattie, who was looking pale and uncertain. Which was unusual for her, because she was one of the most certain people he knew. She seemed to be finding it hard to breathe. All around them people carried on with their shopping, immersed in their own last-minute purchases, unaware of their family drama.

'Hat?'

'Sorry. I just can't stop thinking about Mum.'

'It's going to be OK,' said Simon. 'She's having a bit of a wobble, that's all. She'll be back. Mum loves Christmas.'

Hattie nodded, trying to seem convinced.

'Hey. What about a foot spa?' suggested Luke.

Hattie rolled her eyes. 'That is *so* last century.'

Luke looked wounded. 'I think she'd love one. She's always complaining her feet hurt.'

'That's a brilliant idea, Luke,' said Simon. He didn't want the twins squabbling. They usually got on well, but he could see they were both upset and trying not to show it, which made them querulous. 'Let's all meet back here in fifteen minutes and take a view.'

Hattie wandered into the handbag section. What would Mum like best? Hobo? Cross body? Tote? Suede? Patent? Something neutral or a hot pop of colour? She reached out and picked up a tan bucket bag with red stitching, feeling it for quality and looking inside for useful pockets.

She still felt slightly sick from their encounter with Shirley Booth. She almost felt as if the woman had been talking directly to her. She had definitely looked her in the eye when she gave that spiel about shoplifting habits. Hattie felt paranoid and uncomfortable. Her heart had missed several beats when Shirley had talked about watching people on the CCTV. Her mouth was still dry.

Even drier than it had been the first time she'd stolen something.

She'd done it to impress Kiki. Hattie felt slightly hypnotised by her. Kiki had no veneer. She didn't sugar-coat any of her opinions. She wasn't snaky, like the other girls at school. She didn't have that syrupy icing. She was to the point. You were never in any doubt what Kiki really thought. And that's what drew Hattie to her. Her brutal honesty and her defiance and her shameless lust for adventure. She wanted to be like that too. To not care what anyone thought, and to do whatever you wanted without fear of reprisals. To be daring. Not care about the rules.

She was flattered that Kiki liked her. She was desperate to remain her friend because Kiki was a doorway into a glittering, glamorous world that fascinated Hattie. Her house was like a Hollywood mansion, her parents were supercool and there were always parties and people and music. It was like being in one of the videos Kiki's dad directed.

Kiki was very blasé about it all.

'They're all very shallow,' she said, dismissive. 'They've got no conversation.'

Hattie wasn't sure she had either. But she was swept along in Kiki's slipstream; her anarchic daring. A few weeks' ago, Kiki had insisted they try hitch-hiking.

'My mum used to do it all the time. She went all the way to Switzerland when she was our age.'

'That was in the olden days. It was way safer.'

'No, it wasn't. They had loads more weirdos back then. Mum said everyone was always in love with their teachers and having affairs left, right and centre. Come on. We'll go to Stratford.'

Hattie stood next to Kiki on the main road, hoping that no one she knew would see her, praying that no one her parents knew would see her and report back (that was one of the problems with white and blue hair; you didn't blend in much), and terrified of who would stop to pick them up. They stood there with their thumbs out, and she felt as if she was in a movie, chancing her luck on the interstate highway.

Boringly, it was a middle-aged gardener with an ancient pick-up who stopped. He chuckled at them.

'Very old school,' he said. 'Hop in.'

They climbed into the cab and slid onto the bench seat. Inside, it smelled of rich earth and rain and sweat – not horrible sweat, but the sweat of someone who'd been working hard.

'Do your parents know you're hitchhiking?' he asked. 'I didn't think anyone did any more.'

'Don't get any ideas,' said Kiki. 'I've texted your number plate to my boyfriend.'

The gardener raised his eyebrows. 'I thought I was doing you a favour,' he said, nettled. 'I can drop you here if you want.' He slowed the van down.

'I'm sorry about my friend,' said Hattie. 'She's a bit paranoid.'

Kiki widened her eyes. 'I don't think so,' she chided Hattie, then turned to the gardener. 'Dude, it's OK. I'm just laying the boundaries. So we all know where we are.'

He pushed a tape into his cassette deck by way of reply. The Eagles blared out 'Lyin' Eyes'.

'It's like we've gone back to 1978,' exclaimed Kiki. 'Who has a tape deck in their car? Haven't you heard of Bluetooth?'

The gardener grinned. 'This is vintage. Original.'

Kiki turned the volume right up and started singing.

'You know this?' He looked surprised.

She carried on singing, smiling at him, and he smiled back and joined in, and the two of them started harmonising and Hattie felt the thrill of adventure she'd been missing all her life. Kiki was cooler than cool.

He dropped them off at the roundabout outside Stratford and Hattie and Kiki fell about laughing. Hattie secretly hoped they could just get the bus home, but she wanted to be daring, like Kiki. To push the boundaries and ignore the rules.

Then Kiki had given her an idea last time they went shopping. Indirectly.

'It's not fair us girls have to pay for all this stuff. Guys don't,' Kiki had said, indignant, standing in the chemist with a basket full of toiletries: Immac and shampoo and hairspray and eye make-up remover and five different nail polishes.

Hattie thought she had a point. Luke had a pot of gunky hair wax and some deodorant; that was the extent of his cosmetics. She had shelves full of stuff to keep her looking good. Kiki was right. Why should girls have to foot the bill?

That's when she'd had her brainwave.

Hattie put the tan bag down and picked up the next one: a silver lamé shopper, capacious, with good long handles. She sighed. Why had she tried to be something she absolutely wasn't?

Because she was an idiot. She'd just been trying to impress Kiki. Their first trip out to Inglewood's she'd got away with a flagon of Tom Ford perfume, a silk Ted Baker cardigan and a pair of sunglasses. Kiki'd had no idea what she'd been up to. She had looked on in amazement when Hattie produced them half an hour later in the café down the road.

'It's a piece of cake,' Hattie said airily. 'All the shops pretend they've got all this security but they haven't. You've just got to hold your nerve.'

'I didn't think you were that kind of person.' Kiki had looked at her oddly. At the time, Hattie had thought it was admiration. Now, looking back, perhaps there had been a hint of disapproval?

Yesterday they had gone into Birmingham. Hattie thought about her haul. She'd stuffed it away at the back of her cupboard when she got in last night. She wouldn't be able to explain any of it. A silk scarf by a designer so famous even Lizzy would recognise it. A purse. Hair dye and false eyelashes and some fake tan.

She had to admit it had given her a bit of a thrill. An adrenaline rush. She'd liked the feeling. Hattie was nervous of drugs, which some of the girls at school took; she didn't indulge, mostly because of her competitive ice skating. It was the perfect inbuilt excuse. She told people they had random drug testing at the skating club. They didn't, but at least no one pushed her into it. Sometimes she wondered what she was missing out on, but not enough to experiment.

Kiki hadn't joined in with the shoplifting, even when Hattie told her how easy it was.

'My mum would kill me if I got caught,' Kiki said.

'You won't get caught,' Hattie assured her. Looking back, she realised that Kiki didn't want to do it not because she was scared of being caught, but because she thought it was wrong.

Now, standing in the middle of the handbags in the very shop where she'd committed her first crime, Hattie felt very afraid. What had she been thinking, taking risks like that just to impress Kiki? She thought perhaps she hadn't impressed her that much, after all. And if she got caught shoplifting, she'd jeopardise her place at uni and she'd have a criminal record. She could lose everything.

She felt hot and cold all at once. And she wanted Lizzy. Kind, comforting, unjudgy Mum. She could tell her anything and she never flinched or shouted. She talked things through calmly and gave brilliant advice.

OK, so Lizzy wasn't tall and skinny and cool like Kiki's mum Meg, with her leather leggings and her curated ear. She didn't have access behind the velvet ropes in all the clubs in Birmingham or a white SUV with tinted windows. But she was always there with a smile or a mug of hot chocolate, happy to sit and watch endless episodes of *How I Met Your Mother* on Netflix.

Lizzy was like a comfort blanket. When you grew up, you didn't have it with you all the time, but it was still there, in case you needed its softness and warmth. But they'd been careless with their comfort blanket. Done the equivalent of dropping it out of the pushchair to land in a muddy puddle.

Shame at the things she had done and what they had *all* done, as a family, seeped through Hattie. It made her feel nauseous and shaky. The lights in the shop felt searingly hot and the noise was deafening and the smells – the leather from the handbags, the scent from the perfume hall – became so cloying they seemed to choke her.

'I don't know what machine to choose. There's too many. I need help.' She was dimly aware of Luke in front of her.

'Hat?' He looked worried. He put his arm round her. 'Hat? Talk to me?'

'I feel funny,' she said and flumped against him.

'It's OK,' he said in her ear, his voice gruff. 'I've got you.'

And she felt her knees go from under her, but he didn't let go, her twin brother. He didn't let her go.

22

On their way to Micklestone Candlelight Market, Lizzy and Harley stopped at the Ship Aground to use their wi-fi to Skype Caroline.

'She'll be totally fine with it. I promise you,' said Lizzy. 'God, this place hasn't changed since 1987. Except it doesn't stink of stale fags.'

The pub was exactly as she remembered it. The plate-glass front overlooking the sea, with the breath-taking views. The long bar along the back, with every bottle in the world you could want to drink from. The pool table in one corner and the posh banquettes on one side and the rickety tables on the other. Even the food looked the same: burger and chips, fish and chips, omelette and chips... It hadn't changed because it didn't need to. It was by the sea. Why would it need driftwood furniture and tasteful grey paint and a chalkboard menu? That all cost money, and what the Ship Aground already had was priceless.

Harley called up Caroline on Skype, handed Lizzy the phone then headed off to the bar to grab them a couple of take-away coffees for the car.

Caroline's face appeared on the screen, smiling.

'Hey, Harley.' Then she frowned, peering. 'Lizzy?'

Lizzy beamed into the screen.

'Caroline! Merry Christmas. I'm sorry about Richard's knee. How is he?'

'Well, you know. Moaning and groaning and drinking on top of his painkillers, which he shouldn't be. But . . . why are you on Harley's phone? Or have I cocked something up?'

'Well,' said Lizzy. 'I'll cut a long story short. Basically I got fed up and did a runner. You said I could use the hut so . . . here I am. But I just wanted to double-check it was still OK.'

'Of course. You can stay there as long as you like. And Harley will make sure you've got whatever you want – you've obviously found him. He's your go-to guy.'

Lizzy cleared her throat. This was the tricky bit.

'That's another thing. He's had a bit of a falling-out with his mum's boyfriend. Poor kid. He's really cut up. So do you mind if he stays too?'

'Wow.' Caroline blinked as she tried to take everything in. 'Well, I'm totally happy for both of you to stay there as long as you like. But are you OK, Lizzy? You and Simon?'

Lizzy made a face. 'Basically, I suppose. I just feel a bit used and abused. They're not always very thoughtful, my family. And I've had enough of it. I need some time out. Being here kind of gets you back to basics, and what you really want. Though I still don't know the answer to that . . .' She laughed and gave a little shrug.

'Oh God, who does?' said Caroline. 'I want to run away sometimes, too. I think it's a difficult age, our age. Like . . . if you don't get it right now, you never will.'

'Yes,' said Lizzy. Having verbalised her feelings to

Caroline, she felt even more resolute about what she had done. 'I knew you'd understand.'

'Are you in the Ship Aground?' asked Caroline, leaning forward excitedly.

'I am,' said Lizzy. 'And it hasn't changed a bit.'

'I know. It feels like only yesterday we were in there together. Young, free and single.'

'Over-made-up and drunk,' added Lizzy.

'We were gorgeous. I just wish I'd appreciated it at the time. I thought I was fat!'

'Tell me about it.'

'Well, listen. Come and stay out here when the silly season is over. Get some sun poolside and I'll make you cocktails and we can play Duran Duran at full blast and let our hair down.'

'You're on,' said Lizzy. 'Merry Christmas, Caroline.'

'Merry Christmas, darling Lizzy.'

She pressed end and stood up. 'It's all good,' she said to Harley, who handed her a cardboard cup of coffee. 'So let's go. I want a hot pork roll with apple sauce and maybe a doughnut.'

He looked horrified. 'After that breakfast?'

'It's Christmas! You have to eat your own bodyweight in lard. It's the law,' grinned Lizzy.

The drive along the coast to Micklestone was spectacular. The tortuous road curved across the moors, dense with dry bracken and gorse, the bare brown earth exposed in between. Shaggy brown ponies stood with their heads lowered against the biting winds, sturdy and untroubled by the elements. They were built to withstand an Exmoor winter.

'Brrr,' shivered Lizzy. 'Poor things.'

From time to time they would turn a corner and there would be the sea, dark green and treacherous, miles below them under the black rocks. It was both thrilling and terrifying to watch the waves.

Harley was quiet on the journey.

'I'm worried,' he said, 'that Mum will persuade me to go back.'

'How much longer have you got?' asked Lizzy. 'You can leave home soon. Are you going to uni?'

'I haven't applied,' said Harley. 'Anyway, it's not me I'm worried about. In the long run. I wouldn't be happy leaving her with him. Or River.'

Lizzy glanced at him.

'It's just a feeling,' he said.

Lizzy slowed down as the traffic started building up. She felt disquiet at Harley's situation. She didn't think he was exaggerating, and he didn't strike her as the kind of moody and antagonistic teenager who might provoke an older man's exasperation. Tony sounded unpleasant at best. She mustn't get involved, she told herself, she had her own problems. Though she didn't mind being a sounding board or encouraging him to talk to his mum.

They edged their way into the town amidst all the other cars queueing.

'We'll never get a parking place,' fretted Lizzy.

'There. There, there, there.' Harley pointed at a Mini edging out of a space. Lizzy whizzed up and waited, then reversed neatly in.

The two of them got out of the car and walked along the narrow pavements towards the town. Micklestone was a medieval village on the edge of a steep cliff, locked in another age, with ancient stone buildings, humpbacked bridges and a marketplace overlooked by a rambling castle. Every Christmas it took advantage of its historic perfection and held a week-long market, the cobbled main street given over to vendors and traders and everywhere lit by glass lanterns filled with candles.

'Oh,' said Lizzy, as the magical scene unfolded in front of them. 'Oh, isn't it pretty?'

Harley was scanning the stalls for his mother. There were dozens of them, and the visitors milled amongst them, buying up everything on offer. The air was heavy with the scent of mulled wine and hot chocolate laced with rum.

'There she is,' said Harley suddenly. 'There's my mum. That stall there, on the right. Come on.'

23

'Thank you, sir. And a very merry Christmas to you too!' Leanne handed over the wreath, carefully wrapped in tissue and packed into a cardboard box.

She hadn't been sure about renting a stall at Mickle-stone – even just a small trestle table cost a fortune. And who left buying a wreath until the day before Christmas Eve? A lot of people, it turned out. She had sold six already, which at thirty pounds each had covered her fee. She was now heading into profit, which lifted her spirits no end.

She had various themes for her wreaths: a Highland theme, with lots of tartan; a Scandi theme, with carved wooden hearts; and her favourite, the seaside theme, made with sea-green ribbon and decorated with shells and starfish. They were works of art, and she felt proud when customers ooh-ed and aah-ed over them. She was amazed how much they'd been admired. People liked to be traditional at Christmas but they also liked something a bit different, a little twist. She was surprised how many men had bought them. They shopped in a very different way from women, and were more impulsive, more likely to buy something that caught their eye and pleased them.

She was thrilled with how successful her new enterprise

had been. She'd hit upon the idea in the hopes of making some extra cash for Christmas. She had bought greenery from the wholesaler, boxes and boxes of it. And ribbon and accessories. For the past three weeks she had spent hours making wreaths and selling them at various markets around the West Country. She'd sold out every time.

She had made sure to be careful to hide her money. She did a rapid mental calculation of how much she had made and was pleased with the outcome. She didn't tell Tony, though. She'd lied to him about how many wreaths she had made, and how much profit. She squirrelled the cash away in her handbag – there was a zip with a secret pocket at the very bottom. She didn't call it her running away fund, because if she called it that, it meant admitting to herself that she had something to run away from.

Leanne was starting to realise that perhaps she had made a horrible mistake.

She had thought herself the luckiest woman in the world when she'd moved in with Tony. A three-storey house with a sea view? She only had to walk down to the bottom of the hill and turn right to see the whole of the harbour in Tawcombe.

Moving in with someone was a big commitment and maybe she had been a little hasty after only two months of dating. But it was wonderful to get out of the rented accommodation, to have central heating and her own front door and not to have a row about the bins every week. Most of all, it was nice for River to have a garden to play in. A four-year-old shouldn't be cooped up in a top-floor flat.

And there weren't many men who'd take on a single mum with a toddler and a teenager.

She had been giddy with it all when Tony had first asked her out. Working two jobs was hard, but when Harley had become old enough to look after River in the evenings, she'd bolstered her book-keeping income by doing a couple of shifts at the Spinnaker down on the harbour. It was the locals' pub rather than the tourists', which was why she liked it. She'd started to feel part of the town. Tony was a regular, and she was charmed because he actually bothered to talk to her rather than just look.

In honour of moving to the seaside she had totally embraced the surfer girl look: tiny frayed shorts and singlets with sneakers, kimonos and crocheted tops, floaty flimsy dresses with suede ankle boots. She hoped it wasn't tarty and that she wasn't too old – you had to start being careful at thirty-six – but she worked hard at keeping herself toned.

Her new image was very different from the groomed and polished veneer she'd had for so many years when she'd lived in the city: high heels and styled hair and painted nails. Gone was the sleek black bob and in its place was shoulder-length tousled beach hair, streaked blonde from the sun (well, not the sun, technically, but that was what you were supposed to think). She'd even had a tattoo on her shoulder – a tiny gecko.

If anyone from the old days ever wandered into the Spinnaker – and they might, because she often caught a Midlands accent on the harbour front; Tawcombe was a popular holiday destination – they probably wouldn't recognise her. She'd even changed her name by adding her middle name to it. Lee Anne. Leanne. That had helped her feel like someone new but it still belonged to her. She'd had enough taken away from her without her identity being erased.

Moving away after what had happened had been the right thing to do. She didn't miss Birmingham one bit. It had been a military campaign to get herself out of the city, but she couldn't bear the gossip, couldn't carry on knowing Richie was breathing the same air as her when he'd betrayed her, so she had run as far as she could. And no one wanted the wife of someone who'd been done for fraud to do their books. Somehow her clients had dropped away one by one. In Tawcombe, no one knew. She'd picked up new business quite quickly – she was good with figures.

She'd stayed away from men for the first few months. She was wary, and besides, Harley and River had been through enough without her bringing someone new into their lives. But when Tony had shown interest, she had been drawn to him. Maybe it was because he was older than her – about ten years – although he was still pretty fit. He had money too – not that she was interested in men for the size of their bank balance; no one knew better than she did that it could vanish overnight. But she missed dressing up and going out for dinner. She and Richie had eaten out all the time, but since coming to Tawcombe fish and chips once a week was an indulgence.

Tony owned the arcade in the middle of town, where holidaymakers pumped their spare cash into rows of flashing machines in the hope of a big payout. He had a burger bar too, at the end of the harbour, and a car park by the beach on the road leading out of town. His family had bought them all with cash when the owners were on their uppers. Seasonal cash businesses. The trick was to have more than one: if it rained, the arcade was full; if it was sunny, the car park filled up. Tony was no fool. He was a respected pillar of the community too, captain of the yacht club, on the local council.

In retrospect, she should have thought it odd that he was single and available. And she didn't listen to the warnings given to her by a couple of girls down at the pub. She'd thought they were jealous. That they were warning her off so they could have him for themselves.

It was gradual, Tony's metamorphosis from white knight to something much darker. At first she had wallowed in the luxury of his charm offensive, his compliments and presents and seeming adoration. In bed they were explosive, experimental – great sex had a lot to answer for because it covered up the breadcrumb trail of tiny clues that, when she looked back, had always been there. The jealousy. The control. The tantrums. She'd been horrified the first time: instantly apologetic that she had arrived home half an hour later than she'd said.

Afterwards, in bed, he'd stroked her hair and murmured into her ear that he had been worried, especially when she hadn't answered his text (the signal was terrible in Tawcombe; messages often didn't get through) and she had promised to be more considerate. After all, it was awful not knowing where someone was – she told Harley off for not telling her his whereabouts all the time.

The biggest row they'd had was when she'd told him about her wreaths. He came up with so many reasons why she shouldn't be doing them, it made her head spin. But something deep inside told her she had to stick to her guns. That his objection was symptomatic of something very wrong, and that if she gave in to him, she would never be able to do what she wanted without a fight.

She had won, and she knew she had displeased him, for there was a coldness to him as Christmas approached. She felt sure this was his way of punishing her. But then he would take her by surprise and love bomb her, whisk her out for dinner, tell her she was the sexiest thing on two legs, and because she was feeling her age, conscious that forty was nearer than thirty, because she felt insecure after everything that had happened in Birmingham, she wallowed in the attention and thought everything was going to be all right.

And now, even though her hands were chapped and scratched, she was proud of what she'd done. She even dreamed of having her own lifestyle shop one day. She wasn't sure if Tawcombe was the right place for it: there weren't enough people with money over the winter months in a remote seaside town, but maybe she could make it work if she had a big enough range. She even knew what she'd called it. Anemone-by-the-Sea. Because the sea and flowers were the two things she loved best in the world. It was clear in her head: white writing on a bleached-out sign; chunks of driftwood in the window with flowers woven round them; distressed zinc planters and tubs . . .

She knew she was entitled to her dream. No one could take it away from her. For now, she kept it to herself, tucking it away somewhere and taking it out to look at every now and then.

It was a long way off, though. She didn't have the money to set up a shop, she couldn't imagine Tony being enthusiastic about the idea, and there was River. He wasn't due to start school until next September, which seemed a lifetime away. How could she run a shop when she had a small child to look after? It had been hard enough making the wreaths. She'd had to plonk him in front of the telly, which she hated doing, though she always made up for it by walking him down to the harbour afterwards or trundling him on his scooter to the park. And he'd sometimes had to come with her when she went to the markets. He'd been an angel, but again she'd had to plonk him on a chair with an iPad, and bribe him with cake and hot chocolate, and most of the markets were freezing so he'd got very cold, his little fingers blue by the end of the day. He wouldn't wear his gloves because it meant he couldn't use his iPad. Today, luckily, one of her friends had offered to take him on a trip to see the Christmas steam train. Leanne was going to repay her by babysitting for her another night. Thank goodness for bartering.

Sometimes Harley looked after River but it wasn't fair on Harley to expect him to take care of his little brother. He needed a life of his own. He never minded, though, which almost made it worse. She couldn't have wished for a kinder son. Lots of mothers complained when their boys became teenagers, but Leanne appreciated Harley more and more as he got older. He was thoughtful. And protective.

She didn't want to think about Tony and Harley. Tony was dismissive of Harley; Harley was wary of Tony. They had nothing in common. Harley had inherited Leanne's artistic side. He was dreamy and creative; he loved his music, his guitar, his art. He wasn't Tony's kind of person at all. And that made her uneasy. How could she properly love someone who wasn't drawn to her own flesh and blood?

Again, she hadn't seen it at first, because she'd been besotted. The thrill of her new relationship had masked any misgivings. She didn't pick up on Tony's sneers or the throwaway jibes. And Harley never reacted, so she convinced herself she'd misheard or got the wrong end of the stick.

She tightened the scarf round her neck and tucked it inside her down jacket, shivering. It was freezing, standing still behind the stall. She had on a woollen hat and fingerless mittens and fur-lined boots, but she still felt chilled to the bone. She couldn't leave to go and get herself a hot chocolate. How much longer before she sold out, she wondered?

'Mum!'

She turned and saw Harley in front of the stall, grinning at her, holding out a steaming cup of chocolate topped with a swirl of cream and marshmallows.

'Harley!' Her heart leapt with joy at the sight of him. 'How on earth did you get here?' There were no buses from Tawcombe to Micklestone, and he couldn't have walked.

'It's kind of a long story.' A woman appeared beside him, bundled up in a red woollen coat and matching bobble hat. 'This is Lizzy. She gave me a lift.'

'Hi.' Leanne held out her hand and Lizzy shook it.

'I need to talk to you about something, Mum.' Harley was jittery with anxiety, bouncing from foot to foot.

Leanne looked at Lizzy, alarmed. Surely there was nothing going on between her and Harley? This woman was older than she was.

'Oh God,' said Lizzy, clocking Leanne's bemusement. 'Nothing like that. Don't worry.'

'Then what?' Leanne felt anxiety nip at her stomach. 'Has something happened?'

'Why don't I look after the stall while you two chat?' suggested Lizzy.

Leanne felt wary and nervous. It must be something serious. 'OK . . .' she said, uncertain. 'But just five minutes,' she added. She wasn't happy about leaving a total stranger in charge of her wares, even if Lizzy did have a kind face and seemed very concerned for Harley.

A couple of minutes later, Leanne and Harley were threading their way through the crowds, elbowing their way through the shoppers until they reached a bench in the marketplace. Under the castle ramparts was a queue of children waiting to pet two reindeer who were standing patiently, seemingly unperturbed by the crowds and the music and the lights.

'OK,' she said. 'What's going on?'

'Mum. Calm down. It's all cool.' Harley moved out of the way of a man selling balloons and sat down on the bench. 'But I think it's best if I stay out of the way over Christmas. I don't want to ruin it for you and River.'

Leanne crossed her arms and stared down at him. 'What?'

'I can't deal with Tony any more. The guy hates me. He's just waiting for me to make the wrong move. And I can't handle it. I'm sorry.'

'You can't not be there.'

'I'm scared, Mum.'

'Oh God.' Leanne sank down onto the bench next to him and looked into his eyes. 'Scared of what?'

'Of what might happen. I don't trust him. And I don't trust myself. I'm really sorry.'

'No, *I'm* sorry. I don't know what to do.'

'You don't have to do anything. Just try and understand.' Harley was grasping about for the right words. The words that would make it all clear to Leanne without alarming her too much. 'He's out to get me. I know he is. And he's clever. He'll make it look like I started it. So I'm just going to stay out of the way.' He shoved his hands in his pockets. They were getting numb. 'I'm staying at Mrs Openshaw's beach hut. She's said it's OK. Lizzy's staying there too.'

'Well, I guess that's a nice place to be.' Leanne often brought River over to the beach at Everdene when Harley was working. 'Is it warm enough?'

'Yes. There's a wood-burner.'

'I feel terrible. That you don't feel you can stay. You're my son.' She sighed, her breath exhaled in a misty cloud that was as big as her disquiet. 'I could talk to him?'

Harley looked at her. 'I don't think he would listen. He'd say I was making it up.'

They stopped talking for a moment to watch a woman dressed in gold juggling fire sticks, a bright ring of flames circling around her.

'I can't leave him,' said Leanne. 'We've got nowhere to go. I can't just walk out ... Not with River. We wouldn't be able to find anywhere else at Christmas.'

'I'm not asking you to leave, Mum. It's OK. It's just better if I'm not there. That's the answer for now.'

She put her hands up, cupping his face. He could see her hazel eyes welling up, the tears shimmering, about to fall.

'But I love you,' she said. 'And I want you with me. We're a family.'

Not with bloody Tony there we aren't, Harley thought. Tony was determined to smash them up. He wasn't going to give him the satisfaction.

'Look, if I'm not there, you guys can have a nice quiet Christmas with no stress.'

'How can I? I'm worried about you. This is awful. I don't know how I got it so wrong.'

Harley could see how distressed she was. After everything she had been through with his dad, he didn't want to make life difficult for her again. She was wiping her eyes, her mascara starting to run. He hated seeing her cry. A couple of passers-by looked at her, concerned. Harley grabbed her gloved hands in his.

'Mum, Mum, stop it. Let's get Christmas out of the way then we can make a plan. There's no point in getting upset. The important thing is River has a good time, and he won't, not if I'm there.'

'But he won't, because he'll miss you. And what about your presents?'

'Why don't you come over to the beach tomorrow? We can go for a walk, get something to eat? River loves the beach.'

Leanne thought about it. 'I could tell Tony I'm going out shopping. Getting some last-minute stuff. I can't stay too long.'

'You can do what you like, Mum. Surely?'

'You don't understand.'

'It's not right. He doesn't *own* you.' Harley was getting upset. 'Dad always let you do whatever you wanted. He might have been a crook but he wasn't a control freak.'

'Don't bring your dad into this.' Leanne's tone was sharp. Harley knew he'd overstepped the mark. She never wanted to talk about Richie. It was as if he'd never existed. Harley found it hard, but he understood, in a way. Richie had ruined her life.

Harley wasn't going let another man stand in the way of his mum's happiness.

'I'm sorry,' he said. 'I just find it hard, you know?'

'OK. Look – we'll try and come over to the hut tomorrow. About midday,' Leanne soothed him. 'I better get back to the stall. Your friend seems nice. What's she doing down here?'

'To be honest, I'm not sure, exactly. I think she had an argument or a falling-out with her family.'

Leanne rolled her eyes, but she was half smiling. 'Bloody Christmas. It's got a lot to answer for.'

When they got back to the stall, Lizzy waved a sheaf of notes in glee. 'I sold three,' she said triumphantly. 'These are so gorgeous. Can I buy the last shell one, please? I think it would be perfect for the hut.'

'Of course!' Leanne looked round at the bustling market, the revellers, the entertainers, everyone spending as much money as they could to make sure everything was just so. It was constant, the strive for perfection.

But you couldn't cover over the cracks with presents and food and sparkling lights.

24

'When did you last eat, Hat?'

Never had Simon felt Lizzy's absence more keenly. She was good in a crisis. Particularly if it involved teenage girls keeling over in the middle of a department store. Shirley Booth had come out to see what the commotion was, and he'd seen her looking at him disapprovingly again, as if he was as useless a father as he was husband.

He slid the lasagne into the oven to heat it up. An army marches on its stomach, he thought.

'Oh, I don't know. There were some nibbly things at Kiki's last night. Thai coconut skewers. Pork balls.' Hattie wrinkled her nose.

'You didn't have any breakfast.'

'None of us did,' Luke pointed out. 'You just threw a loaf of bread at us.'

They were all perfectly capable of making their own breakfast, of course, but somehow when Lizzy was there she made breakfast something you wanted to indulge in rather than something to be avoided. There was always a big pot of tea on the go, in the Emma Bridgewater pot they'd got her. And the smell of toast. And bacon if you fancied it. And a bowl of chopped fruit. She didn't force it down you but she made it easy to indulge.

Simon realised that he should have fuelled everyone before they charged off. Then maybe his daughter wouldn't have collapsed in the middle of Inglewood's for everyone to see. She looked a bit better now she'd had a couple of pieces of toast and honey, the colour seeping back into her cheeks.

'We still haven't got Mum anything,' she wailed.

'It's OK. I have got her something,' said Simon, thinking that at least the slow cooker would do if she did get back. 'And we can go shopping in the sales. She'd be much happier with that anyway. We'll get twice as much for the money.'

'That's not really the point, though.' Luke looked pained. 'We need to spoil her.'

Hattie thought about the perfume and the purse hiding upstairs in her bottom drawer but decided not to say anything.

Just then the doorbell drilled through the house, making them jump.

'Do you think that's her? Maybe she forgot her key!'

The three of them headed out of the kitchen and through the living room. Simon flung open the front door.

There stood the man from Ocado, surrounded by boxes.

'Your delivery?' he said. 'This is the golden slot. Your missis must have been on it like a car bonnet to get this one.'

The three of them lugged everything back into the kitchen. Turkey, chipolatas, two stalks of sprouts, cartons of cream, a Christmas pudding. A net of satsumas, a bag of potatoes, smoked salmon, tubs of bread sauce and brandy butter. Danish pastries for breakfast, five different cheeses, chutney. Sausage rolls.

It took them fifteen minutes to put it all away. The fridge was bulging, the shelves groaning.

'I can't face any of it,' said Luke. 'We can't have Christmas lunch without Mum.'

Simon looked at the turkey. Maybe he should put it in the freezer? But then if Lizzy did turn up, they'd be turkey-less. It would take ages to defrost.

He picked up Lizzy's phone which was still on the side, hoping for a clue, even though he knew he was clutching at straws. He saw there was a new voicemail message from his mother.

'There's a message from your gran on here.'

Luke and Hattie looked at him.

He played it back.

His mother's voice came down the line.

'Lizzy? It's Cynthia. I think there might have been a bit of a mix-up. Amanda seems to think I'm coming to you for Christmas Day. But as soon as Amanda told me she was off skiing I made other arrangements. I do hope that hasn't inconvenienced you. Let's make plans to swap presents after Christmas.'

Simon felt his skin crawl with panic; maggots of anxiety creeping up his arms and round his neck. This was his fault. If only he'd remembered to tell Lizzy when Amanda said she was off skiing, none of this would have happened. Now his own mother had taken umbrage. He knew perfectly well she didn't have other plans. He'd meant to phone her earlier, to make sure she was all right and arrange what time to pick her up the next morning. But in all the fuss she'd been forgotten.

'I better go over,' he told Luke and Hattie. He wouldn't just phone because he knew his mother well enough to know that she would tell him she was fine. He needed to see her in person.

'What's up with Gran?' asked Hattie.

'Another block in the Jenga game of life,' said Simon. It was all going to come crashing down if he wasn't careful. Terrible husband, terrible father, terrible son. He was useless.

'But what about Mum?' asked Luke.

'If we don't know where she is, there's nothing we can do. Just make sure someone is here in case she comes back,' said Simon, grabbing his car keys. 'I'll be as quick as I can.'

As he left the house, Luke's mate Hal was lumbering up the path, barely visible beneath the Michelin-man rolls of his green puffa jacket.

'Hey, Mr Kingham.'

Hal pushed back his hood to reveal an enormous set of earphones which he'd pulled down round his neck.

Simon thought about saying this wasn't the best time to visit, but decided there was no point. Hal was a good kid, and the twins might need him.

'Catch you later, Hal,' he said, holding open the front door for him, then running for the car.

'Run away?' said Hal in amazement, sitting in between the twins at the kitchen table. 'My mum freaks out every year and threatens to leave. But I don't think she ever would. What did you *do*?'

'It's what we didn't do,' said Luke. 'We were all supposed to be here last night. To decorate the tree.'

'Oh man,' said Hal. 'That's harsh. No wonder.' He frowned at Luke. 'You were only round at my place. It's not like we were doing anything important.'

'Yeah, we were,' protested Luke.

'Not more important than your mum.'

'You're supposed to be making us feel better, not worse.' Luke crossed his arms and sank down into himself.

'But your mum's a total legend,' said Hal.

'Really?' Hattie and Luke looked at him, surprised.

'She's awesome. She's always smiling. She's never on your case. She's chilled and she's funny and she's kind. You want her to give you a hug. Not in a weird way,' he added hastily. 'She just makes you feel . . . safe. My mum doesn't make me feel safe. I never know if she's going to be in or not. Or whether she'll be too knackered to cook. She never remembers anything. Parents' evening. Permission slips. Dad's better than she is at that stuff.'

'How are we going to find her?' asked Hattie. 'She didn't even take her phone with her.'

The two of them looked at Hal, two little bewildered owls. He spread out his hands.

'It's obvious. Put a shout-out on Facebook,' said Hal. 'That's what Facebook's for, right?'

'What do we say, though?' asked Luke. 'And what will people think?'

'Who cares? It's got to be worth a try.'

Luke and Hattie looked at each other.

'What do you reckon?' said Luke.

'I don't think Dad would like it.'

'He won't know. He's not on Facebook.'

'He'll kill us if he finds out.'

'It doesn't matter, if it gets Mum back.'

The twins turned back to Hal, still unsure.

'What have you got to lose?' said Hal.

'Let's do it,' said Hattie. She picked up her phone and started to scroll through her photos.

'I can't believe it,' said Luke, woebegone. 'I see those missing posts and I always wonder what kind of family the people come from, why they've run away.'

'Stop bellyaching,' said Hal. 'Let's get on with the job.' He'd always been practical and direct.

Hattie found a picture of Lizzy in the garden, smiling at the camera in jeans and a sweatshirt, a trowel in one hand, her curls tied up. Then another of her dressed up ready to go out, her hair down and make-up on.

'Oh, look at her,' she said.

Meanwhile, Luke composed a post.

LOST!
**Lizzy Kingham: has anyone seen our mum?
She's gone off for a few days but we don't know
where she is. And we want her back for Christmas.
Please share.
We love you, Mum!
Hattie and Luke xxxx**

'Does that sound OK?' he asked. 'Not too dark and mysterious? Like we've just . . . mislaid her? Rather than driven her away?'

Hal looked at it, thoughtful. Then he nodded. 'What else can you say? Anyway, everyone loves helping find someone on Facebook. No one will judge.'

'Put my phone number on it,' said Hattie. 'They can call me direct.'

Luke added Hattie's number then hovered over the send button. 'Shall I do it?'

'Go on,' said Hattie. 'At least we're doing something. I can't just sit here and wait. And I don't want to do anything Christmassy.'

Luke pressed send. The post went up and they looked at it in silence.

A little tear trickled down Luke's cheek.

Hattie looked up at her brother. 'Hey, Lukey. It's OK.'

'I hope she's all right,' sniffed Luke, then buried his head in his arms on the kitchen table. 'I was supposed to bring the decorations down for her yesterday and I didn't.'

'Bro, that's totally normal,' said Hal, patting his mate awkwardly on the back. 'I forget to do stuff my mum asks me all the time. Your mum's just having a moment. She hasn't gone off to Montego Bay to be a sex tourist, like my aunt. She came back with a twenty-five-year-old.'

Hattie looked back down at the post on her phone. 'It's had sixteen shares already.'

'It's gonna go viral.'

'Oh God,' said Luke. 'If only I'd helped her. I left all my dirty plates in my room, too.'

'Standard,' said Hal. 'You've seen my room.'

'True,' said Luke, but he didn't feel consoled. He remembered thinking he was late, that it didn't matter, that he'd sort it all when he got back. He was an inconsiderate pig and that was one of the reasons she'd gone.

Hattie's phone went. It was Kiki. Yesterday, she'd have answered it in a flash. Today, she let it ring six times before finally answering.

'Hello?' she said, cautious.

'What's happened to your mum?' Kiki's voice was breathless with the scandal. 'I just saw your post.'

'We don't know,' said Hattie. 'She's just disappeared.'

There was silence for a moment.

'My mum says if there's anything she can do to help, just ask. She thought your mum was amazing. She said she was the nicest person she'd met for a long time.'

Hattie swallowed down the lump in her throat.

'Thanks, Kiki,' said Hattie, and hung up.

She turned away, tears in her eyes. Kiki phoning had brought everything into sharp focus. She had thought Kiki had everything yesterday, gliding around Birmingham in her mum's SUV with the music pumping, sipping champagne in Selfridges.

Now she was starting to realise that it was they who had everything, her and Luke, and it looked as if they were going to lose it.

25

'Smoked almonds!' said Lizzy. 'We need two tins of these. At least.'

Lizzy grabbed the nuts off the shelf decisively and threw them into the trolley. She and Harley were in Lidl, doing a big shop before they went back to the hut. It was surprisingly quiet so they were prowling the aisles for provisions.

Harley looked at the pile of food in the trolley.

'This is definitely the weirdest Christmas I've ever had.'

'It's perfect,' said Lizzy. 'I'm going to go minimum effort on the cooking front. Bollocks to bread sauce, cranberry sauce, brandy butter and all the rest of it.'

She gave a little fist pump.

'I don't mind helping,' said Harley. 'But you'll have to tell me what to do.'

He eyed the two frozen lobsters she had already put in the trolley. Living in Tawcombe, he watched the fishermen bring in lobster pots day after day, whatever the weather, but he'd never eaten one. Let alone cooked one. At least these were dead.

'What's your favourite meal?' asked Lizzy. 'Your absolute favourite, that makes you feel happy? We can have that for Christmas lunch.'

Harley wasn't sure. Then he remembered what his dad used to cook them on a Thursday night, when his mum went to Pilates. All boys together. Comfort food.

'Sausage and mash,' he said, a little unsure whether this would be an appropriate answer.

Lizzy seemed delighted with it.

'Perfect,' she said. 'That is super easy, and I make the best mash on the planet. Half a pound of butter, basically, and loads of salt.'

She laughed and pushed the trolley towards the sausage section. Harley thought she seemed a bit manic, but he didn't really know her – maybe she was always overexcited in Lidl.

'Just plain bangers or shall we have apple ones? Or a mixture?' asked Lizzy. 'Bugger it, let's have both.' She put them in the trolley. 'I better stop. I keep flinging things in. Parma ham. Sticky toffee pudding.' She peered at him. 'Are you OK?'

'No.' He thought he was going to cry. He didn't know why. Whether it was talking to his mum or remembering his dad's sausages. 'No, but yes. If you know what I mean.'

'Oh, I know what you mean,' said Lizzy. 'I've been *no but yes* for ages. Or is it *yes but no*?'

'Come on,' said Harley, grabbing the side of the trolley. 'Let's get out of here before you buy the whole shop.'

Back in the car, Lizzy took a deep breath.

'Are you all right?' said Harley, putting a hand on her arm.

'I don't know,' she said. 'This feels weird. I should be at home. Wrapping presents. Getting in a panic. Worrying about whether the turkey is big enough and if we've got enough chipolatas.'

'You haven't told me,' he said. 'Why you're down here.'

'Everything,' she said. 'Everything and nothing. I feel like I've lost myself. I feel as if everything I do is for everyone else and nothing is for me. And it wouldn't matter if I wasn't there. And now I'm not, I still feel like that. I'm still cross with them all. But I can't help wondering what they're doing.'

'Oh,' said Harley, not sure he understood.

'They all stood me up last night. My husband and my kids. Hattie and Luke. They're about your age. We were supposed to do the tree, but they were all off doing ... whatever.'

'That's pretty mean.'

'Yes. But it's not *just* that. My bloody mother-in-law is coming for Christmas at the last minute.' Lizzy tightened her grip on the steering wheel, feeling her teeth clench at the thought.

'Well, you're not supposed to like your mother-in-law – that's classic, isn't it?'

Lizzy turned and looked at him. He flinched for a moment when he saw the look in her eyes. Suddenly they were cold and hard and he felt a tiny bit afraid.

'She did something terrible,' said Lizzy. 'That I can't ever forgive. But I'm the only one who knows about it. I have to sit there and keep my mouth shut when I just want to say to my husband: *Do you know what she did, your precious mother? Do you know what she did?*

26

Simon arrived at Copperfield Close and punched in the entry code. The gates slid open. He drove in and parked in Cynthia's allocated visitor space.

He headed for the front door, pulling the keys out of his pocket, steeling himself for what he might find. It wouldn't be the first time, though she had been better of late. He never judged her. How could he? She was grieving, and lonely.

Cynthia was lying on the sofa. There was a bottle of white wine in a clear plastic ice bucket on the glass coffee table in front of her.

'Oh, Mum . . .'

She blinked up at him.

'Come on, Mum. You're coming with me.'

Cynthia managed to sit up and then slumped over, putting her face in her hands.

'I miss him,' she said, her voice muffled. 'I miss your stupid ruddy father more than I know what to do with.'

'I know, Mum,' he said. 'But he's not in the bottom of a bottle, you know. He's not going to pop out, like a genie.'

'Nobody needs me,' she said, taking her hands away

and looking at him. She'd cried away her make-up. She was limp with self-pity.

'That's where you're wrong,' said Simon. 'I need you. I really *really* need you. But you're no bloody use to me drunk.'

She leaned back into the sofa, swaying slightly. She gave a little hiccup.

'Lizzy's run away,' he told her. 'We all messed up. We forgot to come home to dress the tree last night, and she's gone off somewhere.'

'Lizzy?' Cynthia struggled to take the information in. 'But that's not like her.'

'Which is why it's so worrying.'

He knelt down next to his mother and took her hands.

'Will you come back home with me, Mum? Help me hold the fort. Be there for the twins. They're both very upset. They feel guilty.' He paused. 'They're blaming themselves but it wasn't their fault. It was mine.'

'Oh, Simon...' Cynthia's eyes were round with it all.

'So I could do with some moral support. Even if I have been a rotten husband and a lousy father and a useless son.'

'You have not!' Cynthia was staunch. 'You're a good man, Simon. You've only ever made one mistake.'

He looked at her. 'What?'

She raised her eyebrows. 'You know. Madam.'

'But I thought you and Amanda were like this.' He crossed his fingers.

'You know what they say,' said Cynthia. 'Keep your friends close, but your enemies closer.' Her face crumpled a little bit. 'She phoned me this morning from the airport. To tell me Lizzy didn't want me to come to you for Christmas.'

Simon stared at his mum.

'Mum. That is absolutely not true. Lizzy was just upset that no one had told her the plans had changed. And that was my fault. I forgot. Because I'm an idiot.' He reached over and put his arms round Cynthia. 'Lizzy's a bit . . . oversensitive at the moment. I think the whole being made redundant thing hit her harder than anyone realised. Being Lizzy, she pretends she's fine. Then when she does have a wobble . . .'

'She's at that time of life though, isn't she?'

'Is she?' Simon asked, remembering Colin's warning.

'I remember it too well,' said Cynthia. 'Don't underestimate it. It can be very dark indeed. Your father was wonderful. Even when I was in the deepest pit of despair, he made me feel like a princess. He was so patient. So kind.'

'He was kind to everyone,' said Simon.

He knew he wasn't as good a man as his father had been, and never would be. His dad had been his hero. Everyone's hero. Neville had time for each person in his life, and was the best he could be for them. A wonderful husband. A wonderful dad. A wonderful employer. A wonderful friend. No doubt he had been a wonderful son too.

Simon sighed. He tried, he really did. But things were harder now. The expectations on both men and women were much higher. And in the process of trying to get one thing right – in Simon's case, at the moment, it was his job – if you took your eye off the ball, everything else collapsed.

This was a wake-up call. His family was falling apart. The one thing they had was each other, but somehow they were all pulling in different directions. He had to glue them back together. Smooth over the disagreements, make sure they were a proper unit, supporting each other. And he had to stand up to Amanda for once. She was not going to be calling the shots any more. Lexi and Mo would always be a priority, but not his ex-wife.

And his mum. He had to look after his mum. He looked around her lounge. It stood to attention, shiny and smart and hushed, like a model pupil. He had thought Copperfield Close was the perfect place for her when they'd chosen it. Safe and secure and efficient. Now, he could see it was all wrong. There was no life. The polar opposite of Pepperpot Cottage, with its bustle and warmth.

'Come on, Mum,' he said. 'Let's get you out of here.'

She got to her feet, uncertain. He looked at her. His heart gave a little twist. He reached out his arms and put them round her. She melted into him for a moment, leaning against him. They didn't say anything, but the gesture said everything. He patted her on the back.

'Go and splash some cold water on your face. Freshen yourself up. I'll get your things.'

'There's something I need to tell you,' blurted Cynthia. 'Something terrible. I can't keep it to myself a moment longer.'

27

FOUR YEARS EARLIER

On a Wednesday, Cynthia spent the day at Leadenbury golf club. It was Neville who'd introduced her to the game some years before. She turned out to be rather better than he was and soon became a fixture at the club and then Lady Captain, albeit somewhat reluctantly, for she didn't much care for responsibility or politics. Wednesday was always a splendid buffet, and she enjoyed some cold king prawns and coronation chicken and a glass or two of wine and a chat.

One or two of the gentlemen players were attentive, but she wasn't interested. She didn't want anyone other than Neville. She'd had the perfect husband. Why on earth would she settle for anyone less now he had gone? She couldn't think of anything worse than having to cope with someone else's demands and foibles.

She might be lonely, but she wasn't desperate.

That particular afternoon, however, she was struggling to get on top of her feelings. Neville had been gone just over a year. It was his birthday and she didn't know what to do with her emotions. They had always made a big fuss of birthdays – lavish presents, funny cards, elaborate cakes, dinners out with friends. The day seemed even quieter and emptier than a usual day, and she was torturing herself. What would she have bought him, if he was still here? What kind of cake would she have made? Where would they have gone for dinner? If only she could control her thoughts.

As she sat in the club lounge after an invigorating eighteen holes, she sipped at her sauvignon blanc. She shut her eyes as the soothing blanket of alcohol wrapped itself around her. With every drop she felt safer, and her thoughts became blurry and less sharp. She accepted another glass from a fellow player, and by the time that had gone down, she felt almost relaxed. One more, she thought, and she would be as right as rain.

She was just draining her third glass, thinking she would get a taxi home if she had another, when her phone rang. It was Lizzy. She hurried outside – mobiles weren't allowed in the clubhouse.

'Oh, Cynthia,' said Lizzy. She sounded flustered. 'I'm in a fix. Could you help me out? I wouldn't usually ask.'

She never asked. She never wanted Cynthia's help. Not like Amanda, who used to ttreat Cynthia as some kind of glorified au pair, there at her beck and call. But perhaps that was why Lizzy had never turned to her when the twins were small – because Amanda seemed to have first dibs. Cynthia had longed to help Lizzy more than anything. But she had never wanted to push herself on her.

'Of course.' Cynthia was delighted Lizzy had asked her. Maybe now that Mo and Lexi were off at uni she could muck in more. Though the twins were growing up fast – they didn't really need looking after these days. It made her feel sad, to have missed out.

'I'm stuck in a meeting,' Lizzy explained. 'I'm supposed to be picking Hattie up from school to take her to the skating rink. Would you be able to take her for me? I'll be finished by half five so I should be able to pick her up afterwards.'

'Now?' Cynthia put a hand on her chest.

'She needs picking up in half an hour. Do say if it's a problem.'

Cynthia tried to gather her thoughts. Of course she wanted to help. This was a breakthrough, Lizzy turning to her. But how much had she had to drink? She tried to calculate – it had been two hours since she'd come into the club house, so surely two of the glasses she'd had were out of her system. Which just left one, which was OK. Wasn't it?

She could hardly tell Lizzy she was too drunk.

'Of course,' she said. 'I'll leave right now.' The twins' school was about twenty minutes away.

'You're a lifesaver,' said Lizzy. 'I'm for ever in your debt.'

Cynthia settled her bill. The bartender seemed to think she'd had four glasses but she didn't have time to quibble. She drank down a glass of water then went to the cloak-room. She looked in the mirror, trying to assess how she felt. Fine. She felt completely in control. A tiny bit muzzy but that was lunchtime drinking for you.

She drove, slowly and carefully, to the school, where Hattie was waiting for her.

'Granny!' Hattie seemed delighted to see her. 'Ooh, can I have one of your Polos?'

They made it to the skating rink with no mishap. On the way, Cynthia loved listening to Hattie babble on about her skating, her next exams, the auditions for the summer extravaganza.

'I'm so proud of you, darling,' she said. 'And grandpa would have been too.'

He would have been, she thought, and felt the familiar prickle behind her eyes.

She set off for home, her head starting to throb, but happy in the knowledge that she had come to the rescue. Perhaps this could become a thing, picking Hattie up to take her skating. Maybe she could watch her practise and then take her back to Pepperpot and stay for supper. A family ritual. Every Wednesday.

Every Wednesday. She liked those words. Perhaps she would suggest it to Lizzy. Or was that being pushy? Cynthia always felt lesser in Lizzy's company. It was nothing that Lizzy did. She was sweetness and warmth itself, but that only made Cynthia feel more uptight than she actually was. She longed to be relaxed and easy-going and spontaneous.

Cynthia decided to take the cross-country route back home, just to be on the safe side. It was easier negotiating narrow lanes than traffic, and she was feeling tired. It was ten minutes to home, and she would have made it. She was sure she was fine, but it had been a little bit of a risk. It was all about metabolism and how much you'd had to eat—

Suddenly the car started juddering and shaking. She wrestled with the wheel in alarm, realising that she had failed to notice the sharp left-hand bend. Instead, she had gone sailing straight on through a gateway and into a field. The car lurched and dropped down a steep bank, plunging its bonnet into the soft earth.

Her heart was pounding. She put the car into reverse, but it was stuck. There was no way she was going to be able to get it out.

Her phone was ringing. It was Lizzy. Cynthia knew it was her only chance of getting out of this without getting into trouble.

'Everything OK?' chirped Lizzy. 'I'm so grateful. I'm just leaving work now so I'll be fine to pick her up.'

Cynthia tried to gather her thoughts. How was she going to explain her predicament without incriminating herself?

'Oh, Lizzy,' she said. 'I'm such an idiot. I missed the bend on the back road and I've got the car stuck in a ditch. Don't tell Simon. He'll be so cross with me.'

'Oh, gosh,' said Lizzy.

'I don't know what to do. I've smashed the bonnet up.' Cynthia was in tears by now.

'You need to call someone to get you out.'

'I feel such an idiot. Would you come and help?'

There was a moment's hesitation. If Lizzy couldn't help, Cynthia wasn't sure what she would do. Stay in the car until she was stone-cold sober? How long would that take?

'Of course,' Lizzy said. 'I'll get one of the other mums to take Hattie home. Where are you exactly?'

Cynthia felt sweet relief as she described where she'd left the road.

'Oh, there,' said Lizzy. 'It's a black spot. I don't know why they don't put up warning signs.'

It made Cynthia feel so much better, knowing it was a mistake anyone could have made.

*

The car was far enough off the road not to be spotted by a passer-by. While she waited for Lizzy, Cynthia did endless calculations in her head. She must be all right by now. What an idiot. Though it was easily done. She kept telling herself she wasn't the first person to end up missing that corner.

She saw Lizzy's car bumping up the field behind her. She parked on the harder ground, then came running over to Cynthia's car. She opened the driver's door.

'Oh goodness. How are we going to get you out?'

'Thank you for coming, Lizzy.' Cynthia smiled up at her. 'I didn't know what to do.'

The smile froze on Lizzy's face. She was looking down at Cynthia in horror.

'You're drunk,' she said.

'What? Don't be silly.'

'You absolutely stink of booze. How much have you had to drink?'

Cynthia was flustered. She couldn't deny it completely.

'I had a lunchtime glass of wine at the golf club,' she said.

'How much?' repeated Lizzy.

Cynthia stared up at her, mute.

'I can phone the club. I'll ask the barman. How much?' Lizzy's voice was icy.

'I don't know.'

'More than two?'

Cynthia shut her eyes and nodded.

'Are you telling me that you picked up Hattie and drove her while you were *drunk*?'

'I was fine. It was over a long period. I felt perfectly

clear-headed.' Even as she spoke, she could hear her words running into each other, muddy.

'Well, we'll see, shall we? We'll get the police.' Lizzy was brisk. 'They'll get your car moved. And if you're not over the limit, you've got nothing to worry about.'

'Please.' Cynthia thought she was drowning in a sea of sauvignon blanc and shame. 'Please don't call the police. Please don't call Simon.'

Lizzy surveyed her mother-in-law with distaste.

'I will never forgive you for this.'

'I just wanted to help,' said Cynthia. 'I just wanted to help you.'

'You could have killed someone. You could have killed *Hattie*.'

'I'm sorry. I'm so sorry.' Cynthia was ashamed to find she was crying. Snivelling, actually. Uncontrollable, heaving sobs.

'Oh for God's sake,' said Lizzy. Her cold distaste was more painful than any anger. 'Go and sit in my car. I'll get on to the garage in Astley. They've got a tow truck.'

Cynthia scrambled out of the car and stumbled over the rough ground to Lizzy's car. She sat curled up in self-loathing while Lizzy phoned the garage and oversaw the removal of Neville's beloved Jaguar. The front was well and truly bashed in, she saw, as the car was lifted onto the low-loader.

'Shame,' she heard one of the garage men say. 'That's a classic, that is. But I reckon it's a write-off.'

Neville would be so ashamed of her. He had zero tolerance for drink-driving. How on earth had she thought she could get away with it?

Once the car had been driven off, Lizzy got into the driver's seat beside Cynthia.

'Please,' said Cynthia. 'Don't tell Simon.'

She hated the sound of her pleading voice.

Lizzy's face was expressionless. She couldn't even look at Cynthia as she put the car into reverse and drove out of the field.

'We won't speak of this again,' she said as she turned onto the road. 'But I will never forgive you for putting Hattie's life at risk. Never.'

28

'Look, Nat!'

It was funny how, wherever you were in the world and however you felt, that first glimpse of the sea always lifted your heart. Why it should was a mystery, for it was a simple joining of land and water, but there was something special about it, something calming and reassuring yet also exciting.

'What do you think, buddy?'

Nat nodded his approval. 'Is that the thea?' he lisped.

'It is,' said Jack. 'And it goes all the way to the other side of the world.'

The car wound its way down the hill, the sunlight bouncing off the surface, dazzling him. Everdene was somewhere totally new to him and Nat, realised Jack. Somewhere with no ghosts, where they could make memories. Just the two of them.

Jack reached for his sunglasses and tried very hard to banish his unwanted thoughts. It was bloody impossible. All he could think about was Fran's excitement, the way she would have woken – she'd have been asleep for most of the journey; she always slept in the car – with her eyes shining.

'*I must go down to the sea again*,' she would have said,

'*To the lonely sea and the sky.*' She had a poem for every occasion. In the back would be her picnic hamper, tartan rugs, a vintage thermos filled with consommé and a Coronation tin full of shortbread. He'd put them all away, her beloved things, in a metal trunk that had belonged to her grandfather, until the day he felt ready to look at them again. Or until Nat wanted to see them. Whichever came first.

He sighed. There it was in front of him. The lonely sea and the sky, stretching out to the horizon, beckoning him with its beguiling blueness. How could somewhere you'd never been remind you of someone? Fran would have made this simple trip to the seaside an adventure. Of course, that's what he wanted to do, too. For Nat. But Jack knew he didn't have Fran's sparkle. Her ability to turn the mere making of a sandwich into an event.

'Egg sandwiches, for the seaside,' she would say, decisive. 'On very soft malted bread, with the best mayonnaise and finely shredded spring onion.'

And there they would be, plump and soft and bulging, individually wrapped in brown paper and tied with string, with each of their names written on them in black spidery writing.

She's gone, Jack reminded himself. As if he needed reminding. This is your holiday. Yours and Nat's. You have to do it without her.

He was doing it again. He was remembering her as perfect when she wasn't. He was forgetting the mess she left behind her in the quest to make the perfect cake, the perfect birthday card, the perfect hanging basket – a permanent trail of crumbs and glitter and mud that he had to clear up. He was forgetting how forgetful she was, how she would fail to turn up to important appointments or fill out important forms. Every year he had to arrange her MOT for her Fiat 500 because she never remembered. He was forgetting how impossible it was to get her up on a Sunday morning to do something. She would slumber for hours under the rose-patterned duvet while he waited, impatient and anxious, reluctant to go and do whatever it was he wanted to do without her, because she made everything more exciting and more interesting.

Jack sighed and looked at the print-out of the instructions on the seat next to him. It was a client who was lending him the beach hut. He'd refused to take any money for it, just told Jack to enjoy it.

Jack didn't know what he would do without his clients. They never ceased to warm his heart, with their kindness and thoughtfulness and generosity. When he had told Clemmie where he and Nat were going, and sworn her to secrecy, she had pointed out that it was karma, that people were kind to him because he always went the extra mile.

'What goes around, comes around, Jack,' she said, and when he rolled his eyes she rolled hers in exasperation at his cynicism.

'Don't let your grief define you,' she begged him. 'Don't become bitter. Try and enjoy yourself. Have some fun.'

And that's what he was going to try and do. He had taken him and Nat out of the equation, away from the norm, and he was going to spend this Christmas as if it was his first, with no nostalgia, none of the rituals and traditions he and Fran had made for themselves or inherited from their families. No gingerbread men. No jigsaws. No fucking fairy lights. A new kind of Christmas.

He swung into the car park. The journey had taken longer than he thought because they'd had to stop twice at a service station. But it was still light. They would unload the car and get settled in, then have a picnic on the beach.

'I need a wee,' said Nat, and Jack thought, of course you do, you poor little lad. It had been over an hour since they'd last stopped on the motorway. He got Clouseau out of the boot and they sneaked round the back of the public loos, which were determinedly closed for the duration of winter, and Jack found a tree and they had a wee, boys together (even Clouseau), laughing conspiratorially (except Clouseau), and Jack thought if Fran was here he would whisper *Don't tell your mother* . . .

When he got back to the car, he wondered how he was going to manage everything, with Nat and Clouseau, and decided he'd have to do it in stages. He pulled out their suitcase, slung two cool bags over his shoulder, then slammed the boot shut.

'Number twenty-four,' he said. 'Beach hut number twenty-four. You'll have to count with me, Nat.'

The three of them made their way out of the car park and down the slipway, past the ice-cream kiosk and chip shop and the surfboard hire and onto the golden sand.

Jack had forgotten how difficult sand was to walk on, especially when you were laden with luggage, and it took them quite a long time to make it down the row of huts. Although it was sunny, there were only a few people on the beach. He supposed most people were at home, getting ready for the big day, ushering in guests who were coming to stay for the festive season or rushing to the shops for gravy granules.

'All right, mate?' he asked Nat, who was plodding along

stolidly in his striped yellow wellies, his bright blond pageboy shining in the sunlight. His hair was getting a bit long, thought Jack, but it suited him. Another week and he'd look the part – a real surfer dude. He'd probably get away with it here, but not in Chiswick. There were so many things to keep on top of with a child. Haircuts, shoe fittings, nit checks, booster jabs . . . He was seriously thinking about creating an app for single dads.

It was hard, being thrown in at the deep end, even if it hadn't been unexpected. But he'd had better things to talk about to Fran than Nat's first dental appointment.

'Are we nearly there?' said Nat. 'Can we go fishing?'

'I think,' said Jack, drawing to a halt outside a pale blue hut, 'that this is us.'

As he felt in his pocket, a woman outside the hut next door waved her hand in greeting. She was attaching a Christmas wreath to the door, the sea breeze messing with her mass of curls.

Jack reminded himself that this was going to be the new him. The start of a new chapter. That his past was to be behind him and he was going to open his heart to new friendships and possibilities.

He raised his hand to return her greeting and pulled the key his client had posted to him out of his pocket. He felt the usual anticipation of arrival at a holiday destination. Was he going to be delighted or disappointed by what he found inside? Would it live up to his expectations? He hadn't even seen photographs, so he didn't have any great preconceptions. At the time, all he had wanted was neutral territory and the offer of a beach hut on the Devon coast was the answer to his prayers.

The door swung open and he and Nat stepped in.

The inside of the hut was painted in ice-cream colours: pale pink and cream and baby blue, with candy-striped deckchairs, bookshelves stuffed with old games and Penguin paperbacks and a table covered in a red spotted oil-cloth. The kitchen had a little dresser loaded with mismatched china. There was bunting strung from the ceiling; lamps in the shape of lighthouses; a mobile of china seagulls.

Jack blinked. It was as if Fran had walked in and decorated it. He could imagine her cries of delight if she saw it. It captured her spirit so perfectly, he thought he might be sick. Or cry. He certainly couldn't breathe.

'Dad!' said Nat, who had found a collection of buckets and spades and fishing nets. 'Look at this!'

'Cool,' Jack managed to choke. He stepped outside the hut and took in great gulps of ozone. He wasn't going to lose it. He'd made it through the whole day without crying so far, which was a record. He squeezed his eyes shut.

'I just thought I'd come and say hello,' said a voice. 'And Merry Christmas.'

He opened his eyes to see the woman from the hut next door standing in front of him. Her appearance was enough to distract him from his potential breakdown. She must be mid-forties, with a mass of squiggly curls that she probably endlessly complained about but were wild and untamed and wonderful. She was in jeans and trainers and a thick coat, wrapped up against the elements.

'Hello,' Jack smiled.

'I'm Lizzy, by the way. I'm staying next door.'

'Dad?' Nat appeared at the top of the steps, wondering where he was.

'It's OK, buddy, I'm right here.' Jack held out his hand for Nat to come down the steps, and turned back to smile at Lizzy. 'I'm Jack and this is Nat. There's just the two of us here for Christmas.'

He waited for her to look surprised or awkward, but she crouched down in front of Nat.

'And how old are you, Nat?' she asked. 'I'd say...'

She looked at him thoughtfully.

'Free,' said Nat.

'Three. Just as I thought,' said Lizzy. 'That's a grand age.'

She stood and gave a wry shrug. 'We must all be mad. It's not really the time of year to come to the British seaside. But it certainly blows the cobwebs away.'

'Yes,' said Jack. 'That's just what I need. All those Christmas deadlines.'

'Is this your hut?'

'A client lent it to me,' Jack told her, then swallowed. 'This is our second Christmas on our own.'

Lizzy nodded. She didn't probe any further. 'I'm on my own too,' she said. 'Well, there's two of us in the hut next door, but we're not *together* together. It's a long story.'

'Snap,' said Jack.

The two of them exchanged a complicit look.

Maybe, over the course of the next few days, he'd be inclined to share his story. To tell this person, with her smiley blue eyes, what had happened, without breaking down or closing up. Not now, though.

'I better go and fetch our things,' he said instead.

Lizzy nodded, then looked at Nat again. 'If you want me to keep an eye on him while you get the rest of your stuff, I'm happy to?'

'Actually . . .' said Jack, assessing her rapidly. It would take him five minutes if he was unencumbered. And Lizzy looked like a kind and responsible person. He trusted her on instinct. 'That would be really helpful. It'd take twice as long with him.'

Just then Clouseau came lolloping down the steps.

'And there's this beast as well. But I can shut him in the hut. This is Clouseau.'

'Oh my goodness, he is gorgeous.' Lizzy fell to her knees and fondled Clouseau's ears. 'Nat, why don't you and I walk Clouseau down to the sea while Daddy gets the rest of your stuff?'

Nat turned to look at her, assessing her with the uninhibited gaze of a three-year-old. He didn't find anything to protest against.

'OK,' he agreed.

'You're very kind,' said Jack.

'Don't worry. I've been there. I've got twins. I used to need eyes in the back of my head,' she laughed.

There was a momentary tussle, when Jack tried to get Nat to put a hat on to protect him from the cold wind, but Nat didn't want to. Lizzy remembered similar struggles with Luke, who hated hats and scarves and gloves and would deliberately lose them, until she'd finally given up the battle. Now he never seemed to be without a hat.

Jack clipped on Clouseau's lead and handed it to her. The little dog looked up at her, his shiny eyes bulging with trust and expectation. Lizzy held out her hand to Nat.

'Come on, then. Let's see how many steps it takes us to get to the sea. How is your counting?'

It was funny, thought Lizzy, as they clomped over the

wet sand, their footprints slurping behind them, how the nurturing instinct didn't leave you just because you'd run away from your family. Surely this moonlit flit had been about her and finding out what she wanted and needed, not taking on board another batch of dependents? Already she felt invested in Harley, and Jack and Nat had piqued her interest. A man on his own with a small boy at Christmas was an unusual thing. The need to look after them was almost primeval.

She wondered fleetingly what was going on at Pepperpot Cottage. The Ocado delivery was scheduled for this afternoon. Oh well, she thought, her heart hardening at what she'd had to go through to get that precious slot. At least they won't go hungry.

Clouseau had sat down on the sand and was looking out across the ocean, unblinking. Lizzy laughed and bent down to pat his head, and her heart melted a bit as he pushed against her hand and looked up at her in appreciation. A dog, she thought, with a sudden flash of inspiration. That's what I want.

'He's lovely, isn't he?' she said to Nat, who put his arms round Clouseau's neck. The dog shut his eyes in bliss.

She'd always longed for a dog but it had never fitted into their lifestyle, not with her working flat out at Craven Court. But maybe now was the time. If she worked part-time, or worked from home, she could have one. She felt a little flip of excitement; the first positive feeling she'd had for a while. The possibility was a revelation: perhaps she needed to come at life from a completely different angle. Work out what she wanted for *her* and then put the practicalities in place.

In the distance, she could see Jack making his way back to the huts, laden with bags.

'Come on, Nat. Your daddy's on his way back. Come on, Clouseau.' She tugged on the little dog's lead and he followed her, endlessly eager to please.

Lizzy walked back towards the huts, laughing to herself. Here she was, on a windswept beach, with a mismatched trio of fellow refugees, none of whom belonged to her, and the meaning of life had just presented itself. She felt as free as the seagulls swooping above her. No responsibility, no timetable, no guilt, no pressure, no being made to feel as if you were slightly mad, no one to raise an eyebrow if you weren't wearing make-up or had odd socks on, no having to nag or chivvy.

Why was it so liberating? So . . . exhilarating?

And then she realised: for the first time in a long while, she was able to be herself. She didn't need antidepressants, she needed space. Time and space.

'Look at Nat's cheeks,' laughed Jack as they approached the hut.

Nat's eyes were bright and his cheeks were pink and his blond hair was standing on end. He looked up at the sky.

'I love the beeeeeach!' he shouted, and Jack and Lizzy smiled at each other over his head.

'Listen,' said Lizzy said to Jack. 'I'm doing lobster mac and cheese tonight. There's going to be plenty if you want to join us. But I won't be at all offended if you say no!'

Jack hesitated for a moment.

'That's really kind,' he said. 'But I think we'll probably just get an early night. It's been a long journey.'

'Of course,' said Lizzy. 'I understand. But if you change

234

your mind, just come over. I always make far too much of everything.'

'Thank you.' Jack smiled and scooped up Nat. 'Come on, mate. Let's get the kettle on.'

The little trio disappeared inside their hut. Lizzy watched after them, wondering. He was such a big, gentle giant, Jack, and the tiny quicksilver sprite that was Nat made him seem even bigger and gentler. Who was the missing person in their life?

29

'What the hell were you thinking?' demanded Simon, talking to Cynthia in the passenger seat as he drove her back to Pepperpot. 'It's the one thing Dad drummed into me. Never get in the car if you think you're over the limit. Get a taxi, or stay the night, or call someone.'

'I know,' said Cynthia, her eyes shut.

'I mean, I got a cab last night. And stopped drinking in good time so I wouldn't be over the limit today.'

'He'd never have forgiven me. I know that.'

'And that's why you got rid of his car? Because you wrote it off?'

Cynthia nodded miserably. 'I was thinking of getting rid of it anyway. It was far too big.'

Simon shook his head. 'I don't know what to say, Mum. I'm shocked.' He sighed. 'Although at least it explains some of Lizzy's behaviour. Why she was so funny about Christmas Day.'

'It's been a strain for her,' said Cynthia. 'Trying to pretend to be nice to me, all this time. And she promised me not to tell you. I don't deserve her loyalty.'

'No,' agreed Simon. 'You don't.'

Cynthia flinched. 'You should take me back home. I can't face the twins.'

Simon didn't answer for a moment.

'It was terrible, what you did,' said Simon. 'I'm never going to think otherwise. But we've got a bigger problem right now. And I think we need to pull together. Get everything out in the open.'

'I'm sorry about Lizzy. I feel as if it's my fault.'

'Yes. Partly. But I think there's other things going on with her.'

'This age,' said Cynthia. 'It's very difficult for women. You would think the difficult bit was when the children were small; when you were run ragged trying to keep all the balls in the air. But when they're about to leave home, and you look in the mirror and you can barely recognise the woman you once were, and your body is doing strange things and you just feel like a useless lump... I can't describe to you how empty it makes you feel.'

'But she hasn't said a thing,' said Simon.

'That's the trouble. It sneaks up on you gradually. So you don't say anything to anyone, but you feel as if you're silently going mad...'

'That's terrible. Poor Lizzy.' He looked at his mum, grateful for her wisdom, and he softened a little towards her. 'I know things are tough for you too, Mum.'

'Don't try and find excuses for me. I need to pull myself together. I've known it for a long time.'

'Don't be too hard on yourself.'

'Nor you,' she said to her son. 'You're a good husband, Simon. Don't start blaming yourself for anything.'

'Oh, there's things I should have done differently. Stood up to Amanda, for a start.'

'We should all have done that. Instead of pussyfooting around her. There's only one person in Amanda's life and that's Amanda.'

Simon was surprised at his mother's harsh tone. He had always seen her as Amanda's ally; had always felt his mother had blamed him for their marriage break-up. It seemed the dynamics of his family were a lot more complicated than he realised. There were more secrets than he'd realised as well. He hoped there weren't too many more nasty surprises lurking.

Back at Pepperpot, there was still no news of Lizzy. The twins seemed happy to see their grandmother, which cheered him a little. They had no need to know of her misdemeanour, but it would be good to have her back in the heart of the family.

Simon flipped on the kettle and sat down at the kitchen table, exhausted. The worry, the emotion, the late night. He supposed he should get supper on the go, but he didn't have the energy to do it himself or even dictate to the twins.

'Why don't we get an Indian?' he said. They loved the local takeaway. It would probably be heaving tonight – people treating themselves before the holiday began in earnest the next day. It was Christmas Eve tomorrow. The house should be filled with jollity and celebration and excitement. What a mess.

'I'll get the menu,' said Hattie.

'Chicken and spinach balti for me,' said Simon, hoping that some food would give him strength.

'Dad!' Hattie turned from the noticeboard, a slip of green paper in her hand. 'Look at this.'

Simon snatched it off her. It was a prescription made

out to Lizzy, dated just the day before. 'Citalopram.' He frowned. 'What's that?'

'I don't know.'

Luke craned his neck to look, typing the word into his internet browser, waiting for the answer to come up. He frowned.

'Citalopram. It's an SSRI.' He looked up at the others. 'An antidepressant.'

'I was offered them,' said Cynthia. 'After Neville died.'

'Oh my God,' wailed Hattie. 'What if she's done something awful? What if she's taken them all?'

'Don't be stupid,' said Luke. 'She hasn't got them, has she? The prescription hasn't been filled.'

'But what if she's been on them for ages? And we didn't realise?'

'We'd know. *I'd* know.' Simon's tone was adamant. But how would he know? He felt a rush of panic. Lizzy could have had infinite bottles of antidepressants stuffed into her handbag and he would have had no idea, because she wasn't the sort of person you'd expect to be on them, and you wouldn't go looking for them.

Events were unravelling too fast for him. He felt as if he was in one of those nine o'clock dramas Lizzy loved watching: some tense domestic thriller where it turned out that the person you loved best in the world wasn't who you thought they were after all.

'Let's phone the doctor,' said Hattie.

'They won't tell us anything,' said Simon. 'Hippocratic oath. Patient confidentiality.'

He knew this much from the telly.

'But if she's in danger...' said Hattie.

'This isn't like her,' said Luke. 'It's so not Mum. How

239

can she be depressed? What's she got to be depressed about?'

He looked distressed and terribly young. A boy who needed his mother.

'Lots of people take them. To get them over blips.' Cynthia tried to be reassuring. 'Like losing your job.'

Simon felt unease claw at him. The kettle whistled to a crescendo, as if sounding an alarm. As it came to the boil, it switched itself off and the sound subsided. They all looked at each other.

'I think,' said Simon, 'we should go to the police.'

30

The police station in Astley had miraculously managed to survive ruthless cutbacks and was tucked away just off the high street, away from curious eyes.

Outside the red-brick Victorian building, Simon hesitated, flanked by Hattie and Luke. Luke was in the depths of an oversized Paddington duffle coat; Hattie was in a tiny kilt with her long legs in red woolly tights. Their clothes hadn't really changed since he used to take them to the park when they were small. They just wore them ironically now. Hattie was even wearing a tam-o'-shanter like one Lizzy's gran, now long gone, had once knitted for her.

Did it make them feel safe, dressing like their toddler selves? Did they know they were doing it? Or was it him being fanciful, wishing them back again as the helpless, dependent creatures they'd once been, not two independent beings about to flee the nest?

He knew their impending departure was distressing for Lizzy. Was that what lay behind the ominous green slip of paper? In true Lizzy style she hadn't even hidden it. There it had been, in plain view, tucked beside the menu from the Bay of Bengal. It was dated yesterday. She'd said nothing about going to the GP, though.

'Let's go in,' he said in a low voice, and the three of them looked at each other, unable to believe that they were here, about to report Lizzy missing.

Simon had been in the station twice before: once when he'd lost his mobile phone, in the days when mobile phones were rare and valuable things; and once to report an incident of road rage, when someone had cut him up by the level crossing. Generally speaking, crime in Astley wasn't high – it was far enough out of the city not to be targeted and was stuffed with people who were naturally vigilant and inclined to spot anything suspicious. Simon and Lizzy took it in turns to attend Neighbourhood Watch meetings, as they liked to think of themselves as responsible citizens. Third time lucky, he thought hopefully as he pushed open the door.

Inside, a small fake Christmas tree gently beamed out a rotation of luminous colours and the station clock was wrapped in gold tinsel. PCSO Melinda Cope was mentally urging the day to finish. It was her first Christmas since her divorce and she couldn't bloody wait to be able to close the station door and head home. Only half an hour to go.

'How can I help?' Melinda liked to try and second-guess what people were coming in for. The three of them looked anxious and subdued, so she hazarded a guess that perhaps the girl had been mugged; maybe on the train. And they were probably trying to keep it quiet from the mum.

'We'd like to report a missing person.'

Ah. An addled pensioner, perhaps? Who'd wandered

off from their sheltered accommodation? Melinda drew a notepad towards her and pulled the lid off her rollerball.

'OK. Do you want to give me a few details? Who's missing?'

'My wife. Elizabeth Kingham. Lizzy.'

'And how long has she been missing?'

Simon cleared his throat.

'We don't know exactly.'

'A day? A week?' Melinda prompted.

'We woke up this morning and she was gone.'

'OK. So . . . when did you last actually see her?'

The three of them looked at each other. Melinda looked at them and nodded encouragement.

'I came home late last night and slept in the spare room,' said Simon. 'Because of my snoring. I didn't want to disturb her.'

'I got home about two but I didn't want to disturb anyone either,' said Hattie.

'And I got back this morning. I stayed at my mate's,' added Luke.

'Basically I got up at half seven this morning and she was gone,' finished Simon.

'We were supposed to decorate the tree with her last night,' blurted Hattie. 'But we all forgot.'

Melinda considered what they were saying.

'So you were all out last night but you don't know if she was there or not when you got home?' She paused. 'No one bothered to check on her?'

They all looked uncomfortable. 'No,' said Simon. 'But only because we didn't want to disturb her. Not because we don't care.'

Melinda nodded, but her eyebrows were heading upwards, her scepticism evident.

'So when was the last time someone *actually* saw her?'

'I left for work at eight yesterday,' said Simon. 'And she seemed perfectly happy.'

'I left the house about eleven,' said Hattie. 'She was fine.'

Melinda frowned and her eyes flickered up to the clock. She opened her mouth to speak but Luke elbowed his father. 'Show her the note, Dad.'

Melinda looked at Simon. He pulled a piece of paper from his pocket. 'She left this.'

'OK.' Melinda scanned the few words with interest, then looked up at the three of them.

'I'm afraid this means she's not technically missing. She's left an explanation for her absence.' She handed the note back. 'And there's nothing suspicious about it. You didn't bother to come back for something she'd arranged. You didn't even notice if she was there when you did come back. I don't want to judge, but maybe she's just fed up with being taken for granted?'

Melinda was all too familiar with the feeling. It was one of the reasons she was relishing her new relationship – she loved the sense of being appreciated and taken into consideration, instead of being at the bottom of the pile.

'Mum's not like that,' said Luke.

'No, she's not,' agreed Simon. 'She's just not the sort of person who gets in a huff. This is totally out of character.'

'We all have a breaking point. Perhaps she's not very good at saying how she feels?' Melinda put the lid back on her pen. 'I can't register her as missing when all the evidence points to her...' She paused for a moment while she looked for her words, then shrugged. 'Running away from Christmas. I can't say that I blame her, either. We've all wanted to do it.'

'There's this as well.' Simon proffered the prescription. 'This is the really worrying thing. We had no idea she'd been prescribed antidepressants. Or even that she needed them.'

Melinda's gave a shrug. 'Antidepressants aren't all that unusual these days.'

'It's unusual for *Mum*,' protested Hattie. 'We're really worried. Mum's always just *there*.'

Melinda sighed. 'I'm afraid there's nothing I can do at this point. Mrs Kingham has left a note saying she is going away for a few days. There is nothing suspicious about her actions. I know it's upsetting, but—'

'Surely you could find out where she is? Track her car via her number plate?'

'I'm afraid the police aren't here for your convenience, sir.'

She handed back the note and prescription. Simon shoved them in his pocket with a sigh.

Putting what had happened into words made it crystal clear. They'd treated Lizzy badly. They'd been too wrapped up in their own selfish little worlds to care about the person who cared about them the most.

'Let's go,' he said to Luke and Hattie.

Melinda watched the three of them leave the station. She hoped wherever Mrs Kingham was, she was sitting with her feet up with a glass of wine and a good book in her hand. Good for her, she thought, having the balls to run away from Christmas. For the past few years, during her unhappy marriage, she'd found it torture too, but now she was reclaiming it for herself. She grinned as she thought about the present she'd bought for her new boyfriend. His eyes were going to pop out of his head.

Simon thought he might cry as they left the police station. He felt judged and he felt foolish and he felt afraid. He knew the others did too. They all looked at each other for a moment, each of them imagining Lizzy in the kitchen with her rabbit slippers on, her curls shovelled on top of her head in a big butterfly clip, wielding a mug of tea, singing along to Crowded House or shouting out the answers to *Pointless* on the tiny telly in the corner. Hattie was right.

Lizzy was always *there*.

31

Back in the sanctuary of the hut, Lizzy found herself making everything look festive. She might have run away from Christmas, but she kept finding it creep under her skin. It was almost automatic. Anyway, it wasn't just about her any more. She wanted the hut to look Christmassy for Harley. She dotted a dozen tea lights around the hut, put three foil-covered chocolate Santas down the middle of the table, found a CD of Frank Sinatra's *Ultimate Christmas* and put it on. By the time she had started preparing the mulled wine, the hut smelled of cinnamon and cloves and brandy and it felt very festive indeed.

Harley put the rest of the shopping away and stoked up the wood-burner.

'This is amazing,' he said. 'I wish Mum and River were here.'

Lizzy was grating mounds of Gruyère to put in the mac 'n' cheese. She wasn't going to think about Simon and the twins. Every time she did she felt a lump in her throat.

'What's the story with Jack and Nat, do you think?' she asked instead.

Harley shrugged. 'I guess we'll find out.'

'Divorced? Maybe it's "his turn" this year,' suggested Lizzy.

While they were waiting for the macaroni cheese to brown, she changed into her favourite cable-knit sweater and skinny jeans and a pair of cashmere slipper socks. She felt windswept from the open air that afternoon and relished the glow it had brought to her skin as she put on a touch of mascara and lip gloss. She ran her fingers through her hair to fluff up her curls. For the first time in a long time, she liked what she saw in the mirror – maybe the sea air suited her or had blown away some of her anxiety. The frown line between her eyebrows seemed to have faded. Cheaper than fillers, she laughed to herself.

Then she curled up on the sofa with a copy of *The Shellseekers* she'd found on a bookshelf. She'd brought books of her own, but somehow the lure of someone else's reading matter was more enticing, and she couldn't think of a better book to be reading at the seaside.

Harley was drumming his fingers on the kitchen worktop. He seemed restless. He felt a bit happier now he had bared his soul to Leanne, but there was something still bothering him.

'Can I ask you something?' he asked Lizzy.

'Of course.'

'Do you think I should visit my dad in prison?' he asked. 'I mean, I'm eighteen now. I can if I want.'

'Do you usually?'

'No. We sort of cut him off when he got put inside. Well, Mum did. But ... I don't know ... Maybe there's two sides to every story. And I never gave him a chance to tell me his side. I only got Mum's. But maybe whatever he was doing was for us?'

'That doesn't make it right,' said Lizzy.

'I know. But I did – do – love him. He's still my dad. Mum made it very difficult for us to see him. She would never take us to visit him. Then when we moved down here, it was impossible.'

Lizzy could understand a mother wanting to protect her children from someone who had committed a crime. But Harley was old enough now to make up his own mind.

'It's never too late, I suppose. And forgiveness is a very powerful thing.'

Lizzy was keenly aware she was being a hypocrite. She was hardly the epitome of forgiveness. She was punishing her own family for their wrongdoings, after all.

There was a knock on the door. Lizzy looked up. She couldn't help wondering if, by some miracle, her family had tracked her down. Did she want that to happen? For a moment, she wondered what on earth she was doing, running away like that. What was she hoping to achieve? Then she remembered how standing alone by the Christmas tree had made her feel small and insignificant and meaningless. This was her way of saying 'I matter'.

Harley opened the door. Jack and Nat were standing on the doorstep, Nat bundled up in a reindeer onesie and Jack bearing a bottle of champagne and a big plate.

'I think I was a bit churlish earlier,' said Jack. 'We'd love to join you, if you don't mind. And I brought this. It's my own gravlax.' He proffered the plate. 'Cured with vodka.'

There were coral pink slices of salmon laid in perfect rows, so thin they were almost translucent, the scent of lime mingling with the aniseed of dill.

'How gorgeous,' said Lizzy. 'We'd love to have you. I've made mountains. Nat, I can make you your own little mac and cheese – you can have it now if you're hungry. I'm not sure if you'd like lobster or not.'

'Oh, he'll eat lobster,' laughed Jack as they trooped in. 'He's well-trained.' He looked around the hut. 'Wow. This is totally different from the one we're in.'

'They're all different,' Harley told him. 'I like the one you're in, though. It's kind of retro.'

'Yes,' said Jack, and took in a deep breath. 'My ... um ... my ... wife ...' He faltered for a moment. 'My wife would have loved it.'

Harley and Lizzy both stared at him.

'She was ... really into ... vintage stuff.' He gulped. 'Could I have a drink?'

Later, when everyone was in a carbohydrate slump and had sunk into the sofas with a glass of wine, Jack bared his soul. Nat was curled up in a sheepskin beanbag, fast asleep, so he could speak without worrying.

'Fran died,' he managed to say. 'Just before Christmas this time last year.'

Harley didn't know what to say. He twirled one of his locks around his finger, a habit when he was uncomfortable. He had known unhappiness in life, but nothing on this scale.

'It's OK,' said Lizzy. 'You can tell us. If you want. Or not. If you don't.'

Jack took a slug of his mulled wine before carrying on.

'They found out – we found out – she had cancer, just after we found out she was pregnant.' He gave a half-laugh. 'We'd sort of given up hope. We'd been trying for quite a while. We were going to give it a break – it can be pretty exhausting, trying for a baby – then talk about options. IVF. Whatever. So it was a bit of a surprise. But not as big a surprise as finding out the real reason why she'd been feeling so terrible. Not the fertility drugs or the morning sickness . . .'

He could remember the appointment. The wonderfully empathetic consultant who had broken the terrible news, her anguished eyes filled with a look that said, 'I'd rather be telling you anything but this.' It seemed to come from nowhere, the diagnosis. A strange new trio of words which strung together meant nothing at first – non-Hodgkin lymphoma – yet the subtext was abundantly clear.

Fran had been sitting there, in a yellow gingham shirt dress and espadrilles. Surely nothing like this happened to girls in yellow gingham, Jack remembered thinking. She had looked puzzled and said, 'Oh. I see.' She didn't raise her voice or start asking questions. She just sat very still.

'What does this mean?' demanded Jack. 'I don't understand. How long has she had it? Why are we only finding out now? Surely there are symptoms? She's been feeling tired, yeah, but—'

'Shh, Jack,' said Fran. 'Let the doctor speak.'

'You have,' said the consultant, 'three options.'

'We're not going to like any of them, are we?' asked Jack, and Fran put a hand on his arm to quieten him.

'You can have chemo now and risk harming the baby – we don't know quite how much damage it can cause, but we can monitor—'

'No.' Fran was emphatic. 'That's not an option. I have spent the last year making sure I don't eat or drink or do anything that might harm a baby. I'm not going to go down that route. Next.'

The consultant breathed in. Option two was clearly going to be even more unpalatable. 'You can abort the baby and start chemo straight away.'

Fran just laughed and shook her head.

'What?' said Jack, frowning at Fran. 'But surely—'

'Option three?' said Fran brightly. 'What's option three?'

'You can wait until the baby is born and start treatment immediately afterwards.'

The consultant's words fluttered in the air. Her voice was so gentle, it seemed impossible that they could hold such devastating news. Fran and Jack waited a moment for their resonance to settle.

'Well, that,' said Fran, 'is the *only* option.'

'No,' said Jack. 'Surely Fran needs treatment straight away?' He looked at the doctor. 'If she wasn't pregnant, would you wait six months?'

'Absolutely not,' said the consultant. 'But it's never an easy decision. We are very aware there are two lives to consider here.'

'One life,' said Fran. 'There's only one life that matters to me.'

'Don't be stupid.' Jack's voice was harsher than he meant it to be.

'Jack,' said Fran. 'It's simple probability.' Fran always solved problems in a scientific manner. 'Option three is the only option that has a no-risk outcome for one of us. Assuming, of course, that at the moment the baby is fit and healthy?'

'It certainly seems to be,' the doctor agreed.

'So if we want to guarantee that one of us comes out of this alive, that's what we go for.'

Jack stared at her. How could she have assessed the risks in such a calculated manner in such a short space of time? His brain couldn't assimilate the horror at all.

'You're mad,' he said to Fran. 'You need treatment straight away.'

'I'm not putting my baby's life at risk.'

'You don't have to decide this minute,' said the consultant. 'In fact, I would advise against it. Go and sleep on it. Take as much time as you want to discuss it. Then come and see me.'

Jack was shaking his head. 'You have to explain to her. I don't think she's thinking straight. She's more important than the baby.'

'No,' said Fran. 'The baby comes first.'

'How come you get to decide that? What about how I feel?' Jack knew he was shouting but he felt the power slipping away from him. He knew Fran had decided; that he wasn't going to be able to talk her round. He wanted the consultant to intervene. Insist, at the very least, that they started treating Fran no matter what the risk. He knew his wife and how steadfastly she stood by her decisions. How stubborn she was. And it was one of the reasons he loved her so very much. 'Help me,' he pleaded. 'Make her see sense.'

'The decision has to be yours,' said the consultant. 'And can I just say, I'm so sorry.'

Jack looked at her and her gaze slid away from his. She couldn't meet his eye, and in that moment he knew how the story was going to play out, that he was not the narrator, that there was going to be no amazing plot twist in the third act, with an end scene where the consultant who'd guided them to make the right choice would be godmother at the baby's christening...

For the next few days, he tried every trick in the book to make Fran change her mind. He didn't care what tactics he used or who he pulled into their dilemma: parents, friends, people he had found on the internet who had been through similar and survived (he didn't mention the ones who hadn't).

At the end of the week, she sat him down.

'I never thought I was going to get pregnant. I never thought I would bring a baby into this world. It is all I want. I'm its mum, and while the baby is inside me I have to do all I can to protect it. And the other thing I refuse to do, if I do die, is leave you on your own.'

'You can't say that. Don't say that,' Jack begged. He couldn't control his tears.

'Jack, you might thank me for making the right choice one day. Do not think I haven't thought it through.' Her voice was shaking with emotion. 'It's an awful decision to have to make, but now I've made it can we please just draw a line and try and make what happens next as –' she flailed about for the words – 'as not-shit as it can be. Even though it's total shit.'

She slumped, exhausted. Her mouth was twitching with the effort of not crying and he saw how much the decision had taken out of her and in that moment he decided to respect her wishes

Now, retelling it all to Lizzy and Harley, he half laughed. 'You don't know Fran. She'd made up her mind and there was nothing I could do. I had to make sure that every day mattered, that the birth was as joyful as it could be, even though we were living with the terror.'

'You were very brave,' said Lizzy.

'No, I bloody wasn't,' said Jack. 'I spent half my life hiding in the bathroom crying my eyes out.' He gave a wry smile. 'She didn't even come out of hospital when Nat was born. She went for treatment straight away. Everyone was amazing. My parents. My sister Clemmie. Our friends. Helping with Nat then helping look after Fran when she did come home.'

He shut his eyes, remembering the madness of those days: nurses and midwives and health visitors and feeding bottles and snatched sleep and vomit and crying and chaos. His wonderful parents and his sister, Clemmie. All he'd wanted to do was hold Fran and tell her everything would be all right, but there was never time for calm; never time for them to hold each other.

She got sicker and sicker and weaker and weaker as Nat grew bonnier and bouncier, but every time she looked at the baby her eyes shone with pride. Nat seemed to give her a reason. Jack suspected that *he* would never have been enough to make her fight as hard as she did against the disease. For nearly three years she grappled with it, always facing it full on, never denying its existence, snarling in its face.

'Fifth of December last year,' he managed to say. 'I was holding her hand and we were listening to Amy Winehouse. She loved Amy Winehouse.'

Lizzy wiped away a tear. Harley got up and took Jack's glass, then went over to the saucepan to top it up. He handed it back to him.

'I'm really sorry, mate. Fran sounds awesome.'

'She was . . .' Jack nodded in agreement. 'And Christmas was her thing. She always made it so special. Which is why I couldn't face it this year. I'm not strong enough. Every bauble, every carol, every bloody *mince pie* makes me think she should be here.' He swallowed and tried to smile. 'And maybe it's not fair on Nat, but I've tried to do the best I can for him. Make it fun.'

'And unlucky for you, you found us,' smiled Lizzy. 'We're running away from Christmas too. But it doesn't mean we can't have a good time.' She looked between Harley and Jack. 'Does it?'

Later, Jack scooped up Nat and took him back to his hut, tucking him into bed. He looked at his little boy fast asleep, those Cheryl Cole lashes resting on his cheeks, one arm flung over the velvety pouch of softness that was Clouseau, who had snuggled up next to him. Their breathing was almost synchronised.

He had done it, Jack thought. He had shared his story for the first time with someone who didn't know it, and he had survived. One day perhaps he wouldn't feel the need to tell it, that it would no longer be such a big part of him, that he wouldn't feel the pressing need to explain his circumstances.

He had made quite a bit of headway recently. He'd been shocked when he looked in the mirror one day a few months ago: shocked at the way his shoulders were slightly hunched, his eyes without light, his mouth slack with despondency. So he'd straightened his shoulders and put on a smile – a real one, not a fake, leering rictus – and just pretending he was OK had made him feel more positive.

Tonight, though, he had felt his shoulders relax and his eyes crinkle with laughter and his mouth turn up at the corners involuntarily. Maybe it had been Lizzy's mulled wine or Nat's excitement at the thought that Father Christmas really would be coming to the beach hut, even though they had no proper chimney, or the strange companionableness of a bunch of strangers sharing their troubles, each of them away from home for a different reason. He had felt relaxed, in the womb of the hut next door, in the depths of the sofa, the wood-burning stove throwing out warmth, the murmur of Harley's husky voice interspersed with Lizzy's laugh.

Perhaps the newness of strangers helped to heal your scars? While he was with his old friends, the wounds stayed fresh and open, because he thought of other times, times when Fran had been there with them all. He hadn't felt that with Lizzy and Harley. He'd been wrapped up in their stories and forgotten his own. He'd been eager to find out more about them. He'd been less selfish, less self-centred, a better person.

Sometimes he wondered how and why his old friends put up with him and his misery, though they did. But maybe now it was time to reach out and bring in some new people. Not that he didn't value his old mates: of course he did, and he could never repay them. But they, as much as anyone, deserved a new Jack. He could see it in their eyes sometimes, pity mixed with – was it boredom? Having to hear his schtick again and again? He tried not to go on, but he didn't have much else to talk about.

It filled him with resolve, not to try new things, but to try new people. The revelation was, he thought, the best Christmas present he could have had.

CHRISTMAS EVE

32

Simon woke with a start on Christmas Eve. He felt ashamed – how had he fallen asleep? What if Lizzy had phoned in the night or even come back to find them all snoring away as if they didn't have a care?

Then he sat up, suddenly attentive, alert as a meerkat. He could hear the pipes starting to click and groan. Someone had put the heating on. The timer had been on the blink for months so they had to turn it on and off manually. It was the first thing Lizzy did every morning.

He strained his ears. He thought he could hear the radio – it would be Radio 2, the chuntering burble of whichever DJ had drawn the short straw, introducing jolly festive tunes. Then he breathed in . . .

Coffee. He could smell coffee.

She'd come back! She had sneaked in without letting them know and was pottering about in the kitchen. She'd be going through her Delia plan, working out what time to put the turkey in tomorrow. There was always a complicated mathematical calculation and she always got up super early, because it took bloody hours. Every year they debated whether to have something else, and every year they had a fifteen-pound bird that took up more time and attention than it surely merited. But it always looked magnificent when she finally pulled it out, all golden and steaming.

He jumped out of bed. Thank God, he thought. They could be normal now. They wouldn't go into it all, they'd just have a wonderful Christmas, and he would be on the lookout for signs, he would take extra care of her and they could sort things out in due course—

He scrambled down the stairs, nearly hitting his head on the beam in his haste, and burst into the kitchen with a wide smile on his face. She was there, with her back to him. She turned with a smile.

He had never felt disappointment like it. It was crushing. Like being plunged into a pool of icy water that took your breath away. He couldn't speak. For there, in front of him, in Lizzy's dressing gown, setting out the mugs on the side as she plunged the cafetière, was his mother.

'I've turned the heating on. I hope that's OK. Did you sleep? . . .' She trailed off as she saw the disappointment on Simon's face. 'Oh, darling. You thought I was Lizzy. I'm so sorry.'

'It's ok.' He gulped. It really was serious if Lizzy had stayed away for a second night. 'I'm so worried about her, Mum.'

'I know you are, but I'm sure she's ok. She'll be back when she's good and ready.'

Cynthia went over to give her son a hug. It was tentative at first, after yesterday and her confession, and they weren't the most demonstrative of families. But he leant into her and she put her arms round him and it felt good, to be a comfort and a support.

'Thanks, Mum,' he mumbled. He was still cross with her, but he needed consolation more than retribution.

Hattie woke up on Christmas Eve and grabbed her phone. Just like she did every morning, only this time it had a purpose. She checked her Facebook page to see if there had been any sightings. The post had been shared hundreds of times. It could be anywhere in the world now. She scrolled through all the messages underneath. Messages from people she had never met, wishing her luck, sending her love.

> Your mum looks beautiful I hope you find her

> Oh my God I can't imagine waking up without my mom on Christmas. Here's hoping.

> Come home Lizzy!! Everyone loves you.

> Sending lots of love and good wishes to your family at this stressful time

Her phone rang. It was Hal.

'I saw you were on Facebook. Any luck?'

'No.' She sighed. 'But thanks for asking.'

'My mum says if you all want to come over here for lunch, you'd be welcome. We always have a big old fish pie on Christmas Eve. It's pretty tasty.'

'You told your mum?'

'Hat, it's all over Facebook.'

'I guess so.' She sighed. 'Thanks. And thanks to your mum. I don't know what we're doing yet.'

'She will come back, Hattie. Your mum's . . . solid.'

Hattie giggled, despite herself. 'She wouldn't thank you for that.'

'You know what I mean.'

'Course I do.' She sighed. 'It's so weird, Hal. The house feels dead without her.'

It did. The air on their floor felt cold: the heating took a while to reach this high up.

'I don't know what to do,' she told Hal.

'Go back to sleep, I guess,' he replied. 'It's not even seven. No one's awake here.'

'How come you're up?'

There was a pause. 'I'm excited,' he admitted. 'I love Christmas. I shan't sleep tonight.'

'Do you still get a stocking?' Hattie giggled.

'Yes. Even though I know my mum's PA gets all the stuff off the internet.'

'That's terrible,' said Hattie, but she was smiling at the thought of ultra-cool Hal rooting through his Christmas stocking in the semi-darkness. She could hear him chewing something.

'What are you eating?'

'I've got a massive Toblerone. My nan gives me one every year. Want me to bring it round?'

'You're OK,' she said, managing a smile. 'Go and make your mum a cup of tea.'

'God, no, she'd die of shock.' Hal laughed. 'Anyway, you've got an open invitation to come round. You're welcome, any of you.'

'Thanks, Hal,' said Hattie softly. People were kind, when it came down to it. She hung up and pulled her duvet over her head. She didn't want to get up. She didn't want to walk through a house without Lizzy in it. There wasn't any point.

Her door opened and Luke stood in the doorway, his hair sticking up on end, the hem of his pyjama bottoms trailing along the floor, his ratty Metallica T-shirt barely covering his midriff. Hattie peered out at him.

'Hey.'

'I can't sleep,' he said. 'What if Mum's run off with someone? I mean, you read about stuff, don't you?' He came over and sat on the edge of her bed. 'Maybe she met some rich dude at the hotel? And she's driven off with him somewhere? Or what if she's been kidnapped? By some weirdo?'

'She left a note, Luke. She's mega pissed off with us and she's ... chilling somewhere.'

'How can you be so cool about it?'

'I'm not. But what can we do?'

They were exactly the same age, but sometimes Hattie felt much older than Luke. Maybe they needed to revert to their childhood habits, for comfort. She shuffled over to give him some room, then grabbed the remote for her telly.

'Let's watch *Flintstones* reruns,' she said, flicking through the channels. 'Hal just called. Said we can go round to his if we want.'

'Nah. Let's stay here in case Mum comes back.'

The two of them snuggled up together. It was, thought Hattie, like when they were tiny and watched telly together on a Saturday morning. Only Mum wasn't going to come in any minute and tell them breakfast was ready. She looked at her phone again, just in case.

Nothing.

33

Jack got up early on Christmas Eve and went into Tawcombe with Nat and Clouseau, to the fishmonger on the quay. He'd checked the opening times on the internet, and it was one of the things he was most excited about, going to buy fresh fish and seafood. He and Nat wrapped up as warmly as they could. The wind had a Baltic bite to it; the temperature had dropped overnight and the skies were brooding and dark.

Jack let Nat stand on the harbour wall and they watched the choppy navy-blue water slapping against the stone. He shivered as he thought of the fishermen out there, battling the elements to bring in their catch. They'd come back here in the summer, he decided. Get a boat. Do some fishing. They wandered along the quay, got two bacon rolls from a kiosk, then bought some fat creamy scallops, bright white cod and bubblegum-pink prawns. He was going to make a chowder, he decided, with chunks of potato and dill. The perfect Christmas Eve dish, heart-warmingly satisfying.

As they walked back to the car, picking their way over the wet cobbles, breathing in the gusts of Atlantic air, Jack thought: I feel, if not happy, then content, that I am doing as well in life as I can expect to right now. He loved his little boy, his little mate. He loved this seaside adventure they were having. Simple pleasures. Fresh air. New people. He had definitely done the right thing, coming here.

When they got back to Everdene, Lizzy and Harley were outside the hut with a woman and a young boy who looked like a mini version of Harley. He must be about a year older than Nat, he guessed.

'Hey, Jack,' said Harley. 'Come and meet my mum. Mum, this is Jack. And Nat.'

'Hi, Jack. I'm Leanne. And this is River.'

For a moment, Jack hesitated. Then he held out his hand and she took it. Leanne was petite, with a classic heart-shaped face and hazel eyes, her hair bleached and tousled. Dressed in a fur-lined combat jacket and ripped jeans, she had a dainty tomboy look going on. The boys both had their mum's grace and delicacy, he noted. What a beautiful family.

'Hey,' was all he could manage, slightly overwhelmed and tongue-tied.

He remembered what Harley had told him the night before. About his dad being inside, and how much he hated his mum's new boyfriend.

'We're going for a big beach walk,' said Lizzy. 'Then we're going to the Ship Aground for carols. Do you want to join us?'

'I would love to,' he said, telling himself it would be good for Nat to have someone his age to play with.

'Oh, a French bulldog,' said Leanne, falling to her knees in front of Clouseau. 'What a darling.'

'That's Clouseau,' said Jack.

'I love dogs,' she said. 'But my Tony's not keen. Maybe I can talk him round.'

Jack felt a tiny flicker in his belly. He examined it, and recognised it as disappointment that she was talking about Tony in such a possessive way. He saw disappointment flitter across Harley's face too. Last night he had definitely expressed hope that his mum might move on. He caught Harley's eye for a moment and gave him a smile of reassurance, then turned to Leanne.

'He's a very good companion,' he told her. 'For me and Nat.' Then realised what was implicit in those words, as she looked up at him, eyes wide with curiosity.

River and Nat had already found sticks of driftwood and were having a sword fight.

'I'll just put this stuff in the fridge,' said Jack, holding up his bag of fish.

Inside, he looked in the bathroom mirror and ran his fingers through his hair to make it stick up a bit like it was supposed to. His hand hovered over his bottle of Acqua di Parma. No, he decided. There was little point.

It was interesting, though, the fleeting feeling he'd had. A flicker of something that made him feel . . . what? That potent mix of adrenaline mixed with something more base. He measured his guilt. Was that flicker a betrayal? He didn't think anyone would say it was. Not even Fran.

He sighed. It was academic, anyway. He couldn't try himself for something that wasn't going to happen: not if Leanne was talking about Tony as if they were an item. Maybe all it meant was that he was still a living, breathing human being. Something he had begun to doubt.

*

268

The six of them walked to the other end of the beach, where Nat and River scrambled on the rocks, poking in the rock pools, their hair damp from the sea mist that was rolling in across the water. Clouseau scampered about, as animated as he ever was. Leanne collected shells, in different shades of grey and pink and cream, filling her pockets.

Lizzy sat on a big lump of driftwood that had washed up on the beach. She had never spent Christmas Eve in the open air like this. Doing next to nothing. Her head as empty as it could be. The relief of not having to keep up a pretence outweighed her guilt at having left her family.

Although she wondered if the relief was starting to wear off, like an anaesthetic. There was something needling deep inside her. She recognised it from when the children were very young, and she and Simon had gone out for an evening or a rare night away. There was an initial excitement and exhilaration, but gradually that wore away. You missed them. And the feeling grew and grew until you had to rush back early, because you couldn't bear it any longer.

Was that sense of loss setting in now? Was that what she was feeling? She felt a chill as the air temperature dropped. Without the sun, it was properly chilly. She shivered and jumped off the log, wandering back over to the others.

Leanne was looking at the boys as the mist thickened round them.

'We should start back,' she said to Jack. 'Before they get cold.'

'We should,' he agreed. 'There is nothing less fun than a cold, tired boy.'

Leanne laughed in recognition. 'You're right there. River!' she called. 'Nat!'

Jack looked at her. He liked hearing her call Nat's name. He didn't always like it when other people took over. He was, he realised, very protective of his son. He should learn to let go a bit. Maybe today was a start.

The boys scrambled off the rocks and came running towards them, accompanied by Clouseau, their faces alight with the joy of it all.

'Pub, I think,' said Lizzy. 'I'm in the mood for a good sing-song. And I need a drink.'

The Ship Aground did Christmas Eve in style. They served Little Donkeys, which was their take on a Moscow Mule: a lethal combination of vodka, ginger wine and lime which had a deadly kick. And they were doing Karol-oke. Anyone who wanted to belt out their favourite Christmas song to a rocking backing track was welcome to take the stage.

People had come from miles to take part in the festivities. Huge plates of sausage rolls and cheese straws were being handed round. There were Christmas jumpers and flashing earrings galore. River and Nat were given bowls of chips, against Jack's better judgement.

Leanne jumped up to take the stage.

'Oh no,' said Harley, grinning and putting his face in his hands. But she was brilliant. She sang 'All I Want for Christmas is You', Mariah Carey-style, and she hit every note.

And there was one moment, as she sang the chorus, when she caught Jack's eye. He felt himself blush, and she just smiled and carried on singing, looking away again. But still smiling.

Harley checked his phone to hide his embarrassment. He scrolled through his various apps, wishing people Merry Christmas and answering messages. As he wound his way idly down his Facebook page, something caught his eye. He stopped and scrolled back up.

It was a picture of Lizzy. With a heartfelt plea from her children: *has anyone seen our mum?* The post had been shared hundreds of times all over the country. He looked at all the messages underneath and all the replies from Hattie and Luke, thanking people for sharing and commenting and saying how worried they were.

He chewed on the side of his thumb as he thought. Would he be betraying Lizzy if he revealed her whereabouts? He thought about how he would feel if his mum went missing. He'd be beside himself, but Lizzy and Leanne were two very different creatures. Leanne was quite likely to be in trouble, whereas Lizzy – he couldn't imagine her doing anything reckless. Running away this Christmas was obviously the most impulsive thing she had ever done.

Her family must be missing her terribly. She must light up their lives with her smile and her certainty and her way of making you feel special even if you didn't think much of yourself. She was drawn to the good in people and didn't tolerate the bad. She was loyal and dogged, and kind. If she was his mum, he would be frantic.

She was laughing as Jack pulled her up on stage to duet with him, 'Fairytale of New York'. Harley took a photo of her, surreptitiously, then thought that probably wasn't what her family wanted to see. Lizzy after two Little Donkeys doing karaoke with a strange man.

He looked over at his own mum. Leanne was looking anxious, checking her phone.

'I need to get back,' she whispered. 'Tony's wondering where I am. But I don't want to go.'

'Then don't,' said Harley. He wanted his mum to stay. This felt right. He saw Jack looking at her, sensing her anxiety. And he thought, maybe—

No. That wasn't going to happen. Leanne was getting her coat on, passing River his, picking up her bag. The party was over.

34

At Pepperpot Cottage, Cynthia had galvanised every-one into action. She wouldn't be able to bear it if Lizzy came home and saw the house shrouded in gloom, without a single decoration. She owed it to her daughter-in-law to make sure everything was as it should be.

Let's be honest, she thought, she owed Lizzy the world. Cynthia was appalled she had felt under so much pressure that she had run away. You never knew the strain people were under, and sometimes it was the sunniest of natures that were hiding the darkest troubles. Whiners and moaners seemed to manage, as if their pessimistic coping mechanism made life bearable.

She gathered them all in the kitchen and gave them a list each of things to do. She sent Hattie into Astley for flowers, got Luke to jet-wash the courtyard and string the outside lights up and got Simon to clean out the fireplace in the living room while she set to restoring order in the kitchen. She turned the radio up for forced jollity and by mid-afternoon everyone had a sense of achievement.

'I think,' she told them, 'we should do the tree.'

They stared at it, not sure. It was, after all, the root of their problems; a six foot reminder of what they had done wrong. But it didn't feel right, not to decorate it. And if

Lizzy did come back, it would be lovely if it was there in all its glory, lights blazing, to welcome her home.

By four, the tree looked more perfect than it had ever done. Hattie had used the ribbon Lizzy had bought to string everything up, and it looked like their tree, but better: all the familiar decorations but with beautiful orange velvet bows, the ends trailing amongst the foliage. Cynthia had strung up all the Christmas cards with the rest of the ribbon and put them round the room.

Afterwards, in the kitchen, Cynthia stood wondering how and if she should cook them all lunch the next day. She felt momentarily daunted. It was so long since she had done it she wasn't sure how she was going to manage. She barely cooked at all these days. But it must be like riding a bike, doing Christmas lunch. And anyway, the hard bit had been done: the shopping. It was all there, in the larder and the freezer and the fridge. And there was Delia to help.

If nothing else it would help to pass the time. Potatoes to peel and vegetables to prepare. Otherwise they would just be sitting around, staring into space.

Her phone rang. She looked at it. Amanda.

What did she want?

She wanted something. She never phoned otherwise. Surely she was swooping down the slopes in Val-d'Isère? What was so important now? She ignored it.

Amanda called again. She ignored it again.

By the third call, Cynthia decided the only way to get rid of her was by answering.

'Amanda!' Her voice had a sing-song ring to it.

'Oh, Cynthia, thank goodness.'

There was a drama. She could hear it in her voice.

'I've done my bloody knee in. I'm on crutches. I'm getting the next flight home. I've left the kids here, but there's no point in hanging about in the chalet while everyone's out on the slopes. I'm at the airport now.'

'Oh dear. Well, that's skiing for you. It's always a risk.'

'Can you send your driver man to come and get me? And can you come over and give me a hand? I can't do a thing. I can hardly even get to the loo on my own.'

Cynthia smothered a smile. She wasn't being cruel. She could tell by Amanda's voice that she was more furious at her week's skiing being cut short than in any particular discomfort.

'Oh, I'm very sorry. I can't help,' she said, her voice sugary. 'I'm at Pepperpot. Getting everything ready for Christmas.'

She wasn't going to tell her about Lizzy's disappearance.

'I'm sure Lizzy would understand.' Amanda's voice was tight with impatience.

'No,' said Cynthia. 'I'm sorry. I'm sure you'll be able to find someone else. I'll try and pop over next week and bring you a casserole.'

There was a shocked silence.

'Well, thank you very much,' snapped Amanda. 'So good to know that you're there in a crisis.'

She rang off. Cynthia put her hand over her mouth and started to laugh, peals of it ricocheting around the kitchen, and she stopped short, realising it was a sound she hadn't heard very often recently, then started again.

'What are you laughing at?' Simon came into the kitchen.

'Nothing,' said Cynthia. 'Just something silly on the radio.'

The house phone on the wall rang. Simon stared at it for a moment, then rushed to it. It might be news of Lizzy.

'Hello?' He listened for a moment, then his lips tightened before he answered. 'Amanda? Just fuck off, will you? I'm not your bloody chauffeur. Sort yourself out. Get a taxi like anyone else.'

And he hung up.

Cynthia looked at him. 'Good for you, darling. Does she really expect you to drop everything?'

'Of course she does. You know she does. And I've had enough.'

Then he looked at his mum and gave a little grin. It was the first time he had stood up to his ex-wife. It felt *fantastic*.

If only Lizzy was here. She'd be proud of him. It darkened his mood again. He looked at the clock. Quarter to six.

'Do you think it's time for a drink?' he asked.

'Not for me.' Cynthia said. 'I've decided. I'm going on the wagon for a while.

'Oh!' Simon was surprised. 'Look, what you did was awful but you don't have to punish yourself. Maybe just cut down a bit.'

'No. I've thought about it. Drinking doesn't make me happy. If anything, it makes things worse.'

Simon felt rather relieved. He had suspected his mother was drinking too much, but had felt awkward about confronting her. And anyway, you couldn't tell people to stop drinking, or even to cut down. They had to do it for themselves.

'Well, that's very brave, Mum. And if you're not, I won't.'

'No, no – you go ahead. I've got to get used to other people drinking round me. Otherwise it's not really giving up, is it?'

'I suppose not.' Simon hesitated nevertheless.

Cynthia went over to the wine rack and pulled out a bottle of Shiraz.

'Come on. It's Christmas.'

'But it's not, is it?' he said sadly. 'Christmas isn't Christmas without Lizzy.'

35

That evening, Jack brought his chowder round to Harley and Lizzy with pride.

'I've made enough for an army,' he said.

The four of them sat round the table, scoffing it out of chunky blue bowls: thick, creamy and unctuous, it tasted of the sea, the fronds of dill giving it an aniseed edge.

'I helped make it,' Nat told Harley and Lizzy proudly, dunking his bread in. Jack had let him drop the prawns and scallops in, one by one.

'Well, it's delicious,' Lizzy told him. 'What a brilliant cook you are.'

The hut felt cosy, but there was a slight air of melancholy underlying everyone's thoughts that evening, each of them very aware of the people who should be there but weren't. Outside, the wind whipped up and threw itself against the glass. No one was quite sure what to do.

'I think,' said Jack, 'I'm going to crash. I expect Nat will be up early.'

'Father Christmas is coming,' said Nat, matter-of-factly.

'He certainly is,' said Lizzy, hugging the little boy to her, relishing the warmth of his body, the smell of his apple-scented hair. 'We'll see you for lunch tomorrow?'

The four of them had decided to pool their resources and share what they had.

'Definitely. If it's not raining, I'll fire up the barbecue,' said Jack.

When Nat and Jack had gone, Harley was hovering, restless, unable to settle. Lizzy wasn't sure what he wanted or needed, but he seemed a bit twitchy. He kept checking his phone. It reminded her of the twins, and she felt a sudden pang.

Perhaps she should send them a message to say she was all right. She was regretting not bringing her phone, because she had no idea what anyone's number was. She could borrow Harley's and call the house phone but she wasn't sure how she would react if one of the kids answered. She'd cry. She knew she would. She could feel it now, her throat tightening at the thought. Maybe she'd ask Harley to track Hattie or Luke down on Facebook and tell them she was all right.

She looked at the clock. If she was at home, they'd have just got back from the crib service in Astley. They went every Christmas Eve. The house would smell of mulled wine and sausage rolls and there would be the usual cluster of people dropping in for a drink on their way home afterwards – Pepperpot Cottage was only two hundred yards from the church, so it had become a bit of a custom. Would they have all gone anyway, she wondered.

No, she thought. They would be relieved not to go. She always had to nag them to get ready. They were usually late and would have to cram into seats at the back of the church. No way would they get there without her chivvying them. Hattie would probably go to Kiki's – crib services were so not cool – and Luke would be at Hal's, and Simon always moaned about going because he didn't see the point when they weren't religious. But then he always ended up enjoying himself and playing host afterwards. She tried to picture what was happening; if they'd all managed without her.

Of course they had. They were probably loving not having to get up or wash up.

She could feel it closing in – that sense of panic and despair that had become so familiar of late. She took another sip of wine and breathed it away, telling herself to relax. She was supposed to be enjoying this taste of freedom. Feeling overwhelmed was quite normal if you'd had a big change.

What she really needed to do was get her head around what she wanted from the future. Work out who she was and where she fitted in. She hadn't had time to think about any of that since she'd arrived. But she was beginning to think perhaps she didn't want to go back to work for someone else and be at their beck and call. Maybe she could set up on her own? There wasn't a lot she didn't know about organising weddings and parties. She had lots of contacts. She could be her own boss. She could work from home or maybe even find an office in Astley. It was a great location; there would be lots of potential clients.

And, she remembered, she had her redundancy money. She'd been thinking about a new car, but that was a waste. She could use it to set herself up. She imagined a lovely office in a converted attic room, perhaps a feature in the local paper that would bring in business.

She heaved a sigh. If it was that easy, everyone would be doing it.

Harley walked over to her.

'Hey,' he said, crouching down by her chair. 'Are you OK?'

'Yes,' she said. 'I'm just ... missing my squad, as Hattie would say.'

'Of course you are.'

'I'm wondering if maybe they weren't as bad as I thought.'

'I bet they're missing you,' he said. 'I would be.'

'Oh,' she said, touched. 'That's sweet. But they're probably not. They're probably just doing their own thing, thinking I'll come back when I've got over myself.'

Harley frowned. 'I think they're probably quite worried. Don't you think you should call them?'

'No. Because I don't really know what to say. I should just go home.' She held up her glass and calculated how much she'd drunk. Probably the best part of half a bottle. It made her think of Cynthia, and she felt a fleeting irritation. 'I can't drive back now, though. I've drunk far too much. I'll go tomorrow.'

Harley's face fell.

'But what about lunch? With Jack and Nat?' He didn't want lunch with them on his own. He wanted Lizzy there. It was selfish, maybe. But it was Lizzy holding them all together. She obviously had no idea how much she affected people. How much they depended on her.

Lizzy smiled. 'Don't worry. I'll stay for lunch. I won't just abandon you.'

Harley put a hand on her arm.. 'I just want to say what you've done for me ... for us ... I can't ever thank you enough.'

She laughed and shrugged.

'What have I done? It's Caroline you've got to thank.'

'You've given me courage. Courage to stand up for myself and do what's right. And look out for my mum.' Harley didn't want to bring the mood down by thinking about Tony. He stood up. 'Will you be ok if I go for a walk? I need some fresh air or I'm going to fall asleep in here.'

'I'll be fine.' Lizzy watched him head to the door, thinking how proud Leanne must be of her son, and hoping they would be able to get their life back on track. It must be hard for Leanne, having divided loyalties, though surely your kids came first?

She felt a pang of conscience. She was a right one to talk. Was she putting her kids first, buggering off like she had? No. She'd been completely selfish.

Harley ran down the steps of the hut and onto the sand. The wind had died down now, blown itself out, and he could hear the sea murmuring a gentle lullaby. He picked up his phone, scrolled until he found the post, hesitated for a moment, then dialled the number.

'Hello?'

'Is that Hattie?'

'Yes.'

'Hi. My name's Harley. I saw your Facebook post? I wasn't sure whether to call. I know where your mum is.'

There was a gasp. 'Really?' Then a note of wariness. 'Where?'

'She's down in Everdene. At her friend's beach hut? Caroline?'

'Caroline? The beach hut . . . ?' It was as if a realisation

282

was dawning. 'In Everdene? Oh my God, she used to love it there. She's told me so many stories.'

'It's an amazing place.'

'Is she OK?'

'She's fine. Absolutely fine.'

'Is she OK, though? Really? What has she said to you?'

'She's cool. She's been looking after us.'

'Us? Who's us?' Hattie sounded suspicious.

'Me and my mum and my brother. And the guy from the hut next door... It's a long story.'

'Did she say what was the matter? We've been tearing our hair out wondering. She's not ill? Or in some kind of trouble?' Hattie's words rattled out like gunfire.

Harley considered his reply carefully. 'I think... to be honest... she's just... tired?'

'Of us?'

'Of life. Everything. Everything and nothing. I think it all closed in on her.' He paused, wanting to be tactful yet firm. 'I think you guys not turning up to decorate the tree was a big one.'

'Oh, poor Mum...' Hattie's voice sounded full of unshed tears. 'We all feel terrible. We're just a bunch of selfish pigs.'

Harley laughed, despite himself. 'Well, maybe.'

'Is she still there?'

'Yeah, yeah – I just walked up the beach to get a better signal.'

'Will you wait? While I go and tell my dad? Can I call you back?'

'Sure. You've got my number.'

'Harley. It's Harley, right?'

'Yeah.' He liked the way she said his name.

'Harley... Thank you. I can't tell you how much this means.' She took in a breath. 'This is the best Christmas present ever. I'll speak to you later.'

Harley put his phone back in his pocket with a smile. He felt suffused with the glow of doing the right thing. He was pretty sure he had done. Lizzy might be planning to head home tomorrow, but her family needed to know she was ok now. Then they could wake up on Christmas morning knowing she was safe. She might think they didn't care, but Harley could tell they did. Very much.

Hattie had sounded a little bit like her mum: warm and funny and a bit scatty but nevertheless in control. Uncertain yet definite. People were often a mass of contradictions, he thought. His own mum was. She was tough in so many ways yet made herself vulnerable, especially when it came to men.

Even he was a mass of contradictions, he thought. He might come across as too cool for school – it was a useful defence mechanism – but deep down he just wanted to feel settled. He was anxious about the next stage of life and what was going to happen to him after he finished college this summer. Maybe you always were anxious, if you hadn't known stability? He should be excited, thinking about art college and where to go and what to discover and new people. But the thought of going away gave him a sharp feeling in the bottom of his stomach. Proper fear.

He thought today was the safest he had felt for a long time. He'd been amongst people he barely knew but they had formed such a strong bond. They all had each other's backs. It had been so special, and he'd wanted every day to be like that. Gentle and full of laughter and generosity.

It couldn't last though. He knew that. He knew by phoning Lizzy's family he had broken the spell, but he'd had to do it. She belonged with them. And Jack and Nat would be going back home at the end of the week. He couldn't just stay here for ever.

And he would have to decide what to do about his dad. The card was still in his pocket. He had got it out several times today. He kept thinking about how his dad must feel, all alone in prison. Wasn't prison enough punishment? You didn't have to lose the people you loved as well.

He had to see him, thought Harley. He wanted to, more than anything. It was deep down inside his DNA, the need. He wanted to see his father again.

36

Simon was sitting on the sofa in the half-darkness, the flickering television providing the only light. The tree was still in the corner but he'd turned the lights out as it got on his nerves, taunting him.

He hadn't shaved today and by this time in the evening the unfamiliar stubble on his face made him look slightly sinister. There was a bottle of red wine at his elbow and a plate of cheese and biscuits, untouched. He'd opened the wine once Cynthia had gone to bed out of respect for her, even though she had carried on insisting she didn't mind.

He'd phoned Mo and Lexi earlier, to make sure they were ok now Amanda had gone home. They were obviously fine, entrenched in a bar somewhere by the sound of it.

'Merry Christmas for tomorrow, Dad,' said Lexi. 'And we'll see you New Year's Eve. We'll be back in time.'

New Year's Eve, thought Simon. They always had a get-together. Open house for anyone who didn't have anywhere else to go. Would she be back by then?

'Great. See you then.'

He didn't mention Lizzy was missing. He knew the two of them would have been straight on the next plane, and he didn't want to spoil their holiday. And what could they do to help? Even he could do nothing. It was so frustrating. All they could do was wait, but the minutes dragged past.

'Dad!' Hattie bounded down the stairs and into the room.

Simon looked up at his daughter. She looked feverish. Excited.

'I've found her,' she said. 'I've found Mum.'

He jumped to his feet, looking behind Hattie as if Lizzy might be there. 'Where is she?'

'She's in Everdene. At that beach hut her friend owns. Caroline?'

'Is she OK?'

'I think so.'

'How did you find her?'

Hattie looked uncertain. 'Me and Luke put a thing on Facebook.'

'Facebook?' Simon frowned. 'So the whole world knows?'

'It doesn't matter, Dad. We found her.'

'Does she know? Have you spoken to her?'

'Not yet.'

Simon grabbed Hattie and hugged her fiercely. 'Thank God,' he said. 'Thank God.'

Luke came into the room. When he saw Hattie in Simon's arms, he panicked.

'What's happened?'

'We've found Mum,' said Hattie. 'Someone answered the Facebook thing. We've found her. She's at her mate's beach hut.'

'Well, what are we waiting for?' asked Luke. 'How long will it take us to get there?'

'Slight problem,' said Simon. 'I'm well over the limit.'

The irony of the situation wasn't wasted on him. He'd have done anything to get in the car and drive to Lizzy, but there was no way he'd risk it.

'We can get gran to drive?' suggested Luke.

'She's fast asleep. And she hasn't driven for a while – I don't think it's a good idea.'

'I think,' said Hattie. 'We should get up first thing and drive down. Surprise her.'

'But what if . . .' All sorts of possibilities were going through Simon's mind. A secret lover. That would be awful. 'What if she's *with* someone.'

The twins stared him.

'She's not with anyone, Dad,' said Hattie kindly. 'Not in that way, anyway. She's just taking some time out.'

Simon sank down on the sofa and put his face in his hands. To his horror, he found he was crying. It was only now he knew she was safe that he could face up to the fear he'd been feeling. The fear and the guilt and the worry.

The twins rushed to sit either side of him.

'Dad!' Hattie hugged him tight. 'Dad, it's ok. Mum's ok.'

'I love her so much,' said Simon, embarrassed but unable to control what he was feeling. 'I don't know what I'd do without her.'

'Well, don't tell us,' said Luke, patting him on the shoulder. 'Tell Mum, you 'nana.'

37

Jack looked at Nat's stocking, which the two of them had laid out carefully at the end of the bed earlier, trying not to think of Fran embroidering the golden N onto the red felt. He had better fill it now. He felt weighted down with the need to sleep: the long journey yesterday and the walk and the wine today and all the emotion were catching up with him. If he fell asleep and Nat woke before he did, the wail of disappointment when he found an empty stocking didn't bear thinking about.

He took the parcels out from the bottom of his suitcase. He stuffed his in first: little things, of the kind he had once enjoyed. A kaleidoscope, a box of Lego, a silly dinosaur hat. Not big stuff, because he didn't want Nat to be spoilt. Just fun stuff that they could do together. He never resented time spent with his son.

Then he took out the last parcel from the bottom of his case.

He held it in his hands, feeling her through the paper, knowing that when she had wrapped it she had been thinking about Nat opening it, knowing she wouldn't be there.

He'd come to the hospice one day, when they knew she hadn't got long. She was sitting up in bed, her head swathed in the ruinously expensive Hermès scarf she'd ordered off eBay. It was emerald green and covered in parrots.

'If I can't treat myself to one now, then there really is no point,' she'd said cheerfully when she'd clicked the 'Buy Now' button.

She was surrounded by a pile of books she had ordered from the local bookshop. They'd hand-delivered them in a big cardboard box. She'd got hold of wrapping paper too: navy blue with tiny silver stars, in thick soft paper that felt almost like fabric.

And ribbon, because she never gave a present that wasn't swathed in ribbon with big fat bows and trailing ends. Her presents always looked important, as if they might change your life.

'I've chosen,' she told him, in that voice that brooked no argument, which she was using more and more, 'a book for every Christmas and every birthday for the next few years. For Nat.' Her eyes were bright, with determination, morphine and tears. 'They're the books I loved, that meant a lot to me, and told me how to live my life.' She held up *The House at Pooh Corner*. 'I mean, who tells it better than Winnie the Pooh? You'll have to read them to him, to start with.' She shuffled through the other books on the bed. 'There's everything he'll need. Roald Dahl. Harry Potter . . .'

She trailed off and they looked at each other. Jack swallowed down a lump. Would Nat one day take comfort from the one thing he shared with Harry: the lack of a beloved mother? At least Nat would have his dad.

'I'm doing tags,' she told him, 'with the date on, so you know what order to give them in. Otherwise all they say is *Love from Mummy*. The books themselves will tell him all I want him to know.'

'Jesus, Fran,' said Jack, thinking that if she was trying to kill him, make his heart stop from the horror of the impending grief, she couldn't have done a better job.

'I just can't bear the thought of him not having something from me to open.' She was making herself busy now, not looking at him, taking her scissors and snipping through the paper: she cut the straightest lines of anyone he knew.

'No,' he said. 'But whatever I get him will always be from both of us.'

She looked up at him and frowned, then pointed her scissors at him.

'You're to meet somebody else,' she said. 'I won't have you moping. I won't mind, you know. It's better than thinking of you being on your own.'

She held his gaze for a few moments, again with that stern look. If she'd had any eyebrows, they'd have been raised for extra emphasis. And then she carried on cutting as if she hadn't said something utterly devastating and unthinkable.

He slid the parcel into the top of the stocking and laid it back on the bed by Nat's feet. It was satisfyingly heavy, as all good stockings should be. Nat stirred slightly and Clouseau raised his head for a moment, then the two of them settled back down.

There was a little round clock in the kitchenette and Jack saw its hands were both vertical. Midnight. It was Christmas Day. He opened the door and stepped outside. The clean cold air made him blink and gasp, whipping away the last remnants of wine. He was enveloped in darkness: as inky black as night should be, but for a small cluster of stars above him, diamonds falling from a broken necklace.

If she was here, he would scoop them up and give them to her. He would give her the diamond stars. He would give her everything.

'Merry Christmas, Fran,' he said into the darkness. For she was Christmas: red velvet and gingerbread and snowflakes and candlelight. He turned his face up to the sky and to his surprise his face was not wet with tears; his heart did not feel cracked in half like a broken church bell.

He might not feel happy, he thought, but he felt hope.

38

Harley was starting to get cold on the beach when his phone finally rang.

'It's Hattie.'

'Hi.'

'Dad says it's too late to drive down now as he's had too much to drink to drive. Not that he's drunk,' she added hastily, 'but he's worried he'll be over the limit. So we're going to leave first thing in the morning.'

'That sounds like a great idea.'

'We should be with you by about midday. I just need you to make sure she doesn't go anywhere. If she knows we're coming she might take off somewhere else. We need to talk to her.' She paused. 'Tell her how much we love her.'

'To be honest,' said Harley, 'I'm pretty sure she knows. I think it's herself she doesn't love very much right now.'

'Who *does* love themselves?' said Hattie. 'I don't. Right now I *really* hate myself.'

'Don't hate yourself,' said Harley. 'You sound great to me.'

He surprised himself rather with his boldness.

There was a little pause. Then Hattie spoke again. Her voice sounded pleased. 'Thank you. You do too.'

Harley felt a little jolt of pleasure. 'She's been amazing to me, you know. I don't know how I'll ever repay her.'

'You won't have to,' said Hattie. 'I know Mum. She won't expect anything. She'll just be pleased that she could help. Oh God, I'm making her sound like Mother Teresa. She's not. Sometimes she drives us nuts.'

'That's what good mums do. Drive you nuts.'

'I guess so,' said Hattie. Then, in a very small voice. 'Can you give her a hug from me? Without telling her it's from me?'

Harley laughed. 'Of course.'

'And you'll call me if she tries to go anywhere, won't you?'

'I am not letting her out of my sight,' he promised.

When Hattie rang off, Harley sat on the step outside for a moment. Part of him was longing to go back inside and tell Lizzy he'd spoken to Hattie. But he didn't want to spoil the surprise. It was important for her family to come and find her. It would prove to her how much they cared.

They should train you at school, he decided, in how to look after your mum. Mums always seemed to know everything and to be invincible, but deep down they needed looking after just as much as anyone.

Frozen to the bone, he went back inside. Lizzy was about to climb up her ladder to get into bed.

'I'm exhausted,' she admitted. 'See you in the morning. And sleep in one of the proper beds. Now we've got Caroline's blessing.'

He laughed, and then leaned in to give her a hug, silently passing Hattie's love to her, and she seemed surprised and pleased by the gesture even though she had no idea of its hidden meaning.

Then he sent Hattie a message to say her mum had gone to bed. A moment later he added an 'x'.

At Pepperpot, Hattie blushed slightly. She hesitated, then started texting again.

So what are you doing there, then? You said it was a long story.

I've run away too.

OMG. What are you all like?

I know, right? We're a right bunch.

He went on to tell her about his mum, and also Jack, and how they'd all become friends.

They carried on texting for hours. It was as if they had known each for ever. They talked about music, and art, because they were both doing Art A level, and the places they wanted to go most in the world (him: Copenhagen; her: Berlin). It was like having a new best friend, but there was something else too. A bond. A sense of belonging.

Hattie hoped she wasn't imagining it. She hoped it wouldn't vanish as soon as she saw him. She didn't know what to expect. He didn't have any pictures of himself on his Facebook page. She'd gone through hers, madly deleting anything that made her look like a dork or an airhead. Especially the photos of her and Kiki dressed up to the nines in sunglasses, pouting.

In the end, she had to say good night.

I need to sleep if we're going to get up tomorrow and come down.

Ok. Looking forward to meeting you.

Me too. Thanks for everything.

xx

CHRISTMAS DAY

39

'Mum! He's been!'

The triumphant cry started Leanne awake. She could see him in the doorway, River in his blue and white flannel pyjamas, holding his stocking aloft with a wide smile.

'Oh, wow,' said Leanne. 'He actually came?'

'Yeah.' River came running over to her side of the bed. 'Can I open it?'

She held out her arms, marvelling at the excitement in his little face as he thrust the stocking at her.

'For God's sake, what's the time?' growled Tony, his voice thick with sleep and last night's drink. He hadn't been pleased that she'd been out most of the day yesterday. She'd had to make it up to him, with wine and attention and fake affection.

Leanne peered at her phone.

'Six.'

'Tell him to go back to bed.'

'But it's Christmas.'

'It's too early. Tell him Father Christmas will take his toys away.'

'I can't say that.'

Tony leaned over and grabbed her arm. 'It's too early.'

For a moment, she froze. She hoped River couldn't see what was happening in the dim light. Tony's fingers were tight. She tried to pull away but he squeezed harder. She knew how strong he was; how much time he spent in the gym doing weights. He could lift her up with one hand – he'd done it, in jest, more than once. But she had always sensed it was a warning. She shut her eyes for a moment, trying to figure out what to do. Who to please. How not to cause a scene.

'You're right,' she whispered. 'I'll put him back to bed. I'll be right back.'

Thankfully he released his grip. She slipped out of bed and picked up River.

'Hey, buddy,' she whispered. 'It's too early yet. We won't be able to stay awake if we get up now. You get back into bed for another hour.'

'How come I can't open my stocking! It's right here,' River protested as she carried him back to his bedroom.

She winced at the shrillness in his voice. 'I know. But Mummy's too sleepy right now. Just one more hour, OK? We'll put the stocking back on the end of your bed. It will still be here when you wake up.'

She slid the little boy back under his duvet. He was a good kid. He always knew when to obey and when to push it. She guessed it was something he'd learned, just as she had. With a bit of luck, he would go back to sleep. She tucked his rabbit in under the bedclothes and he hugged it to him. There was a little frown furrowing his brow, and she felt sad that Christmas morning was off to a bad start.

'Good boy,' she whispered, patting him. 'The sooner you go back to sleep the sooner you can wake up.'

He gave her words careful thought, then wriggled down under his duvet and shut his eyes as tight as he could. She shut her own eyes for a moment, faint with growing unease, sick with the suspicion that they were no better off than they had been the day she'd had the phone call from the police station. She had vowed to keep her boys safe and to give them a better life. She had failed them both. They were trapped. She was going to have to be wily. Strategic. And lucky.

Tony grinned at her as she came back to bed.

'Hey,' he said. 'Come and see what Father Christmas has brought *you.*'

Her stomach turned over. The thought of him repulsed her. She looked at his smirk and felt sour with distaste. She could still feel the pressure from his fingers on her arm.

She bent over him, letting her hair tickle his cheek, blocking her nose to the scent of his cologne mixed with the night's sweat. He insisted on keeping the heating on so it was like a hothouse. Once she had thought it a luxury. Now it stifled her. 'I'll just go to the bathroom,' she whispered in his ear, keeping her tone teasing, laden with promise.

'Hurry up,' he said, reaching out a hand and caressing her thigh. It was all she could do not to shudder. She ran a finger suggestively down his cheek, then with her spare hand behind her lifted her phone off the bedside table.

As she left the bedroom she looked back to see Tony roll over and bury his face in the pillows. With any luck he would fall back to sleep. He was terrible in the morning: it took him ages to wake up properly. She watched the rise and fall of his back for a moment, saw his breathing slow down, then crept to the bathroom.

She looked at her face in the mirror. She was shocked. Her eyes were hollow, her cheeks sunken, her bleached blonde hair lank. She knew she hadn't slept well, but it was anxiety that made her look like this. The stress of walking on eggshells.

'You know what you have to do,' she whispered. 'Don't let yourself down. Don't let yourself and Harley and River down.'

She had to do it now. She knew if she ignored what had happened this time, she would ignore it again. And it would get worse.

She did not want to be with a man who wouldn't let a little boy get up at six o'clock on Christmas morning.

She did not want to be with a man who squeezed her arm so tightly it left bruises when she'd come home later than expected the day before.

She did not want to be with a man who had made her own son run away.

She was scared. Her insides were churning as she made a plan in her mind. She was going to have to hold her nerve. She went to the loo, brushed her teeth, making all the noises Tony would expect to hear.

She opened the lid of the laundry basket and took out yesterday's clothes: hers and River's. She pulled hers back on, then gathered their toothbrushes and toothpaste. She went out onto the landing and listened. She could hear Tony; that heavy breathing bordering on snoring that confirmed he'd nodded back off. River was quiet, so maybe he had too. She crept down the stairs, freezing every time a floorboard creaked, then tiptoed into the kitchen, holding her breath as she opened the door, praying it wouldn't make a noise. She grabbed her handbag off the back of the kitchen chair, stuffing her phone inside it, then checked that her roll of money was still in the secret pocket. Then she popped open the dryer, pulling out all the clean clothes. Luckily it was a mixed load – some of River's tops and jeans, two of her sweatshirts and some cargo pants, and a selection of underwear. She weeded out a couple of Tony's T-shirts but folded the rest neatly and stuffed them into a big canvas shopping bag, squashing her handbag on top.

The kitchen clock said twenty past six. She hurried into the hall, opened the front door and put the shopping bag in the porch. She put her sheepskin boots next to it, and River's little blue Crocs, the ones he went to the beach in. They'd be the easiest to get on quickly. There was no time for laces. She went back into the hall, checking both their coats were hanging on the hook, ready to grab.

She eyed the stairs, biting her lip. Her mouth felt as if she had tried to swallow a handful of sand. She could bottle it now; carry on with Christmas Day as normal. Give herself some time to figure out what to do. Surely that made more sense? Running away with only the clothes they stood up in was impractical. And what were the chances of her getting away—

Stop it, she told herself. You cannot stay a minute longer with a man who makes you feel like this. Every day that passes is a day closer to something bad happening. She remembered the conversation with Harley, the desperation in her son's voice, his fear. He had left them because he was afraid of what might happen. It was up to her to bring them all to safety.

She crept up the stairs and back into River's room. He was in that deep slumber that comes from falling back to sleep in the morning. She would have to wake him and urge him to be quiet; if she picked him up asleep she risked him waking and making a noise. She shook him gently.

'Hey. River. Wake up, baby,' she whispered. 'You must be quiet though.' She put a finger to her lips as he opened his eyes and looked at her. 'Shhhh. We mustn't wake Tony. Or he'll be cross.'

River nodded, solemn. He understood that threat. She hated herself for it.

'Come on. I've got something to show you. A surprise.' She felt mean, luring him with a lie, but she'd make it up to him. 'I'm going to carry you downstairs, but you need to be super quiet.'

She picked up his stocking from the end of the bed, held it up conspiratorially, ssshh-ed him again, then scooped him up. He put his arms round her neck and snuggled in, and the warmth of him made her melt. She had to get away. For River and Harley. For both of her boys.

She pulled him in tight as she went down the stairs, hoping she wouldn't slip on the wood. She made it to the bottom, grabbed their coats, pulled open the front door, piled the stocking into the top of the big bag that was waiting, then started to slide River's Crocs onto his feet, all the time wondering whether there was something she had forgotten.

'Where do you think you're going?'

She looked up and Tony was standing at the top of the stairs, in a T-shirt and pants. She jumped up and slammed the front door shut between them, rammed her feet into her boots and grabbed the bag.

'What's the surprise?' asked River. 'Where's Harley?'

'We're going to go and find him, right now,' she said, her voice strangled with terror.

She ran up to the path to her car. Thank God it was parked behind Tony's and not the other way round. She opened the back door – she never left the car locked – and pushed River in. She'd stop in a bit to strap him in, once they'd got away. She pushed the carrier bag in after him, grabbed her handbag, fishing inside for the keys, pushing aside all her handbag detritus, scrabbling, longing for the relief of her fingers closing round the furry pompom of her key ring. River was on the back seat, his knees drawn up to his chin, staring out of the windscreen with a look of horror.

She turned. She saw Tony in the doorway, holding up her keys.

'Looking for these?' he asked.

She stood up. *Stay calm.*

'Harley phoned,' she said. 'He's in trouble.'

She leaned into the car, took River's hand, pulled him towards her as gently as she could, put her handbag over her shoulder. They could leave the rest.

'Mmm-hmm,' said Tony, his eyes stony with disbelief. 'So why have you taken River's stocking? I thought we were all going to open it? Together?' He started walking towards her. 'You better come back inside.'

She only had a split second to choose whether to stand her ground or run. Her eyes flickered to the houses either side. Should she scream? There was nothing to scream about. He'd done nothing. Yet.

'Hold on tight to me,' she whispered to River. Then she pulled him from the car and turned and ran, as fast as she could. Tony couldn't chase her through the town in his pants. People would be up early – it was Christmas morning. They'd be opening their curtains, looking out.

She didn't have much time. Two minutes at the most before Tony managed to pull on his jeans and his shoes and come after them . . .

She tried to remember her breathing from when she used to train at the gym, but already her lungs felt serrated. Down to the end of the road, round the corner – should she take the short cut down the passage that led to the harbour? No, she should stay in full sight of the public eye. She didn't want to be cornered if he caught up with her. On and on she pounded, wishing she could see someone to ask for help, but there was no one outside. Not yet. She reached the end of the next road and swerved right, not daring to look back. She was at the shops now – maybe the newsagent would be open?

It wasn't. She ran past it, feeling despair rise as that hope vanished. At the end of this road was the harbour. She knew where she could head. Where she could hide.

Everywhere she looked, Christmas lights were twinkling. Everyone in Tawcombe liked to outdo each other with their displays: Santa and his reindeer, huge illuminated Christmas trees and snowmen, all blinking on and off in shades of red and green and gold. It was slightly surreal in the silent mist of early morning. She didn't pass a soul.

She slowed for a moment to look behind her. She couldn't see Tony. She'd managed to keep him off her trail. She turned right, towards the sea. There was a limit to the number of places she could hide before her escape route turned to water...

She was stumbling now, along the harbour front, too exhausted to run. The harbour was almost empty; most of the boats had been lifted out of the water and were stored in the car park until winter ended. The water looked as black as squid ink and she shivered.

At last she got to the Spinnaker. There was a narrow passageway that needled in between the pub and the fudge shop next door. In the summer, the air would be thick with the scent of boiled cream and sugar mixed with the salty sea. Now, it just smelt dank. There was a gate at the front of the passageway that to a passerby would look locked. But she knew from working at the pub that it wasn't; that there was a trick with the latch and you could get in, if you knew how.

She put River down, panting, and fiddled with the latch, her fingers clumsy on the cold metal. There! It was open. She grabbed River and pulled him through the doorway, shutting the gate, sliding the lock back into place until it clicked. Tony would have no idea how to get inside.

She darted into the passageway, following it between the cold damp walls to another gate at the back. She slid open the bolt and went through to the car park behind the pub. There was a high fence barricading off the area where the bins were kept. That would be the perfect hiding place until she could get help. If Tony came down to the harbour, he would have no idea where they had gone. With luck, he would think they had doubled back earlier.

She put River down again, then realised he didn't have his shoes.

'Oh dear me,' she said. 'We left your shoes.' She kept her voice light and sing-song so as not to betray her panic as she lifted him up again.

'Where are we going?'

'Let's go behind here. Shhh. We'll have to keep quiet.'

'Are we hiding?'

'Sort of.'

'Why? Where's my stocking?'

'Just shush for a minute.' She pulled out her phone to call Harley. Please let him answer.

'Mum?'

Her heart leapt with joy at the warmth of his sleepy voice.

'Baby?' She whispered as loudly as she could.

'Oh, Mum! Merry Christmas. My God, what time did River get you up?'

'Baby, I need your help. I've left him. I've left Tony.'

'What? When?'

'We just did a runner. Me and River. I haven't got any of our stuff. He's got my car keys.' Her voice was starting to crack. She choked down a sob.

'Mum. Stay calm. I'm coming to get you. Right now. Where are you?'

'Round the back of the Spinnaker. By the bins.'

'It's OK – I'll be about fifteen minutes. Tops. Just stay there.'

'You know where the car park entrance is? You have to go down the road at the back.'

'Course I do. It's gonna be OK, Mum. Love you.'

'Love you too,' she murmured, but he had already hung up.

'I'm cold,' said River.

'I know, baby. Harley's going to be here any minute. We need to keep quiet.'

'Are we hiding from . . . Santa?' River looked confused.

'No, darling. Never Santa. Now come here. Come inside my coat and keep warm.'

Hurry, hurry, hurry, she urged Harley in her mind. The sea air was cold on their skin. Oh God, she thought, what have I come to? Hiding amongst the wheelie bins at half past six on Christmas morning? Why hadn't she seen Tony's true colours sooner? She was a fool. As soon as Harley got here, she would sort everything out. She'd done it before. She could do it again.

40

Years of listening out for the twins meant Lizzy was fine-tuned to crises. As soon as she heard Harley's voice on the phone she knew there was a problem. She was immediately awake. By the time she'd scrambled out of bed and over to the edge of the platform he was standing at the bottom of the ladder looking up.

'What's up?'

'It's Mum. She's run away from Tony. I need to go and find her. Will you take me?'

Lizzy was already scooping up her clothes.

'I don't even know why you're asking.'

'We need to hurry. She's with River. They'll be freezing.'

'Give me two minutes.'

She slid down the ladder and put an arm round his neck, kissing him swiftly on the cheek as she passed him.

'Merry Christmas, chicken. I just need a wee and to do my teeth.'

'Merry Christmas . . .' He nodded, looking slightly shell-shocked.

'It's going to be OK,' Lizzy called behind her, disappearing into the bathroom.

Harley grabbed his shoes. His heart was pounding but he felt exhilarated. He had to get to his mum before Tony did. The slimy creep would either talk her back round or—

He didn't want to think about 'or'.

Two minutes later Lizzy emerged. 'I'll just get my car keys. I've left them at the top.' She ran for the ladder and scrambled up it. Harley rushed for the bathroom while she looked for them, mentally working out how much time they had already lost.

Soon they were outside in the cold air. It was still dark and damp, the air filled with icy droplets. They stumbled over the sand, running as quickly as they could.

'Sorry,' gasped Lizzy, unable to run as fast as Harley. 'I'm not very fit.'

'It's OK,' he said, wishing for wings. At least ten minutes had gone since his mum had called. His phone went again. He pulled it out of his pocket.

'Where are you?'

'We're on our way, Mum. We're nearly at the car. Ten minutes. Hang on.'

Leanne hung up the phone. She was crouched down with her arms round River as he sat on her lap; she didn't have the strength to stand up and hold him, but her legs were screaming with the effort. He was starting to shiver, poor lamb. As was she, but she thought perhaps it was shock and fear as much as cold.

'Harley's on his way, baby,' she said, and River's face lit up. He adored his big brother. How on earth could she have put Tony first over them?

'I *thought* I heard a little mouse.' A shadow fell over them. Leanne looked up, instinctively pulling River tighter. It was Tony, leering down. 'Look what they put out with the rubbish. I thought you'd be here. I knew you couldn't have just vanished. And everyone brought up in Tawcombe knows the trick with the gate.'

'Leave us alone.' She looked up at him, trying to keep her voice steady.

'I deserve an explanation, don't you think?'

He nudged her with his foot, pushing her off balance. She reached out a hand to stop herself falling over. She felt the gravel cut into her hand and her wrist give way. She bit her lip to stop herself crying out.

'It's over, Tony. Leave us *alone*.'

'Over? After everything I've done for you? I don't think so.'

Leanne shut her eyes and squeezed River tighter. She knew whatever she said would be wrong. That Tony wouldn't listen to reason.

'You'd been put out with the rubbish when I picked you up. I put a roof over your head: you and your kids. That mouthy little brat who looks at me as if *I'm* something he's stepped in. Most people would be grateful. I think you all need reminding who you were, what you were, what you *are*—'

'Tony, I'm grateful. I really am. But it's over. It's not working.'

'What isn't?' He frowned. 'I mean, who paid for all that stuff in his stocking, huh?'

He pointed at River.

She raised her eyebrows and looked at him. 'Father Christmas?' she said meaningfully.

He threw back his head and laughed. River frowned.

'What's so funny, Mum?' he asked.

'What's so funny?' Tony crouched down so he was level with River. 'There's no such—'

'Don't you dare.' Leanne stood up. 'You say one more word and—'

'What?' Tony stood too, and they were now face to face, River beneath them, bewildered.

Tony shut his eyes as if to calm himself, then opened them, his smile sweet, his voice even sweeter.

'Tell you what. Let's go back so River can open his stocking, shall we? Then you and me can talk things over while he plays with his new toys.'

He sounded perfectly reasonable. Calm.

'Can we, Mum?' River tugged at her hand, excited by the prospect.

Leanne sighed. It wasn't fair to put River through this. He should be opening his stocking.

'Come on,' Tony wheedled. 'This is daft. It's Christmas. How about I make you breakfast? Coffee. Bacon and egg.'

How did he do it? Flip from bully to charmer in the blink of an eye? He was smiling at her, all sweetness and light. She swallowed, her mouth dry. The trick now was to play along with him. Play for time.

'You're right,' she said. 'I'm sorry. I over-reacted.'

Tony reached out his arms to River. 'I'll carry you back. You've got no shoes, silly billy.'

River giggled.

'No,' said Leanne, picking her son up herself and tensing for an altercation. 'I'll carry him.'

As she pulled River into her, she saw a car pulling into the car park. Please, please let it be Harley. The car pulled to a halt as Tony turned, and Harley jumped out of the passenger side.

'Oh, look, here comes the cavalry,' sneered Tony.

Harley ran over to them. 'Mum. Are you ok?'

'I'm fine.'

'Come on.'

Tony stepped towards him.

'I think you'll find your mother's coming back home with me. Father Christmas has been, hasn't he, River?'

River nodded, wide-eyed and uncertain. Leanne stood, frozen. She didn't want trouble. She didn't trust Tony not to cut up rough. How was she going to negotiate this? They all looked at each other: Tony looming threateningly, Leanne stock-still, Harley tense and ready to spring, River confused and looking round at everyone.

Lizzy got out of the car and walked over to them.

'Oh,' said Tony. 'Now I'm really worried.' His tone was mocking.

Lizzy looked at him. And frowned. Then the light of recognition came into her eyes.

'Oh. It's you.' She gave a laugh. 'You don't change, do you?'

Tony looked wary. 'What?'

'Tony Brice.' It was a statement, not a question. 'Long time no see.'

'I'm sorry – do I know you?'

'I wouldn't expect you to remember me.'

Tony looked at Lizzy with a twisted smile, as if to say there was hardly anything memorable about her. 'Sorry, love. No. Unless . . . do you work at the Co-op?'

Lizzy drew herself up and fixed him with a knowing look.

'You might remember my friend. Caroline.'

He still shook his head, but he wasn't looking so confident now.

'Well, I've obviously got a better memory than you have,' said Lizzy.

'I really don't know what you're on about.' His voice was uncertain.

'Oh, I think you probably do,' she said. 'The Ship Aground? Summer of 1987? You took my mate home with you. I wanted her to go to the police. But she wouldn't. For some reason she thought it was all her fault.' Then Lizzy turned to Leanne. 'Come on – let's get you both in the car.'

To Harley's amazement, Tony stood to one side as they all walked to Lizzy's car and got in. Leanne strapped River in and did up his belt. She sat back, closing her eyes, shaken. They watched as Tony strode off across the car park, his fists clenched.

Lizzy looked at Leanne in the rear-view mirror. 'You OK? Shall we go?'

Leanne nodded.

Lizzy slammed the car into reverse, backed it up at high speed and did a really impressive three-point turn, tyres squealing, as Tony looked on in amazement.

'Woo hoo!' whooped Harley. 'Check you out!'

'The twins gave me an Advanced Driving course,' grinned Lizzy, 'for my fortieth birthday,' and she changed the car into first and gunned it out of the car park, Tony flattening himself against the pub wall as they drove past.

Tony Brice, Lizzy thought. A leopard never changes its spots.

41

1987

'You know the rules, girls. I'm trusting you not to break them. I'll be back at the weekend. Phone me at six o'clock every evening.'

Caroline's mother was putting the last of her bits and pieces into her bag. The two girls tried to look solemn and responsible, as if they weren't counting the seconds to her departure. They had done it. They had actually managed to convince Mrs Keane that they were grown up enough to be left alone at the beach hut for a few days. They were seventeen, nearly eighteen. They'd finished their A levels. They were almost officially adults.

Caroline's younger brother was furious at not being allowed to stay too. There had been one awful moment when Mrs Keane had thought it might be a good idea. But common sense, thank goodness, had prevailed, and Andrew was going back with her. She and Mr Keane and Andrew would be driving back to Everdene again on Friday evening.

Today was Tuesday.

They had three days on their own. Three days of sun-drenched unsupervised bliss at the beach hut. It was the beginning of August and temperatures were soaring. Everdene was filling up with visitors, and the Ship

Aground was filled with bronzed and intoxicated young people pumping money into the video jukebox.

Mrs Keane left a crisp twenty-pound note on the Formica-topped table. 'I shall expect change,' she told them. 'Don't go mad.'

'We won't,' they promised, mentally calculating just how many cans of Red Stripe they could buy. They could live on Frosties and Pot Noodles and chips. Food was of no great interest to them. Alcohol and lip gloss and a packet of Marlboro were all they needed.

As soon as Mrs K had disappeared from sight at the end of the row of huts, Caroline and Lizzy jumped up and down, hugging each other. Lizzy pressed 'play' on the cassette player plugged in to the corner of the living area. Belinda Carlisle belted out.

To them, heaven really *was* a place on earth.

The two girls were completely different. Lizzy was small, but with the advantage of the long wild curly hair that most girls were having to pay big money for. Caroline was taller, with a netball captain's physique. She had a packet of Sun-In ready for her transformation from mousy to Madonna-blonde.

By mid-afternoon, when the sun was still high in the sky, they were outside on the veranda surrounded by everything they needed, stretched out in bikinis. They had managed to get the cassette player as far as the door, its lead stretched across the beach-hut floor. Lizzy was reading a magazine; Caroline was painting her toenails.

In front of them, the sea shimmered, Rimmel-blue, but they had no intention of going swimming after all the effort they had made. They sipped at their cans of lukewarm lager. It was a waiting game. They were languid with heat and freedom and anticipation. Their eyes honed in on every person that passed the hut. No one escaped unjudged. As the sun started to go down, they were a little peeved that a bevy of Brat Pack lookalikes hadn't paraded past, clamouring for their attention.

'We'll go to the Ship Aground,' said Caroline, inspecting her newly blonde tresses in the mirror, slightly alarmed by the brightness but telling herself it would tone down by the time her mother got back.

'We need change for the video jukebox,' said Lizzy, rooting through her purse, ever the organised one.

By seven, they were in stone-washed denim skirts and tank tops – yellow for Lizzy; pink for Caroline – eyes rimmed in bright blue eyeliner, lips slick with pale pink gloss. They walked along the beach in a cloud of cigarette smoke and Giorgio Beverly Hills that Caroline's mum had foolishly left behind in the bathroom.

All eyes were on them when they entered the pub. Lizzy was under no illusions that it was her igniting anyone's interest. Caroline seemed to radiate on a higher frequency than usual, thanks to her blondeness, the freckles on her cheeks where the sun had kissed her and the lack of parental authority in any proximity. Two Tequila Sunrises increased her confidence even more. She was fizzing, laughing, talking, dancing. Lizzy didn't mind being in her shadow. She busied herself fetching their drinks, buying more cigarettes from the machine, choosing the next song to boom out, the bass line tuning in to everyone's heartbeat, steady, relentless, heavy with promise.

'Hungry Like the Wolf' was playing as Tony Brice walked in. The girls had seen him before at the pub: he was from Tawcombe, a rich family who owned half the town. He loped amongst the crowd, lean, predatory, eyes flickering over limbs and faces, a vulpine smile on his lips. Lizzy saw him before Caroline and shivered with a premonition. She wasn't a fanciful girl given to any sixth sense: it was common sense that told her what was coming.

Local bad boy meets out-of-town good girl. A timeless tale. Only Lizzy suspected this was going to be no sugary John Travolta/Olivia Newton-John unravelling. She wondered about the chances of getting Caroline out of the pub before the inevitable happened.

Zero.

She had to admit Tony Brice was dazzling, his hair even blonder than Caroline's, his caramel skin stretched taut over his muscular limbs. He wore a black jacket with the sleeves pushed up over a white mesh singlet and skin-tight jeans. He walked straight up to Caroline and offered to buy her a drink.

The locals looked at each other, knowingly, and Lizzy wondered what it was they knew. The girls from Everdene smiled at him, hooked their arms round his neck and kissed his cheek, the lads raised their glasses, but they all melted away from him. Caroline, in comparison, was agog, halfway down yet another lurid blue cocktail, her eyes rolling around like the balls on the billiard table, totally in Tony's thrall, unable to see beyond his beauty.

Lizzy approached the two of them, wondering how she was going to handle this.

'We should probably be heading back,' she said brightly. 'We promised your mum we wouldn't be late.'

Caroline swayed as she laughed, poking at her drink with her straw. 'Mum's a million miles away.'

'No. She's coming back tonight, remember?' Lizzy stared at her, willing her to get the message.

'Lizzy. She only left today. How pissed are you?' She leaned against Tony and cackled. Tony put his arm round her and smiled. Lizzy's heart sank as Caroline rested her head on his shoulder. 'You go back if you want,' said Caroline kindly. 'You don't have to wait for me.'

'I'm going to the loo before I leave,' she said. 'Wanna come?'

Caroline was always needing the loo, so she hoped she would get the hint. But Caroline wasn't letting Tony out of her clutches. 'I'm fine.' The insistent bass line of INXS tumbled out of the jukebox. 'Oh my God, I love this!'

She thrust her glass at Lizzy and grabbed Tony's hands, beginning to dance with him. Lizzy shut her eyes in despair. She'd never seen Caroline this drunk. It was obvious she wasn't going to co-operate. She watched in horror as Caroline's movements became more and more suggestive. Everyone was laughing. It was made worse by the fact that Tony was a good mover. He was lithe and slinky next to her, but his smile said it all.

'You should rescue her before it's too late,' someone whispered in Lizzy's ear.

From what? she thought. After all, maybe Caroline should have a bit of fun? It might boost her up a bit. She'd convinced herself she'd flunked her A levels and was dreading results day. Maybe a night with Tony Brice would give her something else to think about.

Lizzy bit her lip. It was agony, sitting in the pub like a spare part, playing gooseberry, but she wasn't going to leave her mate. She sidled up to a group of youngsters, edging next to a girl with a smiley face who looked friendly enough.

'Can I stand with you for a bit?' she asked. 'I want to keep an eye on my friend.'

Caroline and Tony were kissing now. They'd moved away from the centre of the room. Her back was up against a pillar.

'Good luck,' said the girl. 'Tony's a right one. He's only in Everdene because he's been through all of Tawcombe.'

Oh God. Lizzy was powerless. She knew she couldn't drag Caroline out by the scruff of her neck. She'd just have to hang on. Hopefully she would get so drunk she'd pass out. Maybe she should give her another Blue Lagoon with an extra vodka in it to hasten the process?

Stop worrying, she told herself. Caroline's just letting her newly blonde hair down. She doesn't need you policing her.

Lizzy danced for a bit with her adopted friend, who introduced herself as Suzette, pumped some more money into the jukebox, then when she couldn't bear it any longer nipped to the loo.

When she came out, Caroline and Tony were nowhere to be seen.

It was midnight before she got back to the hut. She'd waited until everyone had been thrown out of the pub, then for the gaggles of chattering youngsters to fade away, hoping against hope that Caroline would reappear. She had no idea where she had gone or how she could get in touch with her. She felt slightly sick from too many cocktails and too much sun that afternoon.

In the end she went back to the hut, digging in the

sand for the key tin, and let herself in. She slopped onto the sofa, pulling the scratchy old tartan rug over her, determined to wait up.

She must have dropped off because she was startled awake by someone trying to get in. She jumped up and opened the door. Caroline fell on her neck, sobbing. She looked terrible. Her make-up was streaked down her face and her hair was wild. She had lost her shoes and her feet were bleeding.

'Oh my God,' said Lizzy. 'What happened?'

Caroline stumbled in and fell onto the sofa. Lizzy came to sit next to her, putting her arm round her shoulders.

'I went back to Tawcombe with him. There was a whole bunch of us. He was kissing me all the way there in the back of the car.'

'Who drove?'

'I don't know. One of his mates. We went to his house – somewhere down by the harbour. He took me up to his room. He wanted me to . . .' She couldn't say the words. 'I thought I wanted to. When we were in the pub I thought, he would be the perfect person. To do it with. For the first time . . .' Caroline was overcome with sobs.

'It's OK,' said Lizzy, stroking her back. 'Tell me what happened.'

'When it came down to it, I just didn't want to. He wasn't very nice. He was really rough. I told him I didn't want to and he kept saying I did, that I was being a . . .' She could hardly get the words out. 'A prick tease. He said everyone in the pub could see I was desperate.' She paused, her face crumpled up with the memory. 'I had to fight him off. I was screaming at him and kicking him. He said I was crazy. He pulled me down the stairs and

322

threw me out of the door.' She slumped onto Lizzy, her arms round her neck. 'I've been so stupid.'

'You have not,' said Lizzy staunchly, smoothing Caroline's hair back from her face. 'This wasn't your fault, Caroline. You made a bit of a mistake, that's all. He was a bully. How did you get back?'

'I had to walk back. My stupid shoes gave me blisters.'

Her feet were bleeding. It had taken her nearly two hours to walk back from Tawcombe. She was freezing and shivering and still drunk. Lizzy wrapped her in a blanket, made her a cup of cocoa and then tucked her into bed. She didn't say anything to Caroline, but she felt a little relieved by the outcome of the story. To begin with she had feared much worse. Caroline's ordeal had been awful, of course it had. But thank goodness Tony hadn't forced her into anything. Lizzy's fists clenched as she thought of his arrogant, self-satisfied face. His conviction that he was the best-looking bloke in the room. Well, being good-looking didn't count for anything if you behaved like that.

The next day Caroline didn't wake until four o'clock in the afternoon. Lizzy didn't mind. She spent the day lying on a blanket on the sand reading Judith Krantz, escaping to another world entirely, a glamorous world which nevertheless had its own set of problems. Billy Ikehorn's complicated love life absorbed her completely, in between rehydrating with glasses of lemon squash and eating three packets of Skips, letting the salty sweet crackers melt on her tongue.

When Caroline finally dragged herself out of bed, pale and red-eyed, Lizzy made her spaghetti hoops on toast. Caroline didn't really want to talk about what had happened the night before. She was very subdued. Twice a tear trickled onto her plate.

'Come on,' said Lizzy at six o'clock. 'Let's go and have a drink.'

'There is absolutely no way I'm going anywhere near that place ever again.' Caroline looked horrified at the prospect.

'Why not?' said Lizzy.

'Everyone will laugh at me.'

'No they won't.'

'Yes they will. They were all watching. They saw me dancing with him. And snogging him.' Caroline wailed in despair at the memory. 'And have you seen my hair? It looks terrible. It's gone sort of orange.'

This was true. Yesterday it had looked glamorous. Today it looked brassy. Lizzy looked at her friend: gone was the confident creature of the night before. In her place was a wreck. But wrecks could be restored to their former glory, inside and out.

'You've got to get back on the horse,' she said. 'Come on. Go and have a shower, wash your hair again, put on some make-up. We've only got two nights left before your parents come back down. We are not going to let Tony Brice ruin our fun.'

'What if he's there?'

'Then he'll wish he wasn't,' said Lizzy, her voice grim.

Caroline chewed the inside of her cheek. 'I'm sorry I left you,' she said. 'Last night, I mean. I should've asked if you wanted to come too. Or at least asked if you minded. I'm a horrible friend.'

'Just don't do it again, ok? I was really worried.'

'Oh God, was I really drunk? I must've been, because I can't face anything to drink now.'

'You must have had about six cocktails. I stopped counting.'

Caroline mimed being sick. 'I'm pretty sure I was sick outside his house.'

'I hope he stepped in it,' said Lizzy, then laughed. 'Was it blue?'

Caroline joined in laughing. 'Oh God. Blue sick. All over the pavement. What would my mother say?'

Lizzy put on a posh, disapproving voice. 'Oh darling, really.'

They went back to the pub. Lizzy found the people she'd met the night before, including Suzette who'd been so kind to her. They chatted and drank a couple of bottles of beer and agreed to meet on the beach the next day to play cricket.

Suzette gave Caroline a hug. 'We've all fallen for it,' she told her. 'Tony Brice is a rite of passage in Everdene. He might look like a god and think he's a god but he's a total creep. He only comes over here because no one in Tawcombe will put up with his behaviour. You'll get over it.'

Caroline did get over it. By the time her parents returned she was her old self again and she and Lizzy spent the remaining two weeks having the time of their life, making new friends, swimming, dancing, laughing – the holiday was just as it should be.

Caroline forgot all about Tony Brice. But Lizzy didn't. She never forgot anybody who had done something to hurt people she loved. Even thirty years on.

42

Jack thought his heart was going to burst as Nat opened his stocking. The little boy was quite literally shaking with excitement as he opened the parcels. He was touched by how carefully he unwrapped everything, examining it thoughtfully, smiling up at his dad in appreciation.

'How does he *know*?' he kept asking. 'How does Santa know that's what I wanted? And he's even brought a ball for Clouseau!'

'He's a clever old thing,' said Jack, and then handed him the final parcel, a lump in his throat. 'This,' he said carefully, 'is from your mum.'

Nat looked down at it, nodding, then peeled the paper away.

Dr Seuss. *How the Grinch Stole Christmas*. Jack shook his head with a smile. Talk about a message from beyond the grave. Fran knew him too well. She'd known he would be Grinchy.

'What's it about?' asked Nat.

'It's about a grumpy old creature who steals everyone's Christmas presents. Because he doesn't like Christmas. But in the end, he does. Because everyone loves Christmas, right?'

'Read it.' Nat thrust the book at him.

He pulled his son onto his lap, relishing the very bones of him, feeling the softness of his blond hair against his own cheek. He read him every word, conscious that this was a reminder from Fran to Jack to enjoy himself, despite what had happened. She was a monkey, he thought. But today, her memory was bearable. It was the gentle throb of a healing wound, not a sharp pain.

He looked up as he heard voices outside. He was surprised: it was still early, only just eight o'clock. Clouseau pricked up his ears. Nat's face lit up.

'Let's go and see who it is!'

Nat scrambled off Jack's knee and ran to the door. Jack followed in his wake. Outside he could see Harley and Lizzy. And behind them, Leanne and River. He felt the fizz of surprise; like a tiny silver fish leaping in his belly.

'Happy Christmas everybody!' Nat stood on the step, waving his arms. 'Happy Christmas!'

'Happy Christmas, darling,' said Lizzy, and gave him a hug. 'Hey, Jack. We've got extra guests for lunch. Do you think we can manage?'

Jack came down the stairs with a smile. 'Definitely.'

Leanne looked at him with a wry shrug. 'Gatecrashers. What can you do?'

'Well, luckily I've got a piece of lamb big enough to feed an army.'

'And we bought every sausage in Lidl,' said Lizzy.

Jack looked up at the sky. It was a mild morning, with a blustery breeze. If he wrapped up warm he could cook everything on the barbecue. It would taste so much nicer.

'Shall I make everyone a coffee?' he said.

'Actually,' said Lizzy, 'that would be great. Could you

look after Leanne and River? Me and Harley have got an errand to run.'

'Have we?' said Harley, doing a double take.

'Yep,' said Lizzy.

'Sure,' said Jack. 'I've got apricot Danish pastries, if anyone's interested.'

'Oh my God,' said Leanne. 'My favourite.'

'Good,' said Jack. 'We aim to please.'

He held out an arm to usher her into his hut. Nat and River clomped up the steps behind her, already engrossed in conversation.

'Right,' said Lizzy to Harley. 'Come on.'

Harley followed Lizzy's determined stride back down the beach to the car park. Ten minutes later, they were driving down a row of Victorian houses in Tawcombe set in a sinuous curve above the harbour.

'Most of these are flats,' said Harley. 'But he's got one of the whole houses. He inherited it from his parents.'

Lizzy could see why Leanne might have been drawn to the lifestyle Tony had to offer. The house was large and gracious, in grey stone, probably built as a holiday home for an eminent businessman in the 1800s. She pulled up on the road outside.

'Sure you want me to come with you?' Harley asked. 'Only he might get nasty if he sees me.'

'Let him,' said Lizzy. 'Tony Brice needs to learn that he can't bully people.'

Harley followed her up to the front door. He felt anxious. It was all very well, Lizzy saying Tony needed to learn, but he didn't want to see his nasty side. Not on Christmas morning.

Lizzy pressed on the doorbell, undaunted. After a few

moments, Tony opened the door. He looked red-faced and dishevelled.

'What do you want?' he scowled, then saw Harley. 'What are you doing here?'

'We've come to pick up some things,' said Lizzy, polite. 'Most importantly, River's stocking. I think it's here? And a few clothes to keep everyone going. Until we can collect it all.'

She smiled brightly. Tony stared at her. He was turning everything over in his mind, working out what to do, how to react.

'Harley knows where everything is, so he can give me a hand.'

'He's not coming in here,' growled Tony.

Lizzy crossed her arms with a sigh. 'It would be so much easier if you co-operated.'

'Who the hell are you, anyway?'

'I told you. You brought my friend back here, remember? You threw her out when she wouldn't give you what you wanted. Made her walk home in her bare feet.'

Tony shook his head as if to indicate he had no idea what she was talking about.

'I imagine it probably happened a lot so you're having trouble remembering which one she was. But don't worry. The police can help jog your memory.'

'The police?'

'Assault is assault. Even after all this time.'

'I never touched her.'

'Oh, I think you did.'

Harley could see the odious man trawling about in his memory bank, trying to locate the incident, trying to work out the implications.

'You better come in,' he said eventually. 'You've got five minutes to get what you want.'

'It'll take as long as it takes,' said Lizzy sweetly, breezing past him. 'Come on, Harley. You get River's stuff and I'll get your mum's.' She produced a roll. 'I've brought bin bags.'

It took the two of them about a quarter of an hour to gather most of the things River and Leanne would need. They trooped back down the stairs with bulging bags. Tony was in the hallway, arms crossed, glowering.

'Stocking?' said Lizzy.

'It's still in the back of her car.'

'OK. We'll fetch it on the way past.'

He put out a hand to stop her as she headed for the door. 'I'm guessing . . . that's the end of what we were talking about earlier?'

'Well,' said Lizzy. 'It's not up to me. It was my friend you assaulted. But if I were you I wouldn't give Leanne any trouble. Or Harley.'

They stared at each other for a moment. Harley shifted awkwardly, his heart beating, not quite sure of the dynamics of this exchange. All he knew was that his admiration for Lizzy was growing by the minute. She was fierce.

Then Tony nodded.

'There'll be no trouble,' he said.

'Excellent. Merry Christmas.' Lizzy gave him her brightest smile and swept out. Harley followed her, and they headed for the car, swinging the bags into the boot. Harley nipped back and got River's stocking and the rest of the stuff from the back seat of Leanne's car, then laid it carefully on Lizzy's back seat.

'Bloody hell,' said Harley admiringly as they drove off. 'You don't take any prisoners, do you?'

'Nope,' said Lizzy, then gave a shudder. She was having flashbacks to the Ship Aground, Caroline and Tony dancing to INXS. The smell of Marlboro and sticky cocktails. Tanned skin, white teeth.

Harley was slightly in awe. When he'd first met Lizzy, he'd thought she was a cosy, comfy, mumsy type. She was far from it.

She was a ninja.

His phone chirruped. He looked at it. There was a text from Hattie.

We're just leaving. Merry Christmas xx

He texted back,

Merry Christmas xx

and looked sideways at Lizzy, wondering what she would say when they all turned up.

43

By midday, Harley and Jack were standing outside the two adjoining huts, wrapped up in their coats and hats. River and Nat were playing football and Clouseau was desperately trying to join in, to their great mirth. Jack had fired up the barbecue that he'd found in a cupboard in his hut, and the coals had just reached the perfect temperature.

'This is going to be so much better cooked on here,' he said, throwing the butterflied leg of lamb he had brought down onto the rack. A delicious spicy aroma hit the air as the hot grill seared its lines into the skin. 'This has been marinating for three days, so it should be super tender. We can add the sausages right near the end.'

'This is the craziest Christmas lunch ever!' Harley said to Jack, handing him a beer. 'Man. We should trademark this.'

'We're just a bunch of waifs and strays, really.' Jack took a swig.

'It's Lizzy who's brought us together,' said Harley. 'Imagine if she hadn't turned up? We'd all be sitting on our own feeling sorry for ourselves.' He chewed his thumbnail. 'Can you keep a secret?'

'Well, I don't know,' grinned Jack. 'Try me.'

'Her family are on their way down.'

Jack gave a whistle of surprise. 'OK...' He grimaced. 'Is she going to like that?'

'She told me last night she was going to go home after lunch. I think she's missing them.'

'They can't be that bad. She's not the sort of person who attracts bad people.'

'No.'

Harley looked awkward and Jack realised that perhaps he had been tactless.

'So what's the deal with your mum?' He tried to sound casual.

'She's left the guy she was with. Thank God. I just hope she doesn't go back to him. I don't think she will...'

Jack put a hand on his shoulder. 'She's lucky to have you, mate. You've got her back.'

'I have to, don't I? After what my dad did.'

'You don't have to *be* your dad. You know that, right? You get to have your own life.'

Harley took a swig of his beer. 'I need to figure out a few things first.'

'Sure. And remember – you don't need to figure it all out straight away. Take your time. And if you ever need someone to talk to...'

Harley touched his beer bottle to Jack's. 'Thanks.'

Jack prodded at the meat, then flipped it over. It gave a satisfying sizzle.

'I feel like a different person here,' he said, looking up at the bright blue sky. Above them a cluster of clouds tinged with gold, as if applied by the most patient gilder, hovered next to the sun.

'It's not like this every day,' said Harley. 'There's a *lot* of rain.'

'I don't mind rain,' said Jack.

Standing here in the winter sunshine, wielding his barbecue tools, wearing a striped apron that Lizzy had dug out for him over his coat, he felt like himself again for the first time in a long time. Clemmie had phoned him earlier, to say Merry Christmas, and had sounded suspicious.

'You sound like your old self,' she said. 'What's going on down there?'

'A lot of fresh air,' said Jack. 'And some headspace.'

'Well, good,' said his sister. 'Mum and Dad send lots of love. And a hug for Nat.'

There was a purity to the realisation, a massive sense of relief mixed with optimism. It seemed it was possible, however fleetingly, not to be weighed down by grief and responsibility. He wanted to wallow in the realisation; to lie down and wriggle around with joy. But he had Christmas lunch to cook.

Next door, Leanne laid the table ready for the most impromptu Christmas lunch any of them had ever known. She managed to make it look festive despite the lack of accessories. It was surprising what you could do with an artistic eye, and just laying the table properly gave it a ceremonial air. The cutlery gleamed and the glasses glittered in the candlelight – luckily they hadn't run out of tea lights. Lizzy was boiling up mounds of peeled potatoes to make the mash, which would go with both lamb and sausages, and frying up onions for onion gravy. And then there would be a big bowl of peas. That was it.

'This is definitely the way forward.' Lizzy declared. 'Normally I'd be juggling chipolatas and sprouts and stuffing balls and having a nervous breakdown.'

'Oh, I love all of it,' said Leanne. 'I could spend hours faffing about with decorations.'

'I think the key,' said Lizzy, 'is to do the bits you enjoy and sack off the rest. Here, have one of these. Jack made them.'

She thrust a plate of canapés at her: crostini topped with toasted goat's cheese and walnuts and drizzled with truffle honey. Leanne took one.

'Oh my God,' she said with her mouth full. 'These are amazing.'

'He's a bit of a foodie, I think,' said Lizzy.

'He seems lovely.' Leanne took another, avoiding Lizzy's eye, feeling her cheeks go pink. 'Thank you for this morning, by the way. I don't like to think what would have happened if you hadn't turned up.'

Lizzy leaned back against the kitchen work surface and helped herself to a crostini.

'Be kind to yourself,' she said through the crumbs. 'Don't beat yourself up for falling for the wrong man.'

Leanne sighed. 'I'm a fool. I was completely taken in. I need to dig a bit deeper next time, before I throw myself into it. But it's tough. At the time, it seemed like the easy option.'

'So what will you do?'

'I don't know. We need to find somewhere to live, for a start. Which will be really tricky at this time of year. Especially as I don't have a proper job.'

'Listen,' said Lizzy. 'I'm going to talk to Caroline. Ask

her if you can stay here while you sort yourself out. I'm sure she'll say yes. They really only use it in the summer.'

'Would she really?' Leanne looked amazed.

'I think so.' Lizzy wasn't going to go into details, but she was pretty sure her friend would step up when she heard the story. After all, reaching out to help Leanne was the best kind of retribution for the way Tony had treated Caroline all those years ago. Revenge was an ugly motive, but this gesture had a simplicity and a generosity to it that Lizzy was sure Caroline would respond to.

She wiped her hands on her apron and went to strain the potatoes. The truth was she was anxious to get lunch over and done with. Now she had made her mind up to go home, she wanted to get on the road. It was the first time ever she had woken on Christmas morning without her family and she was missing them. She wondered what they were doing. She knew the food would have arrived, so they wouldn't be starving. But would they have a clue what to do with the turkey? They'd better cook it properly or they'd get food poisoning...

She laughed at herself. She had gone back to her default mode. Worrying about them all. But that was what she did. Looked after them. They were her family. She felt a pang that made her stomach swoop with longing. She wanted to see them. Feel them. Listen to the twins' ridiculous nonsense; feel Simon's stubble on her cheek; scrumple up all the wrapping paper from their presents and put it in the fireplace.

She poked her head out of the hut where Jack and Harley were sharing a beer in front of the barbecue.

'How are we doing? Ok if I mash the spuds?'

336

Jack gave her a thumbs up. 'Nearly done. I'll put the lamb on a plate to rest while the sausages finish.'

Just before one, they all assembled round the table, River and Nat sitting on piled-up cushions next to each other, already the best of friends. Half a dozen people who barely knew each other. Half a dozen people with their stories and their baggage, their mistakes, their broken dreams, their tragedy, their dilemmas, all stuffed into a little beach hut by the sea. The sun streamed in through the window, lighting up their faces. Jack opened a bottle of champagne and they all raised their glasses in a toast, even the little ones who had been given the tiniest splash.

'Merry Christmas!'

'Merry Christmas!'

'Mewwy Cwithmath!'

And they all fell upon the food – the platter of pink lamb with the charred edges and the caramelised sausages and the mashed potato that was the consistency of double cream and just fell off the spoon.

Before he sat down, Jack went outside for a moment, pretending to check the barbecue, but really to take in a deep breath. Christmas was ok. He had survived. More importantly, Nat was having the time of his life: fresh air and seaside and new friends. He could never have predicted that this was the day they were going to have. He'd imagined something quiet and reflective, with just the two of them pottering about and chilling. Not mucking in with this motley crew who were already worming their way into his affections. He went back inside and saw Leanne look over at him, patting the back of the chair next to her. 'Come and sit down,' she mouthed over the hubbub. He hesitated for just a moment. He could sense more change on the horizon. Then he watched as she leant over and helped Nat cut up his sausage. He swallowed, then strode across the room and pulled out his chair to sit down.

Harley watched as Jack leant over and filled his mum's glass up with wine. Her eyes sparkled their thanks. She looked, he thought, a different person. All the strain had gone from her face, and she was laughing, properly laughing. He felt a profound sense of relief. There would probably be tough times ahead, but it would be just the three of them together, without the malevolent presence of Tony. They would figure it out. He would make sure of it.

And in the fullness of time, he would tell her his decision: to go and see Richie. He didn't want to upset her, but it was something he needed to do, if he was going to figure out who to be. The thought of seeing his dad after all this time gave him a strange cocktail of feelings. Uncertainty, excitement, but also a strong sense of looking forward to the future. His dad was out in a couple of years. He wanted him in his life. Not to upset the equilibrium, but to recalibrate it. His dad wasn't just someone who had made a massive mistake, he was a man who had taken his small son to see *Star Wars*. It was that man that Harley was going to see.

At the end of the table, Lizzy looked up at the clock. How soon could she escape? She wanted to do the bulk of the journey before it got dark. She hated leaving all her new friends, but she thought they would be ok without her. Somehow, she felt reassured that Harley and Leanne and River had Jack and Nat next door. Jack would make sure they didn't go hungry, at the very least.

Next to her, Harley glanced at his phone to see if there was a message from Hattie. Where were they? They should be here by now...

44

'Oh wow,' said Hattie as they came down the hill at Everdene.

The bay was preening itself in front of them, knowing it looked its best in the bright winter light, pale turquoise and shimmering, competing with the baby-blue sky for attention. The sea flaunted its waves while fluffy white clouds buffeted around the sky, like a pair of film stars parading around in ostrich feathers.

'I can see why she's come here,' said Hattie. 'Can we stay for a bit? I want to find rock pools.'

'I want to go surfing,' said Luke. 'Those waves are wicked.'

'Yeah, because you're, like, such a surfer.'

'I could learn!'

'Shhh, guys, come on. Don't wind each other up. Where's the car park?'

'Right there,' Hattie pointed. 'And there's Mum's car, look.'

They looked at her little Honda, parked in the corner all by itself. The car Lizzy beetled off to work in, took them to school in; zoomed to the supermarket, picked them up after a party, the radio tuned to Radio 2, which they all moaned about. The Wallace and Gromit air freshener. The piles of parking stickers she never cleared out.

They were all quiet for a moment. The car meant she really was here. Any minute now they were going to see her.

Hattie texted Harley.

We're here. Just coming to the car park.

He sent one back

Ok! We're still having lunch. But there's loads left.

Simon parked up next to the Honda and turned off the engine. 'Right then,' he said. 'Let's go and find your mum.'

His stomach was churning. He was afraid. Afraid that things had gone too far. That she wouldn't want to come back. That he had lost her, through his lack of care, by not noticing or appreciating either what she had done or what she needed. But then he looked at Hattie and Luke and he thought – no. She would never desert them.

Would she?

Lizzy had been careful to only have one glass of champagne with her lunch. Everyone was having seconds, and she longed for them to hurry up so she could bring out the pavlova and the black forest gateau she and Harley had bought. She didn't want to wish their lunch away, but now she had made up her mind, she was longing for home. And family. Pepperpot and Simon and Hattie and Luke. The things that made her *her*.

It had been wonderful though, her time here. And it hadn't been wasted. She had made a difference, she thought, in a small space of time. And she had made friends she wouldn't forget. The bond they had forged between them was unbreakable. It was going to be hard to leave them, but they had their lives to get on with.

And she had to set about rebuilding her own, with the new perspective she had found. She had the germ of an idea in the back of her mind, but she needed to talk it through with someone, and her gut told her that person was Simon. He knew both what she was capable of and what made sound business sense. It was, she knew, time for team-work, time for their marriage to play to its strengths for the foreseeable future, not be a victim of the tiny cracks. Everyone had cracks in their marriage at some point. It was how you chose to deal with them that mattered.

There was a knock on the door. She saw Leanne freeze in fear, wondering if it was Tony. And she saw Jack put a reassuring hand on her arm, as if to protect her.

'I'll get it,' said Harley, who was nearest the door. He jumped up. Everyone had stopped eating, and an awkward silence fell. Jack put a gentle hand on Leanne's arm and squeezed it. Then Lizzy noticed that Harley was grinning. Which was odd...

Harley opened the door. There was a cluster of people outside. Lizzy frowned – the light outside was too bright to see who it was.

Then they stepped into the room and her mouth fell open.

Simon. And Hattie and Luke.

She looked at Harley, who gave a gleeful shrug.

'Merry Christmas, Lizzy,' he said.

She pushed back her chair and stood up, her heart thumping. Everyone was looking at her.

'Lizzy.' Simon walked across to the table in three strides and took her in his arms. As he enveloped her she breathed him in. That familiar scent, of the aftershave she bought him for his birthday, their detergent on his clothes, his shampoo. Him.

'You're crazy,' he said. 'And we're sorry. We're so sorry about the tree. About everything.' He squeezed her so tightly she could hardly breathe.

'*You're* crazy,' she laughed. She looked at Harley. 'Is this why you've been skulking about? Like a cat on hot bricks?'

'Busted,' he said.

'We put a shout-out on Facebook.' Hattie came forward and Lizzy reached out to her. Luke followed, and she pulled them in, the four of them in a big embrace.

'I saw it,' said Harley. 'I thought your family needed you back.'

Everyone looked at Lizzy. She said nothing for a moment, just looked from Simon to Hattie to Luke then Harley. Then she smiled.

'I do,' she said. 'I need my family back.'

She turned to the table. 'Everyone, this is Simon. And Hattie and Luke. This is Jack. And Leanne. And River and Nat...'

Hattie sidled up to Harley. 'Hey,' she said. 'I'm guessing you're Harley.'

He looked at her for a moment, taking in her blue and white hair and her yellow hooded parka and her combat boots. 'Yep,' he said, suddenly feeling shy and self-conscious.

'Dude,' Luke bounded up and grabbed his hand. 'You're the bomb.'

Hattie grinned and rolled her eyes. 'Luke's been watching too many *Breaking Bad* reruns.'

'There's masses of food left,' said Lizzy. 'Come on. Sit down. We can find some extra chairs.'

Jack had already vacated his place and went to plate up some more lamb. Leanne fetched glasses. The little hut was fuller than ever, full of chatter and explanation and hubbub.

Simon was holding Lizzy's hand and wouldn't let go.

'Come outside with me,' he begged. 'I need to talk to you.'

'What were you thinking?' Simon was coming down from the relief of seeing Lizzy and was alarmed to feel anger creeping in. 'We were out of our minds. We had no idea where you were.'

The two of them marched across the sand towards the sea, arms crossed, both defensive after the initial joy.

'I left a note.'

'Yes, but to just disappear like that. And then we found the prescription.'

'Prescription?' Lizzy frowned.

'For God's sake. The anti-depressants? Stuck behind the Indian menu?'

'Oh. Yes. But I wasn't going to take them. They dish them out for anything these days.'

'Yes, but we didn't know that. Imagine how we felt. We thought the worst. That you might be suicidal. The thing is, Lizzy, you knew you were all right. But we didn't. We imagined all sorts.'

'I'm sorry.' They'd reached the edge of the sea. The two of them stood at the water's edge, side by side, both wrestling with their points of view. 'But I just couldn't take it any more. It all closed in on me. Losing my job. The stress of Christmas. Not feeling like me any more. The twins about to go.'

'We could have talked.'

'There were other things. Things I didn't feel I could talk to you about. Things I didn't think were fair.' Lizzy's voice rose in indignation.

'I know.' Simon nodded. 'Amanda. And Mum.'

'Yes.' Lizzy looked fierce. 'I'd had enough. Of coming second. All the time. When—'

She stopped. She still couldn't betray Cynthia.

'Mum told me,' said Simon, quietly. 'Mum told me what happened. And how you'd kept it quiet. And . . . I think you're amazing. To be so kind and so loyal. When Mum didn't deserve your loyalty. I want to thank you so much.'

Lizzy sighed. 'It was awful, what she did. But she was so ashamed. And she was vulnerable. I knew if you found out, it would break her. That she would feel so much less in your eyes, at a time when she already felt lost.'

'Oh, Lizzy.'

'And then when bloody Amanda changed everything at the last minute, it was the last straw. I felt as if everything revolved around her, and nobody gave a stuff about me.' She gave a half laugh. 'Oh dear, that makes me sound selfish and self-centred and a total princess. I know it's not all about me. But it's been hard.'

'Lizzy. I know. And it's all going to change. From now on, you come first.'

'It's not about coming first,' protested Lizzy. 'It's about coming... somewhere.'

Simon took both of her hands and looked at her. 'You come first with all of us. You know that. We were all lost without you. We were nothing. Christmas meant nothing. And here you were, being wonderful Lizzy to a bunch of strangers, making *their* Christmas special.' His voice sounded strangled. He was going to cry. 'We don't deserve you. We know that. We let you down.'

'No, you didn't. It was one of those things. And I was being hypersensitive.' She started to laugh. 'I got arrested for shoplifting. In Inglewoods'. Can you imagine?'

'They sent you a voucher. To say sorry.'

'They did?' Lizzy looked surprised. 'Well, good. I shall spend it on something outrageous in the sales. Leather leggings. I think leather leggings are the way forward.'

She looked down at her not-very-long-or-slender legs and giggled.

Simon grabbed her, his wonderful wife, and pulled her to him. 'Let's go home,' he said. 'Let's go home right now and have the Christmas we should have had all along. You and me and Hattie and Luke. Mum's cooking it all for us. And then we can talk. About changes.

'I've had loads of time to think since I've been down here,' said Lizzy. 'About the future.'

Simon looked worried. What was she going to say?

'It's OK,' she laughed. 'It's nothing major. I just don't think I want to work for someone else, that's all. I want to try something new. My own business.'

'That's fantastic,' said Simon. 'I'm all for it.'

'I'm not going to be a millionaire overnight,'

'We know that money isn't everything,' said Simon.

'Time is far more important. Time and family and . . . the little things.'

'And I was wondering,' she said, sliding her hand into his as they turned and walked back up the beach, 'about getting a hut down here. They come up for sale sometimes. We could rent it out half the time so it pays for itself. Come down here for long weekends.'

'And Christmas?' he grinned.

'No,' she said firmly. 'I loved it, for a change, but Christmas belongs to Pepperpot.'

Harley and Hattie said goodbye on the veranda while Lizzy gathered up her things inside the hut.

'We always have a party on New Year's Eve,' Hattie said in a tumble of words before she could think about what she was doing. 'Well, not a party. Just a bunch of people come round and we play board games and charades. You could get the train up. We can fetch you from the station. You can stay at ours?'

She wanted to make it easy for him. She didn't want him to find an excuse. But she was terrified he would say no. That he didn't feel the same as she did: as if he had discovered someone new who felt like an old friend. Or perhaps even more than that.

'I'd love that.' He nodded and smiled, and she thought she had never seen anyone with eyes that kind of green, like the most beautiful glass.

She knew she had to go. But she reached out her hand, and he reached out his, and they did a kind of awkward funny clasp, squeezing each other's fingers. It said everything that was needed, about how they felt and what might happen.

'See you next week,' he said with a nod, then mimed putting a phone to his ear. 'We'll speak, yeah?'

'I'll call you.' She couldn't bear to tear her gaze away from his, but she knew that this moment was about her mum and what Lizzy needed, and that their time would come.

When the Kinghams had gone, the atmosphere in the hut felt a little flat. There was still a fraction of daylight left.

'I'm going to take the little guys for a walk with Clouseau before it gets dark,' said Jack. Sitting down after a boozy lunch would only make him introspective. 'Anyone want to come?'

'I'll come,' said Leanne. 'I definitely need some fresh air. Harley?'

He shook his head. 'I'm going to do the washing-up,' he said.

Leanne hugged him. 'It's almost like you're perfect,' she said.

'Well, who knew?' said Harley. He felt so happy. This was so different from the Christmas he had feared: one filled with tension and resentment. Washing up was a small price to pay.

As soon as the door shut on River and Nat and Jack and Leanne, Harley got out his phone and his father's Christmas card and typed the name of his prison into Google maps. It was just as he thought. Not a million miles from where Lizzy and Hattie lived. Sometimes, things were meant to be.

The Kinghams drove back in convoy. The twins went with Lizzy, to keep her company, and they played her their favourite new songs on their iPhones and fed her buttermints. They drove into Astley just before seven. The little town was quietly twinkling, its houses filled with people sleepy with food and overindulgence.

And when Lizzy walked back into Pepperpot Cottage, she felt her heart lift because there, in the living room, was her tree, strung with lights and sparkling in the corner, looking just as she had pictured it when she had bought the ribbon. Like their tree but better, the familiar ornaments dangling amongst the branches and making her heart ache with nostalgia.

In the kitchen the table was laid with a tartan tablecloth and candles flickering, and the most wonderful smell of roast turkey mingled with a Jo Malone pomegranate noir candle – Cynthia's present to her that she had decided to unwrap and light because it smelled of Christmas. There was an ice bucket with a bottle of champagne ready to open, a board groaning with cheese and fruit, the pudding on a glass cake stand bedecked with a sprig of holly.

Everything was perfect and just as it should be.

Cynthia was standing in the kitchen in Lizzy's apron, a little hesitant and unsure, conscious that she was one of the reasons Lizzy had run off.

'Have you done all this?' asked Lizzy. She must have done, because turkey didn't cook itself and tables didn't lay themselves and candles didn't light themselves.

Cynthia nodded.

'I hope you don't mind.' She was in Lizzy's space, after all, and she might not like it.

'Mind?' said Lizzy. 'It looks wonderful. And smells wonderful.'

'It should be ready in about half an hour,' said Cynthia.

'I had the twins text me when you were an hour away. So I could put the potatoes in.'

Her voice was shaky with nerves. Lizzy felt a flood of fondness for her. Simon had told her about Cynthia's pledge to stop drinking. What Cynthia had done was wrong, but her crime had grown into something that had got in the way of everyone's life. It had become bigger than the sum of its parts. They both needed to draw a line under it. Forgive. Perhaps not forget, but pull together, talk about things, find ways to help each other live the best life they could.

'Thank you,' said Lizzy quietly. 'I really appreciate it. And I'm glad you're here.'

'Really?' said Cynthia. She felt so unsure. Her confidence had taken a battering over the last few years.

'Of course,' said Lizzy, reaching out to her mother-in-law. 'You belong here. With all of us.'

And as Lizzy hugged her, Cynthia realised that all she had ever wanted was to belong, here in this house, and to be in the heart of the family. Maybe that was possible now, with her secret out in the open and her determination to change.

'I'm so glad you're back,' said Cynthia. 'They were falling apart without you.'

Lizzy looked around the kitchen and felt grateful that the isolation she had felt only a few days' before had vanished; that her sense of being let down and her anger and bewilderment had been replaced by gratitude for her family, and a new set of friends and most importantly a sense of peace.

Suddenly she felt as if she knew who she was again. Not the old Lizzy but a new Lizzy, with a fresh set of challenges and a new beginning, ready to take everyone else with her. For the twins would be facing changes soon too, and they would need her, not by their sides any more, but in the background.

And then she heard the soundtrack from *The Snowman* flooding through the speakers in the room next door, and she laughed and cried at the same time, because the others always teased her for wanting it on and this was their way of saying that Christmas belonged to her.

NEW YEAR'S EVE

45

'It happens every year,' said the woman in a brisk Princess-Anne tone. 'People buy them as Christmas presents and then panic. I always get one sent back, no matter how strictly I vet the purchasers.'

She handed Simon a small ball of pale pinky-gold fur. He took it carefully.

'I'll have to come and inspect your house. Make sure the garden is dog-proof and so on.' She looked at him sternly. She had short blonde hair, blue eyeliner and frosted pink lipstick. She was not to be messed with.

'That's no problem,' he said, and held the creature up to look at it. It stared down at him with bright inquisitive eyes, as if assessing him for suitability. It was like holding a real live teddy bear. The puppy's stumpy legs and plump feet were smothered in ringlets, and he had a black button nose planted in the middle of his face. And dear little ears at half-cock. Simon decided he would do whatever it took to take ownership of him. He knew it was the right thing to do. He'd been on Lizzy's iPad and looked at her search history. She'd mentioned Cavapoos several times over the past year, only Simon knew now he hadn't been paying enough attention. 'I can give you the cash right now if you like.'

'Subject to my approval.'

'Why don't you come tomorrow?' he said. He could ask the twins to get Lizzy out of the house.

'Eleven o'clock?' she suggested, and he agreed. He might struggle to get the twins up at that time on New Year's Day but once they knew why, they'd be out of bed in a shot.

'If everything is satisfactory, you can have him next week. His name is Marmalade.'

'Fantastic,' said Simon, and for a moment he felt overwhelmed with emotion. Marmalade would go a long way to making up for the prosaic slow cooker. It would be chaos for a while, but he thought that a puppy was just what Pepperpot needed to fill the hole that would be left by the twins. And he was in no doubt that Lizzy would agree. No doubt at all.

He left the house with his pocket and heart both considerably lighter. He looked up at the sky. The clouds were hanging low, bulging like hammocks with a heavy man inside. It looked like snow, he thought, and hurried to the car. He was fetching Mo and Lexi from the airport to come to the party. He was excited about seeing them. They were adults now, not children, but they were still kids to him. His kids. Part of his family. His wonderful muddle of a family. And tonight, they would all be together. He couldn't wait.

Hattie stood on the station platform. The wind was whistling along the line and the light was fading. The arrivals board said the train from Birmingham was running three minutes late. It was the longest three minutes of her life. She still couldn't believe he was really coming. She'd been convinced he would change his mind. It was probably a bit of an effort, coming all this way. And they didn't really know each other, even though they had been texting and FaceTiming all week.

Here it was. The dark-green engine slid into the station and drew to a smooth halt. Doors opened and passengers started spilling out, en route to their New Year's Eve destinations, clutching bottles of wine and bunches of flowers and sale bags. She scanned the crowds. She couldn't see him. Had he got out at Birmingham and got the train back to Devon instead of changing for Astley?

And then she saw him. At the far end. Long legs in faded skinny jeans, a pale corduroy jacket over a checked shirt, his hair touching his shoulders, a rucksack on his back. He strode along past everyone, lithe, unperturbed, not showing any sign of anxiety as to whether she would be waiting for him. He was so certain.

'Harley.' She stepped out in front of him and she saw his face light up and he dropped his rucksack then hesitated for a split second before putting his arms round her.

And as she looked up at him, she felt something ice cold fall on her face. Snow. It was snowing. Big flakes like goose feathers fluttering down, nestling in their hair and on their eyelashes. And Harley looked down at her and smiled.

'How did you arrange that?' he asked, his eyes crinkling up in delight, and their lips brushed, as gently as the snowfakes.

Oh, thought Hattie. *This feels like coming home.*

Later, as they walked back to Pepperpot Cottage hand in hand in the snowfall, Harley asked Hattie a question.

'I wondered if you'd do something for me,' he said.

'What?'

'I wondered if you'd come with me. To visit my dad in prison.'

'Oh,' she said, startled.

'You don't have to come in,' he said. 'I just want someone with me when I go. And to know there's someone waiting outside when I come out. I've made an appointment. For the day after tomorrow.'

'Of course I will,' she said, squeezing his hand. 'Of *course* I will.'

The New Year's Eve gathering at Pepperpot Cottage was turning into quite the party. Hal and his parents were coming, and Kiki and her family, and several of their neighbours and friends. Mo and Lexi were in charge of the dance-floor – they'd come back from the slopes with ski tans and all the latest tunes.

Lizzy had even swallowed her pride and invited Amanda. Somehow when you felt loved, it gave you the strength to be gracious, and she felt bad that Amanda's Christmas had been spoiled by her injury. Thankfully, Amanda had declined. But Lizzy felt a better person for it.

And for the party tonight she was experimenting with a new concept: her shoestring philosophy. It was the cornerstone of her business idea: organising parties and weddings on a tight budget. Keeping it simple was the key, and it was amazing how that made everything not only less expensive but less stressful. And yes, she might not make so much profit, but as she and Simon discussed, it was more about making people's dreams come true than fleecing them.

Tonight's theme was green and white, because that

seemed to represent a fresh start for her. It was easy to think of food – Thai green curry followed by key lime pie – and every vase in the house was stuffed with fronds of foliage and armfuls of white roses she had found nearly past their sell-by date in the supermarket.

And she'd bought herself a leopard-skin shirtdress in the sale at Inglewoods'. OK, so leopards weren't green, but as the hostess she was allowed to stand out. And she discovered, for the first time in a long time, that she wanted to, instead of shrinking into the corner unnoticed. Hattie had done her hair and make-up, and it was amazing what a pair of hold-you-in tights and a set of false eyelashes could do for your confidence.

'You look such a fox,' Hattie told her, and she felt a slight thrill at this new image. Not that she would be dressing like this every day, but it was good to know she could pull it out of the bag. She even felt confident next to Meg.

At midnight, they all stood in a circle and sang 'Auld Lang Syne'. She stood between Simon and Harley, her hands clasped in theirs, and she remembered, for a fleeting moment, the little beach hut that had brought about her transformation, and she imagined the sea breeze in her hair as the countdown to midnight began.

'Happy New Year, everyone,' she cried as Big Ben rang out over the speakers. 'Happy New Year.'

And happy new me, she added to herself.

46

Jack was putting the finishing touches to his hot buttered cider. He dipped the rim of two white mugs in lemon juice, then sea salt. He mixed up fresh butter and maple syrup and seeds from a vanilla pod, then gently heated some local cider in a pan with a pirate-dark rum. The cider then went into the mugs to be topped with the butter.

He breathed it in. It was delicious and dark and potent and seductive.

He had already decided he was going to stay another week at the beach hut. He had phoned his client, who had been only too delighted to let him stay on. Work could wait. He realised he hadn't taken any proper time off this year at all. Work was his drug, his anaesthetic, the thing that stopped him thinking, but this week had taught him that there was more to life. And, somehow, it was important to him to spend New Year's Eve down here, to make some resolutions. And changes.

He'd been helping Leanne and Harley organise their life over the past week. It was difficult to set things up during the holiday, but they had made lists of possible accommodation and jobs for Leanne to apply for. He'd talked to Harley about going to art college to do a foundation.

Harley had left his application too late for this year, but he could apply after he finished his exams. Jack talked to him about what university had done for him, how it had opened his mind and introduced him to a whole new world and set of people, and Harley felt more confident about making his own way.

'I've been too scared to leave Mum,' he'd told Jack.

'Your mum,' Jack had said, 'will be fine, and she won't want you to put your life on hold for her.'

River and Nat had fallen asleep on the sofa, a big bowl of spiced popcorn in front of them. The four of them had played games all evening, and now the clock was edging towards midnight.

'Let's go outside on the veranda,' he said to Leanne, holding the two cups. She nodded and picked up her sheepskin coat.

They crept outside and shut the door, sipping on their cider. It was a local tradition for the towns along the coast to let off fireworks on New Year's Eve in a chain. Jack looked at his watch.

On the stroke of midnight the first of the fireworks burst into life along the bay.

'I organised them just for you,' said Jack, and Leanne laughed, leaning against him.

No man had ever made her feel like this before. Usually she would be writhing with insecurity, in a maelstrom of self-doubt, probably starving herself. But here she was, glugging a drink with half a pound of butter in it.

The fireworks were joined by another display further down the coast.

'Oh,' gasped Leanne. 'They're even more beautiful than the others.'

'Sure you're not getting cold?' asked Jack. 'Come here.'

And he put his great big arm round her and pulled her into his chest. And she felt so warm and safe, and filled with a feeling that was ... she wasn't sure. It was so unlike the usual feeling she got with men, which was spiky and fizzy and electric but very unsettling. This was gentle and sweet but intoxicating in its own way, rather like the syrupy, buttery cider she was drinking.

She looked up at him and he was looking down at her, and he gave a slow smile that had a hint of secrecy and mischief about it. And she pushed herself up on her tiptoes, on impulse, and pressed her lips gently against his, and the kiss tasted of apples with an undercurrent of dark rum.

They pulled away from each other, a little startled and a little breathless, laughing.

'I know,' said Jack, 'that we've both had a tough time. And neither of us are probably ready for something big.'

'It doesn't have to be big,' said Leanne. 'But maybe it will be? I don't want to hurt you, though.'

'It's OK,' said Jack. 'I'm fragile, but I won't break.'

Leanne laughed. 'I'll be gentle with you.'

She shivered in delight as he ran his fingers through her hair and cupped the back of her head in his big hands, looking into her eyes.

'I'll be gentle with you too,' he promised. 'I want you to know that. And if it comes to nothing, I'll still be your friend.'

She didn't answer, because she couldn't speak. Her heart felt so filled up with emotion, a brand new feeling that quietened all other thoughts.

And Jack thought – it's OK. He finally accepted that he

wasn't betraying Fran by allowing himself this moment. Loving someone didn't mean you had to be miserable without them for all eternity if you lost them. They didn't own your happiness. You could go on to feel things with someone else.

Behind them, the lights in the beach hut glowed blood-orange and the violet sea murmured her approval and the night air fluttered around them, a little jealous of the kissing. Another volley of fireworks exploded further down the coast but went unseen as both Jack and Leanne had their eyes shut firmly tight . . .

47

'*Hello. I'm Lizzy Kingham. And welcome to Shoestring Events, a new concept in planning your wedding or party or special event. The ethos of Shoestring is to make sure that every penny is money well spent. With over twenty years in the business, I have the experience and the contacts to make sure that your event is the most memorable it can be without you having to spend a fortune. It's not about cutting corners: it's about having the confidence to know what's important, what makes an impact and what will matter when you look back on your special day . . .*'

Lizzy gave a wide smile, then breathed out for a moment.

'How was that?'

'That was great, Mum.' Luke put down the iPad he was using to film her. 'You're a natural.'

'I can't remember everything.'

'It's OK. We can do it in sections. I told you. I'll edit it together.'

Lizzy looked in the living-room mirror. She was wearing her leopard-skin dress again, but with less make-up and low heels. She looked stylish but business-like. Like the kind of woman who started up her own business and collected a knighthood twenty years later. OK, so maybe she was getting a bit ahead of herself with the knight-hood, but she felt excited by her idea.

She felt sure it was a completely original concept: a party-planning business that was not about ripping off customers, but about teaching them how to tailor what they wanted so they could afford it.

The twins were helping her set it up. Luke was doing her website and the promotional video. Hattie was doing the artwork. Simon was putting out feelers for suitable premises. Lizzy was going to get in touch with all the suppliers she had used over the years and talk about how they could get on board with the concept.

Even Cynthia was doing her bit. 'I can do all your admin and accounts,' she offered. 'I used to do it for Neville. It'll keep me out of trouble. And you won't have to worry that I'm on the fiddle. That's the biggest worry about running your own business.'

Lizzy had forgotten about the wealth of insider know-ledge her mother-in-law must have. She had been closely involved in Neville's business, and was shrewd. She would be invaluable while Lizzy was setting up. It wasn't prac-tical to imagine she could do it all on her own.

'Thank you, darling,' she said to Luke now.

She frowned. The twins were looking at each other, giggling. 'What is it?'

Had she said something silly, or got lipstick on her teeth?

'Look behind you, Mum,' said Hattie.

Lizzy turned. In the doorway stood a tiny puppy. A mass of rose-gold curls with fat feet and a quizzical expres-sion.

'Hello,' said a squeaky voice from the other side of the door. 'My name's Marmalade and I've come to live here.'

Lizzy put a hand to her mouth. She couldn't speak.

'Well, go on,' said the voice. 'Come and say hello. Don't be shy.'

Lizzy looked at the twins, then back to the puppy just as Simon appeared in the doorway, grinning.

'He's your belated Christmas present,' he said in his normal voice.

'Oh my God,' said Lizzy, and rushed over, dropping to her knees. Marmalade looked at her with his head on one side and she scooped him up in her arms, kissing the top of his head. 'Oh my God, he's beautiful. Thank you. Thank you so much.' She held him up to look at him more closely. 'Oh, you little darling. Welcome to the mad house. Welcome to Pepperpot Cottage.'

About
VERONICA HENRY

Veronica Henry worked as a scriptwriter for *The Archers*, *Heartbeat* and *Holby City*, amongst many others, before turning to fiction. She won the 2014 RNA Novel of the Year award for *A Night on the Orient Express*. Veronica lives with her family in a village in north Devon.

Find out more at www.veronicahenry.co.uk

Sign up to her Facebook page
www.facebook.com/veronicahenryauthor

Or follow her on Twitter @veronica_henry
and Instagram @veronicahenryauthor

Discover Your Next Read from
VERONICA HENRY

The perfect mix of family, friends and delicious food.

Laura Griffin is preparing for an empty nest. The thought of Number 11 Lark Hill falling silent – a home usually bustling with noise, people and the fragrant smells of something cooking on the Aga – seems impossible.

Feeling lost, Laura turns to her greatest comfort: her grandmother's recipe box, a treasured collection dating back to the Second World War. Inspired by a bit of the old Blitz spirit, Laura finds a new sense of purpose and her own exciting path to follow.

But even the bravest woman needs the people who love her. And now, they need her in return…

A gorgeous escapist read for anyone needing a hug in a book.

Hunter's Moon is the ultimate 'forever' house. Nestled by a river in the Peasebrook valley, it has been the Willoughbys' home for over fifty years, and now estate agent Belinda Baxter is determined to find the perfect family to live there. But the sale of the house unlocks decades of family secrets – and brings Belinda face to face with her own troubled past . . .

'A delight from start to finish' Jill Mansell

Everyone has a story . . . but will they g the happy ending they deserve?

Emilia has just returned to her idyllic Cotswo hometown to rescue the family business. Nightingale Books is a dream come true for book-lovers, but the best stories aren't just within the pages of the books she sells – Emilia's customers have their own tales to tell

There's the lady of the manor who is hiding ε secret close to her heart; the single dad lookin for books to share with his son but who isn't quite what he seems; and the desperately shy chef trying to find the courage to talk to her crush . . .

And as for Emilia's story, can she keep the promise she made to her father and save Nightingale Books?

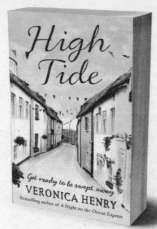

Pennfleet might be a small town, but there's never a dull moment in its narrow winding streets . . .

Kate has only planned a flying visit to clear out the family home after the death of her mother. When she finds an anonymous letter, she is drawn back into her own past.

Single dad Sam is juggling his deli and two lively teenagers, so romance is the last thing on his mind. Then Cupid fires an unexpected arrow – but what will his children think?

Nathan Fisher is happy with his lot, running picnic cruises up and down the river, but kissing the widow of the richest man in Pennfleet has disastrous consequences.

Vanessa knows what she has done is unseemly for a widow, but it's the most fun she's had for years. Must she always be on her best behaviour?

Return to Everdene Sands, setting for the *The Beach Hut*, and discover secrets, love, tragedy and dreams. It's going to be a summer to remember . . .

Summer appeared from nowhere that year in Everdene and for those lucky enough to own one of the beach huts, this was the summer of their dreams.

For Elodie, returning to Everdene means reawakening the memories of one summer fifty years ago. A summer when everything changed. But this summer is not all sunshine and surf – as secrets unfold, and some lives are changed for ever . . .

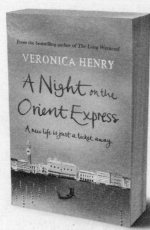

A new life is just a ticket away

The Orient Express. Luxury. Mystery. Romance.

For one group of passengers settling in to their seats and taking their first sips of champagne, the journey from London to Venice is more than the trip of a lifetime.

A mysterious errand; a promise made to a dying friend; an unexpected proposal; a secret reaching back a lifetime. As the train sweeps on, revelations, confessions and assignations unfold against the most romantic and infamous setting in the world.

A short break can become the holiday of a lifetime

In a gorgeous quay-side hotel in Cornwall, the long weekend is just beginning . . .

Claire Marlowe owns 'The Townhouse by the Sea' with Luca, the hotel's charismatic chef. She ensures everything runs smoothly – until an unexpected arrival checks in and turns her whole world upside down.

And the rest of the guests arrive with their own baggage...

Here are affairs of the heart, secrets, lies and scandal– all wrapped up in one long, hot weekend.

Secrets, rivalry, glamour – it's time for the party of the year . . .

Delilah has lived out her tempestuous marriage to hell-raiser Raf in the glare of the media spotlight. Now planning a milestone birthday, she has more on her mind than invitations.

Raf has been offered a part in a movie he can't refuse. But will he succumb to the temptations he's struggled to resist for the last ten years?

Delilah's three daughters are building careers of their own, only too aware that the press are waiting for them to slip up. For the Rafferty girls might look like angels, but they are only human.

It's the perfect recipe for a party like no other . . .

On Everdene Sands, a row of beach huts holds the secrets of the families who own them

'FOR SALE: a rare opportunity to purchase a beach hut on the spectacular Everdene Sands. "The Shack" has been in the family for fifty years, and was the first to be built on this renowned stretch of golden sand.'

Jane Milton doesn't want to sell her beloved beach hut, which has been the heart of so many family holidays and holds so many happy memories. But when her husband dies, leaving her with an overwhelming string of debts, she has no choice but to sell.

How far would you go for love: a white lie, a small deceit, full-scale fraud . . . ?

When Charlotte Briggs' husband Ed is sent down for fraud, she cannot find it in her heart to forgive him for what he has done. Ostracised from their social circle, she flees to the wilds of Exmoor to nurse her broken heart. But despite the slower pace of life, she soon finds that she is not the only person whose life is in turmoil.

It was the opportunity of a lifetime – a rundown hotel in Cornwall, just waiting to be brought back to life

When the rundown Rocks Hotel comes up for auction in Mariscombe, Lisa and her boyfriend George make a successful bid to escape and live the dream. But their dream quickly becomes a nightmare. Their arch-rival, Bruno Thorne, owner of Mariscombe Hotel, seems intent on sabotage.

Meanwhile, local chambermaid Molly is harbouring a secret that will blow the whole village apart. Then an unexpected visitor turns up on the doorstep. It seems everyone in Mariscombe is sailing a little too close to the rocks . . .

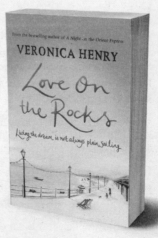

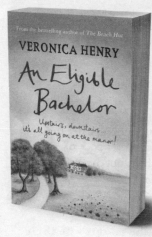

Upstairs, downstairs . . . it's all going on at the manor

When Guy wakes up with a terrible hangover and a new fiancée, he tries not to panic. After all, Richenda is beautiful, famous, successful . . . what reason could he have for doubts?

As news of the engagement between the heir of Eversleigh Manor and the darling of prime-time television spreads through the village, Guy wonders if he's made a rash decision. Especially when he meets Honor, a new employee of the Manor who has a habit of getting under his skin. But Honor has her own troubles – a son who's missing, and an ex-boyfriend who has made an unexpected reappearance . . .

Home isn't always where the heart is . . .

Jamie Wilding's return home is not quite going to plan. A lot has changed in the picturesque Shropshire village of Upper Faviell since she left after the death of her mother. Her father is broke and behaving like a teenager. Her best friend's marriage is slowly falling apart. And the man she lost her heart to years ago is trying to buy her beloved family home.

As Jamie attempts to fix the mess, she is forced to confront a long-standing family feud and the truth about her father, before she can finally listen to her own heart.

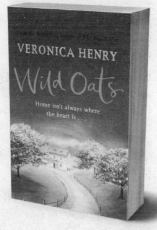

Welcome to Honeycote, and a Christmas no one will ever forget

As the nights draw in, garlands deck the halls and the carols ring out, there are secrets and lies, love and lust all waiting to be unwrapped. After all, it's the most wonderful time of the year...

'Veronica Henry writes like a dream'
Jill Mansell

Originally published as *Honeycote*

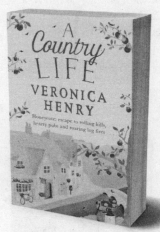

Will an escape to the country be their saving grace... or a recipe for trouble?

WANTED: Enthusiastic couple to breathe new life into a traditional village pub.

When Suzanne and Barney Blake take on the faded Honeycote Arms, it's a fresh start for both of them. But it seems the Blakes aren't the only new arrivals in the village looking for an escape...

Originally published as *Making Hay*

Return to Honeycote in this perfect comfort read, brimming with humour and heart

As the champagne goes on ice and the church bells ring out, it looks set to be a perfect day. But between the bride's clashes with her mother, the groom's cold feet, and a ghost from the past, it seems that trouble has arrived uninvited.

Everyone loves a wedding, don't they?

Originally published as *Just a Family Affair*